KILLIGREW R.N.

Kit Killigrew has been a sailor since he was twelve – he has the sea in his half-Greek, half-Cornish blood. His most recent posting is to the steam sloop *Tisiphone,* part of the West Africa Squadron which is trying to rid the seas of the now illegal slave trade. Rear-Admiral Sir Charles Napier sees in Killigrew someone ruthless enough to infiltrate the slavers, find the slave market owned by the shadowy megalomaniac Francisco Salazar – and expose the British Establishment figure who is one of the slave trade's major investors.

KILLIGREW R.N.

KILLIGREW R.N.

by

Jonathan Lunn

Magna Large Print Books
Long Preston, North Yorkshire,
BD23 4ND, England.

British Library Cataloguing in Publication Data.

Lunn, Jonathan
    Killigrew R.N.

    A catalogue record of this book is
    available from the British Library

    ISBN   0-7505-1664-X

First published in Great Britain in 2000 by Headline Book Publishing

Cover illustration by Fritz Sigfried Georg Melby © Christie's Images by arrangement with Headline Book Publishing

Published in Large Print 2001 by arrangement with Headline Book Publishing Ltd.

Magna Large Print is an imprint of Library Magna Books Ltd.

Printed and bound in Great Britain by
T.J. (International) Ltd., Cornwall, PL28 8RW

For Macer

Eternal gratitude to my father, for smuggling me into the cinema to see *The Three Musketeers* (1973 version) and my first Bond film, *The Man with the Golden Gun,* at an appallingly young and impressionable age; to George 'He's torn our carpet!' MacDonald Fraser for giving the Victorians back their humanity; to John 'The Guvnor' Barry and David 'The Heir-Apparent' Arnold for the music; to Christopher Lloyd for giving me the original idea in *The Royal Navy and the Slave Trade* (London, 1949) and to Hugh Thomas for his exhaustive yet constantly fascinating history of the Atlantic slave trade, *The Slave Trade* (New York, 1997), which introduced me to Pedro Blanco and the Gallinas Barracoon; to Anne Williams and Sarah Keen at Headline for all their work and patience; to Richenda Todd for her excellent editing and fact-checking; to the staff of the S.S. *Great Britain* Project for their kind permission for me to be photographed on board Brunel's masterpiece; and to James Hale for keeping faith while everyone else was jumping ship.

I:

The Prize

You could always tell a slave ship from any other vessel.

The sharks knew that.

Any ship that crossed the Atlantic could expect at least a couple of sharks to follow in her wake in the hope of catching some scraps tossed overboard by the cook. But a slave ship would have a couple of dozen fins slicing through her wake. Sharks were not the most clever of the ocean's denizens but they were patient and they knew from experience that sooner or later there would be deaths on board a slave ship and when that happened there was nothing for it but to throw the body over the side. Often a member of the crew would die, usually from yellow fever, but twice as often it would be one of the slaves. The sharks did not discriminate between black and white. To them it was all food.

The sharks could tell it was a slaver from the stench.

Mate Killigrew could smell it now as he was rowed across from Her Majesty's paddle-sloop *Tisiphone* to the *Maria Magdalena:* a compound of stale sweat, urine, excrement and vomit. Even on Her Majesty's yacht *Victoria and Albert* the sanitary arrangements for the crew were primi-

11

tive at best, and the stench of the effluent which gathered in the bilges could be overpowering to a landsman during high summer. On a slaver, the sanitary arrangements for the slaves were non-existent.

'Sweet Jesus!' one of the rowers gasped as they approached the slave ship. 'What a stench! She stinks like the nethermost pit of Hell!'

'Just keep rowing,' ordered Killigrew. He sat in the long boat's bow, his saturnine face turned towards the *Maria Magdalena*. His mind was already on the deck of the slaver, planning what tasks the prize crew would have to perform once on board, and putting them in order of priority.

There were fourteen men crammed in the *Maria Magdalena*'s long boat. The three officers – Mate Killigrew, Assistant Surgeon Strachan and Midshipman Parsons – all wore navy-blue pea jackets, white kerseymere pantaloons, and peaked caps. He was also entitled to wear the China War Medal but he preferred not to. He was not proud of having taken part in that small but dirty conflict, which some called the Opium War, even though he had been promoted to mate – a halfway house between midshipman and lieutenant – as a reward for his part in the taking of Chingkiang-fu in 1842. That was five years ago now, but still the nightmare of that butchery sometimes haunted his dreams.

The remaining eleven men were all ratings and wore no uniform as such, except that they all drew their clothes from the purser's slops and there was inevitably a uniformity to their white trousers, blue jackets and broad-brimmed straw hats.

Killigrew glanced across to where Strachan sat with his handkerchief held delicately over his nose and mouth. The assistant surgeon was in his early twenties, the same age as Killigrew, with blue eyes behind wire-framed spectacles and a tangle of light brown hair. A graduate of the University of Edinburgh, where he had qualified as a Licentiate of the Society of Apothecaries, Strachan was a relative newcomer in the navy. Killigrew suspected the assistant surgeon could not have graduated very high in his class at medical school, otherwise he would have worked in a country practice: far more pleasant than a paddle-sloop in the Tropics, and far more remunerative than the nine pounds and sixteen shillings a month he earned as an assistant surgeon.

It was two bells in the afternoon watch, or three o'clock, as the landsmen would have it. The *Tisiphone* – 160 feet long from stem to stern, with a single funnel between the two masts – and the *Maria Magdalena* were hove-to alongside one another about fifty yards apart. The sun beat down mercilessly on the shimmering blue sea. Back in Britain it was winter but the Tropics knew nothing of winter and summer, only the dry season and the wet season. It was the dry season now and hardly a breath of air disturbed the sails of either vessel.

During the first part of the chase a fresh off-shore breeze had propelled the swift Baltimore-built barque along at a good twelve knots which the paddle-sloop, with her sails and her engines, had barely been able to match. But the *Tisiphone* had persisted, her crew knowing that as long as they could keep the slaver in sight then time and the doldrums were on their side. Eventually, as the morning gave way to afternoon, the breeze had slackened and died, leaving the *Maria Magdalena* helpless. A blast of chain shot from the *Tisiphone*'s sixty-eight pounder had brought down the slaver's upper spars and she had run down the American colours she had been flying, colours which Killigrew did not doubt were false.

The Stars and Stripes was a good flag of convenience for slavers. Both the British and the Americans maintained an anti-slavery squadron off the coast of West Africa, but the British one was by far the larger and more active of the two. The United States did not have a treaty with Great Britain to allow British ships to stop and search US vessels: the memory of the War of 1812 and its primary cause – the Royal Navy's unjustifiable habit of stopping American merchant ships and pressing their crewmen into service on board British men-o'-war – still rankled with American politicians and admirals who were old enough to remember those days. Thus no vessel of the Royal Navy could stop an American ship, and no vessel of the United States Navy could stop a British one. All the slavers had to do was hoist the Old Glory when chased by a British vessel, or hoist the Union Jack if chased by the Americans. Any Royal Naval officer stopping a ship flying the US flag had to be damned sure of his ground if he did not want to spark off a diplomatic incident.

14

The starboard side of the barque loomed over them and Killigrew glimpsed the surly faces of some of the crewmen left on board. As soon as the *Maria Magdalena* had surrendered, the *Tisiphone*'s captain, Commander Standish, had ordered her master to cross over to the paddle-sloop with a dozen of his crewmen. Those men were now captives under the rifles of the *Tisiphone*'s marines, while the rest of the slavers waited on board the barque for Killigrew and his men to board and take command of the vessel.

'Way enough,' said Olaf Ågård. One of the *Tisiphone*'s two quartermasters, the Swede was the senior petty officer in the long boat. He had served on British ships – first Hull whalers, then Royal Navy vessels – for so long that scarcely a trace of any Swedish accent remained in his voice. 'Toss and boat oars.'

The rowers shipped their oars and allowed the long boat to cover the last few yards under her own momentum until the bow bumped gently against the clipper's side where a rope ladder hung down from the gunwale.

Killigrew went up first. At the top he hooked both hands over the gunwale, heaved himself up and swung his feet on to the deck. There were a dozen sailors gathered there, some looking fearful, others glaring at Killigrew with venom in their eyes. The moment he stood on the deck he unhooked his 'pepperbox' – multi-shot pistol with six revolving barrels – from his belt and levelled it at the sailors. It was not unknown for the crew of a captured slaver to murder the prize crews put aboard her, although they usually waited until the vessel which had caught them had sailed away. But Killigrew was damned if he would take any chances with this villainous-looking bunch.

'Which one of you is in charge?' he demanded.

The sailors exchanged glances. None of them spoke.

Killigrew repeated his question in Portuguese and gestured with his pepperbox. 'Come on, speak up. I haven't got all day.'

'I am,' said one, a heavily built man with greasy black hair and a cast in one eye.

'What's your name?'

'Ramón Barroso.'

'Are you the first mate?'

'Yes.'

The rest of the prize crew gathered on board the *Maria Magdalena*'s deck, armed with pistols and cutlasses, and some of them at once covered the slavers. 'Keep those men under guard until we can get irons on them,' ordered Killigrew. 'I'm sure there'll be no shortage of those on board. Boulton, Evans, Ivey and McFee: you four search the ship for other crewmen and weapons. Mr Parsons, be so good as to run the Union Jack up the jackstaff. Mr Fentiman, make an inventory of what spars we'll need to jury-rig her until we make it to Freetown. You help him, Sails. See what you can find in the ship's stores; what's missing we'll have to bring across from the *Tisiphone*.'

Fentiman and 'Sails' – the chief carpenter's mate and the sailmaker respectively – nodded and went about their work.

16

'I'll check the slave deck,' said Strachan, heading below.

Killigrew gestured at Barroso with the pepper-box. 'Show me the ship's papers.'

'The *senhor capitão* has the papers. He took them across to your vessel to show to your *capitão*–'

'I mean the *other* ship's papers,' said Killigrew. 'I never stopped a slaver yet which didn't have more than one set of papers.' He followed Barroso into the captain's day room where the Portuguese indicated a padlocked strongbox.

'I don't have the key.'

'I do.' Killigrew shot the padlock off with his pepperbox.

Barroso moved to open the strongbox, blocking it from Killigrew's sight with his body. ''Vast there!' Killigrew snapped before he could raise the lid. 'Move over there. Turn your face to the wall, spread your legs and put your hands against the bulkhead. Good boy. Now don't you bat an eyelid.'

He lifted the lid of the strongbox. A pistol lay on top of the papers inside, an old-fashioned single-shot flintlock. Killigrew picked it up and showed it to Barroso. 'Is this what you were looking for?'

Barroso did not reply. Killigrew tucked the pistol behind his belt and turned his attention to the rest of the strongbox's contents. There were no ship's papers, no log, no cargo manifest, no owner's instructions, just a slight haze and a smell of burning in the day room.

There was a knock on the door. 'Who's there?'

17

Killigrew demanded without taking his eyes off Barroso.

'Me, sir. Parsons.'

'Come in, Mr Parsons. What can I do for you?'

'It's the quack, sir. He wants you to join him on the slave deck.'

'All right.' Killigrew seized Barroso by the scruff of his neck, rammed the muzzles of his pepperbox into the small of his back, and marched him out on deck. 'You can go back with your shipmates for now.' He pushed Barroso roughly across to where the barque's other crewmen waited, and then descended through a hatch and down a companion ladder to the slave deck.

Below decks the stench of sweat, urine, excrement and vomit was even worse and Killigrew found himself gagging. Strachan waited outside the door. The sounds of moaning and weeping came from the other side.

'I thought you'd want to see this for yourself, sir,' said Strachan, grim-faced.

Killigrew glanced at him. Strachan had already been aboard several other slavers in his short time with the West Africa Squadron; if he thought this one was worthy of particular attention, then it had to be especially bad. The forewarning braced Killigrew, as much as anything could have braced him for the stench and sight which greeted him when Strachan opened the door.

A wall of hot, stinking air hit him at once, and he had to choke back the bile which rose to his gorge. The one mercy was that the dim lighting prevented him from seeing too much.

If Killigrew lived to be a hundred years of age – which with his career and personal habits was unlikely, he reflected – he would never understand the mentality of slavers. Even if the very concept of slavery had not been entirely contrary to all laws of natural justice, surely it would have made sound economic sense to look after the slaves. True, they would have transported fewer slaves per voyage, but then they would have lost a smaller number on the way and sold a higher proportion of those they had paid for on the African coast.

But instead they packed the slaves on deck as closely as it was physically possible, and on average roughly a third of them died during the middle passage to the New World. 'O brave new world, that has such people in it!' he thought ironically. And it was not even a reflection of the complete indifference to the lives of their slaves, which his various encounters with slavers had taught him was a given. To the slavers, their cargo was not even human, merely a superior form of ape. But the diseases which spread like wildfire through the slave decks of these death hulks – dysentery, smallpox, ophthalmia – could transfer just as easily to their crews, and it was not unusual for a sixth of the crewmen to die as well.

The deck had been split into two levels, with less than three feet of headroom between the two. Like most people Killigrew had seen the graphic plans of slave decks published by the abolitionists, and had read the statistics about how little space each slave had. But those were only pictures and statistics, and could never capture the full horror. There were over four and a half hundred slaves crammed into that cramped, fetid hold, all of them naked and in irons, their ankles raw and blistered where the fetters chafed their flesh. A shallow wave of piss and puke swept across the deck each time the barque rolled. As soon as the door opened, the moans and cries intensified as they jabbered at him in their incomprehensible tongue.

And the worst of it was that the vast majority of them were children.

When the slave trade had been legal, slaves of all ages had been transported to the Americas. But now that fewer ships dared to make the crossing and the supply was strangled, it made more economic sense to import younger slaves from whom the owners would get more years of work. And since children were smaller, the slavers could pack more of them on board.

'Jesus Christ,' breathed Killigrew. 'All right, does anyone here speak English? Speakee Krio? *Est-ce qu'il y a quelqu'un qui parle français ¿Habla español? Fala português...?'* A firm believer in self-improvement, Killigrew had found that there were usually one or two foreign ratings on board most British ships, and one way to pass the time on long voyages was to employ them in teaching him their tongue; in this manner he had picked up the languages of the most common seafaring nations, including Spanish and Portuguese in addition to the French most naval officers learned as a matter of course.

20

'I speak Portuguese,' said one of the older ones, a woman of about twenty.

'What's your name?'

'Koumba, *senhor.*'

'My name's Kit. Now listen, Koumba, I want you to translate what I'm going to say for everyone else here. Can you do that?'

She nodded.

'Good girl. Tell them everything's going to be all right, do you understand? I'm an officer of the Royal Navy, we've come to save you from the slavers. We're going to get you out of here and take you all up topsides as soon as possible, and the doctor here will care for your sick. Then we'll take you back to Africa, all right? But you have to be patient.'

She nodded again.

'Good girl. Be strong. The ordeal's nearly over.'

He went back on deck and gestured for Barroso to approach. 'The keys for the irons. Where are they?'

Barroso grinned. 'The *capitão* has them. He keeps all the *chaves* on him all the time...'

Killigrew shook his head. 'What about the spare set?'

'Spare set, *senhor?* What spare set?'

Killigrew punched him in the stomach. As Barroso doubled up, Killigrew drove his knee into his face. Barroso's head was snapped back and he sprawled on the deck.

The British seamen on deck stared at this display of gratuitous violence, half shocked, half admiring. None of them cared for slavers, of course, but Mr Killigrew hated them with a passion. He knew what they would be thinking: *A rum cove, that Mr Killigrew, most of the time as staid and sober as any English gentleman, yet every now and then prey to the most violent passions. But then he did have a foreigner for a mother, it was said, so what could you expect?*

Ignoring their stares, Killigrew kicked Barroso viciously in the side, grabbed him by the scruff of the neck and hauled him to his feet. Then he smashed his face against the mainmast.

Barroso sank to his knees with blood streaming from his nostrils and a livid bruise weeping blood on his temple. He spat a mouthful of blood on the deck and several teeth with it. Killigrew felt nothing. He had no doubt this was not the first time blood had been spilled on that deck.

'The spare set.'

'Hanging on a ... *o que é* ... *o prego?*'

'A nail?'

'*Sim*, a nail. Hanging on a nail behind the door to the *capitão's* day room.'

'It's amazing how co-operative these people can be when you ask them nicely,' remarked Killigrew. 'Go and fetch them, Mr Parsons.'

As the midshipman scurried off to fetch the keys, Boulton, Evans, Ivey and McFee returned from below decks. 'There's no one else hiding on board, sir,' reported Boulton.

'You're sure? I don't want anyone you over-looked sneaking out once we've parted from the *Tisiphone* freeing their shipmates here so they can slit our throats. Remember the *Felicidade*.'

'Yes, sir.'

The *Felicidade* had been another slave ship

captured by the Royal Navy off the coast of Africa two years earlier: the slavers had overpowered the prize crew and thrown the survivors overboard. Worst of all the slavers had later been captured and despite their guilt having been established, a judicial appeal had ruled that a British court had no jurisdiction over a vessel owned by a Brazilian who had murdered a British prize crew. The slavers had been sent back to Brazil at British expense.

Killigrew turned to the chief carpenter's mate from the *Tisiphone,* who was waiting to report. 'Well, Mr Fentiman?'

'It ain't good, sir. They must've chucked most of their stores overboard when we was chasing 'em. And most of the timbers and rigging that's still home is as rotten as a politician's conscience. There ain't enough rope and timbers on board the *Tisiphone* to replace 'em all. Christ – pardon me language, sir – but we'd need to build a whole new ship to replace this floating coffin. We'll be lucky to get halfway back to Africa.'

'Well, there isn't enough room on board the *Tisiphone* for all the slaves, so we'll just have to make do. Galton, I want you and Evans to row Fentiman and Sails back to the *Tisiphone* to arrange the transfer of stores.'

'Aye, aye, sir.'

Parsons returned carrying a bunch of keys. 'Good lad,' said Killigrew, taking them from him.

'Sir, there's something I think you should see in the captain's cabin.'

'All right.' Killigrew turned to Boulton and handed him the keys. 'I want you and the others

23

to start bringing up the slaves from below. And bring up some irons for these fellows,' he added, indicating the slavers. 'Once we've got all the slaves on deck we can put these swines in their place, let them see how they like it down there. It's a pity there aren't more of them, so they can get a flavour of how cramped it is.'

Killigrew followed Parsons aft to the master's day room. 'What is it, Mr Parsons?'

'It's ... um ... it's difficult to explain, sir. I think you'd better see for yourself.' Parsons echoed the phrase Strachan had used not five minutes earlier before showing him the slave deck. Killigrew wondered what new atrocity awaited him.

Parsons opened the door to the cabin. A handsome black woman in her early twenties stood at the window, gazing out across the sea. Like the slaves in the hold she was completely naked, but better kempt, and Killigrew would have been less than human not to admire her long, lithe limbs and supple curves.

'Ah-ha!' said Killigrew. 'No need for alarm, Parsons. That is what is knows as a "woman". A remarkably fine specimen, at that.'

Parsons flushed. 'I know that, sir...'

Hearing voices, the woman turned and crossed quickly to where Killigrew stood on the threshold. She dropped to her knees at his feet and entwined her fingers in the material of his coat, her eyes pleading. 'Doan' hurt me, mas'er. Please doan' hurt me...'

Killigrew grimaced and gestured helplessly, unsure of what to do with his hands. In the end he settled for patting her on the head and motioning for her to rise. 'It's all right, it's over. No one's going to hurt you. We're officers of the Royal Navy. We're going to take you back to Africa.'

'Oh, t'ank you! T'ank you!' Sobbing with relief, she buried her face in his crotch.

He gently took her under the arms, prised her away, and helped her to the bunk. 'What's your name?'

'Missy, mas'er.'

He shook his head. 'Not the name the slavers gave you. Your *real* name.'

'Onyema.'

'Well, you sit there, Onyema, and I'll send someone to make sure you're not hurt as soon as I've got a moment.' He headed for the door and gestured for Parsons to follow him.

'Do you suppose they … you know…?' asked Parsons as soon as the door was closed.

'I don't doubt it,' Killigrew said tightly. 'You'll often find the master of a slaver picks out the handsomest of the women for his own personal pleasure during the voyage to the Americas. Sometimes he'll let the whole crew do likewise.'

'My God!' stammered Parsons. 'Savages! So this is how the white man brings civilisation to the dark continent.'

'At least she didn't seem too badly knocked about. It doesn't make up for the violation, of course, but in some ways she'll have been better off in the master's cabin than she would have been down in that slave deck with the others.'

The others were being brought up on deck now. Some of the little ones were so sick after

25

only a few hours on board they could no longer walk and had to be carried up. Even before they had been brought on board the *Maria Magdalena,* they might have spent weeks in equally vile imprisonment in a barracoon on the African coast. As each one emerged, Strachan directed one of the seamen from the *Tisiphone* to play water from the ship's pump over their besmirched bodies. Some of the children howled when the salt water entered their sores, but brine was better than excrement.

At length all the slaves were brought up – including half a dozen dead – until the decks were crowded with their bodies: not only the barque's waist, but the forecastle, quarter-deck and poop deck, so that it was hardly possible to move without stepping on one. They lay about listlessly, a few of the children still crying, some of the older ones addressing the navy seamen in their strange tongue – Koumba told Killigrew they were offering their thanks – but most still too drained by the suffocating heat of the hold to do more than lie there. Strachan moved amongst them, checking for any signs of infectious disease and doing what he could for them, while Killigrew directed two of the seamen to rig up a sail as an awning over the waist to provide some shade from the glaring heat of the sun for the sickest of the freed slaves. The slavers, mean-while, were put in irons and carried down to the filth of the slave deck, enabling the marines to stand down at last.

'There's no sign of any disease,' Strachan reported at last. 'I think it's safe to put some of

26

the stronger ones aboard the *Tisiphone*.'

'Good. I'll see to it. There's a woman in the captain's cabin. I don't think she's hurt as such, but I'd be grateful if you could ... you know ... make sure she's all right.'

Strachan nodded. 'Very well, as soon as I've collected some things from the sick berth.'

By now the *Tisiphone* had manoeuvred alongside the *Maria Magdalena*, and as timber, ropes and sails were transferred across one way, about eighty of the slaves were carried across the other. Killigrew and Strachan went back aboard the *Tisiphone*, the latter collecting medical supplies from the sick berth while the former presented himself to Commander Standish.

Standish was in his forties, long overlooked for promotion to post-captain, and Killigrew knew that it rankled. There were men younger than Standish who were commodores by now. It was not because Standish was the kind of pompous, unimaginative officer who did everything by the book to conceal his own incompetence – although he was – but because he lacked the 'interest' of a senior officer: that magical quality which meant all the difference between the advancement and stagnation of a naval career. Without it, it did not matter how bold or efficient an officer was.

Standish stood by the window in his day room, staring out, and he did not turn to face Killigrew as the younger man issued into his office. There was no love lost between the two of them. Another reason for Standish's slow career progression was the fact that he was a graduate of the Royal Navy College at Portsmouth. Most senior officers sneered at college graduates deriding them as 'X-chasers', and preferring the majority of officers who had learned their trade at sea, the way they themselves had done, the way the navy had trained all its officers since time immemorial. That had been how Killigrew had learned, and Killigrew had the 'interest' which Standish lacked. If Killigrew played his cards right he would be a post-captain long before he was Standish's age.

'Fentiman tells me she's in an appalling state, Mr Killigrew.'

'By navy standards, sir, yes.' By any standards, for that matter, but there was not enough room on the *Tisiphone* for all the slaves; the only way to get them back to Africa was to try to sail the *Maria Magdalena* to Sierra Leone, so Killigrew knew there was no point in complaining.

'Think you can make it?' Standish did not sound as if he cared either way, but was obliged to ask out of good manners.

Killigrew did not imagine it would be easy, but he was confident in his own ability and that of the men who had been appointed to the prize crew. 'It shouldn't be too much trouble, sir.' It went without saying that Killigrew's definition of 'too much trouble' meant much more trouble than most other people's definition.

Standish grunted. 'It's now' – he checked his fob watch – 'just coming up to four o'clock. We should reach Freetown some time after noon the day after tomorrow. We'll wait for you there until the morning tide on Monday; in any event, if we have to leave before you get back, I'll leave orders at the prize court.'

Finally some supplies, especially water and fresh fruit, were transhipped aboard the *Maria Magdalena* in an effort to improve the stock of rice and yams which the slavers had taken on board for the slaves. Then Killigrew and Strachan went back aboard the barque and the two ships parted company, the *Tisiphone* tacking eastwards back towards the African coast.

Killigrew felt a pang of loneliness as the paddle-sloop sailed away, but it was only momentary. It was always a thrill for a young man to find himself in command of his own vessel, even if it was only the temporary command of a captured prize. He was never happier than when there was a seaman's work to be done – except when he was in amenable female company with a plentiful supply of good whisky and cheroots, of course – and there was no shortage of work to be done aboard the *Maria Magdalena*.

The first task was to repair the spars and rigging damaged by the *Tisiphone*'s chain shot during the chase, so they could get the barque under way at the earliest opportunity. The simple fact that the slaver was now in the hands of the Royal Navy would not prevent more deaths from occurring amongst the recaptives – as the technically freed slaves were known – and the longer it took them to reach Sierra Leone, the more recaptives would die. The transfer of eighty Africans to the *Tisiphone* had left more space on deck, and the seamen chivvied the ones left behind to leave gaps between them through which they could cross the deck while they worked.

It did not take long to hoist those sails that had not been damaged, and Killigrew at once directed Ågård to take the helm and put her about. The wind had freshened a little now – no more than five knots, force two on Admiral Beaufort's scale – but it was off-shore, against the *Tisiphone*. No sailing ship could head directly into wind, but by bracing up the yards they could travel on a starboard tack, at an angle to the direction they wanted to go, before changing to a port tack. In this way they could follow a zigzag course which would eventually take them to Freetown, but it would be a slow and laborious process – for every ten miles of ocean covered they would actually have to cross fourteen – especially with the winds so light. At least they would pick up speed as soon as they had replaced the upper sails.

Killigrew heard a woman's scream from below decks. He vaulted over the poop-deck rail and landed nimbly on the quarter-deck, narrowly missing one of the Africans who lay there. He kicked open the door, passed through the master's day room into the cabin and quickly surveyed the scene. Onyema sat on the bunk, her thighs pressed against her chest with her arms wrapped around her knees. To Killigrew's right, Strachan pressed himself into the corner of the cabin furthest from the bunk. He was dabbing at a split lip with his handkerchief.

'What the devil's going on in here?' demanded Killigrew. Both Onyema and Strachan began to speak at once. Killigrew waved for silence. 'One at a time. Ladies first.'

'She's no lady,' muttered Strachan.

Onyema indicated Strachan. 'Him me touch–'

'I was examining her, damn it!' snapped Strachan.

'Him touch Onyema paps. Him try touch Onyema cunny.'

'That's a damn lie!' spluttered Strachan. His native Scots burr, usually hardly discernible, became more pronounced when he was upset. 'I had nae even got as far as taking her pulse when the black bitch went crazy on me. She hit me, damn it!'

Killigrew studied Strachan's red face, trying to judge whether he was telling the truth or if it was just bluster. It was unthinkable that a naval officer could act in such an ungentlemanly fashion, but Strachan had not been in the navy for very long and Killigrew did not know him well enough to be sure either way. He could not blame a man for being tempted – Onyema was a fine-looking woman – but a gentleman resisted temptation if his advances were unwelcome. To take advantage of a woman who had just been through the kind of ordeal Onyema had been subjected to was the behaviour of the vilest scum.

'Get out,' he told Strachan.

'You're going to take her word for it over mine?'

'Why should she lie?'

'How should I know? She's crazy. She just went for me all of a sudden.'

'A man's innocent until proven guilty,' Killigrew said tightly. 'I'll allow you that much.

31

Now get out of my sight.'

'For God's sake! You don't seriously think I'd try to take advantage of her? After what she's been through?'

'Get out!'

Strachan stared at Killigrew and apparently decided it would be safest to do as he was told. As soon as he was gone, Killigrew turned to Onyema. 'I must apologise for allowing this to happen. It won't happen again, I assure you.'

'Thank you, mas'er.'

He grimaced. 'It's Mr Killigrew, not "mas'er",' he told her, and then softened. 'Or "Kit" to my friends.'

'Mas'er Killigrew Onyema friend?'

He smiled. 'I hope so.'

'Onyema like Mas'er Killigrew. Mas'er Killigrew, him have kind face. Face woman trust, can.'

Killigrew laughed. 'Well, that's the first time anyone's ever accused me of that.' He opened the closet, hoping to find a shirt he could give her to put on – the sight of her smooth ebony skin was starting to distract him to the point where he could almost sympathise with Strachan – but instead found a woman's muslin shift. He handed it to her. 'Here, put this on.'

She pulled the shirt on over her head. It fitted perfectly. 'Ship go Africa long time?'

'Three, maybe four days.'

'What happen, ship go Africa?'

'We'll take you to Sierra Leone. That's a British colony. There's no slavery there.' Which was not entirely true: ironically, since Sierra Leone had been set up as a colony for freed slaves, it was one of the few places in the British Empire where slavery was still allowed, but only for domestic slaves. But he saw no need to confuse her. 'The British government will maintain you – pay for food and shelter, I mean – for a year. After that, it's up to you. You can stay in Sierra Leone and try to get work, although I don't recommend it. You may decide you're better off going to the British West Indies under a scheme of apprenticed labour. But all this will be explained to you when we reach Freetown.'

'Onyema work Mas'er Killigrew? Onyema servant Mas'er Killigrew?'

He chuckled, but without much humour. 'I'm afraid I can't afford to keep any servants.' His closest living relative, Admiral Killigrew, was wealthy, but he refused to go cap in hand to his grandfather, and lived as best as he could on his navy pay and any prize money he earned.

'Now you must excuse me,' he told Onyema. 'I've got important work to do.'

He made his way into the day cabin, took out the charts and navigational instruments he had brought on board with him and plotted a course to Freetown. When he had finished he stood up, crossed to the window and opened it to let in some fresh air. He wedged himself in the frame, with one foot on the sill, his knee against his chest, and lit a cheroot while watching the sun set the sky aflame as it sank towards the horizon. Beneath the ship's stern the sharks' fins still swam in the wake. When he had finished his cheroot he flicked the butt out and watched the glowing tip arc down through the gloom to the waves.

'That's all you're getting out of me, you bastards,' he murmured softly to himself.

'Mas'er Killigrew?'

He turned his head. Onyema stood framed in the door to the cabin, the light from a hurricane lantern shining through the diaphanous material of her shift to silhouette her nubile figure. She toyed with the stays at the neck of the shift, pulling them down between her breasts – whether by artifice or not Killigrew did not know – to emphasise her cleavage.

'Nothing. I was just thinking out loud.'

'Onyema make Mas'er Killigrew happy?'

'Mas'er Killigrew already happy.'

'Mas'er Killigrew, him have wife?'

'No.'

When a knock sounded on the door before he could say anything more, his reaction was one of relief. He waved her back into the cabin and she closed the door behind her. 'Come in.'

Fentiman thrust his head around the door. 'Begging your pardon, sir, but there's five foot o'water in the well.'

'Five feet!' With that much water in the bilges the orlop deck must have been completely awash. 'My God, it's a miracle we've not floundered already. Set two of the hands to work the bilge pump immediately.'

'Begging your pardon, sir, but I've already done that. It's just that I checked the water in the well when we first come aboard, and there was less than six inches then.'

Killigrew stared at him in incomprehension for a moment, and then took out his fob watch and flicked open the cover. It was nearly five o'clock. 'You mean to tell me we've shipped four and a half feet of water in less than two hours? We must have a bad leak.'

'Yes, sir. I've set Ivey and Lidstone to look for it and I'll be going to help them in a moment, but with that much water coming in we're going to need to man the pump all the way from here to Freetown, and even then I wouldn't care to lay odds on our staying afloat till we arrive.'

'You'd better get on with looking for that leak then, hadn't you?'

'Aye, aye, sir.'

Killigrew followed him out and ascended to the poop deck where Parsons stood yawning besides Ågård at the helm. He glanced up at the tops of the masts. Fentiman and the sailmaker had done a fair job of jury-rigging the damaged upper spars, sails and rigging, but if they had five feet of water in the well then the benefit of the upper sails would be counteracted by the drag of the hull. Boulton and Evans had stripped off their shirts and were working steadily at the bilge pump. The recaptives lay quietly on the deck while Strachan moved amongst them, treating their sores. *Trying to atone for earlier misdeeds,* mused Killigrew.

The sand in the half-hour glass by the ship's bell ran out and one of the seamen turned it over before ringing the bell four times to signify the beginning of the second dog watch. With the help of two seamen Killigrew measured the barque's speed with the log-ship and -line. Then he crossed to the log-board and wrote '2' under the column marked 'K'. 'How's her head?' he asked. There was no reply. 'Mr Parsons?'

The midshipman blinked. 'Wha–?'

'How's her head, Mr Parsons?' persisted Killigrew.

Parsons glanced at the compass in the binnacle. 'East by north, sir.'

Killigrew made the appropriate entry on the log-board, followed by a note of the wind direction, and then turned to Parsons. 'You're asleep on your feet, lad.'

'Yes, sir. Sorry, sir. It won't happen again.'

'It will if you don't get some rest. You've been on duty non-stop since the start of the forenoon watch. Go down to the day room and get your head down.'

'Thank you, sir.' Parsons went below.

Just under two knots, mused Killigrew. The loss of speed would be partly due to the fact the wind had dropped off again, but also because they were wallowing with five feet of water in the bilges. He glanced to where the two men still worked at the bilge pump. At this rate it would take them more than a week to get back to Sierra Leone; and if things were as bad as Fentiman had implied, they would be lucky to stay afloat that long. If Killigrew had known about the leak before they had parted from the *Tisiphone,* he would have asked Standish to tow them into Freetown.

'Something wrong, sir?' asked Dando.

Killigrew forced himself to smile and took out

36

another cheroot. 'I was just wondering … I don't suppose you noticed if there were any women amongst the crewmen from this ship who went on board the *Tisiphone?*'

'Women? No, sir. Leastways, if there was, they were the ugliest women I ever clapped eyes on. Why d'you ask?'

'Just wondering.' He glanced at his fob watch. 'Time to change tack,' he decided.

Ågård nodded. 'Stand by to go about!' he boomed prompting some of the recaptives on deck to raise their heads. 'Haul of all!'

The seamen scurried about the decks, cursing the recaptives who got in their way.

'Hard-a-lee,' ordered Killigrew.

Ågård span the helm to starboard. 'Helm's a-lee.'

As the barque's bow came around into the wind the sails sagged back against the masts. The barque began to lose way and the bow swung to starboard. The hands hauled on ropes to adjust the sails, bringing them around to catch the wind from the other side. The mainsail filled with wind once more as the head continued to come around to starboard.

'Ease the helm,' Killigrew told Ågård, who span the wheel to bring the rudder amidships.

At last the barque came around far enough for the wind to fill the sails from the port tack, and they gathered way once more. The hands adjusted the trim of the sails accordingly.

Ågård was not used to handling the barque and the bows came around too far. 'Meet her,' said Killigrew. Ågård span the wheel to compensate.

'Handsomely does it … helm amidships. Luff and touch her.'

'Aye, aye, sir.' Ågård steered the barque as close to the wind as he could without letting it spill from the sails.

'How's her head?'

'East by south, sir.'

'Keep her so,' Killigrew told Ågård, and turned to Dando. 'Be a good chap and run along to the galley to see if you can find some tea, would you? Make some for everyone who wants it.'

'Aye, aye, sir.' Dando turned away and was about to go below when a thought occurred to him and he turned back. 'Does that include the darkies, sir?'

'Negroes, Mr Dando, and if you can find enough tea for all of them don't let me stop you. Actually, it's about time they had a bite to eat and something to drink, and it seems to me you just volunteered. No more than half a pint of water each. We've only got enough to last us a week.'

'Aye, aye, sir.'

Killigrew entered the master's day room and lit an oil lamp to update the log: even a prize ship had to keep a log. When he had finished he glanced around the cabin. There was not much to reveal the personality of the previous occupant. The only personal touches seemed to be a couple of rather bad watercolours depicting maritime scenes. He found himself wondering if the master had bought them under the mistaken impression they had any artistic merit whatsoever or if he had painted them himself. There was no evidence of any artist's materials in the

38

day room so he had to assume that the former was the case.

There was a knock on the door. 'Come in.'

The door opened and Dando entered bearing two mugs. 'Your tea, sir. I brought some for Mr Parsons too, in case he wanted a cup. Is he in the cabin?'

Killigrew frowned. 'That's a good question.' He had told Parsons to sleep in the day room, but there was no sign of him. Of course, if Parsons had changed his mind and decided to chat to Onyema, there was no harm in that, but then why was there no sound of voices coming from the cabin? It occurred to him that Parsons and Onyema might have found another way to pass the time, and the thought did not shock him too much: after all, the lad had to learn sooner or later, and somehow Killigrew suspected that Onyema would be as good a teacher as any. But the deathly hush from the cabin did not suggest the sport of Venus was in play.

He stood up, crossed to the door, and tapped on it gently. 'Parsons?' When a few seconds had passed without any reply, he tapped again. 'Onyema?'

Still no reply. Killigrew exchanged glances with Dando and opened the door.

The light of an oil lamp illuminated the scene with its guttering yellow flame. Parson's coat was tossed carelessly on the floor while Parsons himself lay on the bed, staring up at the deck head. His pantaloons were around his ankles. There were no marks on him, nothing to suggest a struggle, just the gaping wound in his throat

39

and the blood-soaked bedclothes.

'Sweet Jesus!' gasped Dando.

Killigrew backed out of the cabin and turned and ran out on deck, Dando hard on his heels. 'Turn out the hands,' he snapped, reloading the empty barrel of his pepperbox with a fresh cartridge and ball. 'We've got a murderess on board.'

II:

Floating Coffin

'Evans! McFee!' Killigrew waved across two of the sailors who had pistols thrust in their belts. 'Look lively, you two. Go down to the slave deck and stand guard over the prisoners. No one goes near them, do you understand? Shoot if you have to.'

'Aye, aye, sir!' The two sailors drew their pistols and cutlasses and dashed below.

'What's going on?' asked Strachan.

'It seems I owe you an apology, Mr Strachan.'

'About the captain's belly-warmer? I told you she was mad.'

'Not mad, Mr Strachan. Just very, very cunning. She's one of them.'

'What?'

'One of the slavers, damn it! I was a fool not to see it. She cooked up that yarn about you trying to molest her to sow dissension amongst us. She's been biding her time, waiting for us to drop our guard so she could free her friends.'

Killigrew wondered how he could have been so stupid: the only black on board who spoke English; the absence of any signs of cruelty on her body; the shift in the master's closet that fitted her so perfectly...

He cast his eyes over the deck, mentally

41

mustering the men under his command: Dando and the sailmaker standing by for orders, Quartermaster Ågård at the helm, Boulton and Galton at the bilge pump, O'Connor moving amongst the slaves with a cask of water, and the other two men working at the bilge pump.

'Vast pumping, there,' he told them. 'Check your pistols. Where are Fentiman, Ivey and Lidstone?' Then he remembered: they had gone below to look for the leak. 'We'll have to search the ship, deck by deck. Boulton and Galton, you two stay on deck with Mr Ågård. Sails, you take Dando and O'Connor and start at the bows. Strachan and I will start from the stern and we'll work our way for'ard until–'

He broke off as a scuffle sounded below. They heard a thump, and then the report of a pistol followed by a man's scream, cut off short.

The sailmaker crossed to the main hatch. 'Dick? Johnny?' he called down. 'Are you boys all right down there?' When there was no reply, his expression became grim. 'Looks like they've got themselves a couple of pistols now, sir.'

'Everyone up on the poop deck, chop-chop!' ordered Killigrew.

'What about the recaptives?' asked Strachan, gesturing at the bodies strewn across the deck.

'We'll just have to leave them, that's all...'

Two shots rang out. Killigrew felt something scorch his cheek. A moment later Galton was on his knees clutching his stomach. Killigrew whirled in the direction from which the shots had come from in time to see the slavers rush out of the accommodation hatch behind the mainmast, only a few yards away. He fired his pepperbox twice. Boulton, Dando and O'Connor also fired their single-shot pistols. Three of the slavers went down, falling amongst the recaptives on deck who scrambled to get out of the way, crying out in panic and confusion.

Killigrew fired again, and then the surviving slavers were retreating back down the hatch. He shot one more in the back before they were all out of sight, then grabbed Galton by one arm, hoisted him to his feet and helped him up the companion ladder to the poop deck after the others.

Boulton, Dando and O'Connor quickly re-loaded their pistols and crouched at the rail at the leading edge of the poop, from where they could cover the rest of the barque's decks and hatches. Killigrew reloaded his pepperbox while Strachan crouched over Galton. A dark, thick stain was already spreading over the front of the seaman's shirt. Strachan tore the cloth apart to reveal the wound in his stomach.

'He's been gut-shot,' he said, while Galton groaned in agony.

Killigrew nodded, understanding that the seaman's chances of survival were slim. 'Do what you can.'

'What do we do now, sir?' asked the sailmaker. 'We can't stay up here for ever...' Apart from the fact that the recaptives needed to be looked after, the seamen could not trim the sails from the poop deck. Nor was there any food or water up there.

'It's worse than that,' said Killigrew. 'The ship's sinking.'

Strachan looked up sharply. 'What?' he spluttered in panic.

'Slowly,' Killigrew hastened to reassure him. 'But sinking nonetheless. That's why Fentiman went below with Ivey and Lidstone: they were searching for the leak.'

'I suppose the slavers got them, then, sir,' said Boulton.

'Maybe. I didn't hear anything.'

'Surely the slavers are in the same boat as we are,' said Strachan. 'No pun intended. We may be trapped up here, but they daren't show their faces on deck. If the ship's sinking, they'll drown first.'

'If the water in the hold gets that deep, then we'll be foundering and we'll soon drown with them.'

'Can't we talk to them?'

Killigrew grinned and jerked a thumb towards the hatches. 'You can try it if you like…'

'There's someone moving down there!' hissed Boulton.

'Hold your fire,' ordered Killigrew, and glanced over the rail. 'It's one of the recaptives. Let him up.'

'Him' was a 'her'. Koumba crept up the companion ladder and found herself face to face with the multiple muzzles of Killigrew's pepperbox. Her eyes widened, showing white against the blackness of her face in the twilight. He grabbed her by the arm and dragged her on to the poop deck. She gasped but did not cry out. 'What is happening?' she asked him in Portuguese. 'The slavers – you let them escape.'

Killigrew grimaced. 'Not on purpose, I assure you.'

She jerked her head to where four of the slavers shot earlier lay on deck. 'Two of them are not dead.'

Strachan had finished tending to Galton's wound as best he could. 'I should go to them–'

'You stay where you are, mister,' snapped Killigrew. 'It's them or us now. I can't have you getting shot trying to give them medical attention.'

Strachan looked relieved and did not try to argue.

'We have to do something, sir,' said Ågård.

Killigrew nodded. 'Someone has to go down there and deal with the slavers.'

'Are you mad?' asked Strachan. 'They've had plenty of time to reload their pistols. Whoever goes down will be shot the moment he appears at the top of the ladder.'

'That's why I'm not going down the ladder.' Killigrew crossed to the taffrail at the stern of the poop deck and glanced down.

Strachan stared at him. 'You're going to go down there alone?'

'I'd like one volunteer to come with me.'

Everyone spoke at once. Killigrew waved them to silence. 'Just one of you. Mr Dando, I think.' He turned to the sailmaker and handed him a boat hook. 'Get ready to pass this down to me.' He took off his coat and hung it from a belaying pin.

'For God's sake, man!' protested Strachan. 'There's at least eight of them. Not to mention the bitch that slit poor Parson's throat. Just two of you, against eight of them?'

The sailmaker laid a hand on Strachan's arm. 'Mr Killigrew knows what he's doing.'

'So do I. He's committing suicide.'

'We're wasting time,' said Killigrew. He took a coil of rope from a belaying pin and handed it to Dando. 'The longer we leave it, the more time we give them to cook up a plan.' He crossed to the skylight in the middle of the poop deck and raised it. 'We'll go in through one of the stern ports,' he explained. 'The password is "whisky". Anyone comes up through those hatches without calling that out first, you can blow his head off. Just make sure you don't hit any of those poor negroes. If we're not back in half an hour, you'll know we're dead.'

'Then what do we do?' asked Strachan.

Killigrew clapped him on the shoulder. 'You'll be in command then, so that's your problem.' He jumped down into the master's day cabin before Strachan could protest and landed lightly on the balls of his feet. Dando followed him.

'Belay one end of that rope to that beam,' ordered Killigrew, as he crossed to the window and opened it. Dando made the rope fast and Killigrew dropped the other end out of the window and into the barque's wake.

'Want me to go first, sir?' offered Dando.

'Toss you for it,' said Killigrew. 'Heads I go first, tails you do.' He tossed. 'Heads it is.' Killigrew slipped his double-headed coin back into his pocket. Taking a dirk from a sheath strapped to his ankle he clenched it between his

46

teeth and climbed out through the window, feeling like one of his piratical forebears.

He glanced up and saw the sailmaker at the taffrail above him. The sailmaker lowered one end of the boat hook towards him, but Killigrew shook his head and shinned down the rope. There was a stern port on either side of the rudder. The barque was so low in the water there was barely a foot of freeboard between the water and the sills of the ports. Within an hour water would be pouring through those ports if they did not get pumping again.

The port on the starboard side of the rudder was open, blackness behind it, and–

There was a blinding white flash from the port and a loud report filled Killigrew's ears. Something burned his shoulder and he almost lost his grip in shock. He slipped down the rope until his feet splashed into the water. Gripping the rope in one hand, he took the dirk from between his teeth and flung it through the open hatch. The action made him spin on the rope. As he swung back to face the port, he saw one of the slavers topple out to splash into the barque's wake.

The sharks at once closed in. Killigrew quickly shinned up the rope until he was out of the water. A feeding frenzy erupted below him as the sharks tore at the slaver's body, quickly falling astern.

No more shots came from the stern port, but it was only a matter of time before more of the slavers came to investigate. Killigrew had to move quickly if he did not want to be dangling helplessly when they arrived; next time he might not be so lucky. The overhang from the stern prevented him from reaching the port. He glanced up to where the sailmaker stood at the taffrail with concern on his face.

'Drop it!' hissed Killigrew.

The sailmaker looked puzzled. Killigrew held up one hand, and gestured. Sails remembered the boat hook he was holding. He held it out over the taffrail vertical, and allowed it to fall, straight down, just to one side of Killigrew. The mate snatched it out of the air, near the blunt end. The hook twisted down towards the water and a shark's head emerged, snapping at it. Killigrew jerked it clear, swung it at the stern port and hooked it over the sill. He pulled himself in towards the port and scrambled through.

He was in the after hold on the orlop deck, standing in several inches of water. Footsteps sounded outside and the door began to open. 'Eduardo?' called a voice, and the door opened as one of the slavers entered. He paused on the threshold and squinted into the gloom. 'Are you all right? What happened? What were you shooting at?'

'Me,' said Killigrew, and hit him on the head with the blunt end of the boat hook. The slaver slumped to the deck.

Killigrew was still tying the man's hands behind his back with his belt as Dando climbed in through the stern port after him. 'You all right, sir?' he whispered, glancing at the unconscious man.

'Better than he is.' Killigrew took out his handkerchief and used it to gag the slaver, propping him up in a seated position with his back to a bulkhead so that he would not drown in the water which sloshed about on the deck.

Then he stood up and pressed himself against the bulkhead to one side of the door, listening. The only sounds he could hear were the creaking of the ship's timbers and the sloshing of water.

He drew his cutlass in his right hand and his pepperbox in his left, and the two of them slipped out through the door into the dark bowels of the ship. Down here the slavers had the advantage over them, because they would be familiar with the barque's layout below decks. But so far, he hoped, the element of surprise was on his side.

Killigrew and Dando crept along the deserted orlop deck until they stumbled across something in the dark. Killigrew fell over and sprawled on something soft and sticky. Realising he was lying across the bodies of Fentiman, Ivey and Lidstone, he scrambled back in horror.

All three had had their throats slit from ear to ear. There were no other wounds on them to suggest they had died fighting: the slavers had murdered them in cold blood.

'Bastards,' whispered Dando. 'Begging your pardon, sir.'

'That's all right, Dando. You took the word right out of my mouth.'

They continued along the orlop deck until they reached a companion ladder leading up to the main deck, and paused. They could hear voices speaking Portuguese above.

'What's taking Ferrando so long?' asked one. 'I'm told him to come straight back here.'

'Maybe something happened to Eduardo. I'm

going to check.'

'Do you want me to come with you?'

Please say no, thought Killigrew.

'Yes.'

Footsteps came down the companion ladder. Killigrew and Dando ducked behind the main-mast where it descended between decks to the mast step at the keel. He slipped his pepperbox into its holster and listened to the footsteps splashing through the water. Eerie shadows danced on the bulkheads: one of them carried a lantern. Killigrew and Dando exchanged glances as the two slavers walked past their place of concealment, heading for the after hold.

Killigrew and Dando stepped out behind them. Killigrew hit one with the hilt of his cutlass and Dando laid out the other with a belaying pin. They dragged the two men to the empty slave deck, gagged them and fettered them. Nonetheless they would have to work quickly now, as these two men could quickly raise the alarm by rattling their fetters when they came to.

The two British seamen returned to the foot of the companion ladder. They heard footsteps above and froze.

'Where are Carlos and José?' Killigrew heard Barroso ask. 'Curse them, I told them not to move!'

A face appeared at the top of the steps and Killigrew and Dando quickly ducked back out of sight. 'Carlos? José? Where are you?'

Why don't you come down and find out?

'I don't like it, Ramon...'

'Me neither. There's something strange going

50

on … damn it, some of those English pigs must've gotten below somehow! I'll wager that devil Killigrew is with them. Tomas, Rodrigo, I want you two to go down there and flush the bastards out. Simão and I will stay at the main hatch.'

Tomas and Rodrigo descended the ladder with a lantern. As they headed into the darkness, Dando regarded Killigrew quizzically in the gloom. Killigrew nodded, and as Dando headed aft to take care of the two men, Killigrew went up the companion ladder and made his way to the main hatch. One man crouched beneath the grating, the barrel of his pistol pointed aft towards the poop deck.

Killigrew readied his cutlass. He felt guilty about creeping up on the man and striking him down from behind, but he reminded himself that this man would almost certainly murder him if the opportunity arose. Besides which, with the odds stacked against him, this was no time to fight fair: he would only be giving the advantage to his enemies.

Something clanked behind him and he half turned before a loop of chain was dropped tight around his neck and pulled hard against his throat, choking him. His cutlass clattered to the deck.

'Simão! I have him!'

The man with the pistol turned and levelled it at Killigrew's head. Killigrew kicked at his hand and sent the pistol flying. There was a bright flash as it discharged itself harmlessly into a bulkhead.

Killigrew scrabbled at the chain which bit into

51

his throat but the man who held him was too strong. He tried to draw his pepperbox but the man took both ends of the chain in one hand and clamped the other over Killigrew's wrist.

Simão snatched up the cutlass and came at Killigrew, slashing. Killigrew launched himself backwards and slammed the man behind him against a bulkhead. He gasped and took his hand from Killigrew's wrist. Killigrew drew his pepperbox and shot Simão between the eyes. Then he felt for the other man's side and rammed the muzzles against it, pulling the trigger. The man groaned and the chain became slack enough for Killigrew to break free.

The man with the chain was Barroso. A dark stain spread around the wound in his side, but he was still on his feet and Killigrew guessed he had not hit any vital organs. He swung the chain at Killigrew's hand, knocking the pepperbox away into the darkness.

A lithe, dark shape leaped out of the shadows from one side and crashed into Killigrew's side. Onyema sank her teeth into his wrist. The pain was excruciating. Barroso dropped the chain, snatched up the cutlass and charged forwards.

Killigrew and Onyema rolled over and over on the deck, her teeth still deep in his wrist, her fingernails raking his face, searching for his eyes. As Barroso brought his cutlass down, Killigrew allowed Onyema to roll on top. The cutlass buried itself deep in her shoulder. She gasped in shock. Barroso stared down in horror at what he had done, and then pulled the cutlass free. Onyema screamed and her blood splashed down on to Killigrew.

Killigrew still had the single-shot pistol in his waistband and he levelled it at Barroso. 'Drop the cutlass.'

'I'd do as he says, friend,' growled Dando, appearing behind Barroso. The slaver snarled and tossed the blade to the deck.

Killigrew crawled out from underneath Onyema and unbuttoned his waistcoat. Shrugging it off, he folded it and held it over the awful wound in her shoulder. 'Hold this in place,' he told her. 'I'll send the surgeon down to look at that wound.'

She spat in his face.

'What about my wound?' demanded Barroso.

'I hope you bleed to death,' Killigrew told him, collecting up all the weapons he could find. He turned to Dando. 'The other two?'

'Out like lights and trussed like turkeys, sir.'

'Good work, Mr Dando.' Killigrew made his way to the main hatch. No sooner had he raised his head above the level of the coaming than a report sounded and a bullet bit into the deck inches from his hand. 'Whisky!' he bawled. 'Whisky!'

The men on the poop deck rose to their feet. 'By God, Mr Killigrew!' exclaimed Strachan. 'Is that really you?'

'What's left of me.' Killigrew climbed up on deck. He suddenly felt utterly drained.

'What about Mr Dando?'

'In fine fettle. There are wounded down here for you to take care of, Mr Strachan.'

'Of course, of course.' Strachan hurried down

the companion ladder and crossed the deck to the hatch.

'You'd better go with him, Boulton, in case they try anything,' said Killigrew. 'Help Mr Dando put the slavers back in the slave deck. And watch that woman, too. She's a real hellspite. Sails, you'd better find that leak chop-chop. O'Connor, go with him and help him.'

'Aye, aye, sir.'

Almost fainting with fatigue, Killigrew staggered into the master's day room. Koumba followed him inside. 'Are you all right?'

He lit a candle and grinned. 'I was wondering when someone was going to ask me that.' He stripped off his shirt and examined his shoulder. The bullet which had creased him as he hung from the stern had not gone deep, but he was also bleeding where Onyema had bitten him.

Koumba saw the teeth-marks and her eyes widened. 'What made that mark?'

Killigrew shrugged. 'Onyema – the slave master's woman – bit me.'

'She bit you?' Her eyes widened, and then her face hardened. 'You must kill her, Senhor Killigrew.'

'What?'

'She's a leopard woman.'

Killigrew was too tired to listen to what sounded to him like it was going to turn out to be nonsense. He wondered if his comprehension of Portuguese was not as good as he had supposed. 'A what?'

'A leopard woman. Have you not heard of the leopard people? They have the form of men and

54

women, but in truth they are evil magicians. They have the power to transform themselves into leopards, in which shape they roam aboard at night committing the most terrible atrocities.'

'Superstitious nonsense. You can't go round killing people just because they bite you. I used to know a girl called Eulalia Pengelly, she bit me once when we were children. You're not suggesting *she's* a leopard woman, are you?'

Koumba ignored the interruption. 'The leopard people murder men and use parts of their bodies to create *borfima*.'

'"*Borfima*"?'

She nodded. 'Powerful medicines which give them great wealth. I tell you this: the leopard woman must be killed, before she brings more death and destruction.'

'Nonsense. If she lives she'll get a fair trial in Freetown. As captain of this vessel I have wide-ranging powers, but I'm damned if I'll use them to take the law into my own hands.' A bottle of *aguadiente* stood on the table and he pulled out the cork with his teeth, taking a long pull at the fiery liquid. Then he swabbed away the blood from the wound in his shoulder, poured a little of the *aguadiente* into it, and set it alight with the candle.

Koumba winced as the smell of burning flesh filled the room. 'Is that the white man's magic?' she asked.

'Got to cauterise the wound, keep out infection,' he grunted. The blue flames disappeared and he poured more *aguadiente* over the blackened skin before he repeated the procedure

55

with the teeth-marks in his wrist. She helped him dress both wounds.

'What is the "Royal Navy"?' she asked him.

'The ships of her Britannic Majesty Queen Victoria. And the men aboard them, of course.'

'And is this what you do? Rescue black people from slavery?'

'That's part of it.' Killigrew gently lifted Parsons' body from the bunk and carried it through to the day room where he laid it on the deck.

'Because your Queen Victoria orders you to do this?'

'Yes. And for prize money. And because it's the right thing to do.' He re-entered the cabin and removed the blood-soaked sheets from the bunk. The blood had soaked through to the mattress below, but Killigrew was too exhausted to care.

'The ways of the white man are strange indeed.'

Killigrew thought about that. 'Yes, I suppose they are.'

The sun was streaming through the skylight by the time Dando roused Killigrew with a mug of tea. Killigrew sat up sharply. 'What time is it?'

'Nearly eight bells in the morning watch, sir.'

'Why the devil didn't anyone wake me?'

'The quack said you needed rest, and Sails agreed with him.'

Killigrew climbed off the bunk and pulled his shirt on. 'The ship? Is she still sinking?'

Dando looked dubious. 'We managed to find the leak and patch it as best we can, though there's still some water coming in. We had to use

56

the fore t'gallant to fother her. There was no spare canvas, 'cept the sail we used for an awning. Sails wanted to use that, of course, but the quack overruled him.'

Killigrew thought about it. Taking down the fore topgallant sail would knock a fraction of a knot off their speed and delay their arrival in Freetown by an hour or two, all told. Some of the recaptives might die in that hour, but more would die if they were left on deck without shelter or shade from the tropical sun.

Killigrew took the mug of tea from Dando and followed him out on deck. The recaptives were starting to look a lot more lively than they had done the previous day and Sails was teaching some of the fitter young men the rudiments of seamanship so that they could help to run the *Maria Magdalena* back to port. They spoke no English and he spoke no ... whatever language it was they spoke ... but he seemed to be managing by pointing to various parts of the ship, saying their names over and over until the recaptives repeated them parrot fashion, and by demonstrating himself he taught them some of the simpler chores required in trimming sails. Killigrew nodded thoughtfully. With only eight men left in the prize crew, including the two officers, they would need all the help they could get.

Two more of the recaptives were busy working the bilge pump, and even as Killigrew watched them another recaptive emerged from one of the hatches carrying a bucket of water which he carried to the side and tipped over. No sooner

57

had he carried the empty bucket back down below than a second recaptive emerged with a bucket and did exactly the same thing.

'The only way we can keep pace with the leak, I'm afraid, sir,' explained Dando.

'At least we've got plenty of hands to keep it up,' Killigrew remarked wryly.

To one side several bloodstained sacks about six feet long lay in rows on the deck. Ordinarily Sails would have sewn them up in canvas, but canvas was too precious on board the *Maria Magdalena* to be squandered in the burial of the dead.

'Why haven't those been dumped overboard yet?' demanded Killigrew.

'Mr Ågård said we should wait for you to read the burial service, so we can do it proper, like,' said Dando.

Killigrew counted the sacks. There were a dozen. Had so many really died in the fighting last night? Remembering now, it all seemed like no more than a nightmare. He did some quick mental arithmetic. 'Who are the other four?' he asked Dando.

'I'm afraid Mr Galton didn't last long, sir. And three more of the slaves died as well. Fever. They must've picked it up on the coast.'

Killigrew nodded. 'Are many more of them sick?'

'The quack counted about two dozen. He's put them in the sick bay.'

'Where's Mr Strachan?'

'Up on the poop, sir.'

Still holding the mug of tea, Killigrew climbed

58

the companion ladder to the poop deck where he found Boulton spelling Ågård at the helm. Strachan sat sleeping on the deck with his back propped up against the bulwark, while two sleeping recaptive children nestled on either side of him. Koumba sat opposite him, watching the sleeping doctor with an amused smile on her face. In the light of day he could see that she really was quite presentable now that she had had a chance to clean up, and her broad smile lit up her whole face. As Killigrew stepped on deck she glanced at him and her smile did not falter.

'Good morning, Menina Koumba,' he said in Portuguese, saluting her.

'Good morning, Senhor Killigrew. I trust you slept well?'

'My God, what was I thinking? I slept on that nice comfortable bunk and left a lady to sleep on deck...'

'A lot of ladies slept on deck last night,' she reminded him, nodding to where the other recaptive women sat in the ship's waist. They were chatting amongst themselves, and some of them were even laughing. This morning there was hope in their eyes where yesterday Killigrew had seen only despair, and in that moment he was reminded that everything he had gone through last night had been worth it.

'We couldn't all have fitted on that bunk,' said Koumba. 'Please do not feel guilty about it, Senhor Killigrew. If anyone earned a good night's rest last night, it was you.'

Killigrew grunted non-commitally. Thanks to his carelessness in trusting Onyema, seven

59

members of his prize crew were dead. 'We'd better get the burial of the dead over and done with,' he said.

They rigged up planks from which the bodies could be tipped overboard while Killigrew rooted around inside his sea-chest and came up with his King James's Bible and his Book of Common Prayer. His grandfather had given them to him on the day he had first joined the Royal Navy as a first-class volunteer, aged twelve. 'These were your father's. I know he would have wanted you to have them.'

Inside the cover of the Bible the following had been written in his father's hand, bold and flourishing, yet meticulously precise:

*A gentleman is made, not born. He is defined by his
    actions, not his wealth.*
*A gentleman protects those who cannot protect
    themselves.*
A gentleman respects the feelings and beliefs of others.
*A gentleman is guided by his own sense of justice and
    fair play.*
*A gentleman treats others according to their merit
    rather than their station.*
*A gentleman is not boastful, but lets his actions speak
    for themselves.*
*A gentleman is as careless of the debts he is owed as
    he is careful of those he owes to others.*
*A gentleman does not stand idly by in the face of
    injustice.*
*A gentleman asks no man to do what he is not
    prepared to attempt himself.*
A gentleman takes responsibility for his own actions.

Killigrew knew those lines by heart. He had no way of knowing if his father had merely written them in an idle moment or if he had deliberately put them down so that his son might be guided by them. But like many children deprived of a fatherly role model at an early age, he seized upon any clue towards his father's character and clung to it. Those lines were the strongest clue he had, and all his adult life he had struggled to abide by those rules.

The prayer book was less well thumbed. This was the first time Killigrew had opened it since he had said, 'Thank you, sir, I'll treasure it always.' And he had kept it, if only to prove to himself that he had meant those words. It was not that Killigrew was an impious man as such, it was just that there always seemed to be more important things to do than pray and go to church.

By the time he emerged on deck once more the others were ready. He opened the prayer book at the contents page and was relieved to discover there was a section 'For the Burial of the Dead at Sea.' Killigrew had seen plenty of burials at sea, but this was the first time he had ever been called upon to conduct one himself.

He riffled through the pages until he found the right one. 'Shall we begin?'

The seamen doffed their hats.

Killigrew cleared his throat. '"Forasmuch as it hath pleased Almighty God of his great mercy to take unto himself the soul of our dear brothers here departed, we therefore commit their bodies

61

to the deep, to be turned into corruption, looking for the resurrection of the body, (when the Sea shall give up her dead), and the life of the world to come, through our Lord Jesus Christ; who at his coming shall change our vile body, that it may be like his glorious body, according to the mighty working, whereby he is able to subdue all things to himself."'

He nodded to Ågård, and one by one the bodies were tipped overboard. They hit the water with a splash and went straight under, pulled to the bottom by the iron shot Sails had sewn inside the sacks.

Killigrew passed the prayer book to Strachan and pointed to the next line. 'Perhaps you'd care to read this part?'

Strachan looked a little shocked at being called on to help, but he took the book from Killigrew. '"I heard a voice from heaven, saying unto me, Write, From henceforth blessed are the dead which die in the Lord: even so saith the spirit; for they rest from their labours."'

He passed the book back to Killigrew. 'Our Father, which art in heaven…'

They all joined him in reciting the Lord's Prayer, and when they had finished he read the collect. Then he concluded: '"The grace of our Lord Jesus Christ, and the love of God, and the fellowship of the Holy Ghost, be with us all evermore."'

He closed the prayer book and stood with his hands clasped before him as they stood in respectful silence for a moment with their heads bowed. Then Dando raised a hand to his breast and sang 'How Sweet the Name of Jesus Sounds' in a surprisingly competent tenor.

Afterwards Killigrew sent O'Connor to fetch him breakfast before retiring to the master's day room, checking the log-board on the way so he could update the log. Then, while he was waiting, he took out the chart and calculated their progress so far. It was slow; damned slow.

There was a knock on the door. 'Come in, O'Connor.'

'Not O'Connor,' said Strachan. 'Me.'

'Well, come in anyway. I owe you an apology, Mr Strachan.'

'You mean about the black woman?' Strachan gestured dismissively. 'You apologised last night.'

'All the same…'

'I can't blame you for thinking what you did,' said Strachan, and grinned sheepishly. 'After all, coming in and seeing what you saw… What must I have looked like?'

Killigrew was grateful for Strachan's magnanimity, but he could not bring himself to smile. 'If I'd listened to you last night, perhaps none of those people need have died.'

'And what *would* you have done, if you'd believed me last night? Put her in irons, just for being over-sensitive? It's always easy to be wiser after the event. You can't blame yourself for what happened. It wasn't your fault Parsons and the rest of our men died, and as for the slavers you and Dando killed … well, I don't imagine anyone will mourn their passing.'

'Even blackbirders have mothers, wives…'

'Mothers and wives who'll have given up their

sons and husbands as worse than dead the moment they learned what line of shipping they were in, if they had any milk of human kindness in their breasts. Look at it this way: how many would have died if those men had shipped with a legitimate merchant ship, instead of taking to blackbirding? They knew the risks they were taking. You know, I'm starting to think that for some of those swines cocking a snook at the Royal Navy is part of the thrill of it. Well, they've cocked their last snook at us now, and the world's a better place for their passing. So instead of worrying about their eternal souls, why not give a thought to the three hundred and sixty odd slaves up on deck whom you've saved from a lifetime of servitude and misery?'

O'Connor arrived with breakfast, two bowls of lobscouse: a seaman's stew of *bouilli* beef, ship's biscuits, potatoes, onions and spices. Most landsmen would have turned their noses up at it, but to a mariner it was considered a delicacy. Thinking of the slaves on deck subsisting on a diet of rice and yams, in all conscience Killigrew could not bring himself to eat it. 'Thank you, Mr O'Connor, but I'll just have whatever the slaves are having.'

'That *is* what the slaves are having, sir.'

'You made enough lobscouse for three hundred and sixty-six slaves?'

O'Connor shifted from one foot to the other. 'Well now, sir, I had to take some liberties with the traditional recipe...'

Killigrew picked up a spoon and tasted it tentatively while O'Connor eagerly awaited his approval. He smacked his lips. 'Very good, O'Connor,' he said dubiously. 'It *is* a little different, I'll admit. Rice?'

'Yes, sir.'

'And something else I can't quite put my finger on...'

Strachan tasted a mouthful. 'Yams.'

O'Connor beamed.

'Very good, O'Connor.'

The sailor went out and Strachan spat his mouthful of lobscouse back into the bowl. 'My God, it's disgusting. Even by navy standards.'

'I should eat up, if I were you. It's the only kind of food we're likely to get from here to Freetown.'

'And how long will that be?'

'I've just finished charting our progress. If my calculations are right we're still ninety-two miles from the African coast.'

'Nautical miles, I take it?'

'Of course.'

'I've never understood: what's the difference between a nautical mile and a normal one?'

'About eight hundred feet.'

'More or less?'

'More.'

'Capital,' Strachan said wryly. 'How long's that going to take us?'

'Well, taking into account the fact because we're low in the water and short of a fore t'gallant, and having to tack because the wind's against us, and what wind we can take advantage of is no more than a force two...'

'Don't beat about the bush, Mr Killigrew. Give it to me straight.'

'About five days.'

'Five days! How long do you think we can keep this floating coffin afloat?'

'Oh, about five days, I should say. Of course, we may get there sooner if the wind picks up between now and then.'

'How likely is that, in these latitudes at this time of year?'

'Are you a gaming man, Mr Strachan?'

'Sometimes. Why? What kind of odds would you give us?'

'Very good ones. If you're the kind of man who likes to wager on a long shot.'

'Fire! Fire!'

Killigrew was woken by the sound of shouting and the clump of feet on the deck above his head. He rolled off the bunk, his hand snaking under the pillow to draw out the pepperbox he had concealed there, and took in his surroundings. He was in the master's cabin on board the *Maria Magdalena*. No light came through the tiny porthole, which suggested it was still night.

He had fallen asleep fully clothed but for his waistcoat and tailcoat, so he went straight out on deck. In the early morning light he could see recaptives streaming out of the forward hatch while the seamen on board charged through the recaptives on deck and fought to descend through the crowded hatch, cursing and swearing at those that got in their way.

Smoke billowed out of the hatch.

Panic stirred in the pit of Killigrew's stomach. Of all the dangers a man faced at sea, fire was one of the most terrible.

He descended below decks via the empty main hatch and made his way forward. The smoke became thicker the closer he got to the bows, until it was acrid and choking. The stench was horrible. It smelled like charred pork.

A few recaptives blundered into him in the dark as they fled from the fire. The companion ladder leading up to the forward hatch was still crowded. A few crushed bodies lay at the foot of the ladder, trampled in the rush to get out. Some recaptives were still crawling out through the door of the sick bay, from where the smoke seemed to issue.

Ågård was trying to descend against the tide, a bucket of water held high. He reached the sick bay only a moment ahead of Killigrew, who followed him inside. The smoke stung his eyes and clawed at his throat. Through the thick black smoke he could just make out the fire: one of the cots was ablaze, the flames tinged with blue. There was another odour in the smoke, something Killigrew could not place at first until the smell of burning flesh and those blue-tinged flames reminded him of how he had cauterised his wounds just before going to bed the previous night: *aguadiente*.

He saw with horror that there was a body on the cot being consumed by the flames.

Ågård hesitated only for a moment, and then stepped forward and tipped the contents of the bucket on the cot. The flames were extinguished at once with a hiss, and steam filled the room.

Killigrew stumbled to the ports and opened

them to let in some fresh air. Then he and Ågård started to pick up the bodies of the fever victims who had passed out in the smoke. Strachan himself was there, unconscious, slumped in a chair. Killigrew lifted him over his shoulder and carried him up on deck while other seamen descended to carry out the other victims of the fire.

Two of the recaptives still worked at the bilge pump and Killigrew filled a bucket from the pump before tossing it over the assistant surgeon. Strachan spluttered into life, choking and retching. Killigrew took a ladleful of water from the scuttled butt and poured some of it between Strachan's lips. Strachan coughed and spewed up. He writhed on the deck for a moment and then rose on his hands and knees. 'Wha ... what happened?'

'There was a fire in the sick berth. Don't you remember anything?'

'Fire? No. I was sitting in the chair reading a book ... that's all I remember. I must've dozed off.' He broke off, coughing again, and wiped his sleeve across his eyes. 'A fire? How could there have been a fire? Did one of the lamps fall?'

'Perhaps, but I don't think so.' Killigrew turned to where Ågård was trying to give a small child the kiss of life. But the child was dead. Ågård rose with tears in his eyes, which might have been caused by the smoke, but somehow Killigrew did not think it was just that. For all his rough manners and boisterous behaviour, Jack Tar was a sentimentalist at heart.

'There's three others suffocated from the smoke and two more trampled to death at the

68

foot of the companion ladder,' said Dando, as more bodies were brought out through the hatch. 'There's some more that's badly injured or sickly from the smoke. I think this one's got a broken leg,' he added, indicating a young boy.

Strachan pushed himself to his feet. Killigrew put a hand on his arm. 'Are you going to be all right?'

'I'll have to be, won't I?' Strachan shrugged his arm off and went to tend the injured.

'What happened?' Killigrew asked Dando.

The seaman shook his head. 'I don't suppose I know much more'n you, sir. I were on the poop with Mr Ågård there when we hears screaming from the fo'c'sle. We looks up and sees smoke a-coming from the hatch. Mr Ågård tells Boulton to take the helm and rushes for'ard with me. By the time we gets here the darkies are running out of the hatch. You was already there by the time I got down the hatch after Mr Ågård. Do you think the fire was started deliberate, like?'

'I don't know. Better go and check on the prisoners, Dando.'

'Aye, aye, sir.' Dando descended the main hatch and returned a couple of minutes later to report that Barroso and the other slavers were still securely in their irons and thoroughly frightened by all the clamour.

'Did you put their minds at rest?' asked Killigrew.

'No, sir. Begging your pardon, sir, but I'm afraid I couldn't resist the temptation to tell 'em the ship was afire and we was abandoning 'em to their fate.'

Killigrew listened for a moment. He could just hear Barroso and the others screaming in terror for someone to come and let them out. 'Good work, Dando.'

'Why, thank'ee, sir.'

Killigrew descended to the sick bay once more. Some residual smoke still lingered in the air and the stench was appalling, but the air blowing through the open ports made it possible to breathe in there. The only signs of fire apart from the smoke-blackening on the bulkheads and deck head were the charred corpse on the burned cot, completely unrecognisable except that it might have been a woman.

Killigrew heard a sound behind him and whirled, but it was only Strachan. 'I've tended the wounded as best I can,' he reported. 'We'll need a new sick berth. We can't leave the poor devils out on deck.'

Killigrew nodded. 'Use the master's day room.'

Strachan took in the scene. 'This fire was started deliberately, wasn't it?'

'Yes. My guess is someone poured *aguadiente* all over this poor devil and set her alight. I don't suppose you can recall who–'

'Onyema. But it wasn't the fire that killed her.' Pinching his handkerchief over his nose and mouth, Strachan indicated the crushed head of the charred corpse. 'Her skull was smashed first.'

III:

Reeled In

'You mean someone stove her head in and then set fire to her to make sure?' said Killigrew.

'I'm saying that's what it looks like,' replied Strachan. 'Poor bitch. She probably wouldn't have lived much longer anyway with that shoulder wound.'

'But why?'

'How should I know? Damned savages.' Strachan started to pack his small supply of medicines, surgical instruments and dressings into his bag.

'Even savages don't do something without a good reason. At least, a reason that seems good to them.' Killigrew frowned. 'They used to burn witches, didn't they?'

'Who did?'

'In the Middle Ages, I mean.'

'Oh. Yes. So?'

'Just thinking out loud. I don't suppose you saw anyone nosing around the sick berth earlier, did you?'

'No one who shouldn't have been there; but I told you, I fell asleep.'

'At what time?'

'How should I know? I remember the ship's bell ringing twice ... that would have been at one

71

o'clock, wouldn't it?'

Killigrew nodded and reached for his watch, only to remember it had been in the fob-pocket of his waistcoat which he had given to Onyema to help her staunch the flow of blood from her wound. 'My waistcoat...'

'Hm? Oh, here it is.'

The blood soaked waistcoat had been tossed on the floor. It was ruined, but the watch was still ticking. Killigrew snapped it open. 'Five past four. So our murderous arsonist had about three hours to go about his – or her – work.'

He left Strachan to arrange the transfer of the sick and injured to the master's day cabin and made his way up to the poop deck. Koumba was still there, sitting with her back to the gunwale. 'What happened?' she asked.

Killigrew did not reply, but indicated her to Boulton. 'How long has she been there?'

Boulton glanced at her. 'She's been there since Ågård woke me a few moments ago.'

'When the fire broke out?'

Boulton nodded.

'What's going on?' asked Koumba. 'I don't understand.'

'You stay there,' Killigrew snapped at her, making his way down to where Ågård was helping Strachan and Dando carry the sick to the master's day room. 'How long was Koumba on the poop deck?'

'You mean the negress that speaks Portuguee, sir?' said Ågård. 'I don't think she left the poop deck all night. Oh, except once, to perform the necessary.'

72

'Did she use the heads?'

Ågård shook his head. 'No, she just went down to the waist and pissed over the gunnel, sir. Why? You don't think she was the one who started the fire, do you?'

'Could she have been?'

'No, sir. That was the only time she left the poop, and I could see her the whole time.'

'Did she speak to anyone while she was down there?'

'She might've done, sir, I don't know. It's not like I was watching her or anything. Even a negress is entitled to her privacy. It was only because I was at the helm looking for'ard that I noticed. But she couldn't have started the fire, I'd stake my life on it.'

'Did you see if any of the other recaptives went below?'

'Plenty, sir, but don't ask me to tell you which ones. They all look the same to me. Especially in the dark.'

Killigrew sighed. 'All right. Thank you, Mr Ågård.' He made his way back up to the poop deck, caught Koumba by the arm and hoisted her to her feet.

'What is it?' she asked.

'I want a word with you,' he told her. 'In private.'

'By all means,' she said.

He took a hurricane lantern and dragged her below decks to one of the store rooms where they could talk undisturbed. She regarded him nervously and ran her tongue over her sensuous lips. 'Senhor Killigrew, I do not think you are the kind of man who would take advantage of–'

'Onyema was murdered tonight,' he told her, hanging the lantern from a nail in an overhead beam. When she said nothing, he ploughed on. 'Her skull was smashed in and her body was burned.'

'I cannot pretend I am sorry. She was *evil.*'

Killigrew grabbed her by the shoulders and slammed her back against the bulkhead. 'I know you didn't do it, but I think you know more about it than you're letting on. I think you know who did. In fact, I think you put the murderers up to it.'

'I don't know what you are talking about.'

'Someone poured *aguadiente* all over her body and set fire to it. The way you saw me pour *aguadiente* over my wounds earlier and set fire to that. Why burn her after she'd already had her skull smashed in? To destroy her evil spirit? Is that it?'

'Perhaps I mentioned to some of the other Africans on board that Onyema bit you. Perhaps they surmised, as I did, that she must have been a leopard woman. What does it matter? Whether or not you believe in the leopard people, you cannot deny she was evil. She tried to kill you, tried to kill us all…' She smiled, and pushed her breasts out towards him. 'But that is not the real reason you brought me here alone, is it?' she asked, licking her lips.

He turned away quickly. 'You're no better than she was. You do realise that six others were killed as a result of that fire?'

'God decides who lives and who dies. If

74

Onyema died it was because God wanted to punish her for being a leopard woman. Perhaps God also wanted to punish the six who died for crimes of which we know nothing. Vengeance is mine, saith the Lord.'

Killigrew stared at her. 'You're a Christian?'

She nodded. 'A Catholic.'

'Of course. That's where you learned Portuguese, isn't it? Jesuit missionaries.' He ran his fingers wearily through her hair. 'Get out. Go on. Get out of my sight. And there'll be no more burnings of witches or leopard people or any other superstitious nonsense like that, d'you hear?'

Her head held high, she crossed to the door. On the threshold she paused and turned back to stare at him gravely. 'The leopard people are real, Senhor Killigrew. You *will* believe.'

Killigrew felt a shudder run down his spine, then shook his head dismissively. 'Superstitious nonsense,' he muttered to himself.

The sea was glassy. The sails hung limply from the yards, without a breath of wind to stir them. The heat of the sun was oppressive. The recaptives lay listlessly on the deck; the sailors were not much better off. Killigrew had gambled on rationing the food and water for five days, knowing that they could not stay afloat much longer than that anyway, but even so they were weakened by thirst and hunger.

The only sounds were the creak of the timbers and the squeaking of the pump which two Africans continued to work, knowing that their lives depended upon it now. Killigrew stood at the taffrail where he had rigged up a fishing line. Their only hope now lay in putting the long boat into the water and towing the *Maria Magdalena* to the shore; but he was not convinced his men had the strength for the feat. Still, short of a miracle – the freshening of the wind – it was their only chance. He took out his fob watch and glanced at it. Five minutes to noon. *If the wind doesn't pick up by noon,* he told himself, *we'll have to try it.*

Strachan climbed on to the poop deck, dabbing sweat from the underside of his jaw with a wadded handkerchief. He joined Killigrew at the taffrail. 'We're going to die here, aren't we?'

'Never say die, Mr Strachan,' Killigrew told him with a breeziness he did not feel. 'We're not dead yet.'

'We might as well be, if the wind doesn't pick up soon.' He took Killigrew's telescope and turned it to the east. 'Wait a minute! I can see land!'

Killigrew shook his head. 'Smokes.'

'What?'

'Those are smokes. Low-lying fog banks, Mr Strachan. They're quite common in these waters at this time of year. They can look like land, from a distance.'

'To a landlubber, you mean.'

'I didn't say that. Mind you, if the smokes weren't there – and if my calculations are correct – you would be able to see the coast of Africa.'

'My God, are we that close?'

'It's still about seven miles. It might as well be

seven hundred miles without any wind.'

Strachan had been keeping his voice low, but now he lowered it even more and moved closer to Killigrew. 'But if we're *that* close, couldn't we get in the long boat and row?'

'All three hundred and fifty-seven of us, Mr Strachan?' Sickness had continued to take its toll of the Africans despite Strachan's best efforts; Killigrew had to be content with the small consolation that an average of three deaths a day was not bad for a slaver, even one which a Royal Navy prize crew was trying to get back to a harbour.

'It's pointless us all dying,' murmured Strachan. 'There must be room for twenty in that boat...'

'Twenty-four, actually. Probably more, if you took some of the children instead of the adults. But how do you choose which ones?'

'Well, we Britons should go, naturally...'

'Why "naturally"?'

Strachan thought about it. 'Well, because we've got the guns and I'm a selfish swine.'

'Your honesty does you more credit than your generosity of spirit, Mr Strachan.'

Killigrew's fishing line twitched in the water. 'You've got a bite,' Strachan told him.

Killigrew glanced down. 'It's just a sprat. Not even worth the effort of reeling it in.'

Strachan shrugged. 'I'm not saying we should leave *all* the negroes,' he continued. 'There's nine of us, that leaves room in the boat for fifteen of them. More if we took the children: they've got longer lives ahead of them anyway.'

'Is it your medical training which allows you to

think such things through so coldly and calculating?'

'Just common sense, I'd have thought. Listen Killigrew, if you want to be a hero and go down with your ship that's fine by me. I just don't see why you should want to take the rest of us down with you.'

'I don't intend that anyone should go down with this ship, Mr Strachan,' Killigrew said coldly. 'I've already lost thirty-five people since I took command of this vessel. I've no wish to make it three hundred and fifty-two–'

Killigrew's fishing reel span with a screech. Something big had taken the hook and was moving away fast. 'That's a sprat?' Strachan asked incredulously as everyone gathered around the two of them.

'Something that ate the sprat, Mr Strachan.' Killigrew took the fishing rod from its line and braced himself to fight the fish.

Everyone else was suddenly an expert on deep-water fishing. 'Let it run, sir! Let it run!' urged O'Connor.

'No, fight him!' said Boulton. 'Wear him down.'

'It's a marlin! It's got to be a marlin.'

'No, it's a shark!' Strachan pointed to where a fin cleaved through the water about a hundred yards or so off the stern.

'Good,' said Killigrew. 'Have you ever eaten shark steak, Mr Strachan? It can be surprisingly tasty. In China, the fin is considered a delicacy.'

'Hit him, sir! Hit him now!'

The line went slack and Killigrew at once began to reel it in.

'All right, now reel it in,' Boulton said unhelpfully.

'Why don't you tie the line to the bows, maybe we can persuade it to tow us ashore,' sneered Strachan.

'You've lost him, sir,' said Boulton. 'The line's snapped.'

'No, he's hooked,' said O'Connor. 'He's hooked good and proper.'

'He's gone, I tell you,' insisted Boulton.

The reel screeched as the shark ran again.

'He's running, sir!' said Boulton.

'Let him go … that's it… Right, now hit him! Hard!'

'Sail ho!' cried one of the recaptives Sails had trained to be a lookout.

Killigrew twisted and glanced up to where the African sat on the foretop. 'Where away?'

The African just pointed off the port side of the *Maria Magdalena*. 'Sail ho!' were probably the only two words of English he knew, Killigrew reflected.

He handed the fishing rod to Strachan. 'Here, take this.'

'Wha–? No! No, I don't know anything about this…'

'Boulton and O'Connor will teach you soon enough,' said Killigrew, picking up his telescope. 'They both seem to be experts.'

As the two seamen at once began to bombard Strachan with contradictory advice, Killigrew moved to the bulwark and pointed his telescope to the north, in the direction which the lookout had indicated. He couldn't see any … no, wait, there it was: the upper sails of a ship, the hull down below the horizon. Killigrew descended to the quarter-deck and jumped lightly on to the gunwale before ascending the ratlines to the mainmast top. He paused on the platform about a third of the way up the mast and raised the telescope to his eye once more.

Yes, he could see her all right. A clipper, her sails hanging just as limply as the *Maria Magdalena*'s. Killigrew could just make out three boats in the water before the clipper's prow. They had to be towing the ship.

And she was headed towards the *Maria Magdalena*.

Killigrew slammed the telescope shut and shinned nimbly down the ropes to the deck. 'Vast angling, there!' he roared as he ascended to the poop deck.

Boulton was helping Strachan to reel in the shark while O'Connor readied a boat hook as a makeshift gaff. 'Hold on, Killigrew!' called Strachan. 'We've almost got the blighter! Blood an' 'ounds, he's a leviathan!'

'Belay that! All hands to quarters!'

Boulton and O'Connor at once left Strachan to it, leaving him with a forlorn expression on his face. A moment later the rod was torn from his grip, leaving him with the skin flayed from his palms.

'O'Connor, I'll wager there's a Brazilian ensign in the flag locker,' said Killigrew. 'Fly her upside down from the mainmast, Mr Ågård, see if you can get this pivot gun ready for action. Round shot, if you please, I noticed some in the shot locker the other day.'

'Aye, aye, sir!'

As O'Connor and Ågård hurried off to do Killigrew's bidding, Strachan came across wiping his bloody palms on his handkerchief. 'We almost had him there,' he said petulantly.

'Sorry to spoil your sport, Mr Strachan, but this is more important.'

'What's going on? You look as if you're preparing for a fight.'

'That I am. The ship has the look of a slaver to me.'

'She's not a steamer, is she? I don't see any steam. How is it they're moving while we're becalmed?'

'They're using their boats to tow her.'

'You can do that? Why didn't we think of that?'

'I did. But it's seven miles to the shore and our men are weak with hunger and exhaustion. Pulling a ship of three hundred and fifty tons burthen seven miles to shore is no laughing matter, especially when she's low in the water. That's what they call a counsel of desperation.'

'I'd say we were in pretty desperate straits.'

'I was hoping something would turn up. And it has.' He gestured off the port beam. 'She's headed south along the coast. If she's a slaver that means her slave deck's empty; otherwise she'd be sailing out to sea.'

'And you think they'll give us passage to Free-town?'

'It may take a little persuasion.' Killigrew patted the muzzle of the thirty-two-pound pivot gun on the poop deck.

81

'Do you think we can beat them in a fair fight?'

'Good God, no. That's why we're using guile.' Killigrew nodded to where O'Connor was hoisting the Brazilian ensign to the top of the mainmast.

'That's not a British flag.'

'No.'

'Isn't it upside down?'

'Unofficial sign of distress. With any luck the slaver should come to investigate, which I very much doubt she'd trouble to do if we flew the Union Jack. Take your coat off. You look too much like a naval officer.'

'I'll tell Commander Standish you said that. He's usually weighing off at me for not looking *enough* like a naval officer.'

Killigrew made his way to where Koumba stood in the waist. She had avoided the poop deck ever since Killigrew had confronted her about Onyema's death. 'There's a ship coming,' he told her curtly. 'It's our only chance to get everyone off this floating coffin alive, but if we're going to take her we need her to get close. The only way we can do that is if they think we're just another slaver. That means that all these people have to get out of sight.' He gestured at the recaptives on deck.

'Go back down on the slave deck, you mean.'

'I'm afraid so. We'll put the irons on them but not lock them. Can you explain to them? Make them understand it's for their own protection?'

She nodded. 'I'll try.'

'The slaving fraternity is a close-knit one, sir,' Ågård warned Killigrew. 'If you're going to try to pretend to be the master of this vessel there's a good chance the captain of that clipper will know you're not who you claim to be. He probably knows the real master of the *Maria Magdalena*.'

'I know, but that's a chance we've got to take. Anyway, I'm not going to pretend to be the master of this vessel; you are.'

'Hunh?'

'I'm the only white man on board who speaks more than a few words of Portuguese. If only one of us does any talking it's going to look damned suspicious. So you're going to pretend to be American. You'll never pass for Brazilian anyway, with that blond hair and those blue eyes. Think you can manage a Yankee accent?'

Ågård grinned. 'Waal, Ah guess Ah sure kin try.'

'That's good, but don't overdo it.'

'An American master of a Brazilian vessel?' said Strachan. 'Isn't that going to seem even more suspicious?'

'Brazilian slavers often carry American captains, Mr Strachan,' said Killigrew. 'To go with their false American colours and forged papers.'

Koumba persuaded the recaptives to descend below decks, leaving only two of them on duty at the bilge pump. Dando went below with Koumba to make sure the recaptives put the irons on their ankles so that it would seem to the casual observer that they were secure. They took the slavers, gagged them, and escorted them to one of the store rooms where they shackled them and locked them in.

Killigrew made his way to the cabin to fetch his pepperbox. He passed the sailmaker on the way.

83

'Sails, can you check the level of water in the well for me?'

The sailmaker nodded and made his way to the well. Killigrew entered the cabin and made sure all the barrels of his pepperbox were primed and loaded. He thrust it into his holster and then took the single-shot flintlock, loading and priming that as well. He unfastened his sword belt, loath to part with his cutlass but aware that as navy-issue equipment it would give the whole game away. On his way out he took the keys from the nail on the bulkhead and slipped them into his pocket.

On deck, he met the sailmaker returning from the well. 'How much longer do you think?' Killigrew asked him.

'Half an hour, an hour maybe? Then the water reaches the lower ports. I've battened the ports down, of course, but that'll only buy us a few minutes.'

'How long until the other ship reaches us?' asked Strachan.

Killigrew took another look through his telescope. 'No more than half an hour.'

'That's cutting it damned fine.'

'Assuming, of course, that they trouble to come and investigate.'

'What if they don't?'

'Then I hope we can all swim.'

The clipper troubled to come and investigate.

The men in the small boats towed the clipper to within a cable's length of the *Maria Magdalena* and the master of the clipper – the name painted on the stern was the *São João* – hailed them in Portuguese with his speaking trumpet.

'You are in need of assistance? You seem very low in the water.'

'I'd better pretend to be the ship's interpreter,' Killigrew said to Strachan, and raised his own speaking trumpet to reply. 'We're sinking. We were chased for over a hundred miles by a damned British steamer. We managed to give her the slip in the end, but not before she damaged us below the waterline.'

'You have slaves on board?'

Killigrew was about to reply when Ågård laid a hand on his arm. 'If this turns out to be a US Navy ship posing as a slaver...'

'Don't even think such thoughts,' said Killigrew. 'Don't worry, the Yankees don't have that much imagination.' He raised the speaking trumpet to his mouth. 'Yes. Three hundred and forty-one of them. You can have fifty per cent commission on them, if you'll just get us out of this mess.'

'Seventy per cent!'

'Nothing doing!'

'Killigrew!' hissed Strachan. 'What the hell do you think you're doing?'

'I've got to haggle, or they'll know there's something rum going on.'

'Seventy, or we leave you all to drown!' called the master of the clipper.

'Fifty-five. My owner will kill me anyway when he hears about this.'

The master of the *São João* laughed. 'Sixty-five.'

'Sixty. Any more than that and I'm bank-rupted.'

'Sixty-five. That's our last offer, take it or leave it.'

'You drive a hard bargain, my friend.' Killigrew hesitated, as if indecisive. 'Very well, sixty-five it is.'

'Come on over. We'll talk.'

'All right, but don't let's talk too long. This ship is going down fast, and if we don't get the slaves on board your ship your commission will be sixty-five per cent of nothing.'

Boulton, Dando, Sails and O'Connor swung the *Maria Magdalena*'s jolly boat out on its davits and lowered it into the water. Killigrew produced the flintlock and thrust it into Strachan's hand. 'Here. Stick this in your belt.'

Strachan accepted the weapon dubiously. 'Won't they see it?'

'That's the general idea. They'll think it odd to see a slaver who isn't armed.'

'Will I have to use it?'

'When the time comes you may have to wave it around threateningly. If we can do this without unnecessary bloodshed I'll feel much happier. If you must shoot it, here's how you aim it.' Killigrew clamped his hand over Strachan's and held the muzzle close against his own side. 'Like that. That's the only sure way of hitting your target with one of those things. And remember it's a single-shot weapon, so once you've pulled the trigger you're defenceless. Unless you want to use it as a club, of course.'

Strachan grimaced and thrust the pistol behind

his belt. 'Let's hope it doesn't come to that.'

Killigrew turned to Boulton and the sailmaker. 'Stay away from the pivot guns – they'll be watching you. But if you hear shooting or it looks like we're in any kind of trouble, try to sink the small boats. The important thing is to keep the *São João* here until we're all aboard her – including the recaptives. Without the small boats they're as helpless as we are, until the wind picks up.'

'Good luck, sir.'

'Thank you. And you.'

Killigrew and Ågård shinned down a rope into the jolly boat. Strachan followed them gingerly, lost his grip when he was only a few feet from the boat and sprawled on the bottom boards. Killigrew helped him up, and then Dando and O'Connor began to row them across to the *São João*. Most of the *São João*'s crew were in the small boats riding off the clipper's bows. Strachan wondered when they would return to the ship so that they could start transhipping the slaves; it could not be long before the *Maria Magdalena* floundered. Still, the more slavers there were in the small boats the fewer there would be on the *São João*'s deck for them to deal with.

The jolly boat bumped gently against the clipper's side and a rope ladder was tossed down for them to climb up. Two of the slavers climbed down first to hold the rope ladder for the others as they climbed up. They stayed in the jolly boat after Strachan had climbed up on deck after Killigrew, Ågård, Dando and O'Connor and began to row it back to the *Maria Magdalena*.

Someone on deck said something in Portuguese to Ågård. Killigrew turned and saw a middle-aged man with silver hair and a tanned face wearing tolerably good clothes. He guessed this would be the master of the *São João*.

'Hey, Barroso!' Ågård called to Killigrew in an execrable attempt at an American accent. 'Come over heah and translate whut the Sam Hill this dude's saying. Whut else do I pay you fuh, Gawdamnit!'

Killigrew turned smoothly away from the gunwale to obey, but the silver-haired man held up a hand. 'You only speak English, Captain?' he asked Ågård.

'The only language Ah know is American, suh.'

'Ah, an American. I was wondering what that accent was supposed to be. Of course – an American captain would help to convince any ships of the Royal Navy that tried to stop you that you are an American ship. Very clever. Allow me to introduce myself: I am Raimundo da Silva, master of the *São João*, out of Pernambuco.' He held out his hand delicately.

Ågård shook it a lot less delicately. 'Abram Tyler, at your service. And this heah's mah first mate, and translator, Senhor Ramón Barroso, and mah ship's doctor, Tex Polk.'

'Er ... howdy,' said Strachan.

'Well, gentlemen, shall we retire out of this fatiguing sun into my day room and seal our bargain with a drink while my men tranship your slaves – or perhaps I should say *our* slaves – to my ship?' He gestured to where the slaves were being

88

brought up on to the deck of the *Maria Magdalena*. Killigrew noticed that the use of whips was much in evidence and he stifled a wince. 'I have an excellent bottle of sherry–'

'Let's stay out here, shall we?' suggested Killigrew.

'You do not trust me?' Da Silva smiled. 'That is very wise. I respect a cautious man...'

A commotion broke out on board the *Maria Magdalena*. Some of the slaves, outraged at having their hopes of freedom dashed by their apparent transfer to another slaver, started to struggle. A couple of shots rang out, and two young recaptives fell to the deck.

'Have your men take care, Senhor da Silva,' warned Killigrew. 'That's valuable merchandise.'

'So you do not have your cargo broken to the lash yet, eh? Personally, I always find a couple of dead niggers a most excellent investment. It encourages the remainder to be still for the rest of the passage. But tell me, Senhor Barroso, I always thought my old friend Capitão Videira was master of the *Maria Magdalena*.'

'Capitão Videira fell ill,' Killigrew explained smoothly. 'The owners employed me to stand in for him on this voyage.'

Da Silva turned to his first mate, a burly man with black curly hair and a greasy, matted beard. 'You see, Figueroa? Did I not tell you it could not be Videira you saw led in chains from the deck of that British paddle-sloop we saw in Freetown two days ago?'

Killigrew realised the game was up.

89

IV:

Land Sharks

Killigrew drew his pepperbox from its holster and touched da Silva beneath the jaw with the muzzles. In the same instant he felt the cold touch of a pistol muzzle behind his ear.

'I believe this is what is known as an *impasse*,' da Silva said coolly. 'You shoot me, and Figueroa shoots you.'

'I think not,' Strachan said somewhere behind Figueroa, and Killigrew felt the gun taken away from his ear. Ågård, Dando and O'Connor also drew their pistols and covered the slavers close by.

Da Silva's face turned grey. 'Royal Navy?' he spat.

'In the best traditions of the service,' agreed Killigrew.

With da Silva and his first mate at pistol point, they waited until all the recaptives and the rest of the prize crew had been transported from the *Maria Magdalena* to the *São João*, only moments before the former floundered and keeled over, turning turtle.

As the slavers were herded down to the slave deck, Killigrew marched da Silva back into the day room. The ship's papers were made out in French, Spanish, Portuguese, Danish and

English – both British and United States. Killigrew did not doubt there was a different flag in the bow locker for each of the different nationalities represented amongst the forged papers. There was also a cargo manifest: even now the slavers still carried out their trade by the book, as if it were all still perfectly legal and above board.

He cast his eyes over the manifest. The cargo consisted of *aguadiente,* copper wire, cotton goods, gunpowder, iron pots, looking glasses, muskets, rum and tobacco; all of them typical goods of exchange for the slave trade. According to the owner's instructions they were supposed to take them to the Owodunni Barracoon to exchange them for a cargo of slaves to be transported to Bahia.

'Where's the Owodunni Barracoon?' Killigrew asked da Silva.

'I have never heard of it.'

'Really? You were supposed to be sailing there.'

Da Silva took out a cigar and struck a match to light it. Before he could apply the flames to the cigar's end, Killigrew had snatched the cigar from his mouth, crushed it in his hand and tossed it out through the window.

'You shouldn't have done that,' da Silva said with an infuriating mildness. 'That really was a waste of a fine Havana cigar. I suppose you think you are very clever, eh, young man?'

'Clever enough to defeat you, if that counts for anything,' retorted Killigrew.

Da Silva chuckled. 'Defeat me?' He shook his head. 'Oh, no, my friend. Perhaps you have won

91

this battle, but you can never win the war. You know as well as I do that once we get to Freetown you will have to let us go. You have no power over foreign nationals. Why you persist in stopping our ships is a mystery to me.'

'Because it's our duty?' suggested Killigrew. 'Both as officers of the Royal Navy and as decent human beings.'

'Humanity is a relative concept, my young friend.' Da Silva crossed to the open door and gestured at the recaptives being brought back on board the *São João*'s decks from the boats. 'To you these cattle are human beings. To me they are no more than apes. Apes that can be trained to take their rightful place in the service of a higher form of life.'

'That counts you out, then. Compared to you, even a slug is a higher form of life.'

Da Silva was unperturbed. 'You English make me laugh. Always so arrogant, so convinced that you are in the right. What gives you the prerogative to interfere in the trade of other nations, to act as the self-appointed watchmen of the seas?'

'What gives you the right to trade in human flesh?'

Da Silva sighed mockingly. 'Such passion and idealism in one so young. One day, when you are my age perhaps, you will come to understand that nothing in life is as clear cut as you seem to think it is…'

'Oh, I think that when it comes to issues you'll find the inhumanity of the slave trade is as clear cut as they come.'

'Perhaps. Perhaps you are right. But being right makes no difference. You know what is important?' He reached into his pocket.

Killigrew put a hand on the grip of his pepperbox. Da Silva smiled, and slowly drew out a fistful of gold coins. 'This. This is what is truly important. This is why you will never end the slave trade. Because men will always love this more than they love justice. You could take this – share it with your men, if it makes you feel better – and let us go.'

Killigrew stared at the coins as they glittered in the sunlight. With the money that da Silva had in the palm of his hand, Killigrew could buy himself out of the navy and set himself up for life in a comfortable town house in London. He licked his lips, and then took the money from the slaver's hand.

The smile that started to spread across da Silva's face froze as Killigrew tossed the money out of the window. 'You shouldn't judge other people by your own standards, da Silva.'

'You're a fool. You should have taken the money. I will still be free within days of our landing at Freetown.'

Da Silva's self-assured smugness was so irritating that Killigrew struggled to suppress the urge to smash his face in. 'We'll see,' he said tightly.

'It is the ruling of this court that since the *Maria Magdalena* and the *São João* were separate ships with separate owners, the two cases must be dealt with separately.' Of the three admirals who sat on the panel of the court of mixed commissions, it was the Dutch one – the neutral one, the others being British and Portuguese – who read out the summation and verdict. He at least had the decency to look regretful at the verdict that he and his colleagues had reached.

The courthouse in Freetown was a dry, dusty place with pretensions to civilisation. It was a long way from civilisation, but it was even further from the blood-soaked deck of a slaver.

'Firstly, the *Maria Magdalena*. The captain of the arresting vessel, Commander Standish of Her Majesty's paddle-sloop *Tisiphone,* has presented no conclusive evidence that the crew of the *Maria Magdalena* were at any time engaged in the trading of slaves…'

Killigrew kept his face impassive, merely closing his eyes for a moment. He refused to give da Silva and Videira the satisfaction of seeing that to him the verdict was like a dagger being twisted in his guts. But the *Tisiphone*'s other mate, Eustace Tremaine, leaped to his feet. 'No evidence!' he protested. 'What about the slaves, damn it?'

'Sit down, young man, or I'll have you in contempt of court,' snarled the British admiral, a fat, red-faced, gouty old man.

'I *am* in contempt of a court which takes the word of a gang of murderous slavers over and above that of four officers of the Royal Navy!'

The British admiral banged his gavel. 'Sit down! I *shall* have order in this court! You will conduct yourself with the decorum becoming an officer of the Royal Navy.'

Killigrew reached up and took his friend by the arm, gently pulling him back into his seat.

The Dutch admiral continued. 'Since there is no concrete evidence to convict the crew of the *Maria Magdalena*, it is the verdict of this court that Captain Videira and his men are to be released at once. As to Captain da Silva and his crew, we likewise find that since the only evidence that he and his men were engaged in the slave trade other than the slaves which Mate Killigrew himself shipped aboard from the *Maria Magdalena*–'

Tremaine banged a fist against the table. 'But this is farcical! You can't deny the existence of those slaves in one case, and then use them as evidence in another! If you'd only get some of them in here to testify–'

The British admiral banged his gavel again. 'Silence! If you had been here earlier, young man, you would understand that the testimony of natives is inadmissible evidence. As indeed were the papers which Mate Killigrew claims to have found on board the *São João*, papers which Captain da Silva claims were planted in his cabin by the aforementioned Mate Killigrew. The court therefore finds the captain and crew of the *São João* innocent. They are to be released at once, and the Portuguese vessel *São João* to be surrendered back to them by the Royal Navy at the earliest convenience.

Videira and da Silva shook one another's hands, and then the hands of their plump and over-paid lawyers. Videira's lawyer rose to his feet. 'Your lordships, I would like the record to state that not only will my client be suing Mate Killigrew for the loss of the *Maria Magdalena,* but he will also be pressing the families of the honest mariners so callously slain by Mr Killigrew to sue him for excessive brutality in the execution of his duties.'

At the back of the court, the seamen of the *Tisiphone* present groaned.

'That is a private matter between yourself, the families of the dead seamen, and Mate Killigrew,' the Dutch admiral remarked drily. 'It is no concern of this court. We will now adjourn.'

Killigrew went outside and leaned back against the wall of the courthouse. He looked at his hand and saw that it was shaking. He clenched it into a fist, and then lit a cheroot to calm his nerves.

Tremaine followed him out. The same age as one another, Killigrew and Tremaine were good friends. They both resided in the gun room, but since they were in opposite watches they rarely saw one another, like the eponymous heroes of Mr Morton's new farce, *Box and Cox.* They had grown up together in Falmouth and shared the same dream of becoming captains in the Royal Navy like their fathers. But when they had reached the age of twelve their ways had parted, Tremaine attending the Royal Naval College at Portsmouth while Killigrew had gone straight to sea as a first class volunteer.

There was a self-mocking rivalry between the two of them – college graduates were often derided for their more theoretical approach to seamanship – and they played up to it, but each was secretly jealous of the other. Tremaine envied the kudos Killigrew enjoyed amongst his superiors for being an officer raised in the old tradition of hands-on experience; while Killigrew knew that times were changing and that one day the college graduates would run the navy. Already the navy was becoming more and more scientific. Steamships might lack the romance of sail, but there could be no doubt that one day they would supplant them altogether.

'Damn it, what a travesty!' huffed Tremaine, outwardly more upset by the verdict than his friend. 'That wasn't justice, that was a farce!'

Killigrew shook his head. 'It's not a question of justice, it's a question of law. The two are rarely the same thing. Forget it, 'Stace. It's not important. What's important is that most of the negroes we found on board the *Maria Magdalena* are saved from a life of slavery. That's what counts.'

'Yes, but you'd think you'd get some gratitude out of it, instead of being treated as though *you're* the criminal.'

Strachan came out next. 'Damnably sorry, Killigrew. Outrageous verdict. Listen, about that private action Videira's lawyer was talking about. My uncle Andrew is a QC, I'm sure I could persuade him to accept your case.'

'Thank you, Mr Strachan. I may just take you up on that offer–'

Standish steamed out of the court, red in the face. Seeing Killigrew, he rounded on him angrily. 'Well, I hope you're satisfied, young man. One middy and four of my best hands killed; a slaver I went to a considerable amount of trouble to catch only for you to sink it, cheating me and the rest of the crew of our share of prize money; and for what? So I could stand up in that court and be made a fool of, a laughing stock! All I can say is, I hope Videira's land-shark *does* bring that personal action against you. I won't defend you, for one. Perhaps it will teach you not to be so damned zealous in future.' As Standish had repeatedly informed Killigrew, if there was one thing he could not abide it was a *zealous* officer. 'I mean, what in the name of all that's holy did you think you were playing at?'

'My duty, sir?'

'None of your jaw now, laddie! I shan't have it, d'ye hear? I shan't! You're a disgrace, Killigrew! A damned disgrace! Carrying on like some kind of latter-day buccaneer. Well, let me tell you there's no place for buccaneers like you in today's Royal Navy. If you'd followed proper naval procedure and brought the *Maria Magdalena* straight back here, instead of rushing off trying to catch another slaver, then Parsons and the others might still be alive...'

As much as Killigrew wanted to smash Standish's face in, there was part of him which could not help wondering if the commander was right about him being responsible for the death of the five men who had been under his command as part of the *Maria Magdalena*'s prize crew.

The two slaver captains emerged from the court with their lawyers, laughing and joking. Seeing the four naval officers, they smirked. 'See you in the civil courts, Mr Killigrew,' called Videira.

'How are those high-minded ideals of yours now, Mr Killigrew?' asked da Silva. 'A little dented, perhaps?'

Killigrew's temper finally snapped. He lunged for da Silva's throat, but Strachan and Tremaine both caught him and hauled him back before he reached the slaver. 'Easy, Killigrew, easy,' said Strachan.

'I'm not finished with you,' Killigrew snarled at them. 'I'm coming after you, and all your kind.'

'I hope that's not a threat, Mr Killigrew,' said da Silva's lawyer. 'The courts here take a very dim view of threatening language.'

'There'll be a reckoning yet.'

Da Silva smiled. 'I shall await that day with interest.'

Killigrew watched the two lawyers hurry their clients on into the hustle and bustle of the streets of Freetown, and sighed. He wished he could learn to control his temper, widely supposed to be a legacy from his Greek mother. She had been a fighter in the Greek War of Independence, and quite a firebrand by all accounts. That had been where she had met his father, of course. Captain John Killigrew had served as an officer in the Royal Navy during the war against Napoleon and afterwards became a sailor of fortune, serving with his old patron Admiral Lord Cochrane in the Chilean, Brazilian and Greek navies in turn.

'Are you all right, Killigrew?' asked Tremaine.

Killigrew nodded and banged a fist against the side of the courthouse. 'Damn those scum! Da Silva was right, damn his eyes. He's going to go straight back on board the *São João* and pick up a cargo of slaves further down the coast, and it's as if there's nothing we can do to stop him!' He sighed. 'Oh, well. Standing here grumbling isn't going to help matters.'

Strachan nodded. 'Gentlemen, as a fully qualified apothecary, it is my recommendation that we repair at once to the nearest hostelry, partake of intoxicating liquors, and indulge in the company of the lowest sort of females that Freetown can boast of.'

'Capital notion,' said Killigrew. 'Let's go.'

When Killigrew had finished dressing he left a guinea on the bedside table and glanced back to where the prostitute, a freed slave, sat at her dresser, touching up her hair in preparation for her next client. Most of his sexual liaisons were with prostitutes – striking up a relationship with any other kind of woman in a port could only end in heartbreak for one or both parties, and possible ruin for the lady if it resulted in pregnancy – but that night he went downstairs feeling uncharacteristically ashamed. *Aguadiente,* copper wire, cotton goods, gunpowder, iron pots, looking glasses, muskets, rum, tobacco: it was all the same. The rape of a continent.

A brawl between the Tisiphones – it was traditional for sailors from a ship to be known by its name – and the crew of an American frigate had been in full swing in the saloon below when Killigrew had headed upstairs, but it was over by the time he returned. Here and there a few unconscious bodies snored amidst the wreckage of tables and chairs, while a slave swept up the broken glass. 'Goodnight, Mas'er Killigrew.'

'G'night, George.'

Just another night at Maggie's Place, he thought to himself.

George suddenly remembered something. 'Oh, Mas'er Killigrew? Wait there a minute, mas'er. I have something for you.' He scurried into the back room. Killigrew was curious enough to wait until he returned; it did not take long. George re-emerged carrying a tall black beaver hat. 'Mas'er Standish, him done left this in Missy Molly's room last night.'

'Did he, by God? Don't worry, I'll see that he gets it back. Thank you, George.' Killigrew tipped him a shilling and went outside.

He paused on the veranda and leaned on the rail, watching the people coming and going for a while until he had finished his cheroot; Krumen as naked as the day they were born, Muslim traders in elegant long blue robes of fine country cloth, and Creoles dressed in European clothes wholly unsuitable to the tropical climate. It was barely eight o'clock, but already things were winding down in the town. Freetown was so shameless it practised its debauchery during daylight hours; it had to get up to go to chapel early the next morning.

Freetown was a city of contradictions: a young settlement with an air of tumble-down decrepitude about it. None of the whites who came to his fever-stricken coast expected to live more than a few years, so no one bothered to invest much time or money in building to last or even repairing that which collapsed. To landward, green-carpeted mountains, slashed here and there with scars of red earth, and dotted with the homes of the colony's wealthier whites, provided a backdrop to the port, rising up until they disappeared into the low-lying clouds which wreathed them. Houses of wood or stone, washed white or yellow, with green-painted jalousies beneath their verandas and wide-caved shingle roofs, crowded towards the sea. The dusty streets, which turned into rivers of mud during the wet season, were broad, and prolific gardens provided microcosmic reflections of the jungles which crowded around the edges of the settlement. St George Cathedral dominated the town – not that the town needed much to dominate it – with turkey-buzzards perched on the roof during daylight hours, and chapels of every conceivable Protestant sect jostled for space with countless rum-houses.

Freetown had been set up on the coast of Sierra Leone as a colony for freed slaves nearly sixty years ago. In those days its population had consisted of four hundred negroes and sixty prostitutes, and while its population had expanded considerably since then – particularly with the arrival of black settlers from Nova Scotia, of all places, in 1797, and of Cimaroons from Jamaica in 1800 – the general tenor of the place had changed little. Most of the town's permanent inhabitants were, as its name suggested, freed slaves. They were maintained at the British government's expense for a year and then left to fend for themselves. Some opted to go to the West Indies as apprenticed labourers or

102

to serve in a black regiment; for those who stayed behind in Sierra Leone there was little choice but to become a labourer, and despite Freetown's steady growth there were always more labourers than there was labour for them to perform.

The white population of the town was no more than five hundred, although that number was bolstered by a constantly fluctuating tide of seamen: sailors from the vessels of the various navies which patrolled the coast for slavers, and to make sure the flags of their countries were known throughout the world; and the crews of captured slavers. The combination of men from rival navies, freed slaves and disgruntled slavers made for a volatile mix, and it was not unknown for African tribesmen to raid across the river and kidnap freed slaves to sell them on to the white man once more.

Yes, Killigrew was going to miss Freetown when he got back to England in a few weeks' time. But there was something else that saddened him about his imminent departure from the West Africa Squadron: the feeling that he was only just beginning to find his feet and the sense that the squadron's work in suppressing the slave trade, far from being over, was only just begun.

He took a final drag on his cheroot and headed back for the wharf. He had not gone a hundred yards when he heard someone groaning down an alleyway between two shacks. He went to investigate. 'Hullo? Are you all right? Who's there?'

A man was sprawled amongst the fetid rubbish, pawing feebly at the ground.

'What's up? One too many to drink? I know the feeling. Come on, let's have you...'

As he tried to turn the man over he saw the glint of moonlight on a blade and jumped back, but slowly, too slowly, his reactions dulled by alcohol. He felt no pain, but when he glanced down at himself he saw that the fabric of his shirt was sliced through and blood was seeping from a long, thin line scored across his chest.

The man came at him again. Killigrew knew no better cure for drunkenness than danger. He dodged back from the man's next lunge and caught him by the wrist. Spinning the man away from him, he slammed him against the side of a shack and twisted his arm up into the small of his back until he dropped the knife. He punched him in the kidneys to make sure, and the man sank into the rubbish with a groan.

He turned to the mouth of the alley and saw three shadowy figures blocking his path.

'You know something, my friends?' asked Barroso. 'If I could have just one wish fulfilled, it would be to catch Senhor Killigrew alone down a darkened alley. And it looks as if it has just come true.'

V:

Pursuit

Killigrew reached for his pepperbox only to remember that he had left it on board the *Tisiphone*. He glanced back down the alley for an escape route at the other end, but there were three more burly figures blocking off his only escape route. He cursed himself for his carelessness in leaving ship unarmed; and for walking right into Barroso's trap.

'Get him!' snapped Barroso.

The six men charged down the alley from either end. Killigrew weighed up the odds and charged to meet Barroso and his friends. As Barroso pulled out in front, he swung some kind of club at Killigrew's head. Killigrew ducked beneath it and drove a fist into Figueroa's side. The slaver doubled up. Killigrew span him around and used his back as a stepping stone to launch himself up towards the roof of one of the houses adjoining the alley. He caught hold of the eaves and swung himself up just as the other slavers converged beneath him, grasping for his ankles and bumping into one another. Killigrew's feet scrabbled against the wall for a moment and he trod on a head to push himself up. He ran up one side of the shingles and then down the other, leaping across the narrow alley

105

on the far side of the building.

He landed easily on the next roof. Behind him, Barroso and his friends were coming round the first house, shouting to one another. Killigrew surmounted the next apex and began to run down the slope on the other side. The next alley was a good ten feet wide. He measured the steps of his pell-mell descent, putting his right foot on the edge of the roof and launching himself into space, his hands clawing at the air as he sailed through the darkness. He was aware of the alley yawning beneath him, and then the other roof rose up to meet him.

Made it.

His feet landed squarely on the shingles, and then they collapsed under the impact. He fell through with a splintering crash, landed on a counter and fell forward. He hit the floor, rolled over and rose quickly but unsteadily to his feet, bruised, scratched and dazed.

He could hear the shouts of the slavers outside growing louder, their footsteps soft on the compacted earth of the street. He looked around for something he could use as a weapon.

He was in a millinery shop.

He unbolted the back door and rushed out. A moment later something slammed across his stomach and knocked the breath out of him. He doubled up and fell down in winded agony, and his assailant brought the plank of wood down on him again. He rolled on to his hands and knees so that it hit him across the back, knocking him flat on his stomach, and then a foot connected with his ribs.

'I've got him! He came out the back!'

Killigrew rolled on his back and kicked the man in the crotch. The man gave a high-pitched scream and dropped the plank. Killigrew scrambled to his feet and ran down an alley just in time to meet Barroso and three more men coming to meet him. He knocked down one with a right cross, and then they were on him, raining blow after blow. He felt his legs crumple and slid to the ground. The slavers gathered in a circle, kicking at him savagely. He heard more footsteps running up – how many of them were there? – and a cry of 'Remember the Alamo!'

Remember the Alamo?

A shot rang out. Killigrew felt something smash into his head and then…

Someone was slapping him gently on the cheek. After the beating he had been taking only seconds earlier it was a distinct improvement. Was he still alive, then?

'It's a Limey navy officer, Loot!' exclaimed an American accent.

'I think you must be mistaken, Charlie,' said another voice, the rich and melodious tones of the Deep South with a hint of Creole thrown in to spice it up. 'British naval officers are always far too dignified to be found brawling in back alleys,' it continued mockingly. 'No, this must be some fellow who stole the uniform of a British navy officer. Maybe we should hand him over to the authorities. What do you say, Charlie?'

Killigrew reached up and grabbed the first thing that came to hand: Charlie's throat. 'Hey, take it easy, *amigo!*' gasped Charlie.

'Who are you and what do you want?' rasped Killigrew, still woozy from his beating.

'Lieutenant Jean-Pierre Lanier, of the United States' frigate *Narwhal* at your service, sir,' said 'Loot'. 'My companions and I are merely acting in our capacity of good Samaritans, so if you would be so kind as to release my bosun's throat I should be much obliged to you.'

Killigrew let go of Charlie's throat and the American sailors helped him up. 'My apologies. I wasn't sure whose side you were on. Mate Christopher Killigrew, of Her Majesty's paddle-sloop *Tisiphone*. Sorry about half strangling you there,' he added to Charlie.

'That's oh-kay, *amigo*. It'd take more than one Limey to half strangle me.' Charlie shook him by the hand, and from the strength of his grip Killigrew knew he spoke the truth.

'I'm sure you could easily have sent off those bully-boys without our assistance, but I know how you Lime-Juicers think we Americans are always holding back when it comes to suppressing the slave trade,' Lanier said with a hint of amusement in his voice.

'You came along in the nick of time, and there's no denying it,' Killigrew told him. 'I'm indebted to you.'

'Not at all, sir, not at all. It was our pleasure.'

Killigrew tried to take a step but his knees gave way and he would have fallen to the floor if Charlie had not caught him. 'Hey, take it easy, *amigo*. You sure you're oh-kay?'

'I'll be all right in a minute,' said Killigrew. 'I just need to...'

'Nonsense, nonsense,' said Lanier. 'You need to sit down and get a good stiff drink inside you. Mr Killigrew, I should be honoured if you would be a guest in the wardroom of the *Narwhal* tonight. In fact, I must insist upon it.'

'In which case, it would be churlish of me to refuse,' Killigrew said cheerfully, although he was still a little suspicious. There was no love lost between British and American seamen – assuming these *were* American seamen, for it was so dark Killigrew could not make out what Lanier was wearing. Crimping was still a common practice in some of the world's less salubrious seaports, and it would be too embarrassing if he woke up the next morning and found himself pressed into service as a common seaman on an American vessel. But there were four of them, and he was in no condition to resist.

It was only a few hundred yards to the wharf overlooking St George's Bay where the USS *Narwhal* rode at anchor. Further out, Killigrew could see the *Tisiphone*. Two American seamen waited by the *Narwhal*'s launch, tied up at the wharf's single wooden jetty. As soon as he saw them he felt reassured: he had seen the American frigate enter the bay earlier that day, and knew then that these men were genuinely US Navy, and unlikely to provoke a diplomatic incident by kidnapping an officer of the Royal Navy.

Once on board the frigate Lanier took Killigrew to the wardroom where he struck a match and applied it to an oil lamp which he hung from an overhead beam. He was in his mid-twenties, tall and rake-thin, with a lean jaw and high cheekbones which gave his face an angular, wedge-shaped look. The wardroom was not unlike that of the *Tisiphone,* except that there was slightly less head-room, and a daguerreotype of President Tyler hung on the bulkhead in place of a portrait of Queen Victoria. Killigrew was helped into a chair and a black servant took his hat while the ratings made their way back to their own quarters.

'Two whiskeys, Skip,' said Lanier. 'Then be so good as to rouse Mr DeForest from his bunk and have him attend to Mr Killigrew here.'

'Yes, sir.' The black poured out two glasses of rye whiskey and put them on the table before silently slipping out of the wardroom.

'Mr DeForest?' asked Killigrew.

'Our ship's surgeon,' said Lanier, and raised his glass. 'To Her Britannic Majesty Queen Victoria.'

Killigrew raised his own glass. 'To President Tyler.'

'I'll overlook the fact that you did not rise to salute our president, sir, and ascribe it to your current condition,' Lanier said coldly.

'My apologies,' Killigrew said quickly. 'In the Royal Navy it's the custom to give the loyal toast seated. Ever since the last king rose too quickly to accept it on board ship once, and banged his head on a beam.' Lanier smiled, and Killigrew rose to his feet. 'To President Tyler and the United States of America. Your health.'

'And yours.'

They downed their drinks. Killigrew gasped as the liquor churned a fiery wake down his throat.

'Good God, what is that?'

Lanier grinned. 'Kentucky rye whiskey, Mr Killigrew. It's an acquired taste.'

'Pass me that bottle. I think I may just have acquired it.'

The black returned with a middle-aged man dressed in a nightshirt and nightcap. 'Well! If someone had told me there was a celebration in progress, I might not have cursed poor Skip here quite so heartily for rousing me from my beauty sleep which, the good Lord knows, I'm in need of.'

'Mr Killigrew, may I introduce you to our surgeon, Mr DeForest? 'Bones, this is Mate Christopher Killigrew, of the *Tisiphone*.'

'Pleased to make your acquaintance, sir,' said DeForest. 'Sweet Jesus! You look like you've gone twenty rounds with Ben Caunt.'

Killigrew smiled at the reference to the boxing champion, and then winced as his split lip split again. 'Twenty-one, actually.'

'What you need is a good stiff drink,' said DeForest, and the black refilled Killigrew's and Lanier's glasses while pouring out a fresh one for the surgeon. 'What are we celebrating, anyway?'

Lanier glanced at Killigrew, and then raised his glass in a fresh toast. 'The end of the slave trade.'

'I'll drink to that,' said DeForest.

Killigrew glanced at the black servant and left his glass on the table.

Lanier grinned. 'Yes, Mr Killigrew, Scipio's a slave. I said death to the slave trade, not slavery.' He turned to the servant. 'Hey, Skip. You realise, of course, that Sierra Leone is a British colony

111

and there's no slavery here? All you have to do is step off this ship, and you'll be a free man. I won't stop you.'

Scipio beamed. 'Why, thank you, sir. But I've already been ashore today and I didn't think much of what I saw. No, sir, I'm quite happy where I am, thank you all the same.'

'Then again, Scipio's a domestic slave,' said Lanier. 'And since Sierra Leone's one of the few colonies where the British allow people to keep domestic slaves he wouldn't be free anyway, as I understand it.'

'If it were up to me it would be a very different story, I can assure you,' said Killigrew.

Lanier shook his head. 'It's the cruelty I despise, Mr Killigrew, not the principle of slavery. There are no whips on my father's plantation, I can assure you. We feed our slaves well, give them clean and adequate accommodation, and they're grateful for it. They work all the harder knowing they're well looked after.'

'I don't doubt it, but I'll wager it's a different story on some of your neighbours' plantations.'

'True, but then I'll wager they're no worse off than the negroes you British transport to the West Indies under your system of apprenticed labour. You ask Scipio here: slavery doesn't have to be unpleasant.'

'For myself, it's the principle as well as the cruelty.'

Lanier shook his head again. 'We're all slaves to something, Mr Killigrew.'

'And what is it that you are a slave to, Mr Lanier?'

112

Lanier's face cracked into a grin. 'Why, to duty, of course.'

'I'll bet being a slave to duty is a damned sight more comfortable than being a slave to a plantation owner with only a loose understanding of your noble but discriminating bill of rights.'

Lanier shrugged uncomfortably. 'How about you, Mr Killigrew? What are you a slave to?'

'I don't know. I'll have to think about that one.'

'Say, I thought this was a celebration,' protested DeForest. 'Seems I was mistaken. Sounds more like I've walked into a debate on slavery. If I'd wanted that I could've gone to a meeting of the Society of Friends.'

'Agreed,' said Lanier. 'But not at two bells in the first watch. Let's at least put our differences behind us and drink to what we have in common: our contempt for the slavers.'

The three of them raised their glasses.

'That's what we need to do,' said DeForest. 'It's high time our navies learned to put their differences behind them. The War of 1812 was a long time ago. We'll never beat the blackbirders until we learn to work together.'

'It's a nice idea, but it's been tried before,' said Killigrew.

'It has?'

Lanier nodded. 'A few years ago the captain of the USS *Grampus* tried working with the captain of HMS *Wolverine*. The idea was that since only US Navy ships can stop American vessels, and only the Royal Navy's ships can stop British vessels, they'd sail together. If a slaver hoisted a

US ensign then the *Grampus* would stop her; and if they hoisted the Union Jack, then the Royal Navy did the honours.'

'What went wrong?'

'Oh, it worked just fine,' said Lanier. 'Until our government heard about the arrangement and declared it *ultra vires*. Those damned fools in Washington think that asserting the freedom of the seas for American vessels is more important than stopping the slavers. Personally, I don't see what the problem is. I'd be happy for Royal Navy ships to stop and search American merchantmen when and where they pleased. If the merchantmen are engaged in an honest trade, then they've nothing to fear.'

'It's not only your politicians who are at fault,' said Killigrew. 'If statesmen like Lord Palmerston didn't take such a high-handed attitude with the diplomats of other nations, then perhaps those other nations might be a little bit more co-operative.'

The Americans could not disagree with that. DeForest swabbed Killigrew's cuts and bruises, cleaned and bandaged the cut across his chest – it was too shallow to justify stitches – and they drank several more toasts together before having the crew of the *Narwhal*'s jolly boat row Killigrew back to the *Tisiphone*, where the men of the anchor-watch carried him to his berth.

Killigrew was awoken at dawn by a squad of marines shuffling into the *Tisiphone*'s gun room and singing a rousing chorus of 'Early in the Morning'. He fell out of his hammock and crouched on the floor, holding his head which throbbed agonisingly despite his not having banged it on the way down.

He glared up at them. 'And to what do I owe this dubious pleasure, Corporal?'

'Begging your pardon, sir, Commander Standish's orders. He said it would teach you not to rouse him at little one bell by coming on board singing "The Star-Spangled Banner".'

'Did I do that?' It was all coming back to him: not slowly, but memory after drunken memory crashing helter-skelter into a skull too numbed to cope with them all. 'Did I remember to salute the quarter-deck as I came on board?'

'Yes, sir. And you doffed your hats.'

'Hats?'

The corporal pointed to where Standish's beaver hat, now thoroughly battered, sat on Killigrew's sea-chest. 'You were wearing your cocked hat and had that in your hands, sir.'

Killigrew massaged his temples. 'I must say, this is a revelation. I never knew Commander Standish had a sense of humour.'

'I believe it was Mr Tremaine's suggestion, sir.'

Killigrew glanced across to where Tremaine's hammock was stowed. 'Was it, by God? I shall bear that in mind.'

The corporal coughed into his fist. 'Begging your pardon, sir, but Commander Standish presents his compliments and requests you present yourself in his day room at six bells.'

'I don't suppose he told you what it was about, did he?'

'No, sir.'

115

'What time is it now?'

'Four bells, sir. In the morning watch.'

'Thank you, Corporal. Dismissed. Oh, send the ship's barber in here, would you?' Killigrew's hands were shaking too much for him to want to risk shaving himself. 'And tell him he'd better have a mug of tea in his hand when he gets here. Two, if he wants one himself.'

'Aye, aye, sir. Shall I have some food brought down to you?'

'No thank you, Corporal. Just some tea.'

Shaved, dressed, and with some tea inside him, Killigrew began to feel human again. He made his way to the captain's day room where another marine stood on guard. The marine knocked on the door.

'Who is it?' called Standish.

'Mr Killigrew here to see you, sir.'

There was a pause, the sound of feet on the deck – Standish striking up a pose in front of the window, guessed Killigrew – and then: 'Enter.'

The marine opened the door and ushered Killigrew inside. Predictably, Standish stood at the window gazing out. 'I've had a complaint from one of Freetown's saloon-keepers, Mr Killigrew. A demand for payment for damages, in fact. Something to do with a brawl?'

'Yes, sir. There were some American sailors in there and when the Tisiphones met them I understand things got a little out of hand. They were just blowing off steam.'

'To the tune of fifty pounds, Mr Killigrew. I thought I banned all shore leave for the ratings? Aside from the risk of contracting yellow fever, I

116

will not have my men brawling...' Standish turned away from the window and his face became grim when he saw the bruises on Killigrew's face.

'I ran into some of the men from the *São João* on my way back to the ship last night, sir.'

'I suppose you were at Maggie's Place too, were you? What were you doing there?'

'That's not the sort of question a gentleman answers, sir.'

'That's not the sort of hostelry a gentleman frequents, Mr Killigrew. I don't suppose you ordered any of the Tisiphones you saw at Maggie's Place to return directly to the ship, did you?' Standish frowned and tried to peer past Killigrew to see what he held behind his back in his left hand.

'I felt it would have been hypocritical of me to tell them to leave when it must have been obvious I was there to have a good time myself.'

'Damned right. You shouldn't have been there at all. You're a disgrace, man. Exceeding orders, brawling with common seamen, coming back on board roaring drunk in the small hours of the morning. You needn't think that I shall be asking you to join me on my next command when we get back to England, Killigrew... Damn it, man, stand up straight! What the devil are you holding in your hand?'

Killigrew held out his empty palm. 'Nothing, sir.'

'Your *other* hand, damn it!'

'Oh! I'd almost forgotten. Your hat, sir.' Killigrew dusted the beaver hat off with his sleeve

117

and proffered it to Standish.

'My topper! I've been looking all over for that. I thought perhaps that damned fool Gibbons had put it away somewhere. Where on earth did you find it?'

'Maggie's Place, sir.'

Standish turned puce. 'Get out, Killigrew.'

'Yes, sir.'

'Sail ho!'

'Where away?'

'Two points on the port bow.'

Killigrew skipped up on to the *Tisiphone*'s port-side paddle-box, extended the telescope and raised it to his right eye, looking in the direction the lookout at the masthead had indicated. 'Can you make her out at all?' called Standish.

'Two-masted, rakish, square-rigged ... could be a Baltimore brig, sir.' When a good breeze was blowing Baltimore brigs were amongst the fastest ships on the sea, including steamers, and as such were beloved of slavers.

'Can you see an ensign?'

'None flying, sir. I don't believe she's seen us. No, wait a moment: she's altering course slightly; turning to windward.' Killigrew lowered the telescope and snapped it shut before descending to the deck once more.

'Damned suspicious,' said Standish. 'She must be a slaver.'

'*Too* suspicious, if you ask me,' said Killigrew. 'Sir.'

'And what the devil is that supposed to mean?'

'It's as if she's trying to provoke our interest by

acting suspiciously, sir. She could be trying to draw us away from the African coast to give other vessels – the real slavers – a chance to slip past us. When I was on board the *Dido*–'

'When you were on board the *Dido,* when you were on board the *Dido,*' Standish echoed pettishly. 'I was serving on this station years before you were on board the *Dido*, Killigrew. Believe you me, merchant ships have better things to do than lead Her Majesty's vessels on wild-goose chases, be they slavers or otherwise. Give chase, Mr Darrow. Full press of canvas.'

'Aye, aye, sir.' The boatswain relayed the orders, and the topmen in the rigging unfurled those sails which had previously been furled.

'She looks like a trim vessel to me, sir,' said Killigrew. 'Hadn't we better wet the sails?'

'Damn you, Killigrew. How many times must I tell you not to instruct me in my duties?'

'My apologies, sir.'

Standish turned back to the boatswain. 'Dampen the sails, Mr Darrow.'

'Aye, aye, sir.'

The *Tisiphone* was back in her old cruising grounds off the Guinea Coast, a few miles to the south of the Sierra Leone peninsula. Killigrew could see the low outline of the coast off to windward; a landsman might have mistaken it for a bank of low-lying cloud on the eastern horizon. Beneath an azure sky the sun glistened on the waves and shone dazzlingly on the paddle-sloop's pale deck. There was a slight haze in the air, caused by the red dust blown out to sea by the Harmattan winds. The north-east trade wind blew a moderate breeze from the land, filling the *Tisiphone*'s sails from the port quarter.

Beneath their sponsons the paddle-wheels hung lifeless in the water, and no smoke issued from the funnel. Standish rarely used the engine, partly because it made sense to conserve coal for when it was really needed, but mostly because he had learned his trade on sailing ships and was not used to having the benefits of a steam engine at his command. In fact, he disdained to use the engines unless he really had to, and even then did so grudgingly. Besides, all that soot made a dreadful mess of his beautiful sails.

Killigrew continued to watch the suspect vessel through the telescope. When he had gauged the relative speeds of the two vessels, he would be able to calculate how long it would be before the other vessel came within range of the *Tisiphone*'s bow-chaser; assuming the paddle-sloop could out-run her prey, which was by no means a given. The *Tisiphone* had perhaps half a knot on her quarry, if they maintained their current course and the wind did not change; it would be about twelve hours before they came within range. A stern chase could be a long and tedious business, and by now even the most inexperienced mid-shipman on the paddle-sloop knew better than to rush down to the gun room to sharpen his dirk.

In the meantime the day-to-day running of the ship continued as normal. The crew still had to be mustered, the deck holystoned, the rigging maintained, the crew's clothes washed, the log-board filled in, dinner eaten, marines paraded, seamen exercised with cutlasses and small arms, noon sighting taken. All the while they drew closer and closer to their prey, and more and more men began to glance towards it more frequently. By the end of the forenoon watch it could be seen clearly from the deck with the naked eye.

The hands tried to give out an air of calm indifference but they fooled no one, not even themselves. The air of tension on board the *Tisiphone* was tangible; muted, at first, but increasing as the wearing of the hours brought the brig cable by cable closer to the paddle-sloop's guns. There was fear there, for it was not unknown for a slaver to put up enough of a fight to kill or maim navy seamen, although on the West Africa Squadron there was a greater risk of death from yellow fever than there was from action. But mostly there was excitement: a long drawn-out stern chase was a chase nonetheless, a break from the monotonous routine of cruising, the chance to do some fighting and break some slavers' heads, and the possibility of prize money.

At midday Killigrew went below to dine in the gun room with Tremaine, Strachan, the captain's clerk and the *Tisiphone*'s two surviving midshipmen. Even though all of them were thinking of the ship they were chasing – with the possible exception of the clerk – there was a tacit agreement between them not to speak of it. Since there was little else to discuss, conversation was stilted.

After luncheon Tremaine and Midshipman Radmall went up on deck and Strachan went to the sick bay, refilled with a fresh batch of cases of yellow fever after their last run ashore. The clerk had paperwork to attend to in the captain's day room, leaving Killigrew, off duty until the first dog watch, in the gun room with Midshipman Cavan. He knew he would not be able to sleep so he turned to his sea-chest for something to read. His bookmark was stuck between the pages of Gordon's *The Economy of the Marine Steam Engine,* but he knew that in his present state of mind he would not be able to concentrate on the technical information. Virgil's *Aeneid* seemed a better proposition, even on a second reading.

Cavan drew his cutlass from his scabbard and began to sharpen it. The grating of the whetstone against the edge of the blade soon became irritating. 'For heaven's sake belay that scraping, Mr Cavan.'

'Sorry, sir. I just wanted to be ready for when we board her.'

'It'll be a couple of hours before she's in range, even. And I don't see Standish choosing someone as young as you for the boarding party.'

'But how am I ever to become experienced enough if I never get the opportunity because of my lack of experience? Can't you speak to the captain for me?'

'By God, Cavan, you're a bloodthirsty young shaver, aren't you? Are you really so keen to feel the edge of your sword biting through flesh, spilling blood and snapping bone?'

Cavan pulled a face. 'I hadn't thought about it like that, sir.'

'Well, I suggest you do. Better to come to terms with it now rather than when you're face to face with some slaver in the thick of a mêlée. Because if the idea of killing a man gives you pause for thought, then just remember that pause may be all the time your opponent needs to slice your head off.'

'Oh! I wouldn't have any qualms about killing a slaver.'

'Well you should. They've got rights, the same as any other man.'

'Even criminals?'

'They're not criminals until they've been proved criminals in a properly constituted court of law. Our job is to bring them before that court, not to inflict our own justice. D'you understand me?' As he spoke the words he had believed in for so long, he found they had a hollow ring to them now.

Cavan hung his head. 'Yes, sir.' Then he perked up. 'But it's all right to kill them in self-defence, isn't it?'

Killigrew smiled. 'That it is, Mr Cavan.'

'*Please* won't you speak to Commander Standish, sir? I have to get some experience of fighting sooner or later.'

'Later rather than sooner, believe me. Anyway, even if I did think you were ready, my talking to Standish wouldn't do you any good. You know how he hates having to go along with anything I suggest.'

'How old were you the first time *you* killed someone?'

'Sixteen, as I recall. Two years older than you are now, so don't worry, you've got plenty of time.'

'How many men have you killed?'

'Does it matter?'

'You were in Syria, weren't you, sir? And at the storming of Chingkiang-fu during the China War?'

Killigrew grunted but refused to be drawn. He was not ashamed of the battles he had fought against pirates and slavers, but the China campaign was not one he was proud of. At least in Syria the cause had been just, fighting alongside the Ottoman Turks against the rebel Viceroy of Egypt, Ibrahim Pasha. He remembered storming the Boharsef Heights with the combined force of the British Naval Brigade and the Turkish soldiers. He remembered marines and Turks falling dead on all sides around him as they dashed across the open ground to engage the Egyptian Musselmen. And then, with the smell of blood in his nostrils and the memory of the atrocities the Egyptians had inflicted on the Lebanese fresh in his mind, he had been amongst the enemy, his cutlass whirling as he avenged the murder and rapine. Sometimes the nightmare still came back to haunt him, and in his dream he was watching himself from a distance. For it had not been Midshipman Killigrew who had taken part in the assault – as an officer of the Royal Navy he had been far too civilised to engage in that kind of savage bloodletting – but someone else, caught in the grip of an uncontrollable rage. And of all the horrors that had terrified him in that campaign, the one fear that still came back to haunt him was the fear that that Killigrew might not be dead but still locked deep within him, ready to emerge given sufficient provocation and to inflict atrocities as grim as any he sought to avenge. It was sobering to think that for all he was a product of the most civilised nation on earth he was just as capable of savagery as the most primitive Patagonian cannibal or Borneo head-hunter.

'What's wrong?' asked Cavan, snapping him out of his reverie.

Killigrew forced himself to smile. 'Nothing. I was just thinking, that's all.'

'About what?'

'Merely reflecting on human nature.'

'Oh.' Cavan shrugged.

The afternoon watch wore on. The ship's bell tolled the half hours, marking the slow dragging of time, with a lifetime between each bell. Killigrew could see the tension etched in every line of Cavan's young face, and at last he tapped him on the shoulder.

'Relax. Put the slaver from your mind. A watched kettle never boils, and a watched slaver is never overhauled.'

'That's easy for you to say, sir. Dash it, how can you be so cool-headed at a time like this?'

'A naval officer is cool-headed at all times, Mr Cavan. It's a question of self-control. There's an old Chinese proverb: Any man who would conquer the world must first conquer himself.'

The hands were clearing the deck for action by the time Killigrew emerged on to the quarter-deck at four o'clock. The bedding stowed on deck was now draped over the rails to provide some protection against flying splinters in case the enemy opened fire on them.

The brig was less than a mile off the port bow and the *Tisiphone* continued to overhaul her. 'Still no sign of any colours, sir,' said Killigrew, eyeing the brig through the telescope.

'All right,' said Standish. 'Let's see if we can wake them up, eh? Fire a blank shot, Mr Jeal.'

'Aye, aye, sir.' The gunner made his way to the bow-chaser on the forecastle.

One of the disadvantages of paddle-steamers was that the paddle-boxes on the sides took up so much space it was impossible to fit them with a broadside. To counteract this, the navy equipped them with bigger guns. The *Tisiphone* had three guns in all, two thirty-two-pounders and the bow-chaser in the forecastle: a sixty-eight-pound pivot gun.

A silence fell over the decks of the *Tisiphone*, just as if they were about to engage in a gunnery exercise. The gunner and his crew loaded the sixty-eight-pounder with a blank cartridge and primed it with a friction tube. They then cranked it up to its maximum elevation. The gunner's mate took the lanyard in his hands while the gunner glanced back to where Standish stood on the quarter-deck.

Standish nodded.

'Fire!' ordered the gunner. His mate jerked back the lanyard and the sixty-eight-pounder boomed, belching a great mushroom of pale-grey smoke from its muzzle.

The brig ran an ensign up her jackstaff. 'She's showing her colours, sir,' called the lookout.

'Can you make them out?'

Killigrew already had the telescope raised to his eye. 'Claiming to be a Yankee, sir.'

'Don't they all?' sighed Standish.

The brig showed no signs of stopping. Within half an hour they were within six cables – two-thirds of a mile, just within the extreme range of the sixty-eight-pounder – of their quarry. 'Ask Mr Jeal to give them a warning shot,' Standish ordered Cavan.

'Yes, sir. I mean, aye, aye, sir.' The midshipman saluted and scurried the length of the deck to the forecastle.

The gunner and his crew sponged out the gun, loaded her with a cartridge and a sixty-eight-pound round shot, over eight inches in diameter. The gunner's mate inserted a fresh priming, the crew aimed it at a spot in the water alongside the brig – they were too far away and at the wrong angle to fire the traditional shot across the bows – and cranked it up to maximum elevation. 'Ready.'

'Fire!'

The pivot gun boomed and the shot screeched through the air towards the brig. It ploughed into the water on the starboard side of the vessel. The message to the crew of the brig was clear: *You are within range of our guns.*

'Is she heaving to?' called Standish.

The lookout was silent for a moment as he peered through his telescope, waiting for some indication of the clipper's next move. 'No, sir. She's bearing away.'

The brig's bows went about; she turned four points to starboard so that she ran south-west

127

with the wind full abaft. 'Stay with her,' ordered Standish.

'Aye, aye, sir.' The quartermaster span the helm, mimicking the brig's turn. But now the brig had the wind full abaft and the paddle-sloop began to fall astern.

'That's odd,' remarked Killigrew.

Standish said nothing, refusing to give Killigrew the satisfaction of asking him what was odd and waiting for him to elaborate; but Killigrew knew how to play that game too, and it was Standish who broke first. 'What is it?' the commander asked with a sigh.

'She must've known she could outpace us with the wind full abaft. Why not bear away the moment we gave chase?'

'I really couldn't say. Why don't you ask her master when we catch her?'

'Perhaps I shall.' Killigrew snapped the telescope shut.

The gunner and his crew quickly reloaded the pivot gun and were ready to fire before the brig slipped out of range again. But there was no point in firing a warning shot – the brig already knew they were there – and a shot aimed at the vessel could only hit the hull at that range and risk killing any slaves on board.

'We're going to lose her, sir,' prompted Killigrew, seeing Standish's indecision.

'I can see that! Tell Mr Muir to start up his engines. She can beat us with sails alone, but not with sails and steam.'

Killigrew crossed to the engine-room telegraph and signalled full speed ahead. If Standish had expected smoke to billow from the funnels and the paddle-wheels to start churning the water immediately, he was disappointed. After perhaps a minute, one of the greasy, grubby denizens of the engine room emerged on deck and tugged at his forelock. 'Begging your pardon, sir, but we'll have steam up just as soon as we can,' he announced in a thick Geordie accent.

'What the devil's the delay? Start the engines at once!'

'Can't start the engines with cold boilers,' said the engineer. 'We've got to light the fires in the furnaces and boil the water until we've got enough steam pressure, like.'

'How long will that take?'

'Two hours maximum.'

'Damned steam engines. More trouble than they're worth. Just ... just do your best, Mr Muir.'

They should have lost the brig then. But as soon as the vessel was two miles away, she changed back to a southerly course and the *Tisiphone* began to overhaul her once more. As soon as the paddle-sloop came within range, the brig ran before the wind and slipped away again. They went through this pantomime several times as the sun sank towards the horizon.

'She's leading us a merry dance,' the *Tisiphone*'s second lieutenant remarked to Killigrew on one side of the quarter-deck, out of earshot of Commander Standish, in his aristocratic drawl. Lieutenant the Honourable Endymion Hartcliffe was the younger son of the Duke of Hartcliffe. A stout moon-faced man in his late twenties, he had a vague manner which belied the decisiveness and tenacity he could show when necessity demanded. 'I'm inclined to think you were right, Killigrew: she *is* only a decoy.'

Killigrew nodded. 'While the real slaver is getting further and further away, sir.'

'We'd better catch them soon. It will be dark within an hour or two and they'll easily give us the slip.'

VI:

Breaking the Circle

The sun had just kissed the horizon when suddenly the engines' valves hissed and the machinery clanked into life. The deck shuddered and vibrated beneath their feet and the paddle-wheels turned in the water, slowly at first but then with increasing speed, twenty revolutions a minute. The water beneath the paddle-boxes churned and the *Tisiphone* surged forwards.

From that moment it was all over. The brig turned to the south-west, but even with the wind full abaft and her sails drawing well with moderate breeze meant she could manage no more than four knots to the *Tisiphone*'s eight. Within minutes the paddle-sloop was close enough to fire chain shot at the brig's masts, and even as the gunner's crew prepared to fire, the brig ran down her colours and hove to, backing her fore topsail while leaving her fore-and-aft sails set. The *Tisiphone* ranged alongside, stopped her engines and boxed her sails.

Standish called across to the brig – the name *Leopardo* was painted on the stern – and ordered the master to lower his sails and come on board at once.

'No intende inglese.'

'Parlez-vous français?'

'*No intende.*'

'No intende, no intende,' Standish muttered irritably.

'Would you like me to try, sir?' offered Killigrew.

'Don't bother, Mr Killigrew. I'll address them in the common tongue of the seas. Sergeant Rennie! Have your men fire at his jib halyard block.'

'Aye, aye, sir.' The sergeant of marines saluted Standish and then turned to where his corporal and ten privates were arrayed on deck, resplendent in their scarlet coats and white crossbelts, their rifles already primed and loaded. 'You heard the captain, lads. Present arms! Ready ... take aim...'

'Begging your pardon, Sarge,' said the corporal. But what's...'

'The block on the rope supporting the triangular sail at the front,' hissed Standish.

'I've got it,' said the corporal, and he and his men levelled their rifles with more confidence.

Standish rolled his eyes. 'I must have the only marines in the whole blasted regiment who don't know a halyard from a hole in the ground,' he sighed.

'Fire!' roared the sergeant. The eleven rifles boomed as one.

The rope above the halyard block parted and the jib collapsed and folded itself over the brig's forecastle.

There was a polite round of applause from the seamen who stood idle on the *Tisiphone*'s deck. 'Belay that!' snapped the boatswain.

'Oh-kay, oh-kay!' the man on the brig called peevishly. 'We give in!'

Standish raised his speaking trumpet to his lips once more. 'May I congratulate you at the rapidity with which you have acquired a grasp of the English language?'

'Go to Hell!'

Standish turned to the other officers on the quarter-deck. 'Fluent, isn't he?'

A boat was lowered from the clipper and a dozen of the sailors rowed across. Even as they were taken aboard and covered by the rifles of half a dozen marines, the *Tisiphone* lowered one of her cutters and Lieutenant Hartcliffe, Mate Tremaine, a dozen seamen and the rest of the marines rowed across to the *Leopardo*.

The leader of the men from the *Leopardo* brushed aside the rifles and marched straight on to the quarter-deck, heading for Standish. Killigrew quickly thumbed back the hammer of his pepperbox and levelled it at him.

The man stopped short and glared at Killigrew. He was only a couple of years older than the mate, a tall, heavily built man with dark hair and a Quaker's beard, his upper lip clean shaven. He wore a black frock coat and a low, round hat, his clothes dark and drab. Nearly everything about him screamed 'Quaker'; the Society of Friends had been foremost amongst the slave trade in the first part of the previous century, until they had seen the light and become foremost in the fight for its abolition. But there was nothing Quaker-like about the eyes he now narrowed at Killigrew: they glittered menacingly in the twilight, as black

133

and soulless as a shark's, warning Killigrew not to underestimate him.

The man put one hand on the grip of his own pistol without drawing it from its holster. 'Where I come from, mister, it's not good manners to point a gun at a man unless you aim to use it.' He spoke with the nasal twang of a New Englander.

'I aim to use it all right, if you give me cause. Put your hands in the air.'

The man studied Killigrew, as if trying to gauge whether he really would use his gun. Something in Killigrew's mien assured him that the mate was in earnest, for he raised his hands.

'All right, Killigrew, that's enough of that,' snapped Standish.

The man turned to him. 'You the captain?'

'Yes. You the master of that brig?'

'No. The captain's resting in his cabin,' the New Englander said with studied insolence. 'I'm the chief mate.'

'What's your name?'

'Coffin. Eli Coffin.'

'You're from Nantucket?' asked Killigrew.

'What makes you say that?'

Killigrew shrugged. 'Coffin's a common name there. That's not the sort of name one forgets in a hurry.'

'It had better not be,' growled Coffin. 'What did this man say your name was? Killigrew? Well, I don't aim to forget that name in a hurry, either.' He turned back to Standish. 'Now, mister, perhaps you'd care to tell me what you think you're doing?'

'I'd've thought that was pretty obvious.

Stopping and searching you.'

'It may have escaped your attention, friend, but that's an American flag flying at our jackstaff. And these are American papers,' he added, thrusting a sheaf at Standish.

The commander did not even glance at them. 'Forged, I don't doubt.'

Coffin grinned triumphantly. 'Maybe a stiff letter from our State Department to your Foreign Office will convince you.'

'I'll believe it when I see it.'

'Oh, you'd better. Because when my government hears that a British warship stopped a United States vessel engaged in its lawful business, then there's going to be trouble. Your government's going to be looking for a scapegoat to save them from an embarrassing diplomatic faux pas, and guess what, my friend? You just put your head in the noose.'

Hartcliffe and his men soon returned. 'Not a trace of any slaves on board, sir.'

'What?'

'We searched the whole blessed ship, sir. No slaves, no shackles, no evidence at all, rot it.'

'What did I tell you?' demanded Coffin, grinning from ear to ear.

'Then why did you run the moment you saw us? Why didn't you heave to the moment we hailed you with a blank shot?'

'We figured maybe you were pirates.'

'Damn you, man! You could see the British ensign at our jackstaff clear enough, couldn't you?'

'They could've been false colours.' Still

smirking, Coffin tucked his ship's papers back inside his coat. 'I hear that's a common trick in these waters.'

'There are no pirates in these waters, Mr Coffin. The Royal Navy sees to that.'

'Is that so? And what do you call stopping and boarding a ship illegally using the threat of arms, if not piracy?'

'If you return to your ship you'll find nothing's been removed or damaged, apart from the jib halyard,' Standish said stiffly. 'And we've wasted no more of your time than you have of ours.'

'Good day to you, gentlemen. Your Admiralty will be hearing from our government in due course.' Coffin nodded to his men, signalling for them to follow him back down to the *Leopardo*'s boat.

'She's a slaver, all right,' said Standish, watching the boat row back to the brig. 'And as for that insolent swine, he deserves a good flogging.'

'It'd take a brave man to administer it,' said Killigrew. 'I've met some dangerous men in my time, but that one...' He broke off as a shudder ran down his spine.

'Stuff and nonsense. You can't tell if someone's dangerous or not just by talking to them for five minutes. Well, I suppose you're gloating now, Mr Killigrew? Go on, then. Tell me you told me so.'

'Gloating isn't really my style, sir, but if you're ordering me to...'

Standish turned his back on Killigrew. 'You have the con, Lord Hartcliffe.'

'Yes, sir.' Hartcliffe was a good naval officer, and yet somehow he could never bring himself to say 'aye, aye sir'. Standish, who always became fawning and obsequious in the presence of nobility, even when they were his subordinates, was not going to argue.

'I take my hat off to you, Mr Killigrew,' said Hartcliffe when Standish had gone below. 'You *knew* it was a decoy, didn't you? And now the real slaver is far beyond our reach,' he sighed.

Killigrew rubbed his jaw and cast his eyes to leeward. 'Not necessarily, sir.'

'Face facts, Mr Killigrew. She has several hours start on us already…'

'We have steam up. The wind's been blowing a steady nor'easter at about thirteen knots all day. The other ship can't have gone more than forty-five miles, even if she was faster than the *Leopardo*. And she'll have run south-west before the wind, to get clear of our patrols as quickly as possible. I'll bet she's no more than fifty miles west-nor'-west of us.'

'That's still a deuced big lead.'

'My guess is that she'll stay on that course for another two days. If we headed west-sou'-west at full steam I'll wager we'd cross her path within seventeen hours.'

'Assuming she set out from the same point we did, more or less.'

'Why else would the *Leopardo* have gone to so much trouble to lead us on a wild-goose chase?' asked Killigrew. He nodded to where the brig's crew were taking their boat aboard and making sail once more. 'The other ship must've been out of sight of us, but within sight of the *Leopardo*. That would put her right on the Guinea coast.

The *Leopardo* must've signalled to her somehow, telling her to stay in port until she could draw us away.'

'I don't know, Killigrew. It's a big ocean out there. It'd be like looking for a needle in a blessed haystack.'

'We can narrow down our search. After all, we know roughly where she started from, roughly where she was headed and roughly how fast she travelled.'

'That's an awful lot of "roughlys", and there's no place for "roughly" in navigation.'

'All right, I'll admit that the chances of us finding her are slim. But what have we got to lose? Time? We're as well cruising for slavers out here as we are a couple of miles off the coast.'

'I suppose you're right. But Standish will never go for it. Not if it's your idea. Not even if I tell him it was mine.'

'So don't tell him. You know as well as I do he won't be up again before the forenoon watch. He said you had the con. He didn't say where you should take it.'

Hartcliffe stared at him. 'Rot it, Killigrew, you're going to cost me my commission!' he said with a grin. 'Cram on all sail, bosun! Steer a course west-sou'-west, Mr Ågård. Order the engine room to give me full steam ahead.'

Killigrew smiled and went below with the sailing master to the chart room to plot a course for their quarry and a course to intercept. As twilight turned into dusk, the *Tisiphone* steamed off after the sun below the horizon.

The sun had gone all the way around the globe and risen abaft of the *Tisiphone* by the time Standish emerged on deck the following morning at the start of the forenoon watch. He gazed about, searching for the land, and doubtless noticed that the paddle-sloop was sailing westwards, further into the Atlantic. Hartcliffe and Killigrew had been searching the horizon in vain for a glimpse of their quarry ever since first light. Now they were ready to give up the chase and head back to the coast.

'Where the devil are we?' Standish demanded of Hartcliffe.

'Er ... fourteen degrees and ten minutes west, six degrees and twenty-nine minutes north, sir,' Hartcliffe replied.

'Where the devil's that?'

'About a hundred and ten miles off the Guinea coast, I think sir.'

'A hundred and ten... We're in the middle of the Atlantic Ocean, damn your eyes! Are we lost?'

'No, sir. We ... I thought that since the *Leopardo* was obviously a decoy, we could perhaps try to calculate the course of the ship she was attempting to decoy us from and intercept her...'

'Don't lie to me, Hartcliffe. This hare-brained scheme smacks of Killigrew to me. Well, Killigrew? This is your doing, sir.'

'Yes, sir. You didn't give us any instructions before you retired last night, so I thought–'

'You *thought*, did you? You do a damned sight too much thinking for my liking, Mr Killigrew. Perhaps you should have *thought* about the possibility that there was no other ship, and that

139

even if there had been the chances of us being able to find her in the middle of the Atlantic Ocean were so astronomical–'

'Sail ho!'

'Where away?' Hartcliffe called up to the lookout.

'Two points on the starboard quarter.'

'Behind us?' exclaimed Killigrew, climbing on to the starboard paddle-box. 'She's making poorer time than I anticipated.'

'It's probably not the same ship,' muttered Standish. 'The devil take it! That ship probably never even existed in the first place.'

'Perhaps not, sir,' admitted Killigrew, his telescope raised to his eye. 'But this one has the look of a slaver all the same.'

'Well, since she's abaft of us … and since we have to go back that way anyway … I suppose there's no harm in our going to investigate her, whatever ship she may be,' Standish admitted grudgingly. 'Put her about, Mr Watmough,' he told the quartermaster, and turned to Midshipman Radmall. 'Have the engineer start up the engines.' With both the *Tisiphone* and the other ship sailing with the wind directly abaft, putting about meant turning head on into the wind.

The engine still had steam up, and within moments the paddle-wheels plashed into life. The *Tisiphone* turned in a tight circle, her bows coming around to meet the vessel coming up behind them.

A moment later the other ship likewise turned her head into the wind, and Killigrew got a good look at her sideways-on. He lowered his telescope and snapped it shut. 'It's the *São João.*'

'Don't be ridiculous, man. You can't possibly tell at this distance.'

'It's the *São João,*' insisted Killigrew, jumping back down to the deck.

The clipper turned her nose as close to the wind as she dared, trying to get away, but it was hopeless. Sailing on a port tack, with the wind coming in off the port bow, her speed was greatly reduced. The steam-powered *Tisiphone* was little troubled by such considerations and quickly gained on the other vessel.

The clipper continued to turn in a broad circle, trying to get the wind behind her once more so she could slip past the *Tisiphone* beyond the range of her guns. The quartermaster at the helm adjusted the course and moved to intercept her. Within minutes they had closed to within three miles. The clipper completed its turn, running free before the wind, but even with its sails drawing well it could not outpace the steam-powered sloop.

'We've got the blackguards!' exclaimed Hart-cliffe, forgetting himself in his excitement.

Standish scowled and nodded. 'Clear the decks for action. Man the foremost quarters on the main deck.'

The hands scurried across the deck, bracing the sails, draping hammocks over the rails, and loaded the guns. It was another bright, cloudless day, the sun glittering on the sea. The wind had picked up during the morning, blowing a fresh force five, and the clipper had a bone in her teeth

141

and cut a feather, as seamen referred to the foam at the stem and the wake respectively of a fast-moving ship.

Killigrew took up position in the bar, the wind whipping at his clothes. Spume bounced off the paddle-sloop's stem. The glittering waves raced past, and he could see flying fish skipping over the surface, racing the *Tisiphone*, while porpoises swam before the bows, launching themselves exuberantly out of the water as if leading the paddle-sloop. Standing in the forecastle, Killigrew felt himself share in their exultation. The *Tisiphone* had a knot and a half, maybe two knots on the *São João;* with less than three miles between them and the *Tisiphone* closing fast from astern, the slaver would be in range of the bow-chaser within an hour and a half. He hoped da Silva was on board, and wished he could have seen his face when his lookout had sighted the *Tisiphone* lying ahead of him when he must have supposed her to be far behind.

He raised his telescope again. In grim contrast to the porpoises racing the *Tisiphone*, a dozen sharks' fins cut through the clipper's wake. She had slaves on board, of that there was no doubt.

The time passed quickly as the two ships raced across the ocean, but it could not pass quickly enough for Killigrew. Excitement coursed through every vein in his body. Da Silva and his crew had already escaped him once; this time they would not be so lucky. Taken with slaves on board, they could not escape being condemned by the prize court.

The gunner fired a blank shot. The clipper

hoisted the Stars and Stripes but showed no sign of stopping. Raising his telescope once more, Killigrew could make out the crew throwing casks, spars, timber and coils of rope overboard. They were trying to lighten the load in the hope that they might still outrun the *Tisiphone*.

The gunner's crew reloaded the pivot gun, and waited for the *São João* to come within range. The *Tisiphone*'s bell marked off the half-hours. Killigrew made sure his pepperbox was fully loaded.

'Tell the captain we're in range now,' the gunner ordered one of his men, just when Killigrew felt he could bear the tension no longer. 'We can't elevate high enough to hit their spars, but I reckon we can put a shot close enough to them to give the men on the poop a shower bath. Maybe that'll persuade them to give up.'

The order came back within moments. 'Commander Standish says to fire when ready.'

The gunner checked the aim and elevation of the bow-chaser one last time and then hauled on the lanyard. The gun boomed and a few seconds later the shot plunged into the water abaft of the *São João*'s stern, sending up a great plume of water which drenched the men on the poop. A great cheer went up from the men of the *Tisiphone*, and the gunner's crew reloaded.

The clipper showed no signs of heaving to. The crew must have guessed the *Tisiphone* would not fire to hit at that range – a shot penetrating the hull would most likely kill many of the slaves tightly packed below decks, which rather defeated the object of the exercise – so they pressed on, still hoping the paddle-sloop would abandon the chase.

But the *Tisiphone* had the smell of blood in her nostrils and was not going to give up now. Within a quarter of an hour the paddle-sloop was close enough for the pivot gun to fire chain shot at the clipper's mast. The gunner's crew fired shot after shot, working with monotonous regularity. As the chain shot screeched through the air towards the clipper, the other crew retaliated with a pivot gun of their own, a twenty-four-pounder located on their poop deck. But their firing was as erratic as it was sporadic. Every now and then a plume of water would rise up in the *Tisiphone*'s vicinity; sometimes close enough to splash the deck, sometimes as much as a cable's length away. They did not hit the *Tisiphone* until she had almost ranged alongside her, and then a round shot smashed through the *Tisiphone*'s wooden hull close to the bows.

Killigrew felt the deck shudder beneath his feet and a moment later word came up from below: the shot had smashed through the sick berth and killed three cases of yellow fever, as well as cutting off the attendant's leg. A growl of anger ran through the *Tisiphone*'s crew. 'Why don't they give it up? They can see we've got the rate on them.'

The wind was freshening, increasing the *São João* pace. The two vessels were neck and neck for speed. 'Cram on all sail!' ordered Standish. From the tautness in the commander's voice Killigrew could tell that even he was caught up in

144

the excitement of the chase, and determined to avenge the deaths of the three men in the sick berth.

Then the crew of the clipper began to throw their cargo overboard.

Killigrew did not believe his eyes as the first pair of fettered Africans were thrown over the side, their screams echoing faintly back to the *Tisiphone* above the sound of her paddles in the water. He raised the telescope, pressing his eye hard against the eyepiece. He could see the men on the clipper's deck clearly enough, marching the slaves up through the main hatch two at a time with whips and guns. As the slaves realised what their fate was to be they tried to put up a struggle, but they were either shot or clubbed to the deck. Dead or alive, their bodies were heaved unceremoniously over the side as the crew tried to lighten their load and dispose of the evidence at the same time.

The heavy iron fetters on the Africans' ankles pulled them straight under the surface as soon as they hit the water. Killigrew could imagine them screaming as they were dragged down to the ocean floor, their lungs filling with water, struggling, drowning helplessly. He felt sickened. He knew there were few forms of life lower than a slaver, but they were human beings after all, and it astonished him that any man should be so bereft of humanity that he could so callously slay his fellow men – in such large numbers – to save his own hide for what would probably amount to no more than a loss of employment for a few weeks.

Not all the slaves thrown overboard drowned. The sharks quickly caught on to what was happening and they too raced forwards, snatching at the sinking bodies, ripping them to shreds in a feeding frenzy which left a scarlet slick in the *São João*'s wake. As one pair of Africans was thrown overboard, an especially large shark lunged out of the water to snap at them before they even hit the surface. On the clipper's deck, the slavers saw this and laughed. They even tried to aim the next pair of slaves so that they fell into the gaping maw of the next shark which tried that trick. Ranks of vicious teeth snapped on limbs, tearing flesh and snapping bone. The screams of the slaves became more frenzied; even those still in the hold were screaming in terror now.

'Jesus!' said a seaman standing close to Killigrew, and the mate made no attempt to berate him for his blasphemy.

'Bastards!' agreed another.

Still the slaves were brought up, kicking, struggling, only to be beaten down and tossed overboard. Ten, twenty, thirty, forty … more and more, until it seemed the whole sea was red with blood. More sharks came from miles around, drawn by the smell. Killigrew clenched his trembling fists until his fingernails drew blood from his palms. Until the *São João* hove to there was nothing he could do but look on impotently. It was not even worth lowering any boats in an effort to pull the Africans from the water: they would either sink or be torn to shreds long before the boats could get to them; besides which, it would have necessitated stopping the paddle-sloop, allowing the clipper to get further away and giving the crew time to drop even more slaves over the side.

Finally a shot from the *Tisiphone* brought the *São João*'s mainmast crashing down in a tangle of sails, spars and rigging. Immediately the clipper lost way and the paddle-sloop overhauled it and hove to alongside less than a cable away. The slavers realised they were beaten and quickly hauled down their false colours.

There was so much confusion on the slaver's deck there seemed little point in calling across with the speaking trumpet and ordering them to send a boat over. One of the *Tisiphone*'s cutters was lowered into the shark-infested waters. This time it was the turn of Lieutenant Jardine and Midshipman Radmall to go aboard the captured vessel with a crew of seamen and marines. Killigrew slipped into the boat behind Strachan without waiting to be invited.

As the cutter pushed off from the *Tisiphone*'s side, Standish appeared at the rail above them. 'Killigrew? What the devil are you doing down there? I didn't tell you to go aboard with the prize crew. Come back here at once!'

Killigrew sat in the stern sheets with his back to the *Tisiphone*. The rowers had already propelled the cutter halfway across the distance between the two ships. He pretended not to hear.

'Do you want us to bring him back, sir?' called Lieutenant Jardine.

'No. But he comes back with the cutter, you understand me? I don't want any more farces

147

such as happened aboard the *Maria Magdalena*, do you understand me? I'm going to get my share of prize money out of this.'

The sharks paid no attention to the boat. There was already enough fresh meat in the water to satisfy every shark off the Guinea Coast. Moments later the cutter bumped against the side of the clipper and a rope ladder was thrown down to them.

Killigrew went up first. Whoever had dropped the ladder had returned to help the other men try to cut free the men who were trapped beneath the tangle of spars and rigging on the deck. One of the slavers had his legs crushed underneath a spar, and a tide of blood spread around him on the pale deck. Killigrew looked at him and felt no pity whatsoever.

Jardine took control of the situation while Radmall went to hoist the Union Jack from the jackstaff and Strachan went below to the slave deck.

'Hey, Killigrew! You gonna stand there looking like a dumb sonuvabitch or you gonna help me?'

It was Barroso, trapped beneath some rigging but otherwise unharmed. Killigrew crossed to where he lay and drew his cutlass, raising it above his head. Barroso flinched, but Killigrew only hacked through the rigging.

The slaver grinned as Killigrew sheathed his cutlass and helped him to his feet. 'You can't hurt me, right? You've arrested me, now you gotta deliver me to the prize court in Freetown, right?'

'Wrong.' Killigrew rammed his fist into Barroso's stomach. The slaver doubled up and sank

148

to his knees with a gasp of agony.

'Aw, come on! You're not still angry about the other night in Freetown, are you?'

'No, I've forgotten all about that. Now I've got a whole new list of scores to settle with you.'

Killigrew hauled Barroso to his feet and ran him across to the side. Caught off balance, the slaver realised Killigrew's intention too late to do anything about it. He hit the rail and toppled over. He screamed, convinced he was going to fall into the shark-infested waters, but then he bumped against the side and found himself hanging upside down, a rope fast around his ankle. He gazed down into the bloody water only a couple of feet below his head, and craned his neck to where Killigrew stood at the rail above him.

'*Jésus*, Senhor Killigrew! You *loco* sonuvabitch!'

'What's the matter, Barroso? Lost your sense of humour? You seemed to find plenty to laugh about when you threw those slaves to the sharks earlier.'

'What slaves? Ain't no slaves on this ship. We're engaged in honest trade.'

'It's true.' Killigrew turned to see Strachan emerging from the hold, his face ashen. 'There are no slaves on board. The swines must've thrown them all overboard. No slaves, no shackles, nothing. Not even enough extra water butts to convict them of slaving.'

'You mean, they're going to get away with it *again?*' asked Radmall.

'All right, that's enough,' said Jardine. 'Let him up, Mr Killigrew. You've had your fun. Killigrew?

Where are you going? Come back here. Come back here at once! You get back on that cutter *now*, mister...'

Killigrew ignored him and marched into the roundhouse. He found da Silva seated behind the desk in his day cabin, looking as calm and self-assured as ever. 'Ah, Senhor Killigrew. Is it not the custom to knock before entering a room in England?'

'You son of a bitch.'

Da Silva smiled. 'So how are those high-minded ideals of yours, Mr Killigrew? Have they been dented at all yet?'

Killigrew kept his clenched fist at his side. 'Get up. Stand up, you filthy son of a bitch.'

'Are you threatening me, Senhor Killigrew? I think you are in enough trouble already. You're wasting your time, you know. I have papers which prove I'm engaged in legitimate commerce – see for yourself...' Da Silva opened the drawer at his right-hand side.

Killigrew's pepperbox appeared in his hand. 'Stop that. Move away from the desk.'

'For God's sake! You know as well as I do that you are not going to shoot me.'

Killigrew levelled his pepperbox at da Silva's forehead. 'Do it! Get back – right back. Against the window.'

Da Silva sighed ostentatiously and did as he was bidden. Killigrew stepped up to the deck and glanced into the drawer. There *were* papers in there, weighed down by a pistol.

'You think I was going for my gun? Ah, now you are just being foolish, Senhor Killigrew. I don't

150

need a gun to protect me from *you.*' He smiled broadly. 'I have the law to do that for me. You know as well as I do what happens now. You take this ship into Freetown as a prize. But there is no physical evidence that we were ever engaged in the slave trade, so the court lets us go. I keep telling you that you are wasting both your time and mine.'

Killigrew knew da Silva was speaking the truth, and the truth hurt so much he wanted to smash the slaver's smug face into pulp.

'And in a few weeks' time I am back at sea aboard this very ship, and you are cruising for slavers in your ship. What will you do if our paths cross once more, I wonder? Force us to go through this whole charade again? There must be some way we can break this ridiculous vicious circle we find ourselves in.'

'Oh, I can think of a way,' said Killigrew.

'And what is that, pray tell?'

The sound of the shot was deafeningly loud in the close confines of the cabin. The window behind da Silva shattered, leaving a large jagged hole in one of the panes, with the slaver's blood and brains spattered around it.

VII:

Beached

Three chandeliers hung from the ceiling of the ballroom: a main one in the centre flanked by two slightly smaller ones. The thousands of beautifully crafted pieces of crystal caught the light of the candles and cast it into a thousand coruscating rainbows. Huge gilt-framed oil paintings adorned the walls, depicting scenes of naval battles, and rich drapes of red velvet hung across the windows. All of this magnificent opulence paled into insignificance, however, once contrasted with the gathering.

There were perhaps two hundred people in the ballroom, with a fairly even split between men and women and a broad range of ages from sixteen to eighty, with débutantes, midshipmen and sons of financiers at one end of the scale to dowagers, financier's fathers and admirals at the other. Ornately uniformed footmen stood at the doorways while waiters moved amongst the guests with trays of drinks. The women wore magnificent full-skirted dresses of silk and velvet and fluttered fans, while the men were clad in full-dress naval uniform or civilian evening wear: black trousers or pantaloons, white waistcoats and cravats, and tail-coats. In the middle of the floor dancers moved about with slow and sedate steps, going through the intricate patterns of a quadrille to the strains of a full orchestra. A heady odour pervaded the room, a cocktail of scent, pomade and sweat.

The hostess, Lady Grafton, stood close to the door where she could greet her guests. A nod of acknowledgement was neither more nor less than etiquette demanded for Killigrew, but after excusing herself from the guests she was talking to she came across to greet him in person. She was in her late twenties, a handsome, Junoesque woman. 'I don't believe I've had the pleasure, sir...'

'Killigrew, your ladyship. Christopher Killigrew, lately of Her Majesty's paddle-sloop *Tisiphone*.'

'Ah, yes. Admiral Killigrew's grandson. I'm pleased to make your acquaintance.'

She offered him a gloved hand and Killigrew took the tips of her fingers lightly in his, bowing low with practised elegance. She received his bow with a curtsey. 'The honour is all mine, ma'am.'

'I understand you are recently returned from the Tropics, sir?'

'Yes, ma'am. The West Africa Squadron.'

'Are you are in good health?'

'Never felt better, ma'am.'

'I'm so pleased to hear it. You must excuse me, I have other guests to greet. I do hope we shall have a chance to get to know one another better.'

'Indeed, ma'am.' As he watched her move on, he decided that a worse fate could befall a man than to find himself in her bed. Nor would it do his career any harm, provided the lady's husband

153

did not actually catch him there.

He helped himself to a champagne flute from a passing footman and surveyed the gathering, looking for someone he recognised. He was used to such gatherings, having attended balls and levees at various governors' mansions and suchlike in the far-flung outposts of the Empire, and he usually felt at ease. But now he was strangely uncomfortable. He had only been back in England for a few days and he was still adjusting to shore life, where the threat of an encounter with slavers at any moment did not provide that added *frisson* of constant excitement. *This isn't real,* he found himself thinking, and then caught himself. *It* is *real – it's just a very different reality from the one off the Guinea Coast.*

It was not a question of which he preferred – he was equally at home in both – but after five years at sea he was due for a rest. He told himself to relax and enjoy the evening. But not too much: there was work to be done. The *Tisiphone* had gone to Woolwich to have her boilers replaced, and the crew had been paid off. Killigrew was on half-pay until he could find himself a berth on a new ship, and for that he needed the interest of an influential patron. He was in no hurry to do so, but he did not want to spend the rest of his life ashore.

'Hullo, Killigrew. Out of rig?'

Killigrew was not dressed in uniform. He had been in uniform for five years now and, keen to wear something different for a change, had used some of the money from being paid off to purchase himself some new evening clothes:

154

black trousers, white waistcoat and a mulberry tail-coat, the muslin cravat at his throat knotted with careless elegance.

He turned and saw Tremaine standing there, now dressed in the uniform of a lieutenant. Both he and Killigrew had undergone the examination shortly after they had arrived back in England. Tremaine had stayed on board the *Tisiphone* as far as Woolwich, where he had been examined by Standish, newly promoted to post-captain (by God, there was no justice) and two other captains on board a ship of the line. Bearing in mind his own strained relations with Standish, Killigrew had thought it prudent to leave the *Tisiphone* at Portsmouth, and had undergone his own examination on a ship anchored in Spithead.

'How did your examination go?' Tremaine asked him coyly, obviously wondering if the fact that he was in civilian clothes meant he had failed.

'Not bad,' said Killigrew. 'You'll never guess who was on my panel.'

'Who?'

'Captain Crichton.'

'Good God! Not "Nose-Biter" Crichton?'

Killigrew was of above average height, but Crichton had towered above him when he had leaned over him to address his questions during the examination. Killigrew's examination for midshipman had been a simple enough affair: he had been made to write out the Lord's Prayer from memory before the doctor had told him to take off his clothes and jump over a chair, after

155

the completion of which task he had been given a glass of sherry to congratulate him on being in the navy. But the examination for lieutenant was a much more serious business.

'You are the officer of the watch, sir,' Crichton had said. 'It is blowing fresh, and you are under double-reefed topsails and t'gallants. Mark that! The captain comes on deck and asks how the wind is. You make the proper response. He then puts his hand into his pocket and produces a small leather case. Mark that! He opens it and presents you with a cigar. Now, sir – quick – which end would you put into your mouth? Quick! Which end?'

'The twisted end of an Havana, sir, and either end if a cheroot,' Killigrew had replied without hesitation.

'Right, by gad, sir! You have presence of mind. I have no further questions to ask.'

'Did you pass?' Tremaine asked him now.

'With flying colours, apparently.'

'Why, that's capital!' Tremaine pumped him vigorously by the hand. 'Not that I ever doubted you would, of course.' He lowered his voice and raised his glass to his lips: 'So come on, Killigrew. See anything you fancy?' he asked before sipping.

Killigrew smiled. 'I've not yet looked.'

Tremaine grinned. 'Miss Spencer's here to-night.'

'Oh, Lor!' groaned Killigrew. He had already encountered Miss Spencer at a dinner-dance a couple of nights earlier, and found her to be a tedious, simpering ninny, an increasingly common breed these days.

'Don't you like her? She's very pretty. And her father owns half the cotton mills in Lancashire.'

'What would I want with cotton mills?'

'It's not the mills, it's the income that comes with them.'

'If I wanted a good income I'd've gone into trade myself, as you well know. God knows, Uncle William is always pressing me to swallow the anchor and become managing director of his company. Anyway, I'm not here to find a prospective wife. It's a posting I'm interested in. There are a lot of influential people here tonight, 'Stace, so make sure you're on your best behaviour if you don't want to swallow the anchor prematurely.'

Tremaine adopted a tone of injured innocence. 'Don't I always? I've got my eye on Mrs Fairbody.'

Killigrew arched an eyebrow. 'A married woman?'

'A widow. Still young, mark you, and deuced pretty. Her husband died of the Bengal flux a year ago. She's only just out of mourning. But her father's as rich as Croesus, so the suitors are going to be queuing up. Fortunately I've already arranged to have the fifth waltz with her.'

'How very enterprising of you. And does she fit her name?'

'See for yourself.' Tremaine nodded to where a blonde woman wearing a pink silk ball gown was surrounded by admiring beaux, like a first-rate ship of the line at anchor with tenders, gigs and bumboats swarming round her. 'A lovely creature. I must congratulate you: your taste is impeccable. Good luck to you.'

'Would you like me to introduce you?' Tremaine said, clearly out of politeness and terrified that Killigrew would say yes.

'No, thanks. I wouldn't want to cramp your style. You know what they say: two's company, three's a crowd.' *And seventeen is a positive mob.* 'Have you seen Old Charlie?'

'Rear-Admiral Napier? I think he's by the fireplace in the library saloon with all the other old bores.'

'Old fogies they may be, 'Stace, but they're also very influential.'

Killigrew took his leave of Tremaine and made his way to the library saloon. There were no ladies present, just the older men – senior naval officers, financiers and politicians – seated in armchairs around the fireplace, smoking fat cigars and drinking brandy or whisky while pontificating.

Sir Joshua Pengelly, a short, stocky, bow-legged man and the owner of a successful shipping company, was holding forth. 'Palm oil!' he declared. 'That's the thing. It's one of the biggest crops on the African coast. If we can persuade the tribes to stop warring with each other and selling their captives as slaves, and instead to devote their energies to the production of palm oil, why, then we'll have the whole problem of slavery licked. And it's a sound investment, too. These days everything's steam powered, and engines need lubrication. You mark my words, if you've got some spare money and any sense at all, you'll put it all into palm oil.'

'It's a nice idea,' said the host of the evening as he stood with his back to the fire, his hands clasped behind his broad backside, inadvertently lifting the tails of his coat into a tuft like the plumage of some strange but dowdy bird. 'But you're ignoring the basic laws of economics. Demand creates supply. If you want to end the slave trade, you have to cut off the demand, and that means abolishing slavery in Brazil, Cuba and the United States. A task which is quite beyond the powers of our government.'

As a young man, Sir George Grafton had made his fortune in the China Trade, shipping opium from the Honourable East India Company's estates into the Celestial Kingdom in exchange for tea. It had not been easy. The Chinese, ignorant heathens that they were, seemed to object to having opium smuggled into their country, and the British government in London was slow to understand what was obvious to every trader in Canton: the Chinese needed a sound drubbing to show them who was in charge. So Grafton had left the China side of his business in the competent hands of his junior partner and retired to Britain, where he had bought himself a safe seat in Scotland in a by-election. He had never visited the constituency – it was a dismal, dreary place, by all accounts – but that had not mattered, since all the landowners wealthy enough to possess a vote there lived in London, so it was in that great city he had had his campaigning done for him.

Once safely ensconced on the government backbenches, he had been perfectly placed to

159

lobby for what Britain's trade needed: war with China. The Celestials were a backward people, having spent the last two hundred years living in peace and creating great works of art: they were no match for the steamers and shell-guns of the British Expeditionary Force. After much slaughter, the Chinese had been forced to sign the Treaty of Nanking, opening five ports to Western trade and ceding Hong Kong to the British.

After that Mr George Grafton esquire had become Sir George by dint of his generous contributions to the coffers of the Whig party, and the mercantile shipping company Grafton, Bannatyne & Co. had gone from strength to strength, winning lucrative government contracts to run prison hulks and convict ships to transport thieves, Irish rebels, Chartists, trade unionists and other such undesirables to the penal colonies in Australia.

Sir George Grafton was one of the Whigs 'nautical' members of parliament, although his only qualification to speak on naval matters was the fact that he had most of his money invested in merchant shipping. But with the Whigs in power it was necessary for Killigrew to cultivate the patronage of men like Grafton, no matter how offensive he found their politics.

'Only because Palmerston takes such a high-handed attitude,' said Sir Joshua. 'It's all very well being *right* all the time, but sometimes it helps not to be so self-righteous about it. It doesn't win friends. It's not that there aren't plenty of people in those countries who are as

160

opposed to slavery as Wilberforce ever was. But every time they try to speak out, the vested interests just wrap themselves up in their flags and say that the anti-slavers are grovelling to us British.'

'Quite right too,' said Grafton. 'So they should. Damned foreigners.'

'Yes, but perhaps they don't quite see it that way.' Pengelly glanced up, saw Killigrew, and at once rose to his feet. 'Why, it's young Christopher, isn't it? Oh, ho, but not quite so young any more, eh? Glad you could make it, Kit. Forgive me if I don't get up, my damned gout's giving me blue murder these days. Sir George, may I present Mr Christopher Killigrew?'

'Sir George.' Killigrew acknowledged the MP with a cautious nod.

Grafton nodded absently without even glancing at him.

'Pull up a chair,' said Pengelly. 'Get yourself a drink.' He waved across a footman, and indicated Killigrew.

'Whisky, please,' said Killigrew. The footman nodded and hurried off.

'You know Sir Charles, of course,' continued Pengelly.

'Bless my soul, of course I know Kit Killigrew,' said Rear-Admiral Sir Charles Napier, KCB, GTCS, KMT, KSG, KRE, MP. He was sixtyish, a portly man with a double chin and scraggly grey bushy sideburns. He was in full dress uniform, decorated with the Order of the Bath, the Grand Cross of St George of Russia, and the insignia of the Second Class of the Order of the Red Eagle of Prussia. This brave display was in sharp contrast to the thick dusting of snuff on his tail-coat and the way his cravat was clumsily knotted.

He looked like a genial, harmless old buffer, which was exactly what he was: a genial, harmless old buffer who had once taken on three French ships of the line in nothing more than a gun-brig, delaying them long enough for the rest of the English fleet to catch them; a genial, harmless old buffer who had fought as a sailor of fortune in the service of Queen Maria of Portugal against the usurper Dom Miguel, defeating his navy at sea and then – fancying himself an amateur general – giving his army a sound drubbing by land; and a genial, harmless old buffer who less than seven years earlier had exceeded his orders in dictating his own terms to the Viceroy of Egypt.

'Killigrew was one of the middies on board the *Dreadful* during the Syria campaign; and a damned useful aide-de-camp ashore. Blew up the magazine at Acre, so he did; and when I landed with my men the next day, we found Killigrew here sitting amidst the smoking ruins with the *Dreadful*'s schoolmaster and a couple of others, taking tea as coolly as if they were on the lawn at the Naval Academy! Good to see you, Killigrew. Still only a mate?'

'Recently promoted to lieutenant, sir.'

'Why, congratulations! Splendid stuff! Not before time either, I might add.' As the footman returned with Killigrew's whisky, Napier ordered another round of drinks to celebrate. 'Got yourself a posting yet?' he asked at last.

'Not yet, sir.'

'Well, we'll have to see what we can do,' Napier said with a wink which was meant to be encouraging.

Killigrew smiled, although he did not welcome the thought of Napier's patronage as much as he felt he ought to. Despite his respect and admiration for the rear-admiral, Killigrew knew that Napier was not popular at the Admiralty because of his eccentric ideas on abolishing the flogging of seamen and encouraging the building of steam vessels, and his tendency to air them at every available opportunity.

'Kit's just back from the West Africa Squadron,' said Napier. 'He can tell us all about how to suppress the slave trade from the sharp end. Can't you eh?'

Killigrew smiled tightly and glanced down into his glass. 'One tries to do one's duty.'

'If you want my opinion, the West Africa Squadron is no more than a waste of men and money,' said Grafton. 'I intend to bring a private members' bill to the House of Commons to have the squadron disbanded.'

'Abolish the West Africa Squadron?' spluttered Napier. 'My dear sir, if you abolish the West Africa Squadron, who will suppress the slave trade? Surely you do not suggest that we leave it to the French or the Americans?'

'No man opposes the evils of slavery more vigorously than I,' said Grafton. 'But one must face facts. It is forty years since we declared the slave trade illegal and our navy set about suppressing it. Have they succeeded? Not at all. If anything, the West Africa Squadron's attempts to suppress it only make it worse for the slaves. Did you know, when slave ships find themselves pursued by a navy vessel and have no hope of escape, they throw their slaves overboard to drown, in order to dispose of the evidence?'

'And you would let such men carry on their trade unhindered, sir?' Killigrew was careful to keep his expression mild, although inside he seethed with rage at the very suggestion. 'Believe me, sir, if you saw such a thing happen you would feel very differently about it.'

'Ah, but you've been too close to the issue to consider it objectively,' Grafton said with a dismissive wave of his hand. 'Such decisions are best left to wiser heads here in England–'

Napier slammed down his glass. 'Stuff and nonsense.'

Grafton blinked. 'I beg your pardon?'

'You heard me, Sir George. Stuff and nonsense is what I said, and stuff and nonsense is what I meant. By God, if there's one thing I've grown heartily sick of during my time as a member of parliament, it's pompous asses blethering on about subjects of which they are clearly in utter ignorance. Nothing but fools and idiots, sir!'

'Sir Charles! I must protest.'

'You must protest? *You* must protest? After I spent five years listening to damned fools taking up issues not because they believed in them, but because they knew that by backing them they could promote their own careers? Pursuing half-baked policies drawn up in complete ignorance

164

of the maladies which they sought to remedy–'

'I can see you are a passionate man, Sir Charles. But you must understand that there is no place for passion in the art of government. These things must be considered logically, in the cold light of reason. If there were no West Africa Squadron, the slavers would have no reason to throw the slaves overboard.'

'Yes,' said Killigrew, rising to his feet. 'Then they could go on to sell their cargoes into a lifetime of slavery in the Americas and reap rich rewards from the vast profits. Is that your solution, Sir George?' he demanded heatedly.

Pengelly quickly stood up and took Killigrew by the arm. 'This is all very interesting, gentlemen, but if you'll excuse Mr Killigrew and myself, there is someone present I'm keen to introduce him to. I'm sure we can resume this debate at a later date. At the Gresham, perhaps.'

Grafton nodded grudgingly, clearly annoyed at being prevented from having the last word, and at having to concede it to a young whipper-snapper like Killigrew at that.

Killigrew turned to where Napier sat. 'Sir Charles.'

'We must have luncheon sometime,' said Napier.

'Thank you, sir.' Killigrew left Grafton out of his leave-taking, in a calculated snub which he knew he would later regret, although for now he was too angry to care.

Hobbling on his gouty foot Pengelly steered him out of the library saloon and back into the ballroom. 'Sorry to drag you away, Killigrew,' he said. 'Between you and me I was really rather enjoying that. I think you and Sir Charles had Sir George squarely on the ropes. But I couldn't afford to let you ruin your career for the sake of my own entertainment, now could I?'

'No, sir. I'm obliged to you for your timely intervention. I must apologise to Sir George for my outburst...'

'Good Lord, I hope not. Grovel to that pompous ass? You'll do no such thing. Let the matter rest. He'll have forgotten all about you come tomorrow morning; and there are plenty of other people who can help you in your career. Now I wasn't lying when I said there was someone I wanted you to meet. You remember my daughter Eulalia?'

'Eulalia? How could I forget?' *I still have her teeth marks in my arm.*

'Well, she's here tonight, and I just know she's eager to renew your acquaintance...' Pengelly gazed around the throng and then shook his head. 'Damn it, where's the girl got to? You wait here and I'll see if I can find her.' Pengelly plunged into the crowd and left Killigrew to sip his whisky in peace.

But peace was never something Killigrew seemed to be able to enjoy for long. He looked up and saw Tremaine heading towards him from one direction and Mr Spencer heading towards him from another, with his simpering ninny of a daughter in tow.

'Killigrew, have you seen Mrs Fairbody?'

'Good evening, Mr Killigrew,' said Mr Spencer. 'My daughter was wondering if she might have

166

the pleasure of the next dance?'

Miss Spencer giggled and fluttered her eyelashes over her fan at Killigrew.

'Of course she may,' he said, taking her by the hand. Then he put her hand in Tremaine's and gently pushed them both towards the centre of the floor. Mr Spencer gaped and turned puce, at a loss for words. The orchestra struck up a lively polka, and Miss Spencer shrugged and gripped Tremaine tightly, sweeping him around the floor. Tremaine mouthed curses at Killigrew over her shoulder. Grinning, Killigrew shook his head and slipped through another door before Mr Spencer could find his tongue; or before Tremaine could pester him about Mrs Blasted Fairbody, for that matter.

The French windows were open so he went outside and stood on the terrace, leaning against the stone balustrade which faced across the ornamental gardens. The cool night air was fresh after the tobacco fug of the library saloon and the sweaty atmosphere of the ballroom, so he stood there a while, sipping his whisky and smoking a cheroot, reflecting.

It went against the grain for Killigrew to toady to anyone, but he had chosen the navy as his career and that was an end to the matter. He had every intention of retiring on an admiral's pension, and he knew that in order to achieve his aim he would need patronage. If that meant toad-eating the likes of Sir George Grafton, then it was just too bad. He had made his bed; now he had to lie on it. When he had achieved flag-rank, he could starting working to make sure that men were promoted because of merit rather than patronage.

He thought about the West African Squadron. Glad as he was to be given a break in England, part of him still wished he was back there chasing slavers. He did not like leaving a job unfinished, and even after three years he felt he had hardly made any impact at all on the slave trade. Perhaps Grafton was right; perhaps the West Africa Squadron was a waste of time...

'Excuse me, you haven't seen Christopher Killigrew, have you?' he heard Mr Spencer's voice ask someone in the room behind him.

Killigrew hurriedly drained the last of his whisky and vaulted over the balustrade, landing lightly in the flower-bed below. He slipped behind a yew hedge and made his way through the shadows to the gazebo. He was about to sit down on the bench when he perceived someone already sitting there in the darkness. 'My apologies. I was unaware that this gazebo was already occupied...'

'Sit down,' said a woman's voice. 'There's plenty of room for two.'

'May I ask what you're doing out here all alone?'

'The same as you,' she responded. 'Hiding.'

He smiled, and sat down on the bench opposite her. As his eyes adjusted to the gloom he was less than devastated to recognise his co-fugitive as Mrs Fairbody. He raised his cheroot to his lips and was about to puff on it when he hesitated. 'I ... er ... hope you do not object to the smell of tobacco.'

168

'Not at all. As long as it's reasonably good quality.'

'Oh, the best,' he assured her. He tucked the cheroot in the corner of his mouth and stood up to bow. 'Christopher Killigrew at your service, ma'am.'

She stiffened. 'Not … *Kit* Killigrew?'

He frowned. He did not know many women in England, and if he had inadvertently slighted her in some far-flung port he was sure he would have remembered. 'I'm sorry, ma'am, I don't believe I have the pleasure of your acquaintance.'

'Perhaps not; I was wondering if you still had my teeth marks in your arm.'

He stared; he may even have gaped. *'Eulalia?'*

They both stood up and hugged each other. 'Kit! After all these years. How long has it been?'

'Eleven years?'

'Eleven years.' They parted and she put her hands on his arm, holding him at arm's length so she could look him up and down. 'And look at you now. Quite the young gentleman.'

'And look at *you*. A friend of mine pointed you out to me earlier as Mrs Fairbody. I never guessed for a moment that it was you.'

'Tush! And after you told me that you'd love me for ever.'

He held up a hand. 'I refuse to be held accountable for anything I said below the age of twelve. I was still a minor, don't forget. Anyway, you were the one who got married.'

'Only after you ran away to sea.'

After the deaths of his parents, Killigrew had been raised in the austere environment of

Killigrew House under the stern eye of his grandfather. Rear-Admiral Killigrew had never approved of his son marrying a foreigner, and to him Kit was the product of that unnatural union. If he could have left the care of his grandson to the Naval Benevolent Society he would have done, but there was no question that the society could be lumbered with one more orphan when the child had a well-off grandparent still living.

Kit had hated Killigrew House. His grandfather was as much of a martinet in his own home as he was reputed to have been on board his ships, and Killigrew had often been beaten for playing with the children of the local fishermen. Then, shortly before Kit's fifth birthday, the Comte Duchargny – an impoverished nobleman who had been forced to flee his native land during the terror of the French Revolution – had turned up on the doorstep of Killigrew House offering his services as a private tutor. The Rear-Admiral had accepted, reasoning that an aristocratic tutor was just what was needed to instil discipline in the unruly child, and Kit's education in all the gentlemanly studies – Greek, Latin, French, fencing and dancing – had commenced.

The comte's methods had been unconventional to say the least. Even though he was in his sixties, he remained nimble and spry, and in the midst of a bout with épées he would shoot questions at his young pupil. If Kit answered incorrectly, then the comte's blade would slip under his guard and give him a stinging blow. Nowadays Kit often joked that he had had a simple choice between

170

becoming fluent in the Classics or becoming an adept swordsman, and he still could not hear Latin verbs conjugated without instinctively reaching for a sword.

But he liked the old *comte*. What his grandfather had never known, because he had never taken the trouble to find out, was that the *comte* was an old friend of Kit's father. As a young man, the *comte* had been one of those liberal nobles who had renounced their aristocratic privileges one fateful night in 1789, little imagining what it would lead to. Four years later his parents had been beheaded in the Place de la Guillotine and the young *comte* had barely escaped the same fate. He had served with the French Royalist forces against Napoleon, but when the French monarchy had been restored in 1814 it had been too much of a return to the bad old days of the *Ancien Regime* for his liberal tastes. He had become a solider of fortune and it had been while fighting for Chilean Independence he had met Captain Jack Killigrew.

The *comte* told Kit stories about his adventures with his father in Chile, Brazil and Greece, and in an effort to explain the principles they had been fighting for he had introduced him to works by Rousseau, Wollstonecraft, and Burke. Then, when Kit was twelve, his grandfather had found a copy of Thomas Paine's *The Rights of Man* in his room. After a brief enquiry, the *comte* – seventy now – had been sent packing.

Kit had always been terrified of his grandfather, but his rage at his tutor's dismissal finally gave him the courage to stand up to his grandfather and the two of them had had a blazing row, the ancient naval officer versus the precocious twelve-year-old. The only thing they were both able to agree on was that they could no longer live together under the same roof, no matter how wide that roof might be, and that since Kit was now old enough to join the navy as a first-class volunteer, it was high time he did so. Killigrew had been relieved just to get out of the oppressive atmosphere of his grandfather's house. Certainly it had never been a home to Kit, and since that day he had had no communication whatsoever with his grandfather. Nor had he ever looked back.

'Still in the navy?' asked Eulalia.

He nodded. 'I've just been promoted to lieutenant.'

'Congratulations. You know, even after all these years, I still find myself sneaking a peek at papa's copy of the *Naval Gazette* to see if you've been mentioned.'

'And have I?'

'Not since that business in China. I was so proud! When I went back to school the next term I took the cutting to show all my friends. They refused to believe that I'd known Midshipman Killigrew, the hero of Chingkiang-fu. And then, after that, nothing. Where've you *been* all these years, Kit?'

'After China I was posted to the West Africa Squadron for three years. I've only just returned. What about you? Who was this Mr Fairbody? Or would you rather not talk about it?'

'Oh, I don't mind. It's over a year since he

passed on. This is only the second time I've been in Society since I came out of mourning; it's funny, rather like having to go back to square one in snakes and ladders. I think Papa wants me to get married as soon as possible. I can't think why, Mr Fairbody left me … comfortable, so it's not as if I'm an imposition on him.'

'You're still young. You should get remarried.'

'Oh, I dare say I shall, some day. But not the moment I come out of mourning. It's all right for you men. You're not expected to get married until you're thirty or so. It's different for us women, Kit. For us it's straight out of school and into marriage.'

'You didn't care for Mr Fairbody?'

'Heavens, did I make it sound like that? Peter was a good husband. He was Father's choice rather than my own, but I didn't protest.'

'Handsome?'

She grinned mischievously, her teeth shining white in the gloom. 'Devilishly. But … oh I do envy you, Kit. You've been off to see the world, gone to places I can only dream of or read about.'

'You could too, you know. If Mr Fairbody left you a moderate legacy, what's to stop you from travelling?'

'I expect I shall. I just need to pluck up the courage, that's all. That's why I don't want Papa to rush me into getting remarried. You know, I get the feeling he's already got someone in mind for me.'

'Yes,' said Killigrew. 'And I think I know who.'

'You do?'

He nodded. 'I was talking to him earlier. He

173

said there was someone he wanted me to meet and asked me if I remembered you.'

She laughed. 'That's so like Papa. Childhood sweethearts reunited.'

'Would that be so terrible?'

'Oh, Kit! Don't take this the wrong way, but ... I'm just not ready to dedicate the rest of my life to a man. Don't tell me you came here looking for a wife?'

He shook his head. 'As you said yourself, I'm a little too young to be worrying about marriage. It's a ship I'm after.'

'Ah. I've heard it said that naval men were married to their ships. That's why I'm not sure I want to marry a naval officer. No offence intended. But if and when I do get remarried, I don't intend to share my husband with three thousand tons of wood and a thousand horny-handed seamen.'

'Perhaps you should think about marrying the captain of a gun-brig. That way you'd only have to share him with a few hundred tons of wood and ten dozen horny-handed seamen.'

She laughed. 'You would not by any chance be in line for a posting to command of a gun-brig now, would you, Kit?'

He grimaced wryly. 'Right now I'm not even in line for the command of a dinghy. Still, perhaps we could go riding together next week? Catch up on old times?'

'I didn't know you were a horseman.'

'Oh, I'm never happier than when I'm in the saddle. Shall we say Friday morning?'

'Hyde Park?'

'Where else?'

'It's a little public, isn't it? Some people might get the idea that you're courting me.'

'Would that be so bad? If you're serious about not wanting to get married, it might help discourage some of your more ardent beaux if they think they're out of the running.'

'You *are* keen to get the bit between your teeth, aren't you?'

'I just thought that since *you're* not in any hurry to get married, and *I'm* not in any hurry to get married, we could not be in a hurry to get married together.'

She smiled. 'All right. Friday it is. Nine o'clock?'

'Better make it half past ten. I have an appointment at nine.'

'Not with some other woman who's not in any hurry to get married, I trust?'

He shook his head. 'Not unless she's a fellow of the Ethnological Society.'

'Did you say "Leopard People"?' Professor Llewelyn glanced up from behind the desk and pushed his spectacles back on to the bridge of his nose with a forefinger.

'I know it must sound crazy...' Killigrew told him apologetically.

'Believe me, young man, when you've studied ethnology as long as I have, then *nothing* sounds crazy.' Llewelyn picked up the fat, dusty tomes which lay under his desk and carried them across to an empty bookshelf. They had titles like *Seven Months with the Temne*, *Mating Rituals of the Kissi*

175

and *Up the Niger by Canoe*. When he had placed them all on the shelf, he stood and stared at the spines, tapping a pen against the side of his nose.

'Let me see, I think I recall reading something somewhere about leopard people. Professor Phillpotts would have been the chap to ask. He was the real expert of West African cultures. Especially the Mende. In fact, now that I think about it, I seem to recall he said something about investigating the local myths and superstitions last time he left for the Guinea Coast. Unfortunately he never came back.'

'You mean he…'

'Died? Good Lord, no. Nothing like that. No, while he was on the steam packet he met some gypsy girl who was travelling to Spain with a circus and fell in love with her. Extraordinary behaviour. His wife was most upset. No, the last I heard of him, he was taming lions somewhere in central Europe.'

'The leopard people, Professor,' prompted Killigrew.

'Hm? Oh, yes. Let me see now, the Mende. Here we are: Gimson's *Encyclopaedia of the Peoples of Africa*, Volume Two. When in doubt, turn to Gimson, that's what I always say.' He rifled through the pages until he came to the entry he sought. 'Here we are: "the Mende is a large tribe which lives in the interior of Africa near the Guinea Coast. They are a handsome, negroid people" – have you ever noticed how these books never described a people as being ugly? – "who exist in a quasi-feudal society at a primitive stage of development. One interesting feature of their culture is the prevalence of secret societies..."'

Killigrew had never heard of a culture which did not have some kind of secret society. In China they had the Triads, in India they had the Cult of Thuggee, and in Europe and America there was Freemasonry. 'What sort of "secret societies"?' he asked.

'It doesn't say. Presumably because they're secret, hm? Ah, here we are: "One interesting facet of Mende culture is the belief that certain people have the power to transform themselves into leopards through witchcraft. These leopard people are said to use parts of their victims to make *borfima*, magic potions which render the users rich and powerful. There exist in Mende societies witch doctors known as Tongo Players. There men claim the power to identify leopard people in their human form, using primitive and ornate rituals. It is believed that deaths caused by real leopards are ascribed to the handiwork of the leopard people and that the Tongo Players take advantage of this superstition to dispose of unpopular members of the community. When an individual is identified as a human leopard, he is beaten severely and then burned to death." That's all it says, I'm afraid.'

'Sounds like the witchfinder general of Jacobean times,' said Killigrew.

'Yes, they're a primitive people, aren't they?'

'Civilisation is relative in my experience, Professor. What must they think of the white men who come in ships to kidnap their people and carry them away by force across the great ocean

177

to a life of eternal slavery?'

'Yes, but *they're* just ignorant. Where did you hear of the leopard people?'

'From one of the recaptives on a slaver I was bringing in as a prize. The master's mistress bit me in a fight, and when one of the slaves heard about it she started talking about leopard people, and how the woman must be destroyed. The next thing I knew, the woman who bit me hard had had her skull smashed in and her bed set on fire.'

'Good heavens. She wasn't a negro, this captain's mistress, was she?'

'Yes, as it happens she was.'

'How extraordinary.'

'Not really. It was a pretty savage fight. Life and death, that kind of thing.'

'No, I mean the master of this slave vessel taking a negress as his mistress.'

'African women are no different from European women, in my experience, barring the colour of their skin.'

'Oh, I wouldn't go that far. You're aware, of course, that in the bush these people often go around...' Llewelyn looked about surreptitiously, as if worried that someone might overhear him, although as far as Killigrew could tell they were the only two people in the room. '...completely unclothed. Including the women. The negro may be similar to the Caucasian anatomically, Mr Killigrew, but up here?' He tapped his forehead. 'They must exist in a state of permanent – if you'll forgive the expression – *physiological arousal.*'

'You've never been to Africa, have you, Professor?'

178

'No. But I've read all about it. In books.'

'If you had, you might find it so humid that you'd feel more comfortable wearing fewer clothes than we are accustomed to wearing in our more temperate climes. It's the garden of Eden, Professor, where man lived in healthy innocence, taking no shame in the human form until he partook of the fruit of knowledge.'

'I'm afraid that's one fruit I've eaten too much of ever to get back to Eden, Mr Killigrew,' Llewelyn said wistfully.

'I fear you may be right, Professor. Thank you for your assistance. It's certainly been an ... educating experience.'

'Not at all. Glad to be of service. You're not going back there, are you?'

'To Africa? Well, I don't have any plans as such yet...'

'If you did learn anything more about these beliefs, I should be grateful if you could let us know about them if you return.'

'*If* I return?'

'Well, you might decide you're so happy living in primitive bliss in the garden of Eden that you never want to leave,' said Llewelyn. 'On the other hand, you might die of yellow fever. They don't call it the white man's grave for nothing, you know.'

179

VIII:

A Game at Billiards

Killigrew quit the offices of the Ethnological Society and returned to where he had left his hired horse in the care of the crossing-sweeper at the junction of Queen Anne Street and Harley Street, tipping the sweeper every bit as generously as he had promised. When he was going to be sued by Videira's lawyers for every penny he had, a few extra crowns here and there did not seem to matter: better to give it to an honest crossing-sweeper than a slave captain and his pettifoggers.

It was a bright, crisp day in mid April and he enjoyed the ride through Mayfair's elegant streets to Hyde Park Corner. He reached the statue of Achilles on the dot of half past ten. There was no sign of Eulalia, but it would have been unladylike for her to arrive on time; that would have smacked of over-eagerness. She kept him waiting no more than ten minutes, arriving in the company of her maid acting as chaperone, both of them mounted. She looked even more lovely by day than she had done the other evening, the sunlight picking out the golden tresses pinned beneath a high-crowned riding hat perched at a rakish angle. Seeing him, she smiled.

'Good morning, Mr Killigrew. Your appointment at the Ethnological Society went well, I trust?'

He touched the brim of his top hat with his riding crop. 'Not as well as I'd hoped, ma'am,' he said, a little disappointed by her reversion to a more formal form of address than that which they had enjoyed the other night. He supposed it was due to the presence of the maid.

They at once set off at a slow, steady pace along Rotten Row, mingling with the other genteel riders, while the maid followed behind them at a discreet distance. The London Season was getting into its stride and the sandy track was busy with aristocratic young swells trying to catch the eyes of genteel ladies, and officers of the Household Cavalry showing off their latest mistresses.

'You were not able to learn anything more about those primitive native superstitions, then?' asked Eulalia.

'Nothing I don't already know. Would you believe that their foremost expert on Africa had never ever been there?'

'Forget about Africa, Kit. It's behind you now.'

'I know. But it is still there.'

'Is it a beautiful country?'

'The parts of it I saw were – once you get out of Freetown, of course. But those were only on the coast. It's such a vast continent. I've not even scratched the surface' He frowned. It was not the continent whose surface he wished to scratch, it was the slave trade. And he would do a damned sight more than just scratch it, if only he had the chance.

'You seem troubled.'

'I was just thinking.'

'About what?'

'The slave trade.'

'Fie on you, Christopher Killigrew. You come out riding with me, and all you can think of is the slave trade?'

'If you had seen some of the atrocities I have' He shook his head. She did not want to hear of such things.

'It's not your problem any longer, Kit. Forget about it. Let someone else worry about it. Or do you think you're the only man in the whole world who can do that?'

'There are very few men who even seem to have the inclination.'

'You need something to take your mind off it,' she told him. 'Some vigorous exercise will do the trick, I think.'

'Oh?' he said, arching an eyebrow, but before he could come up with any suggestions she had turned her horse off the path and goaded it into a gallop, dashing off across the grass. He cursed under his breath and urged his own horse after her. The strollers of the lower orders cheered to see a fine woman galloping along so bravely, and laughed at the young gentleman who was hard pushed to keep up with her, using one hand to hold his top hat in place. If he was able to keep level with her it was only because she rode side-saddle. The maid was left far behind.

They passed along the bank of the Serpentine and crossed over the bridge, where pedestrians forced her to slow down, enabling him to catch up with her at last. She turned to smile at him, her cheeks flushed with exhilaration.

'So you *can* ride,' she acknowledged, and laughed merrily. 'You know, Kit, you haven't changed one bit. You always did have to excel at everything you attempted.'

He frowned. 'Do you think so? I've never thought of myself as competitive.'

'But that's what's so infuriating about you. It isn't a question of being better than anyone else. It's as if you already know that you're the best at everything you do, accept it without arrogance, and compete against yourself because there's no other competition.'

He shrugged. 'I've always felt that if a job's worth doing, it's worth doing well, if that's what you mean. If it makes you feel any better, there are plenty of things I'm hopeless at.'

'Such as?'

He thought for a moment. 'Gardening.'

She laughed.

'No, truly. Every kind of vegetation I touch withers and dies.'

'I don't believe you've ever tried your hand at horticulture in your life. If you did, I'm sure you would have a garden which would make the gardens at Kew look like a costermonger's vegetable patch.'

Red-faced and dripping with sweat, the maid caught up with them, which stifled the conversation from then on, but it was pleasant enough to amble through the park on horseback beside Eulalia. It seemed that scarcely a few minutes had passed before the bells of St Paul's in

183

Kensington were tolling half-past eleven and Killigrew took out his watch.

'Am I boring you?' asked Eulalia.

'Not at all. I wish I could stay longer,' he said, with genuine regret. He could not remember the last time he had enjoyed a young woman's company so much. 'But I have an appointment at twelve. Perhaps I may be allowed to enjoy the pleasure of your company again some time?'

'When did you have in mind?'

'How about this afternoon?' he found himself saying.

She laughed. 'All right. Your appointment is for luncheon, I take it? Shall we say two o'clock at Gunter's Tea Shop?'

'Better make it three,' he told her. 'I'm dining with Rear-Admiral Napier.'

He left Hyde Park at the same place he had entered, by the statue of Achilles, and rode up Piccadilly to St James's Street, where he had an arrangement with the landlord of the White Horse Cellar Coaching Inn for the stabling of his hired horse. It was only a temporary arrangement, for he had no idea how much longer he would be staying in London. He had only been in the city for a few days but already he was growing bored, and if it had not been for the possibility of a closer acquaintance with Eulalia Fairbody then he might have had a hankering to get back to sea.

There was not time for him to return to his own club to get changed, so he made his way directly to the United Service Club on Pall Mall. He was about to present himself to the porter in the hallway when he saw Napier coming down the stairs from above, deep in conversation with another gentleman who was smoking a cigar. The rear-admiral walked with his feet turned out, limping from one old war wound, and stoop-necked from another. He was too involved in his conversation with his companion to notice Killigrew.

'Can I be of assistance, sir?' asked the porter.

'It's all right, I'm here to see Sir Charles,' Killigrew told him, nodding up the stairs.

'And you are?'

'Christopher Killigrew.'

'Very good, sir. Sir Charles is expecting you.'

At the foot of the stairs Napier and his companion took their leave of one another, shaking hands warmly, and then Napier hailed Killigrew. 'Hullo, Killigrew. Come on up.'

Killigrew followed Napier up the stairs. 'That was Mr Brunel, the celebrated engineer,' Napier told him. 'Do you know him? Very clever chap, young Brunel. He's helping me with the designs for a new steamship I'm working on.' More than a quarter of a century ago, when steamships had seemed nothing more than a novelty, Napier had designed and built a small fleet of steamers for the River Seine at his own expense to prove how practical they could be; and only the previous year another vessel of his design, the first-class steam frigate HMS *Sidon,* had been launched and completed.

'Another steam frigate, sir?' asked Killigrew.

'No, no. She's not so big as the *Sidon.* A sloop. Well, a surveying ship.'

'Steam powered?' Killigrew asked in some surprise.

Napier nodded. 'Most of the navy's exploring ships are still sail-powered only; and all our charts are drawn up with sailing ships in mind. Steam vessels have completely different requirements, as I'm sure you'll appreciate. When steam supplants sailing ships altogether, as I have no doubt it will, then all the old Admiralty charts will be out of date. My new ship will be just the thing to update them; and being steam-powered, she'll have no difficulty navigating narrow creeks and inlets.'

They entered the reading room and sat down at a table, Napier ordering drinks for them both from a waiter. 'Yes, I've got big plans for my little surveying ship. I'm trying to design her to be something of a jack of all trades, you see. The danger is that if you try to compromise too much you end up serving no useful purpose at all. I don't want her to be a jack of all trades and master of none. And I'll need a crew of energetic officers to run her,' he added with a wink. 'Mind you, I can't see her being ready for at least another three years, so you've got time to get another posting under your belt before then. Who knows? By then you may have been promoted to post-rank.'

Killigrew smiled. 'That would be too much to dream of.'

'Why not? You're a capable and energetic young man. You'll be how old three years from now? Twenty-six, twenty-seven? Worse men than you have been promoted to post-captain at a younger age.'

Killigrew was pleased to think that Napier thought him worthy of the command of a vessel which was obviously a pet project of his. But just because Napier had designed another ship, there was no guarantee that the Admiralty would approve its construction, or that if they did they would approve Killigrew's appointment to the crew when it was ready. Besides which, all of that seemed a long time in the future and Killigrew knew he had no chance whatsoever of obtaining post-rank within three years if he spent them all ashore.

They dined heartily – Killigrew had a young man's appetite, and that Napier was a good trencherman was testified to by his stout girth – and talked of the navy, the problems with manning and the slowness of promotion, and of steam engines and the relative merits of paddle-wheels and propeller screws. While all these subjects were close to the hearts of the two naval officers, Killigrew sensed that none of this was why Napier had asked him to luncheon; a hunch which was confirmed when Napier told the waiter they would take coffee in the billiards room.

'D'you play billiards? Splendid game. Very scientific, d'ye see? It's all about *angles*.'

'I'm afraid I never was much good at trigo-nometry, although I have played billiards on occasion,' admitted Killigrew.

'Splendid! We shall play a game or two, and talk while we do so.'

The billiards room was empty at that time of

the day. Killigrew took two cues from the rack and offered Napier his choice. Then the two of them stood side by side at the baulk and each strung a ball up the table, bouncing them off the top cushion so that they rolled back towards the lower cushion.

'Ha! I win,' said Napier, when his ball came to rest nearest the bottom cushion. 'Although I suspect you let me, out of deference to seniority. Well, no matter. I shall break the balls, and you'll soon see I've no need of a handicap. I must warn you, Killigrew, I've been playing this game a good deal of late, and though I say so myself I've become rather a dab hand at it. First to score one hundred? I'll take spot white,' he added, placing that ball in the baulk and lining up a shot. He at once knocked Killigrew's ball into one of the pockets. 'First hazard to me, I think,' he said smugly, lining up his next shot. 'By the way, you do realise that Captain Standish thinks you murdered Captain da Silva in cold blood?'

'Oh?' Killigrew said cautiously. When Lieutenant Jardine had entered the day room on board the *São João* to see da Silva's corpse stretched out on the deck and Killigrew with a smoking revolver in his hand, Killigrew had merely indicated the pistol in the open drawer of the desk and allowed Jardine to draw his own conclusions. 'Has he said anything?'

'Good heavens, no! Not as such. Standish is no fool; at least, not that much of a fool. He knows perfectly well that it could never be proved that you murdered da Silva – which you didn't, of course – and that if he said so publicly you'd be well within your rights to call him out. And we both know how *that* would turn out. No, he's just made some ... shall we say *insinuations*. Oh, damn and blast!' he added as he missed a shot.

Killigrew stepped up to the table and took a shot.

'Oh, well played! Now, if it was up to me, I'd shoot every last slaver and be done with it. But you know what these damned Whigs are like: can't kill a man without a fair trial, and all that. As if there were such thing as a fair trial! Which reminds me, I read your report to the Slave Trade Department at the Foreign Office. Interesting reading. You're not the first naval officer on the West Africa Squadron to hear of this Owodunni Barracoon, either; although the information you found on the *São João* has helped to narrow down its location to within two hundred miles.'

'With all the creeks and inlets on that stretch of coastline, it should only take the entire squadron a couple of years to find it – if they dedicated all their energies to surveying that stretch of the coast, that is.'

'Which they won't, of course. The only thing we know about the Owodunni Barracoon is that it lies somewhere between Sierra Leone and Monrovia, it's run by a man called Francisco Salazar – Portuguese or Brazilian, no one knows for sure – and it seems to have picked up most of the slave trade which was lost when Denman and his colleagues destroyed the barracoons on the Gallinas, Sherbar, and Pongas rivers. In fact the department estimates that over twenty thousand slaves are shipped from this one barracoon to the

189

Americas every year. Can you imagine it? Twenty thousand men, women and children, every year? Why, at an estimate of one-third dying *en route*, that's nearly seven thousand killed on the middle passage alone; and the rest condemned to a life of misery and degradation. Oh, capital shot, Mr Killigrew! I gather from the support you gave me in our rather heated debate with that pompous ass Sir George the other night that you feel rather passionately about the slave trade?'

'I'd give anything to see it stopped,' said Killigrew, concentrating on his next shot.

'Anything?' Napier chuckled. 'I wonder'

'If you'd seen some of the atrocities I witnessed last month alone, you'd understand why I feel so strongly about it.'

'I dare say. But there are plenty of other men in the squadron who've seen sights every bit as atrocious as the ones you've witnessed, yet precious few of them seem to have your zeal for crushing the slavers. Well played! You're better at this game than you let on, Mr Killigrew. It is as well you're not a member of this club; I do believe you are what they call a "shark". Tell me, if you had the power, how would you go about stopping the slave trade?'

'There are a number of ways...' said Killigrew, taking another shot and potting Napier's ball once again. 'And I'd use all of them.'

'Go on.'

'Well, the most important thing is to abolish slavery in the Americas.'

'True. But given that this is beyond our powers?'

'Discourage the African princes from selling the slaves to Europeans; make other forms of trade more profitable. Like that palm oil Sir Joshua is so keen on. I'd use carrot and stick techniques. The carrot is the vast profits they could realise from palm oil; the stick is stepping up the activities of the West Africa Squadron. We should smash the barracoons as they did a few years ago, before Captain Denman was taken to court. Damn the law! If a merchant has goods at a barracoon, then he's aiding and abetting the blackbirders at the very least. His goods should be forfeit. I say we smash their barracoons and smash their goods and smash their ships until we've forced them out of business.' He struck the cue ball savagely and managed to sink all three balls.

'An eight stroke, by God! But will putting the barracoons out of business be enough, do you think?'

Killigrew stared at the green baize while he considered the question. 'No,' he decided. 'To tell the truth, the trade is just too damned profitable. It's the men who make the real money out of it we have to hit. The investors.'

'Very good!' Napier beamed like a teacher listening to a favourite pupil.

'But they're all foreigners so they're beyond the reach of the British law.'

'Supposing I were to tell you that one of the biggest investors in the slave trade today was an Englishman; and not only an Englishman at that, but a leading member of the Establishment?'

Killigrew almost dropped his cue. 'Who?'

Napier chuckled. 'My dear boy, if we knew his name you could rest assured the whole world would know about it by now. No, all we know are a few hints we've picked up here and there from reports such as yours handed in to the Slave Trade Department. But a definite picture is beginning to emerge. We even have a scrap of a letter of instructions to a slaver captain written on the House of Commons own headed note-paper!'

'A member of parliament?'

'Makes one think, does it not?'

'You don't suppose it could be...?'

'I know what you're going to say; don't say it. We need proof before we go making any accusations, otherwise we'll just ruin both our careers. And that's where you come in, Mr Killigrew.'

'I?'

'I want you to become a blackbirder.'

Killigrew miscued. Unmindful of the balls clinking on the baize, he looked up at the rear-admiral in astonishment.

'Yes, you heard me correctly,' Napier told him. 'The tighter we clamp down on the slavers, the more organised they become. The only way we're going to get the proof we need is to infiltrate their ranks.'

'You mean join the crew of a slaver under an assumed name?' Killigrew shook his head. 'It's a nice idea, but it will never work. The blackbirders are as thick as thieves, and I've crossed swords with so many there's too great a risk that one of them will recognise me as a naval officer.'

Napier nodded. 'I suspect that's the mistake I made with the last naval officer I sent on this mission.'

'You mean you've tried this before?'

'Yes. You remember Lieutenant Comber, don't you?'

'Comber? Yes, he's a good man.'

'Ah ... *was* a good man.'

'Please tell me he's working as a lion-tamer somewhere in central Europe.'

'Eh? No, no. I fear it more likely that Lieutenant Comber is currently somewhere at the bottom of the Atlantic Ocean. But I won't make the same mistake with you as I made with him.'

'No?'

'No. I intend for you to join a slaver under your *real* name.'

'I know you well enough by now to know there's method in your madness, sir, but I fear you'll have to explain it to me.'

'We'll make it look as if you've been dismissed from the service in disgrace; guilty of something so vile that you'll never be able to get honest work on any ship again, navy or merchant. What more natural than for you, embittered and twisted, to seek revenge by signing on with the kind of crew which the navy works so hard to foil?'

'What more natural than the aforementioned crew should take the opportunity to thrash the living daylights out of me as soon as we're at sea, just for devilment?'

'Not if we pick the right captain, Mr Killigrew.

One clever enough to realise the distinct advantages he'll enjoy from employing an ex-naval officer – one with a grudge towards the navy – on board his vessel. A man who is completely familiar with all the tactics the navy employs.'

'It might work,' Killigrew allowed. 'You have such a captain in mind?'

'There's an American, a man named Caleb Madison. He's the master of the *Madge Howlett*, a Baltimore-built brig out of New York. She lands at Liverpool two or three times a year and loads with manufactured goods ostensibly destined for Havana. Cotton textiles, gunpowder and muskets, looking glasses, copper wire, kitchen utensils'

'All the usual goods in the slave trade.'

'Precisely so. A brig playing between Liverpool and Havana could make the crossing more than four or five times a year. Furthermore, our consul in Havana keeps a close watch on shipping which might be involved in the slave trade and sends regular reports to the Slave Trade Department. He's never seen any ship named the *Madge Howlett* land there.'

'So she's changing her name between Liverpool and Havana.'

'Or sailing directly to the Guinea Coast. But the *Madge Howlett* belongs to the Bay Cay Trading Company, the same company which owned several other ships which have been condemned as slavers; one of which contained the fragment of the letter with the House of Commons heading. There's a mass of paperwork and red tape between the Bay Cay Trading

Company and its real owners, but I'm willing to stake my life that if you berth on board the *Madge Howlett* for a voyage, you'll learn something which will lead us to our high-placed slaving investor.'

'That's easy for you to say, sir,' said Killigrew, lining up his next shot. 'It's not your life that will be at stake.'

'I know I'm asking you to undertake a perilous enterprise, Mr Killigrew, and believe you me, I'll not think any the less of you if you decline my offer.'

'And if – *when* – the voyage is ended and I return to England? I'll have my naval rank reinstated and my honour restored?'

'A hundred fold. You're going for a ten stroke? You'll never make that shot, Mr Killigrew. A guinea on it.'

'What odds will you give me?'

'A hundred to one.'

'And what odds would you give on my even *surviving* a voyage on a slaver, never mind finding out the information you require?'

'I'll not beat about the bush, Killigrew. About the same.'

Killigrew took his shot, striking first the red ball and then the spot white, pocketing both before his own ball slipped slyly down the top pocket.

''Pon my soul! Done it, by Jove!' exclaimed Napier. 'Which takes your score up to'

'A hundred and one. My game, I believe.'

They replaced their cues in the rack and went downstairs and outside, waiting on the steps while the porter stepped out into the street to flag down a passing hansom for the rear-admiral.

A young girl – no more than eleven or twelve, gauged Killigrew – approached them with a bundle of heather. Her face was scrubbed, but there was grime around her neck and behind her ears, and her out-sized clothes were grubby and patched. 'Buy some lucky heather, kind sirs?' she asked.

'Oi! I've told you before!' growled the porter. 'We don't want your sort round here. Hop it!'

Killigrew waved him away. 'I think I'm going to need all the good luck I can get if I'm going to undertake this enterprise.'

Napier was delighted. 'You accept, then?'

'Did you ever doubt I would?'

'Capital fellow!' Napier clapped him on the back. 'I know you won't let me down.'

Killigrew handed the girl a sovereign in return for a sprig of heather.

'I can't change this, mister!' she protested.

'That's all right,' said Killigrew, smiling benignly. 'Keep the change.'

'Coo! For this much change I'll suck your sugar stick,' she offered.

Killigrew's smile grew thin. 'That won't be necessary. Why don't you buy some food for your family?' She nodded and ran off up the street.

'You realise, of course, she'll probably spend it on gin?' said Napier.

'If I had to live by selling heather and performing lewd acts on strangers, I'd probably spend all my money on gin, too,' said Killigrew.

'To return to your enterprise,' said Napier. 'If, as I suspect, the man we're after is high up in

196

London Society, then there's a good chance he may have spies in all manner of unexpected places; such men usually do. For your own safety, I suggest that the fewer people know of this, the better.'

'How many people did you have in mind?'

'Ideally, just the two of us–'

He broke off at the sound of horse's hoofs clopping on the cobbles and they both turned to see a gig come racing down Pall Mall, a young swell standing with the reins in one hand while he lashed the horse's flanks with a whip held in the other. As the gig careered down the thoroughfare the man swayed on his feet, and it was only a drunkard's luck which kept him from being pitched into the road. The porter, standing halfway into the road to flag down a hackney, had to leap aside to avoid being knocked down.

Further up the road, the flower-girl was not so lucky. She heard the horse's hoofs and the rattle of the wheels on the cobbles, turned to see the gig bearing down on her, and froze. Killigrew launched himself towards her, but it was purely instinctive reaction and he was too far away to do anything.

The driver of the gig did not even see the girl. She squeaked briefly before falling under the horse's hoofs, and then one of the gigs wheels bounced over her chest. The man in the gig fell back into the seat, giggling drunkenly, unaware that anything untoward had occurred, and the gig veered off Pall Mall on to Cockspur Street.

Killigrew reached the girl's body. Plenty of other people walked past, but none troubled to stop. She was barely conscious, and the blood which bubbled past her lips indicated that at least one broken rib had pierced a lung. Killigrew cradled her head in his lap and looked up at the passersby. 'Someone fetch a doctor, for God's sake!'

A fit of coughing racked the girl's body, and she lay still. Napier stood over Killigrew and put a hand on his shoulder. 'It's too late, Killigrew,' he said softly. 'There's nothing anyone can do.'

Feeling shaken, Killigrew pushed himself to his feet. He was not unaccustomed to the sight of violent death, but it was not something he associated with the genteel streets of St James's. 'We'd better fetch a constable,' he told Napier. 'Someone has to give that fellow's description, though I doubt they'll catch him.'

Napier nodded. 'No need for us both to wait. You must have things to do.'

'So must you, surely? And more important than what I'd had planned for this afternoon.' Killigrew glanced at his watch: it was nearly three o'clock.

Napier smiled. 'You had plans? Concerning a young lady, perhaps? No need to keep her waiting. You run along.'

'All right. When the police get here, give them my name. If they do catch that swine, I'll be happy to stand against him in the witness box. I'm staying at the Army and Navy.'

Napier nodded, and after one last regretful glance at the dead girl, Killigrew headed up Regent's Street. As he made his way towards Piccadilly Circus, he thought about her. There were those who would have said the death of one reduced to such circumstances was probably for the best, but Killigrew would have dismissed them as self-righteous asses. He felt sick. He had been so close to the incident, perhaps if he had been a little more vigilant he could somehow had prevented it. But there had been nothing he could do – how he hated to be an impotent bystander! – and it was done now anyway.

As he turned off Piccadilly and headed up Berkeley Street, he forced himself to put the girl's death from his mind and tried to think about the mission he had agreed to undertake for Napier. He wondered how he could inveigle Captain Madison into taking him on board the *Madge Howlett*. Killigrew had little taste for the duplicity which would be required of him to maintain his imposture, although he had confidence in his ability to carry it off, and it would be well worth it if it would enable him to bring some of the men foremost in the slave trade to justice. And it would be exciting; more exciting than cruising off the Guinea Coast on the *Tisiphone*, and certainly more exciting than mooching around in London. Yes, the more he thought about it, the more he realised he was looking forward to the adventure.

He reached Berkeley Square with a couple of minutes to spare, although Eulalia was already there, seated in a calash parked with the top folded down a short distance from Gunter's Tea Shop. There were several other carriages parked nearby, and waiters moved back and forth between the tea shop and the carriages delivering ice creams and sorbets. There was no sign of the calash's driver; Killigrew guessed that Eulalia had sent him off on some errand. Gunter's was popular with the younger members of Society, and the only place Killigrew knew of where a gentleman could talk to an unescorted lady without giving rise to scandal.

'Are you all right, Kit?' she asked as he approached. 'You look pale.'

'I saw a nasty accident just now,' he explained. 'A young girl knocked down by a gig.'

'Good heavens, how awful! Was she all right?'

'No. She died.'

Eulalia looked shocked. 'It's more genteel to say she "passed on", Mr Killigrew.'

'And not referring to her death directly makes it all right, does it?' he asked heatedly, removing his top hat to run his fingers through his hair in agitation.

'I'm sorry. You are right, of course. It will not bring her back. I forgot I was dealing with a plain-speaking navy man.'

'No, I'm the one who should apologise. It was not my intention to address you so intemperately, ma'am. I was angered by what I saw, and improperly expressed my anger towards you.'

'It is not improper to be angry, if the anger is justified,' she allowed, and smiled. 'But we are becoming formal once more, are we not? I think two people who played together as children might be permitted to address one another by their Christian names.'

He smiled and waved across a waiter, ordering

them both a sorbet. 'So, are you going to tell me what all these mysterious appointments you keep having to leave for are?' she asked, when they had finished eating and the waiter had taken away the bowls once more.

'Oh, I'm just doing some work with the Slave Trade Department at the Foreign Office,' he told her absently, mindful of Napier's injunction not to discuss their plans.

'Still trying to suppress the slavers, Kit?'

'I have to. I'm sorry if I seem obsessive about them, but if you'd seen what I saw...' Even there, in the leafy surroundings of Berkeley Square, the mental image of the slavers being thrown off the *São João* had lost none of its impact.

'You had a bad time with the West Africa Squadron, didn't you?'

'I? No. I can think of no place better for a young naval officer wishing to see some adventure, both for its own sake and with an eye to getting noticed by his superiors. Nor can I think of any cause more just to fight for.'

'Does it come to fighting?'

'Indeed, yes. They're a rough crowd, the slavers: murderous scum who'll stop at nothing.' *And the only way to beat them is to play by their rules,* he found himself thinking.

He felt a raindrop on the back of his hand, then another on his cheek. 'It's starting to rain,' said Eulalia.

'Let's get the top up,' he suggested, unclipping the folded-down hood.

'Let me do it,' she insisted. 'I'm afraid there's a knack, and if you're not careful you'll tear ... oh!'

she finished, as he raised the hood effortlessly and clipped it into place. She laughed. 'Oh, Kit! You really are the most infuriating man I've ever met!'

'What do you mean?'

'Because you're too good to be true. Are you going to stand there all day and get soaked?' she added, opening the door for him.

'I'm not sure it would be seemly of me'

'Don't be silly. Look, here comes Giles,' she added, nodding to where her coachman emerged from the tea shop. 'He can chaperone us.'

Killigrew climbed in beside her while the coachman took his place on the driving board and got soaked. 'Where to, ma'am?'

'Better take me back to my club,' said Killigrew. While he would have been happy to spend all day in Eulalia's calash, he was concerned for her reputation despite the presence of her coachman, although inside he despised the new-found prudery of Society and longed for the days of the old king's reign, when a gentleman might do as he pleased and Society be damned. 'The Army and Navy, in St James's Square.'

The coachman glanced at Eulalia, who nodded, and he flicked the tip of his whip at the backs of the horses. They clipped through the rain-soaked streets at a comfortable pace.

Killigrew found himself staring at Eulalia until she blushed, but he could not take his eyes from her face. 'What are you staring at?' she asked at last.

'A Kit may look at a queen.'

She smiled; he knew it was a bad joke and

202

worthy of no more, and appreciated the fact that she did not go out of her way to laugh at the jest. She was a rare woman, of that there was no doubt. When so many of Society's young ladies were brought up to be brainless girls interested only in home-making, it was a delight to meet someone like Eulalia who had a brain to match her looks and was not afraid to let it show. He suddenly realised that if he and Napier went ahead with the rear-admiral's plan to get Killigrew shunned by Society, then he *would* feel unhappy about it. Like her, he did not much care what Society thought of him, but the thought of being in her ill-graces was more than he could bear.

Could it be that he was in love with her?

Of course he was. Hopelessly, stupidly, pointlessly. Had she not said she was in no hurry to get married? But then neither was he. Was there any chance she would wait for him?

Of course not, if Napier's plan worked.

'Eulalia?'

'Mm?'

'If something happened ... if I were accused of some terrible crime, and found guilty and shunned by Society, would you think any the less of me?'

'What a strange question! Well, I suppose it would depend on the crime ... and whether or not you had committed it.'

It was an intelligent response, as he would have expected of her. 'But would you believe in my innocence when everyone else was convinced of my guilt?'

'Of course.'

'You say that, but is it just because you think that is what I want to hear?'

She laughed. 'When have you ever known me to say something just because I thought it might please *you* to hear me say it?'

'True,' he admitted with a rueful grin.

'Why, have you done something or rather, been accused of something?'

'Not yet.'

'Not yet?' she echoed, and then dug an elbow into his ribs. 'Oh, you're just teasing me!'

The calash pulled up in St James's Square. 'Here I must take my leave of you,' said Killigrew, climbing out into the rain. 'Perhaps I can see you again some time?'

'I've taken a box at Her Majesty's for the Season. My father and I are going with some friends to see Jenny Lind in *Roberto il Diavolo* next month.' Already celebrated on the continent, the silvery voice of the Swedish Nightingale had London Society in a froth of anticipation. 'I'm sure I can squeeze you into my box,' she added.

'I can think of no way I'd rather spend an evening.'

'I'll have an invitation sent round,' she told him, and ordered the coachman to drive on. He stood there on the pavement outside the Army and Navy Club and grinned like an idiot as the rain dripped from the brim of his hat until the calash had disappeared from view. Only then did he realise he was getting soaked through by the rain, and he hurried up the steps and into the club.

The porter looked up from where he sat in his lodge, and the expression on his face when he recognised Killigrew told the young lieutenant that something was wrong. 'There's a couple of gentlemen here to see you, sir,' explained the porter, the tone of his voice implying that he considered the visitors to be anything but gentlemen. 'I told them you were out and asked them to leave their cards, but I'm afraid they insisted on waiting.' He jerked his head to where two men sat on chairs in the lobby.

Both wore greatcoats and hats; one was a stout man of middle height, aged about sixty, with sharp eyes set in a round face, and half-whiskers; the other a red-headed, bony man with a turned-up nose. 'That's quite all right, Josephs,' Killigrew said, as the two men rose to their feet. He went to greet them.

'Mr Killigrew?' asked the sharp-eyed man. 'I'm Inspector Blathers, and this here's Sergeant Duff. We're from the Detective Department at Scotland Yard. We're given to understand that you may be able to assist us in our inquiries into the death of a young flower-girl who was knocked down on Pall Mall earlier today.'

'Oh, that business. Yes, I shall be delighted to give you whatever help I may.'

'Would you mind accompanying us to Bow Street Police Court?'

'Is that really necessary? I'm soaked to the skin and I wouldn't mind changing out of these wet things. Couldn't I drop by later to give you a description of the man responsible?'

Blathers and Duff exchanged glances. 'Oh, we

already have a full description of the man. And his name.'

'His name? Why, that's splendid! Fast work, I must say. Who is he?'

'The name we've been given is Mr Christopher Killigrew.'

IX:

The Pall Mall Child-Killer

'This is ridiculous!' Killigrew protested as he was pushed forcibly into the cell at Bow Street Police Court. 'I was there, yes, but it wasn't I who drove the gig. Ask Rear-Admiral Sir Charles Napier. He was there; he saw the whole thing. He'll vouch for me.'

'We already have,' said Blathers. 'As a matter of fact, he was the one who gave us your name.' He slammed the cell door, turned the key in the lock, and walked away.

'Gave you my...' stammered Killigrew, and then felt relief flood through him. At last what had seemed like a terrible misunderstanding had been explained. The rear-admiral was certainly a fast worker; but then, the timing of the girl's death had been too good to ignore. It was notoriously difficult to find witnesses in such cases; the only man who could deny that Killigrew was responsible was the driver of the gig, and he was unlikely to come forward.

It was perfect. If a gentleman like Killigrew pleaded guilty to manslaughter then he had every chance of being let off with a hefty fine – which suddenly struck him as unfair, although now was hardly the time to complain – but the repercussions would be more far-reaching. The navy would dismiss him for conduct unbecoming the character of an officer and a gentleman, and Society would shun him as a child-killer.

As would Eulalia.

He felt a momentary pang. But she would believe in his innocence – wouldn't she?

And then he could inveigle his way aboard the *Madge Howlett;* and with any luck return to England a few months later, honour redeemed, to have his rank restored, and he hoped, able to point the finger at whoever was behind the slavers.

Assuming, of course, he was let off with a fine. Assuming he was successful in joining the crew of the slavers. Assuming the slavers did not see through the imposture and slit his throat and throw his body overboard as soon as the *Madge Howlett* was out at sea.

Killigrew realised he was not alone in the cell. He turned in time to see three heavily built men rise from the bench. They were not smiling. 'So, you're the bastard who killed that little girl on Pall Mall today?' snarled one.

Killigrew guessed that now was probably not the time to plead guilty. Such men rarely found themselves in a position where they could beat up a member of the gentry – assuming they were not rampsmen who did so for a living, which was not entirely improbable from the look of them – and any man would naturally want to inflict some kind of punishment on someone guilty of such a crime. 'Accused,' he said. 'There is a golden thread running through British justice which says a man is innocent until proven guilty–'

Two of the men quickly moved forwards, grabbed Killigrew by the arms and slammed him back against a wall while the third rammed his fists repeatedly into his stomach. Fire exploded in Killigrew's midriff. A fist smashed into his face and threw his head back against the wall, cracking his skull. His eyes rolled up in his head and the two men released him, allowing him to slump to the floor, then the third kicked him in the mouth.

'That'll teach you not to go around killing little girls,' he snarled.

Killigrew tried to get up but a boot slammed into his side and he collapsed to the floor again.

'Break 'is bleedin' neck, 'Arry.'

As the man came at him again, Killigrew barely managed to roll away from the blow. He spat out a mouthful of blood and crawled into the far corner.

'Still got some fight left in you, eh?' snarled Harry.

Killigrew pushed himself unsteadily to his feet and turned in time to see Harry swinging a fist at his head. Then the rampsman's eyes widened in shock as Killigrew's hand came up as fast as a striking cobra and stopped the fist in its tracks. Killigrew closed his fingers over the fist, squeezing tightly until Harry gasped, and then began to twist. Harry turned away from him in an effort to relieve the pressure on his shoulder, and Killigrew punched him in the kidneys.

Harry fell to the floor with a grunt. One of the other men came at Killigrew. The naval officer punched him in the stomach once and the man doubled up in winded agony. Killigrew hit him on the back of the neck and lifted his knees into his face. The man lay still.

Killigrew glanced at the third man, who backed into the furthermost corner and raised both hands placatingly. Killigrew knew he need expect no more trouble from that quarter. He glanced down at his trousers. There was blood where he had kneed the second man in the face, and the fabric had ripped. 'Damn it!'

'My missus'll mend it,' offered the third man. 'Be good as new, it will. I'll give you her address.'

'Mr Killigrew?' called the gaoler. 'You made bail.'

Killigrew looked up in surprise from where he sat on the bench in the cell. 'No I didn't!' he protested. He had been in the police cell for nearly a week now and his clothes were ragged and filthy. Bail had been posted at a hundred guineas, the same amount that Napier owed him after their wager, but as an impecunious naval officer Killigrew preferred a couple of week's board and lodging at her majesty's expense and some cash in hand at the end of it.

The gaoler was not having any of it, however. 'Come along, Mr Killigrew. There's a gentleman waiting to see you.'

The gentleman was the lawyer who had posted his bail, a burly, prematurely-balding man with deep-set eyes beneath bushy eyebrows. He gave Killigrew his card. 'May I ask the name of my benefactor?' asked Killigrew.

'You may ask,' said the lawyer. 'But I can only reply that I am not at liberty to divulge my client's name.'

'My grandfather,' guessed Killigrew. 'Probably worried that I'll bring the family name into disrepute.'

'I could not possibly comment on that,' said the lawyer, gnawing the side of a forefinger. 'However, I have been instructed to engage Sir Abraham Haphazard, QC, MP, to speak at your trial.'

'But you cannot instruct a barrister to act as my counsel without my consent.'

'True.'

'Then you may kindly inform your client that it is my intention to conduct my own defence.' Even if the danger of being acquitted had not been entirely at odds with Napier's plans, Killigrew would not have accepted help from his grandfather even if his life had depended on it.

'That is entirely your prerogative,' admitted the lawyer. 'Although if I were your lawyer then I should advise you against it. Still, you seem to be a young man who knows his own mind. If that is your last word on the subject, it remains only for me to inform my client that I have done everything within my power to carry out his instructions. Good day to you, Mr Killigrew.'

'Mr Killigrew, you are hereby charged with manslaughter; to whit, that on Friday the fourteenth of April in the year of our Lord eighteen hundred and forty-seven, while incapacitated through over-indulgence in alcohol, you did drive down Pall Mall in a gig with wilful negligence, and that furthermore by doing so your actions resulted in the death of Elizabeth

Williams, a minor. How do you plead?'

Killigrew rose to his feet. 'I wish to lodge a plea of guilty to both charges, m'lud, but would also like to plead mitigating circumstances.' He glanced up towards the gallery. Eulalia was there with her father and Eustace Tremaine, although as soon as Killigrew announced his guilty plea the three of them rose to their feet with expressions of disgust on their faces. Killigrew knew he could not blame them for their reaction, but it was still a knife in his heart that Eulalia could really think him guilty of such a crime.

'Very well,' said the judge. 'Does the counsel for the prosecution still wish to call its witnesses?'

The counsel for the prosecution stood up and bowed. 'If it pleases m'lud, counsel for the prosecution would like to demonstrate that there are no acceptable mitigating circumstances for a crime so heinous as that of which Mr Killigrew now stands accused.'

'Very well. Pray continue.'

Killigrew stood in the dock feeling dazed. He knew that in effect the whole trial was no more than a sham, although the fact that he was the only one who knew so was not very reassuring. His only consolation was the sealed letter from Napier brought to him by the solicitor appointed on his behalf. The letter had briefly confirmed that this was all part of the plan, and that while no one except himself and Napier knew the truth of the matter, Chief Justice Denman – the father of the author of the *Instructions for the Guidance of her Majesty's Naval Officers Employed in the Suppression of the Slave Trade* – had assured

Napier that if Killigrew pleaded guilty then he was unlikely to receive any sentence tougher than a fine of a few guineas, which Napier had agreed to pay – admittedly out of the money he owed following Killigrew's final shot in their game of billiards.

'Call the first witness.'

'Will Mr Simon Gubbins please take the stand?'

An elderly and filthy-looking man entered, evidently unnerved by his surroundings, and swore to tell the truth, the whole truth and nothing but the truth. Killigrew was glad that as the accused he had not been sworn in; he was not much of a church-going man, but even so he would have been uncomfortable about perjuring himself on the Bible, albeit in a noble cause and at no one's expense but his own.

'You are Mr Simon Gubbins, of Blue Gate Fields, London?' asked the counsel for the prosecution.

'Yes, sir.'

'And can you tell us where you were at ten minutes to three last Wednesday?'

'Yes, sir. I was on Pall Mall. Looking for pure.'

'And did you see the incident–'

The judge held up a hand, interrupting the counsel for the prosecution, and leaned forward to address the witness. 'I'm sorry, could you repeat that? What were you looking for?'

'Pure, your honour. Dog-muck. That's what I do. I'm a pure-finder.'

The counsel for the prosecution closed his eyes as if in pain. Normally he would ask his witness

213

what they did for a living if the respectability of their profession would lend credence to their testimony. Mr Gubbins being a pure-finder, the prosecution had felt that his profession was best left unmentioned, unless the defence were so crass as to raise the issue.

'Let me make sure I understand you correctly,' said the judge. 'You were looking for excrement?'

'That's right, sir.'

'And what did you intend to do once you had found it?'

'Why, put it in me bucket, your honour. That's what I always do. Then, when I've got a full bucket, I takes it down to one of the tanneries in Southwark. They'll give you a good price if it's the right kind of pure. They like the white, limey kind best of all; they use it in puring the leather, I'm told, though I ain't never seen it done myself. That's why we calls it "pure".'

'And this is how you make your living?'

'Yes, your honour. It may not be much of a living, but it keeps the wolf from the door.'

'That's as maybe, but I don't think I shall ever feel comfortable in the saddle ever again,' said the judge, and a polite titter ran around the court. 'Pray continue with the cross-examination of your witness,' he told the counsel for the prosecution.

'Thank you, m'lud. Mr Gubbins, did you see Elizabeth Williams knocked down?'

'Yes, sir.'

'And did you get a good look at the man driving the gig which knocked her down and ran over her?'

214

'Why, yes, sir. I told you before, didn't I?'

'For the court, please.'

'I saw him, all right. A moment later he almost ran me over, too, so I got a good look at his face.'

'And can you see him in this courtroom today?'

Mr Gubbins had a good look around. 'No, sir.'

'Try again, Mr Gubbins. And I suggest you pay particular attention to the gentleman standing in the dock.'

Gubbins peered at Killigrew. 'No, sir. 'Tweren't him. Definitely not.' The counsel for the prosecution looked stunned; if he was not careful, thought Killigrew, he was going to lose this case. 'He was there, all right, but he weren't driving the gig. He–'

'Just answer the question: yes or no,' snapped the counsel for the prosecution.

'No.'

'I have no further questions for this witness, m'lud. May I respectfully request an adjournment?'

'You may,' said the judge. 'And I shall respectfully decline it. Since the accused has already pleaded guilty, I really don't see why this case should take more than a few minutes and I have a luncheon appointment at one. Does the defendant wish to cross-examine the witness?'

'Yes, m'lud,' said Killigrew, reflecting that when the accused had to help the prosecution prove their case it only went to prove just how complete an ass the Law could be. 'Mr Gubbins, have you ever drunk alcohol?'

'I am an occasional imbiber, sir, but then who isn't? I only ever drink when it's cold, to keep

215

the chill out.'

'There are a great many pure-finders on the streets of London, are there not?'

'Oh, yes, sir!'

'And not many dogs.'

'Sadly, no, sir.'

'So there must be a great deal of competition to find pure.'

'Oh, yes, sir. It can be quite a dog-eat-dog business.'

'Which means you must have to get up very early in the mornings.'

'Yes, sir. When it's still dark.'

'And still very cold at this time of year. So it would be natural for you to fortify yourself with a nip of something alcoholic before going out in the morning?'

'Objection, m'lud!' protested the counsel for the prosecution. 'The defendant is putting words in the witness's mouth.'

'Since the defendant seems to be doing a better job of prosecuting your case than you are, I hope you won't think me too harsh for overruling your objection,' the judge said drily. 'Continue, Mr Killigrew.'

'Mr Gubbins, had any alcohol passed your lips on the morning of the fourteenth? And may I remind you that you are under oath?'

'Well ... maybe just a drop or two...'

'Yes or no, Mr Gubbins.'

'Yes.'

'Thank you. No further questions, m'lud.' Killigrew resumed his seat.

'Does the counsel for the prosecution have any

further evidence it would like to present?'

The prosecutor looked flushed. 'No, m'lud.'

'Very well. Mr Killigrew, is there anything you would care to say by way of a plea for mitigation?'

Killigrew rose to his feet once more and read out his prepared statement.

'I only wish to say that no matter how great a punishment you seek to impose on me, it will pall into insignificance besides the burden of guilt which now tortures my conscience; and that as a God-fearing Christian, I know I will receive my due punishment in the next life as well as in the present. Furthermore, I wish it to be known that I have now sworn off alcohol for the remainder of my days.' He crossed his fingers behind his back before he said the last part.

'Very well. The jury may now retire if it wishes to consider its verdict. In summation I can only draw attention to the fact that, despite the hesitancy of the prosecution's sole witness, the accused has pleaded guilty, and I therefore direct you to find Mr Killigrew guilty as charged.'

The jurymen briefly exchanged a few whispered words, and the foreman rose to his feet. 'We have considered our verdict, m'lud.'

'And how do you find the accused, guilty or not guilty?'

'Guilty, m'lud.'

'Christopher Iguatios Killigrew, this court finds you guilty as charged. In view of your hitherto blameless reputation, and the sterling work done by you in the service of Her Majesty's Royal Navy, this court does not consider that a custodial sentence will be appropriate in this instance. Fined fifty guineas.' The judge banged his gavel like a salesman at an auction.

As he walked out of the court, Killigrew felt almost as guilty as if he really had been responsible for the girl's death. And meanwhile the man who had killed her was walking free, without any danger of ever being brought to justice. Of course, if Napier had not decided to take this opportunity, then it was unlikely that the man would have been in court; but all the same, Killigrew had been guilty of perverting the course of justice.

Justice? After that farce, he was no longer sure what justice was. *Fifty guineas,* he thought bitterly. If he had been a member of the labouring classes he might have been given ten years' hard labour, or transportation to New South Wales. So much for justice.

He was just about to leave the courthouse when a young midshipman stopped him. 'Lieutenant Killigrew, sir?'

'Yes?'

Red-faced, the midshipman said nothing more but merely handed him a letter. Killigrew noticed the Admiralty stationery at once. He ripped it open. The letter was polite but none the less curt: would Lieutenant Killigrew consider himself under open arrest until he presented himself to a court-marital to be held on board HMS *Icarus* at Deptford at ten hours *ante meridian* on Friday the seventh of May, yours faithfully, Vice-Admiral Lord Richardson, etc., etc. It was dated that very day; the letter must have been written the day before, and the midshipman given instructions to hand it to Killigrew as soon as a verdict of guilty was returned. 'You may tell his lordship I'll be there,' he told the midshipman, who saluted and turned on his heel.

Killigrew took a hansom to St James's Square and bounded up the steps to his club. He went straight past the porter in his lodge who called after him. 'Excuse me, sir? Letter for you.'

Killigrew returned to the lodge to take the letter from him. He was about to tuck it inside his coat when the porter called after him once more. 'I think you'd better read it now, sir.'

The letter was from the secretary of the Army and Navy Club and written in the same polite, formal but curt tone as the letter from the Admiralty. Following an extraordinary meeting of the club's executive committee it had been unanimously decided that Lieutenant Killigrew was no longer a fit and proper person to be a member of the club.

'Your dunnage has already been packed sir. I'll fetch it for you now, shall I?'

Dazed, Killigrew nodded. He had expected it, of course, but it still hit home. He had joined the Army and Navy as soon as he had been promoted to midshipman, but this was his first stay there and he had only been in residence a few days. Nonetheless, it was his only home and now that too had been taken away from him.

He took his sea-chest and made his way to the White Horse Cellar Coaching Inn. From the looks he got there from the innkeeper and his wife, it was clear that news of his arrest and trial had spread with astonishing swiftness, and while the innkeeper was not too proud to have a disgraced naval officer living under his roof, he did not treat Killigrew with the same deference he had done previously. Not that Killigrew cared for the deference; it was the civility he missed.

To his complete lack of surprise he heard nothing from Eulalia over the next few days. He called on her at her father's house in Knightsbridge on more than one occasion, but she was never in; or if she was, she was not receiving. Knowing that there would no longer be a place for him in her box at Her Majesty's Theatre, he managed to get a dress circle ticket through the good grace of an opera dancer of his acquaintance in the hope that he would at least get a chance to speak to Eulalia. He was not sure what he was going to say to her. He did not want to tell her all the details of Napier's plan, more because he did not want her to worry about him than because Napier had told him to tell no one. The force of the pang he had felt seeing her walk out of the courtroom had told him that he loved her; if he could not trust the woman he loved, whom could he trust?

There were several people of his acquaintance in the gas-lit finery of the theatre foyer when Killigrew arrived on the night; all of them studiously avoided meeting his gaze. Indeed, whichever way Killigrew turned, an avenue seemed to part through the crush for him. He tried to find the situation amusing, but could not.

He was unable to find Eulalia and her party before the last bell rang, and went in to watch the opera. Jenny Lind's singing was unquestionably delightful – for once *Punch* had got it right when they said that to call her the Swedish Nightingale was a compliment to the bird – but even her dulcet tones were not enough to distract Killigrew from his troubles. He was more concerned to speak to Eulalia, whom he could see seated in one of the boxes with her father, Tremaine, and several others Killigrew knew only vaguely. He studied her through his opera glasses – God, she looked lovelier than ever – but could not catch her eye as she concentrated on the stage.

At last the first interval came and he made his way through the crush to the saloon. Many of the people in the boxes would remain there and have their drinks brought to them, but Killigrew guessed that Mr Pengelly and his daughter would prefer to stretch their legs and socialise with the other opera-goers in the saloon.

He guessed correctly: he was standing by the bar when Eulalia entered with her friends. They were chatting gaily, Eulalia laughing at something Tremaine had said. Then they saw Killigrew and froze for a moment, before Eulalia abruptly led them off in another direction.

Killigrew headed off through the crowd after them. 'Eulalia! I need to talk to you, to explain! For God's sake! Just a minute, that's all I ask...'

She did not even turn her head. Tremaine broke off from the group to block Killigrew's path. 'Damn it, Killigrew, I'd've thought that you of all people would have had the taste and decency to know better than to remind Society of Mrs Fairbody's former connection with you.'

'I just want to explain...' Killigrew said desperately. 'Can you at least give her a message from me?'

'Oh, really! Stay away, damn you, or I'll be forced to call you out.'

'Then call me out!' snarled Killigrew, knowing that he could beat Tremaine any time he pleased, with sabre or pistol.

Tremaine knew it too. He blanched and backed away. Some instinct stopped Killigrew from following. Tremaine was right, of course, as far as he understood the situation, and Killigrew could hardly blame him for that. To have pressed the matter any further would have embroiled Eulalia in an ugly scandal, and that was the last thing he wanted.

He returned to the bar, and when the third bell summoned the audience back to the auditorium he ordered another whisky. He was in no mood to sit through any more of *Roberto il Diavolo*. He was the only one left in the saloon when the second act began; a moment later Sir Joshua Pengelly entered surreptitiously, with an embarrassed look on his face. 'Mr Killigrew?'

'Sir?'

'Look, I'm sorry I had to cut you dead earlier, but you understand...?'

Killigrew nodded.

'I'm dreadfully sorry about what happened. For you, I mean. You're a good man, I know. You made a mistake, that's all. I ... I understand you've forsworn alcohol? I'm sorry there's not much I can do for you now, but perhaps in a year's time or so, when the scandal has died down, I can have you appointed as an officer on

222

board one of my steamers...?'

'That's very kind of you, sir, and I'd be honoured. But a year is a long time, and anything can happen in–'

'Your whisky, sir,' said the barman, placing a glass at Killigrew's elbow.

Killigrew shrugged sheepishly. 'Force of habit,' he said. 'I meant to order soda water...'

Pengelly just shook his head grimly, turned away with an expression of disgust and hurried back towards the auditorium.

Killigrew finished his drink and went outside, dining alone in a chop-house – none of London's more fashionable restaurants could find a table for him any more, even if he booked in advance. Even in the chop-house, he was aware of people nodding towards him and muttering to one another under their breath. He could imagine what they were saying: 'That's Lieutenant Killigrew, that is, the Pall Mall child-killer. You can tell he's a villain just by looking at him – that swarthy complexion, a touch of tar-brush in him, they say. Not really an *English* gentleman at all.' Thanks to his mixed heritage he had had to put up with that kind of remark during his early days in the navy, and although he had not been troubled by such taunts in recent years he had no doubt they would all be dredged up and used to account for his sudden disgrace.

He knew the opera was due to finish around half past ten and after he had paid his bill at the chop-house he found himself ambling back towards the theatre, he was not sure why. The Haymarket was crowded with prostitutes, lining up on the pavements like cabbies queuing for fares. Several of them called out to him – they at least were not too proud to accept the custom of the Pall Mall child-killer, he mused wryly – but he merely shook his head.

'Killigrew?'

He turned. It was Strachan. 'Hullo, Mr Strachan. What are you doing here?'

Strachan blushed. 'Oh, just ... er ... taking the night air.'

'Are you sure you want to be seen talking to the Pall Mall child-killer? Everyone else in Society is snubbing me these days, you know.'

'Well, I'm not sure that I qualify as a member of Society yet. What happened, Killigrew? The papers said you pleaded guilty to manslaughter.'

Killigrew nodded. 'It's true.'

'That you killed that girl? Or that you pleaded guilty?' Strachan asked shrewdly. 'I know you, Killigrew. That's just not the kind of thing you'd do...'

'Perhaps you don't know me as well as you thought you did.'

Strachan shook his head. 'No. I may not be the brightest fellow on God's earth, but I've always been a good judge of character. And I think there's something deuced rum going on here. What happened? Were you framed?'

Killigrew just shrugged. He was pleased that at least someone did not believe the pretence, even though he himself had confessed to the crime; he just wished it could have been Eulalia instead of Strachan.

'Look, Killigrew, it's obvious that whatever's

224

going on you don't want to talk about it – or you can't. That's up to you. I just want you to know that anything I can do to help, just let me know. Money, a letter of recommendation, anything within my power. Here's my card. Don't hesitate to get in touch, all right?' Strachan moved on, embarrassed by his own effusion, but Killigrew called after him.

'Mr Strachan?'

'Aye?'

'Thank you.'

Strachan shrugged. 'You know what they say. A friend in need...' He turned and disappeared into the crowd.

A friend indeed, thought Killigrew, and then had to move quickly to avoid being engulfed as the patrons emerged from the theatre. He quickly took one of the hansoms waiting for trade before they were all snapped up. 'Where to, guv?'

'Do you mind if we just wait here a moment?'

'I'll have to charge you waiting time.'

'Fine.' Killigrew was more intent on the crowd than on what the cabbie was saying.

A slatternly-dressed woman stood on the running board so she could thrust her bosom at him. 'Looking for company, handsome?'

'Yes, but not yours, I'm afraid.'

'Impudence!' The woman stepped back on to the pavement and turned to her friends. 'Bleedin' window-shopper.'

Killigrew saw Eulalia emerge from the theatre with her friends. They said their goodbyes amongst the crowd, and then she got into a carriage with her father and Tremaine. 'Follow that carriage,' Killigrew ordered the cabbie. 'But discreetly, if you please.'

'All right, guv.' The cabbie flicked the tip of his whip across his horse's back and the hansom rattled off across the cobbles after the carriage as it headed up the Haymarket towards Piccadilly Circus.

'Is that young lady your missus, then?' the cabbie asked as they headed west along Piccadilly towards Hyde Park Corner. He evidently thought that Killigrew was a cuckold tracking his wife in the hope of catching her in *flagrante delicto* with her young escort.

'Mind your own damned business,' said Killigrew, seeing no reason to disabuse him of that notion.

At last the carriage pulled off Knightsbridge into the grounds of the Pengelly mansion. 'Pull up just down the road,' Killigrew told the cabbie, taking out his pocket telescope and squinting down the drive to where Eulalia and her father were climbing out of the carriage underneath the mansion's portico. Killigrew was terrified that Tremaine would also get out and go inside with them, even though the rational part of his mind knew that that would be unthinkable. But the rational part of his mind was in abeyance that night, as his act in trailing Eulalia back to her home – and what he planned to do next – demonstrated.

Tremaine did not get out of the carriage, which pulled back down the drive and out of the gate once more, heading back towards Mayfair. Killigrew waited until it was out of sight and then climbed out of the hansom, paid the cabbie his fare and tipped him generously. As the carriage rattled off into the night, Killigrew walked along the pavement until he came to the next turning and cut down a side street which looped around the back of the mansion. The street was unlit and deserted at that late hour, but Killigrew nonetheless looked about to make sure he was unobserved before he jumped up and grabbed hold of the top of the eight-foot-high brick wall which surrounded the grounds. His feet scrabbled against the brickwork, until at last he was able to haul himself over and drop down amongst the bushes on the other side.

There were lights on at the back of the house, in the kitchen downstairs and on the landing above. Enough light filtered out to enable Killigrew to navigate his way across the lawn to the back of the house. There were bars on the ground-floor windows and the only door led into the kitchen where Killigrew could see the cook making cocoa, but a stout iron drainpipe leading up to the guttering at the eaves provided easy access to a landing window on the first floor; easy, at least, for a vigorous young man who had spent a goodly part of his teenage years skylarking about the rigging of a man-o'-war. He stood on the stone window ledge and held on to the drainpipe with one hand to steady himself while with his other he took a clasp knife from his pocket and opened the blade. He eased it into the gap between the sash windows and slid the catch open. Then he pushed the sash up, slipped through and stepped lightly on to the landing.

The first floor was silent, the only sounds from below the gentle murmur of voices: Eulalia and her father, although what they were saying was none of his business even if he could have made out the words, which he was too much of a gentleman to try to do. *A peculiar type of gentleman,* he reflected, *who breaks into a lady's bedchamber at night.* The gas lights were low, but bright enough for him to find his way.

Six doors led off the landing. The first he tried was a bedroom, well furnished but obviously unoccupied. The next room was distinctly feminine without being girlishly so; since Eulalia lived alone with her father, it had to be her room.

He took off his hat as he entered. There were no pictures of the late lamented Mr Fairbody, which did not surprise Killigrew: whatever her feelings had been towards him, she was not the type who would spend the rest of her days pining for a departed husband. In fact there were no pictures at all, only a sampler above the bed: 'The wrath of man worketh not the righteousness of God – James i, 20'. The needlework looked recent, but somehow Killigrew did not think that Eulalia had stitched it: she was not the kind of woman who could find pleasure in menial, repetitive tasks.

He put down his hat on the dresser, lit the oil lamp on the bedside table and sat down. He did not have long to wait. There were footsteps on the stairs, and then: 'Goodnight, Papa.'

'Goodnight, my dear.' A door opened and closed across the corridor while Killigrew watched the doorknob turn. He rose to his feet as the door opened and Eulalia came in. She had closed the door behind her and was halfway across the room before she saw him standing there. She froze in shock.

'Get out of here before I scream,' she said at last.

'If you were going to scream, you would already have done so.'

She snatched one of the pillows off the bed and threw it at his head. 'God damn you, Kit Killigrew. Infuriatingly right as ever.'

He pulled the pillow down from his face. 'Sorry. And sorry for breaking in here, but I had to talk to you and there was no other way.'

She put her hands on her hips. 'Did you kill that child?'

'No.'

'Then why did you plead guilty?'

'It's a long story.'

She indicated a carriage clock on the mantelpiece. 'You have one minute to convince me.'

'I'm going to join the crew of a slaving vessel so I can find out who's financing their voyages and where the slaves are coming from. I'm too well known amongst the slavers as an officer of the Royal Navy, so the only way to do it is to pretend that I've been disgraced and am after a petty revenge by working for those men I previously tried to catch. When Rear-Admiral Napier and I saw a child knocked down outside the United Service Club, it seemed like a perfect opportunity, so I confessed to the accident.'

'And you really expect me to believe that?'

'Frankly, no. But it *is* the truth. How am I doing for time?'

'You've still got about half a minute. And a long way to go before you convince me.'

'Remember a couple of weeks ago, when you gave me a ride back to the Army and Navy, and I asked you if you'd think any the less of me if I were accused of some terrible crime, and found guilty and shunned by Society? If you would believe in my innocence when everyone else was convinced of my guilt?'

'So this is what all that was about?' He nodded. 'Look me in the eye and tell me you were in no way responsible for the death of that child.'

'I was in no way responsible for the death of that child.'

She took two quick steps to where he stood and embraced him, burying her face in his shoulder. 'Oh, Kit! I knew you could never have done such a thing. But when you pleaded guilty I thought ... to tell the truth I didn't know what to think.'

He held her close. 'It's all right. I understand. I'm sorry I couldn't warn you before, but Sir Charles told me I was not to tell anyone. He thinks that the financier may be a member of the British Establishment.'

She stiffened, and then broke away to stare at him. 'Someone we know, perhaps?'

'Perhaps. But we need proof before we can make any accusations.'

'Won't it be dangerous?'

'Only a little bit.'

She turned away. 'You're trying to stop me from worrying about you. Of course it will be dangerous. For the love of God, Kit! If the slavers find out you're a spy, they'll kill you!'

'They can try.'

'It's too dangerous, Kit. What if something happens to you? I couldn't bear to think that I might never see you again.'

'I thought you weren't in a hurry to get remarried? There are plenty of other men out there. Eustace Tremaine, perhaps?'

She turned back to him and seized him by the lapels. 'I don't want Eustace Tremaine,' she said fiercely. 'I want–'

She broke off, and he tried to save her the embarrassment of having to finish the sentence by kissing her. It was a wasted effort, however, for the way she kissed him back finished the sentence more eloquently than words might have done. The next thing he knew she was trying to pull of his coat without breaking off the kiss while he fumbled with the fastenings at the back of her gown. So great was his passion that it required reserves of willpower he had not previously known he possessed to break off and back away. 'Slow down!' he protested.

'What's wrong?'

'Are you sure you want to do this?'

'No. My head says no, but the rest of me says yes, *yes*.' She blushed at her own passion, and lowered her eyes demurely. 'Do not misunderstand me, Kit. I loved my husband as a dutiful wife ought to. The feelings I have for you are stronger, but I'm not sure they're feelings of love. I … I think I'm … I'm weak, Kit. You'll have to help me be strong.'

He shook his head. 'You don't need me for that. You're the strongest woman I've ever known,

Eulalia, and you're intelligent enough to realise that if there's something you want to do which will be to no one else's detriment, there's no reason on earth why you shouldn't.'

She considered his argument for a moment, and then turned away from him. For a moment he feared she was going to tell him to leave at once and never return.

'Help me take off this gown, Kit.'

She bit him in the shoulder at the end. If she had been trying to stop herself from crying out it did not entirely have the desired effect, for he yelped in surprise and pain; she bit deep. She always had. But he did not mind. *Nothing can ever be this perfect again,* he told himself. *I wish I could die right now.*

The two of them subsided on the mattress and lay entangled in one another's limbs, gasping for breath like two shipwrecked sailors washed up on a sun-kissed beach.

After a few moments Killigrew became aware of a knocking sound on the door. 'Eulalia?' called Sir Joshua. 'Are you all right?'

Flustered, she raised a hand to her chest, visibly trying to catch her breath. 'What? Yes, I'm fine, Papa. I was ... I must have been having a bad dream.'

'I told you not to have the Stilton so late at night.' His shuffling footsteps sounded on the landing and a moment later his bedroom door closed.

Killigrew and Eulalia stifled giggles, and then she looked up at him with wonderment in her

232

eyes. 'That was ... strange. I felt so scared and yet ... I never wanted it to stop. Oh, Kit! Why did it have to stop?'

'Sorry. I'm only human.'

Smiling, she reached up and touched him on the cheek. 'You're a god, Kit. A perfect Greek god. An Adonis.'

'That'll be my mother's nose.'

'Is ... is it always like that, between men and women?'

'I've never known it *quite* like that,' he admitted, and frowned.

'What's wrong?'

'I don't believe that matches are made in heaven, that two people are meant for each other. Life doesn't work like that. People just drift through life ... sometimes they connect, more often they don't...'

'I think we connected just now.'

'That's what I'm thinking. I know you're not in any hurry to get married...'

'Yes. On the other hand, it's a woman's prerogative to change her mind.'

'I can't afford to marry you yet. But when I'm a post-captain...'

'How long will that take?'

'It depends. If I can pull off this mission to expose the slavers...'

Her face fell. 'I love you, Kit. The truth is I loved you before tonight. In fact I think I've loved you since we were children. I don't want to lose you.'

'Promise you'll wait for me, and I'll promise to come back alive.' He took off the small medal he wore around his neck and put it around hers.

'What's this?'

'A St Christopher.'

'I thought only Catholics wore saints' medallions.'

'And Greek Orthodox Christians.'

'You're not Greek Orthodox, are you?'

'No, but my mother was. She gave it to my father, and he left it to me. St Christopher is one of the patron saints of sailors.'

'Hadn't you better keep it? You're the one who's going to sea.'

He shook his head. 'I want you to have it, as a symbol of our engagement. May I consider us engaged, or would that be presumptuous of me?'

'You'd better,' she said gruffly, and then kissed him and grinned impishly. 'Must you go? I'll be so afraid for you. Haven't you already done more than your fair share towards suppressing the slave trade?'

'How much is a fair share?' He shrugged. 'Believe me, I'd much rather stay here in London with you. But I have no choice. My pleading guilty to the killing of that poor child may have been a ruse, but the trial was real enough.'

'You can pay the fine, can't you? I shall gladly lend you the money if you cannot.'

'There's more to it than that. I have to restore my reputation in the eyes of Society. My honour.'

'Pooh to Society. Your honour's intact in my eyes. Isn't that all that matters?'

He shook his head. 'If we're to be married I'll need a good steady income, and for that I'll need the good opinion of the navy.'

'Haven't you already got that?'

He grimaced. 'Not for much longer.'

HMS *Icarus* was a small frigate anchored in Greenwich Reach; these days larger ships could only navigate so far up the Thames with difficulty, if at all. Deptford had only been chosen as a venue because it was traditional to hold courts-martial on board ship and the town was convenient for London; Killigrew had no doubt it was the admirals' convenience that they had in mind rather than his own.

On the appointed day he presented himself in full dress uniform at the wharf where a jolly boat waited to row him out to the ship. The seamen on deck stared at him impassively as he made his obeisance to the quarter-deck. He recognised the faces of a few hands from the *Tisiphone*, men who would usually have grinned and knuckled their heads to him; these men now just stared as impassively as their new shipmates. Killigrew had told himself that he did not care what other men would think of him when he was disgraced, so long as he knew in his own heart that he was blameless; but seeing the condemnation in that lack of expression on their faces, he realised he had been wrong.

The court-martial was held in the *Icarus*'s great cabin before a panel of no less than nine admirals, including a straight-faced Napier. Killigrew presented himself before them, tucked his cocked hat under one arm and bowed first to the president of the court, Vice-Admiral Richardson – a smooth, white-haired, sharp-faced man – and

235

then to the rest of the panel. The judge advocate recited the court's authority to assemble and then explained the circumstances which had led to its being convened. The rest of the trial was mercifully brief. Even if Killigrew had been of a mind to contest the accusation, the facts of the matter were clear: he was charged with conduct unbecoming the character of a commissioned officer of Her Majesty's navy; he had been found guilty by a civilian court of manslaughter through drunkenness and wilful negligence.

'Lieutenant Killigrew, have you anything to say in your defence?' asked Richardson.

Killigrew hesitated. Even though this was all part of the plan he had hatched with Napier, the court was real enough and its decision would be binding. He could not merely declare his innocence at a later date, even with Napier to back him up; in the eyes of the Admiralty, he would have to do something pretty extraordinary to redeem himself. It would not be enough just to spend a voyage on board a slaver: he would have to come up with some hard evidence to prove that the enterprise had been worth while. But he hesitated only briefly, for he had thought this through countless times in the preceding days, and he grinned inwardly, knowing that the need to pull of a spectacular success would only be an added encouragement to him, as if he needed any in his fight against the slave trade. He stood up, his back as straight as a propeller-shaft, and looked Vice-Admiral Richardson in the eye.

'No, sir.'

'Very well. In which case I see no need for this

court to adjourn to consider its verdict; the facts speak for themselves.' He glanced at the other members of the panel to make sure that they were in agreement, and saw only nodding heads. 'Lieutenant Christopher Iguatios Killigrew, it is the solemn duty of this court to find you guilty of a most gross breach of conduct. Your behaviour proves you to be wholly unfit to hold either your current rank or any other rank within Her Majesty's navy. Therefore you are hereby stripped of your rank and commission and dismissed the Service...'

Even though it was all part of the plan and entirely expected, it was like being kicked in the chest by a mule. He had lost his home, his friends and now his career. The only thing left for him to lose was his life. Indeed, the navy was more than a career to him, it *was* his life. If he failed in his mission now, then he might as well end it all.

He was stripped of his lieutenant's epaulette – they had already taken his cutlass – and rowed back to the wharf. He went back to the White Horse Cellar Coaching Inn and took off the uniform he was no longer entitled to wear. He folded it carefully and put it in his chest, wondering when he would be allowed to wear it again. If ever.

X:

The *Madge Howlett*

He stood in the shadows beneath the eaves of a tavern near Liverpool docks and waited. The sound of raucous singing accompanied by an accordion came from another tavern further along the waterfront. He could not make out the words, but he knew the tune and did not doubt that they were singing one of the lewder versions of that classic sea shanty, ''Twas on the Good Ship *Venus'*. The sound of an accordion seemed strangely archaic: for some reason it always made him think of how the navy must have been in the days of his father's youth, when Napoleon's fleets threatened the shores of Britain.

It contrasted with the sound of a steam-powered crane lifting bales of cotton fabric on to a clipper in the harsh glare of limelight, for time was money and the sooner the cotton cloth produced in the mills of Lancashire could be returned across the Atlantic to the country from which the raw cotton had come, the sooner the credit could be transferred to the British banks, and whichever company delivered its goods first could corner the market while it waited for the others to catch up.

American cotton, produced by slave labour. Perhaps da Silva had been right: it was easy for the British to be holier than thou about the slave trade, but they still profited from it indirectly. And at least one Englishman – one very important and well-respected man – still profited from it directly. And that man was as responsible for the slaves thrown over the side of the *São João* as da Silva himself had been.

I don't know who you are, Killigrew thought to himself, *but I'm going to find out. And when I do, there's going to be a reckoning.*

The door to one of the taverns opened, spilling firelight across the cobbles with a hubbub of voices, and a man stood framed in the doorway, so tall he had to stoop to accommodate the tall, rather old-fashioned stovepipe hat he wore. Killigrew could only see the man's silhouette, but he had spent so much time studying him through a telescope over the past two days it was enough to recognise him by.

As the man walked away from the tavern, two heavily-built shadows detached themselves from a pile of bales of cotton stacked on the quayside and quickly moved to block his path. 'Can I help you gentlemen?' asked the man with the American accent.

'We were wondering if you could spare us the price of a drink,' one of the shadows asked gruffly.

'Sorry. The First Epistle of Paul and Apostle to Timothy: "For love of money is the root of all evil: which while some coveted after, they have erred from the faith, and pierced themselves through with many sorrows."'

'We asked for money, not a sermon. Give us

239

some or we'll break your head open.'

The American took a step forward, when anyone else would have backed away in fear. As he did so a light from a window fell across him, revealing a face which, though weather-beaten, was otherwise wholly unremarkable, except that he was smiling in a situation which offered him nothing to smile about. The smile crinkled the crow's feet at the corners of his eyes, but there was no humour in those eyes: they were like hard chips of flint and managed to make even his smile seem menacing.

He chuckled ruefully. 'Well, I guess that puts a whole different complexion on the matter, doesn't it?' he said, reaching into a pocket. 'How much did you want?'

'All of it.'

'All of it? What are you planning to drink, champagne?' He took out a fistful of sovereigns and threw them on the cobbles at the feet of the two men.

Clever, thought Killigrew. *One of them bends down to pick up the coins, and the American kicks him in the head, leaving him with one opponent instead of two.*

But the menacing men were wise to that trick and both ignored the coins. They attacked fast, one of them trying to grab the American. Instead of turning to flee, he suddenly moved in to meet them. He swung his fists and managed to land a couple of blows which would have decked an ordinary man.

But neither of these men were ordinary. They received his blows with little more than grunts,

240

and then one of them pinioned the American in a full-nelson, holding him fast while the other twisted in front of him to pummel him. The American kicked savagely at his kneecaps, but the attacker was expecting it. He side-stepped easily and rammed a fist into the American's stomach.

Killigrew decided it was time to intervene. He left the shadows and moved silently across the cobbles, stepping up behind the man who drove his fists repeatedly into the American's stomach. He got one hand on the man's shoulder and span him away from his victim, paying him in his own coin by driving a fist into his gut. The man gasped and swung at Killigrew's head, but Killigrew ducked beneath the blow and hit him in the stomach again, before clipping him on the jaw with a fast uppercut. The man's head snapped back and he went down.

The other man threw the American against a stack of barrels and charged towards Killigrew. The young man awaited his attack, adopting the classic pugilistic pose with both fists raised ready to strike. When the man reached him, Killigrew stepped aside at the last moment and tripped him up with an extended leg which sent him sprawling on the cobbles.

Something – probably the first man – slammed into Killigrew from behind and threw him against the wall of the tavern. Killigrew rammed his elbow into the man's midriff and broke free. They faced one another, circling warily, and then Killigrew stepped in close and tapped the man twice on the chin with his left. The man was evidently something of an expert pugilist, for he glanced to his left, expecting Killigrew to follow up with a right, which was when Killigrew decked him with a left cross.

He turned to see the second man advancing on him again, when suddenly the American loomed out of the darkness, holding a cask above his head which he brought down sharply against the second man's head.

'Are you oh-kay?' asked the American, once it was clear that neither of his attackers was in any hurry to get up and resume the combat.

Killigrew nodded, resting with his hands on his knees, breathing hard. 'Thank you.'

'No, thank *you*. I'm not entirely sure I could've handled them both if you hadn't stepped in. Tough little sons of bitches, weren't they?'

Killigrew crouched down to gather up the coins, and held them out to the American, who gestured dismissively. 'Keep 'em.'

'What I did I did out of Christian charity, not out of hope of a reward.'

'I know. That's why I'm giving you one.'

'I thank you for your kindness, but I'm not in need of charity.'

The American looked him up and down, taking in his unshaven face and the threadbare clothes he had purchased from a second-hand shop in Monmouth Street. 'Well, at least let me buy you a drink,' he said, taking back his money and gesturing towards the tavern.

Killigrew licked his lips as if torn between pride and thirst. 'All right,' he said.

They went inside and crossed to the counter.

'Back so soon, Cap'n?' asked the tavern-keeper.

The American grinned. 'You know me, Jake. I just can't stay away.'

'What can I get you?'

'The usual, please, and whatever my friend here is having.' He indicated Killigrew, whom the tavern-keeper looked up and down suspiciously.

'Well? What's it to be, young feller?'

'I ... I wonder if I could have a cup of tea?' stammered Killigrew.

The American and the tavern-keeper laughed. 'Where did you find him, Cap'n? At a temperance meeting?'

Killigrew shook his head. 'No. I ... I had an accident recently. I'd been drinking and ... well, I'd rather not talk about it, if it's all the same with you.'

'I'm sorry, I didn't mean to pry. If it's tea you want then it's tea you shall have. I'm sure Susie must have some tea in the kitchen?' he asked the tavern-keeper, who nodded and poured out a glass of whisky for the American before disappearing into the back. 'My name's Madison, by the way. Caleb Madison.' The American offered his hand. He had a surprisingly powerful grip.

'Kit Killigrew.'

'Killigrew, Killigrew,' mused Madison. 'I'm sure I've heard that name somewhere recently.'

Killigrew hung his head as if embarrassed. 'It's a common enough name in Cornwall.'

Madison's smile did not falter, but there was suspicion in his eyes. 'But we're not in Cornwall. And you don't have a Cornish accent.'

243

'No, well, I came from a good family. The tavern-keeper called you "captain". Am I to assume then that you are a fellow mariner, sir?'

'United States merchant marine. I'm the master of the *Madge Howlett.*'

'That fine Baltimore brig tied up in front of the Goree warehouses?'

Madison nodded. 'You know your ships. You're a sailor too? Which vessel are you with?'

'I'm between ships at the moment,' Killigrew responded with poorly-concealed circumspection. 'I, er ... I don't suppose...?'

Madison shook his head. 'I'm sorry, I've got a full complement right now.'

Killigrew nodded hurriedly, as if embarrassed that he had enquired.

'You said "came",' said Madison.

'What?'

'You said you "came" from a good family. Most people would've said: "I *come* from a good family", but you said you "*came* from a good family". What happened? Did you disown them? Or did they disown you?' Madison was grinning, as if to make light of the matter, but his eyes watched Killigrew's face carefully, missing nothing.

Killigrew grimaced. 'They disowned me. I don't mean to be rude, but I'd really rather not discuss it.'

Madison held up his hands. 'I'm sorry. You helped me out just now, and all I can do is ask impertinent questions. Please forgive me.'

The tavern-keeper returned with a mug of tea which he plonked on the counter before

Killigrew. 'Thanks, Jake. Put it on my slate.'

'Right you are, Cap'n.'

Madison turned to stand with his back to the counter and cast his eyes across the gloomy tavern as he sipped his whisky. And expression of pain crossed his face. 'Goddamn it!'

'What's wrong?' asked Killigrew.

'There's one of my crew over there. He's supposed to be on watch tonight. I'm sorry, will you excuse me for a moment?'

'By all means.' Killigrew turned back to the counter and sipped his tea while watching Madison in the etched-glass mirror behind the shelves there. Madison crossed to where a man sat at one of the tables, wedged between two buxom serving girls. The man – dark-haired, olive-complexioned – was if anything perhaps below average height, but everything about him suggested bulk. He had the kind of physique which gave the impression of being as wide as it was tall – and impression which in this instance was not too far from the truth – and as far as Killigrew could see very little of it was flab.

The man looked up and grinned as Madison approached. Killigrew could not hear what they said above the hubbub of voices in the tavern, but whatever Madison said prompted the man to glance to where Killigrew stood at the bar. Killigrew saw the words 'Don't look now, you fool' form on Madison's lips, and the man quickly turned his head back to face his captain. He pursed his lips, and then rubbed his jaw as if trying to think. Then he nodded confidently, and spoke at length, prompting Madison to glance surreptitiously at Killigrew.

Got you hooked, you bastard, thought Killigrew. *Now to reel you in.*

'Get out of here, you idle dog!' Madison said, unnecessarily loudly. 'I don't pay you to sit idling in a tavern, consorting with loose women! Get back to work!'

'Sorry, Cap'n.' The massively built man squeezed out from between the wenches, the very image of contrition. He took his leave of them and hurried out.

Madison returned to where Killigrew stood. 'As a seaman yourself, you'll understand the importance of keeping good discipline amongst the crew.'

Killigrew nodded. 'Absolutely. In the navy we used to–' he said, and then broke off sharply as if he had said too much.

'You're in the Royal Navy?'

'Used to be. The bastards chucked me out,' he added savagely, and then looked embarrassed, as if he had revealed too much.

'Yes, your "accident".' Madison drained his glass, set it on the counter and turned to Killigrew. 'Well, my thanks to you once again, Mr Killigrew. That was a right Christian thing you did, and I'm much obliged to you. You have a place to stay tonight?'

Killigrew nodded. 'The Spotted Dog, up along the way.'

'I'm sorry I couldn't give you a berth on my ship, but as I say–'

'Think nothing of it. There's a steamer leaving for the Orient tomorrow, I understand they're looking for hands.'

'The SS *Ophelia?* I wouldn't recommend a voyage on her.'

'Why not?'

'Captain Jacobs has one of the worst reputations for cruelty on the seas.'

'I fear I'm not in a position where I can afford to be choosy about whom I work for.'

'Wait a couple of days. Something better is bound to come alone. Besides, a man with your experience could do better than a berth as an ordinary seaman on a steamer. With your background and training, I'd've thought that ship's captains would be queuing up to have you in their crews.'

Killigrew grimaced. 'Unfortunately I have what you might call a ... a reputation.'

'Your accident?'

Killigrew nodded.

'It wasn't at sea by any chance, was it?'

'No. It had nothing to do with the sea. But as soon as I'd got a criminal conviction for what was only an accident those hypocritical swine at the Admiralty decided it was the perfect opportunity to get rid of me. I never was one of them, not really. My mother was Greek; the bastards never tired of reminding me of the fact.'

'Maybe you should think about getting a berth on a foreign vessel. Countries like Brazil and Cuba are always happy to have European officers on board. It lends them ... shall we say, an air of respectability?'

'Slavers sailing under false colours, you mean.'

'Ah. You disapprove of slaving, I take it?'

247

Killigrew pursed his lips. 'It's against the law in this country. Not that I have a high opinion of the English law. I never really thought about it. I spent three years sailing with the West Africa Squadron, but I can't say I cared for the work. Sometimes I think we did more harm than good.'

Madison regarded Killigrew with a mixture of astonishment and amusement. 'Are there many more in the navy like you?'

'Unfortunately not. Pah, I'm better off out of it.'

'You'll certainly get better pay in the merchant service, once you find yourself a berth. And you strike me as a singularly intelligent young man. I'm sure you'll be oh-kay.'

'You're probably right. Well, thanks for the drink. Perhaps I'll see you around?'

'Perhaps. I was supposed to sail three days ago, but the damned harbourmaster's saying there's some irregularity concerning my ship's papers – which is a damned lie – and I can't leave until I've been cleared. Each day my ship rots in this port is costing me a fortune, and not doing me any favours with my owners, either.'

'Have you tried bribing them?'

Madison shook his head. 'He's one of those self-righteous ones, the kind who'd take great pleasure in throwing the money back in my face.'

Killigrew shook his head. 'Try sending him a crate of fine wine. Just as a gift. Let the *quid pro quo* remain unspoken.'

'You think that would work?'

Killigrew shrugged. 'Compare the cost of each day you're stuck in this harbour with the cost of a crate of fine wine. It's got to be worth trying, hasn't it? Who's the harbourmaster here, Jack Tolliver? I think I knew him vaguely in the navy. I seem to recall he's rather partial to a glass of Madeira.'

'You know, I think I'll give that a try. Thanks for the advice, Mr Killigrew. Once again, I'm in your debt.'

Killigrew watched him leave and sipped his tea to hide his smile.

He finished his mug of tea and left about five minutes later. As he made his way along the waterfront he heard his footsteps echo where there should have been no echo. He stopped abruptly and pretended to read a poster advertising a dinner-dance at the local assembly rooms. Out of the corner of his eye he caught a glimpse of a shadow ducking out of sight behind him. He smiled to himself and went on his way until he reached the Spotted Dog, a tavern which was on the right side of respectable, but only just.

'Evening, Mr Killigrew,' said the pot-boy who, in his capacity as night-porter, let him in.

'Evening.' Killigrew touched the brim of his hat and went upstairs to his room. It was small but comfortably furnished. He lit the oil lamp and took off his hat, drew the curtains, and sat down at the table to write a letter and smoke a cheroot. When he had finished he dried the ink with blotting paper – afterwards burning the blotting paper over the ashtray so the ink could not be deciphered by means of holding it up to a mirror – folded the letter and put it inside his coat. He stubbed out the cheroot in an ashtray, put out the light and slipped out of the room.

He made his way to the water closet at the end of the dingy corridor. It was unoccupied, so he closed the door behind him without locking it and stood on the seat of the commode to open the window. There was no light in the water closet so he had no difficulty observing the alley below. It was deserted. He opened the window all the way and climbed out on to the ledge. Then he jumped into the night.

It was only one flight down. He hit the ground, rolled over and rose quickly to his feet. A couple of cats scavenging amongst the rubbish ran off with a hiss, startling him, but they were the only creatures to have observed his unusual mode of departure. He dusted himself off and went on his way, sticking to the shadows.

The Fouled Anchor was on the wrong side of respectable, but dressed in his second-hand clothes and grubby after rolling in the alley at the back of the Spotted Dog, Killigrew's arrival excited no interest whatsoever. He made his way upstairs and tapped gently on one of the doors.

'Who's there?' asked a voice.

'Tom Bowling,' said Killigrew.

The door opened and one of the men who had attacked Madison earlier stood there. The other sat before a mirror, wrapping a bandage about his own head. Killigrew slipped inside without waiting for an invitation. Corporal Summerbee of the Royal Marines quickly closed the door behind him.

'Are you fellows all right?' Killigrew asked them.

'Nothing that won't soon heal up,' said Summerbee. 'How did it go?'

'Splendidly. You did very well. I was utterly convinced.'

'So was I, sir. You didn't tell us he was such a tough customer.'

'I didn't know it myself. Hope I didn't hit you too hard there, Private Whitehead.'

Whitehead grinned. 'Hardly felt a thing, sir. Unlike when that Yankee bastard brained me with a keg. Begging your pardon, sir.'

'That's all right.' Killigrew took out the letter and handed it to Summerbee. 'I want this delivered to Rear-Admiral Napier. There's no reply necessary. I've got one more task for you. There's a house of ill-repute in Leopold Lane, at number sixty-nine. There should be a package for you to pick up there.'

'What sort of package, sir?'

'The kind that has two arms and two legs. Don't worry, he'll have been drugged to the gunnels, so you won't have any difficulty handling him. Take a wheelbarrow and a blanket to throw over him. Then take him to where the SS *Ophelia* is docked and deliver him to one of the boatswain's mates. He'll pay you a shilling. You might as well keep it between you. That should be all. Once again, thank you for all your help. When this is over I shall be writing a letter of commendation to your commanding officer.'

'I just hope that when this is all over, a letter of commendation from you is worth having, sir. For your sake, as well as for our own.'

'So do I, Summerbee. So do I.'

'Sir? Rear-Admiral Napier didn't tell us what any of this is about – although I think I can guess – but whatever it is, good luck with it anyway.'

'Thank you, Summerbee. That's much appreciated.'

Killigrew opened the door and was halfway across the threshold when he heard the corporal mutter under his breath, 'God knows, you're going to need it,' and Whitehead sniggered.

Killigrew's steps faltered only momentarily before he set his jaw and continued on his way.

The following day Killigrew sat down to luncheon and awaited his visitor. He dined alone, an impressive spread of roast mutton, potatoes and sprouts with lashings of gravy on the broad plate before him, a pot of tea steaming at his elbow.

Cheer up, Kit, he told himself. *If you don't succeed in pulling this off, you can always change your name and start a new career on the boards.* But it was difficult to imagine Eulalia being happy married to anything so disreputable as an actor.

Even though he expected company, there was no sign of it at the table, which was set for one. He was just tucking in when the door opened and Madison entered with an agitated look on his face. He gazed about the room, saw Killigrew, and at once came across to speak to him, holding his hat before him.

'Good day to you, Mr Killigrew. And how is my good Samaritan?'

'Very well, thank you. And you?'

'The same. May I join you?'

Killigrew gestured to the chair opposite him. 'Pull up a berth. Tea?'

'Thank you kindly.'

Killigrew twisted in his seat to address the landlady, who waited attentively by the dresser. She had not heard of the disgraced Christopher Killigrew, but despite his clothes she could tell that her guest was a gentleman. 'Could you fetch another cup for my friend, Mrs Hines?'

'Of course, sir.' She took down a cup and saucer and laid them on the table before Madison. 'Milk and sugar?'

'Thank you.' As soon as she had retreated to her earlier position, Madison turned back to Killigrew. 'You seem to be dining well.'

'Mm. As it happens, I've had a bit of good joss. A friend of mine is an acquaintance of Mr Brunel, the eminent engineer. It seems Mr Brunel will be looking for a new second officer for the *Great Britain* as soon as he can get her floated again.' Brunel's revolutionary transatlantic steamer the SS *Great Britain* had run aground in Dundrum Bay the previous year.

'Assuming they can get her off,' Madison pointed out. 'They've been trying for months.'

'This *is* Mr Brunel we're talking about,' said Killigrew.

'That's a good point.'

'The pay is excellent, and ... well, if one must serve in the merchant navy, then there can be few finer or more prestigious vessels to serve on than the *Great Britain*.'

Madison's face fell.

'Is something wrong?' asked Killigrew.

Madison cleared his throat. 'First of all I want to thank you again, Mr Killigrew. I took your advice and had a case of Madeira sent to the harbourmaster's office first thing this morning. Now maybe it's just co-incidence, but come noon I get a message from one of his boys telling me that I'm cleared to leave harbour whenever I please.'

Killigrew smiled. 'The British way of doing things, Captain Madison. It's a very genteel form of corruption. So, when do you sail?'

Madison grimaced. 'Well, that's just the problem. You remember last night I told you I had a full complement?' Killigrew nodded. 'Well, this morning my second mate had disappeared.'

'Does he drink? Take it from me, Captain, intoxicating liquor does terrible things to a man. Perhaps you should try having your men search all the waterfront taverns and gin palaces.'

'I already tried that. I understand the crimps were busy last night shanghaiing hands for the *Ophelia,* and I fear Mr Cutler may have been caught in their net.' Madison ran a finger through his thinning hair. 'If it was just one of my hands it wouldn't matter. But my second mate...? Men like that are difficult to replace.'

'Oh, I say! What rotten bad timing. If you'd come to me a few hours earlier I could have volunteered my own services – if you'd've accepted them.'

'Of course I would! That's why I came here this afternoon. I'm in a pickle, Mr Killigrew. I've already been stuck in this port for four days; I can't wait any longer.' He leaned across the table and lowered his voice. 'I'll pay you twelve dollars a day.'

'US dollars?' asked Killigrew, and Madison nodded. Killigrew carefully put down his knife and fork and dabbed at his lips with his napkin. 'Mrs Hines, it seems to me I'm being remiss. Unlike myself, Captain Madison here enjoys a glass of wine, in moderation. I wonder if you could fetch us a bottle? No, better still make it champagne, since I'm celebrating my new good fortune.'

'I don't think we have any champagne, Mr Killigrew.'

'Couldn't you send your son out to fetch some?'

'I could if he were here, Mr Killigrew, but I'm afraid he's run off for the day.'

'Oh that *is* a shame...'

'I could run out myself and get some, if you wouldn't mind keeping an eye on the place while I'm gone. The wine merchant is just down the road, I wouldn't be gone more than ten minutes.'

'Not at all, Mrs Hines. That would be awfully decent of you.'

She hurried out. Killigrew leaned back in his chair and looked Madison straight in the eye. 'Where are you bound?'

'Cuba, by way of Africa.'

'The Guinea Coast?' Madison nodded. 'You're a blackbirder, aren't you?'

'I kind of gathered last night that you had no principled objections to the trade.'

'In principle no. But in practice...? I've been humiliated by the Royal Navy enough as it is,

255

Captain Madison. What if I should be on board your ship when it was stopped by a Royal Navy vessel? As a British citizen they could take me and put me on trial. We have the death penalty for slaving in this country now, you know.'

'But it's never been enforced. Besides, my ship's clerk is a very skilled individual, Mr Killigrew. He can ... shall we say "arrange" some US papers for you. Not that you'll need them. The *Madge Howlett* is the fastest ship in the Atlantic. There's not a vessel in the Royal Navy that can catch her, not even a steamer. And I'll wager twelve dollars a day is a good deal more than you're being offered for this job on the *Great Britain*.'

'I couldn't tell you until I'd checked the current exchange rate. But there's also the prestige of working for such a well-respected company.'

Madison nodded sadly and for a moment Killigrew feared he might have overplayed it, but then the American looked up with determination in his eye.

'Prestige? Tcha! I know your sort, Mr Killigrew. You're a sailor. One of a long line of sailors, I'll be bound. Which would you prefer? The stuffy, formal atmosphere of a transatlantic steamer with its starched collars, grubby engines, tedious, middle-class passengers with their foolish questions, and a life that's regulated by a strict timetable, repeated again and again, voyage after voyage? Or the life of a fast merchant brig, with a free and easy attitude, no dress code, and the possibility of some excitement?'

'It's a tempting offer, Captain Madison. I can't

deny I've a hankering to put the stuffy world of civilised society behind me. But what about you? Are you sure you want an ex-naval officer on board? One who spent three years serving on the West Africa Squadron?'

'That's why I'm so keen to have you in my crew, Mr Killigrew. We've been blackbirding for many years now and we know most of the tricks. But you understand the naval mind. You know the navy's tactics and her ships. You know who the captains are of each ship, and which ones will pursue a slaver to the ends of the earth and which ones will give up after the first couple of hours. And from talking to you last night I got the impression that you'd jump at the chance to use that kind of knowledge against them.

'I'll lay it on the square and on the level for you, Mr Killigrew, because I like to think of myself as a straight-dealing man and if we're going to be working together – which I hope we are – I wouldn't want us to get off on the wrong foot. I've been checking up on you. You had a promising career in the navy until you made one little, tragic mistake, and then they took it all away from you. Well, here's your chance to pay them back. By proving that no matter how many steamers they put in their West Africa Squadron, they'll never end the slave trade. What do you say?'

Killigrew sat back and lit a cheroot, shaking out his match and tossing it into the fireplace. He blew out a long stream of blue-tinged smoke and watched it curl lazily towards the oak beams overhead as if deep in contemplation. 'Twelve dollars a day?'

Madison nodded. 'Half in advance, the rest when we reach Havana. And if it works out oh-kay then you can stay in my crew for as long as I'm captain of the *Madge Howlett*.'

'Are you sure you trust me that much?'

'I'll be honest with you, Mr Killigrew: no, I'm not. This is only the second time I've spoken to you; and while my instincts tell me I can trust you, I know a man's a fool if he relies on his instincts alone. So I'll tell you straight: you cross me once, boy, and I'll kill you. It's as simple as that.' Madison's eyes glittered as he leaned across the table once more. 'You breathe so much as a single word of our activities to the authorities, then no matter where you run, where you hide, I'll find you. No matter what it takes, I'll track you down and kill you, and as God is my witness you'll be a long time a-dying.'

Killigrew was in no doubt that Madison meant every word of it and was perfectly capable of carrying out his threat, but he managed a smile nonetheless. 'Well! You're certainly candid, I'll say that much for you.'

Madison smiled. 'I don't mean to scare you … aw, heck, yes, I *do* mean to scare you. Because if I'm wrong about you, then that's the only guarantee I've got that you'll keep your mouth shut. But something tells me I can trust you.'

'Well then, I hope I can prove myself worthy of your trust,' said Killigrew as the front door opened and the landlady returned with the champagne. 'And here's Mrs Hines, right on cue. Let's drink to our first voyage together, if you don't mind raising your glass with a man drinking coffee.'

Madison only stayed for one small glass of champagne – Killigrew guessed the American was not much of a champagne drinker, but ordering the bottle had been a suitable ruse to get Mrs Hines out of the house so they could talk in private – before he left, promising to send one of his men to help Killigrew with his things. As soon as he had gone, Killigrew settled his account with Mrs Hines and went upstairs to pack his sea-chest. It was a small chest for an officer, being only large enough to contain his sextant, writing equipment, clothes, washing things, and a couple of novels by Dumas, and Virgil's *Aeneid*.

Oh, yes. And his pepperbox, of course.

Finally he sat down, wrote a brief note, and laid it carefully on top of everything else in the chest. It was addressed 'To whom it may concern', inviting the finder to feel free to riffle the chest's contents while assuring him he would not find anything of interest unless he was a fan of Mr Dumas. Then he locked it with the key he wore on a chain around his neck, although he did not doubt there would be someone on board skilled enough to pick the lock so they could examine its contents at the earliest opportunity. He did not expect the presence of the pepperbox to raise too many eyebrows amongst such men.

He was carrying the heavy chest downstairs in both hands when Mrs Hines appeared at the foot of the steps. 'That gentleman's come to help you with your things, Mr Killigrew.'

'That gentleman' was the same squat, muscular man Killigrew had seen Madison talk to in the waterfront tavern the previous night. 'Meester Killigrew?' he rumbled.

'Yes.' Killigrew held out his hand and almost had his fingers crushed to a pulp when the man shook it.

'I am Manoel Duarte, the bosun of the *Madge Howlett.*' He spoke with a thick accent that Killigrew guessed was Portuguese. 'Capitão Madison send me to take you to the ship. You have your things?'

Killigrew indicated the chest he had put down to greet him. Duarte bent over, grasped one of the handles, and hefted it on to his shoulder as effortlessly as if it had been empty and made of paper. 'We go.'

Killigrew tipped his hat to Mrs Hines. 'Thank you for a thoroughly pleasant stay, Mrs Hines. I shall be sure to stay here next time I'm in Liverpool.'

She blushed and curtseyed. 'If you don't like us, tell us. If you do, tell your friends. That's our motto, Mr Killigrew.'

'And a fine one it is too. I shall be sure to recommend you.'

'We go,' insisted Duarte.

'Uh … we go,' Killigrew echoed to Mrs Hines, who giggled.

The waterfront was crowded at that time of day, but Killigrew had no difficulty following Duarte through the crush; he carved a path through the sea of bobbing heads like Moses parting the Red Sea.

Killigrew had not recognised the *Madge Howlett* when he had first laid eyes on her a couple of days earlier, which was unfortunate because that was the kind of mistake which might have cost him his life. But although he had a good eye for ships, one Baltimore brig looked pretty much the same as another built to the same specifications, while a simple readjustment of the sails and rigging could change the appearance of a ship entirely, unless one was looking for one ship in particular. Killigrew had been looking for the *Madge Howlett*, so when he had seen that name painted on the stern he'd assumed that was what he had found.

The *Madge Howlett* was a two-masted brig, about a hundred feet from stem to stern, the deck looking uncluttered without as many men or guns as a man-o'-war would have had. Killigrew had already studied her through his telescope, although this was the first time he had seen her close to and he noted with approval that she was in good condition, the brass fittings well polished, the decks holystoned until they shone palest yellow in the spring sunshine, the sails furled neatly under the yards, and the rigging neat and well maintained without any 'dead men' – untidy rope's ends – dangling loose over the sides. It was clear that Madison ran a tight ship; not as tight as a navy vessel, perhaps, but tight nonetheless.

There were perhaps a dozen men at work on deck, preparing to set sail. All had dark, Latinate looks and Killigrew guessed that if there were any genuine ship's papers on board they would prove that the *Madge Howlett* – if that were her real name, which he very much doubted – was in actuality a Cuban or Brazilian vessel.

Madison emerged on to the deck. 'Ah, there you are, Mr Killigrew. Welcome aboard. Now that we have permission to sail we'll be leaving just as soon as the chief mate returns.'

'He's not on board?'

Madison shook his head. 'I sent him down to London on an errand for me. He was due to catch the three o'clock train back, so he should be here within the hour. As soon as we're safely under way I'll have him fill you in on the details of your duties, but basically I'll expect you to take charge of navigation. The rules on board are fairly simple. There's a strict hierarchy on board. It runs from God to me to the chief mate to you to Senhor Duarte here. I expect orders to be carried out promptly and efficiently, and so should you. Do you speak Portuguese?'

'A little.'

'Good. Most of the men speak some English, but they can be a little slow to understand in that language. They're a good bunch on the whole. As far as punishment goes, I don't want to have to undermine you by overruling any of your orders, so if you're not sure of anything I suggest you clear it with me first. If that isn't convenient, you could do a lot worse than allow yourself to be guided by Duarte here. We've been sailing together for over ten years and he has my complete confidence; I suggest you give him yours. You'll get the hang of how I like things run soon enough.' He turned to the boatswain. 'Manoel, perhaps you'd like to show Mr Killigrew to his cabin and then give him a quick guided tour of the ship before we set sail?'

'*Sim, senhor capitão,*' growled Duarte.

'Thanks.' Madison clapped Duarte on the shoulder and turned back to Killigrew. 'Manoel here may not have much in the way of social graces, but I assure you he's loyal and reliable, and that's all I ask of my men. Dinner will be in my stateroom at eight; I'll introduce you to the other ship's officers then. Dress is informal at all times, although I expect certain standards of hygiene from my men which I doubt you'll have difficulty abiding by. Cleanliness is next to Godliness. As for the rest of the men, I dare say you'll get to know them soon enough. Manoel, when you've shown Mr Killigrew around the ship take him to the chart room so he can familiarise himself with the course I've plotted.'

'*Sim, senhor capitão.*'

Killigrew followed Duarte below deck to his cabin. It was the first time he had ever had a cabin on board ship. He indicated the second cot. 'I'm to share this cabin with the chief mate?' he guessed.

'*Sim, senhor.*'

'All right. Just put my dunnage down over there. I'll unpack later. Shall we take a look-see at the rest of the ship?'

Killigrew followed Duarte out of the cabin. 'I might as well leave my hat in the cabin,' he said. 'Wait here, I shan't be a moment.'

Killigrew went back inside the cabin, took off his top hat and placed it on top of his chest. Then he plucked a single hair from his head and stuck it over the catch of the chest so that any attempt

263

to open it would dislodge the hair. Then he went outside and followed Duarte on a guided tour of the ship.

The *Madge Howlett* was little different from any slaver Killigrew had been aboard in terms of layout – officer's quarters below the quarter-deck, stores in the bows, and a large hold running the whole length of the ship – but a good deal cleaner and less noisome. Killigrew doubted its current state would last long once they had slaves on board. The hold was piled high with bales of cotton cloth, rolls of copper wire, the long low shapes of crates of rifles, barrels with the word 'GUNPOWDER' stencilled on their sides, and various other boxes and crates. Killigrew wondered which boxes contained the shackles, handcuffs and padlocks. He also noted about three hundred empty barrels, enough to carry water for all the slaves for the duration of the middle passage, as well as a large stack of timber which could easily be used to make a slave deck.

There was an open hatch with a grating in the deck head, and Killigrew glanced up as a shadow from a man fell through.

'Everything stowed securely?' the man asked, another American. 'Good. That you, Manoel? The cap'n tells me you've got our new second mate with you. Well, stand forward out of the shadows, mister. Let's have a look at you.'

Killigrew took a pace forward and gazed up through the grating at the chief mate. Their eyes locked, and the man's eyes widened as he recognised Killigrew.

'You!' exclaimed Eli Coffin.

XI:

Blackbirders

'Hold him fast!' snapped Coffin. 'I'm a-coming down.' He disappeared from sight, and Killigrew at once felt Duarte's massive hands grip him by the arms. He made no attempt to resist; it would have been useless anyway.

It was not until Killigrew had seen Eli Coffin that he realised he had seen the *Madge Howlett* before, albeit with a different name and a different figurehead on her prow. Once he had been given the Coffin connection, he realised at once that she was merely the *Leopardo* under another name.

Coffin's feet clumped down the companion ladder from the forward hatch and a moment later he appeared in the hold. He was not smiling.

'You know this man, Senhor Coffin?' Duarte asked ponderously.

Coffin hawked and spat on the deck. 'Yeah, I know him. He's a goddamned British Officer.'

'An *ex* British Officer,' corrected Madison, entering behind Coffin. 'I take it you two are already acquainted, then?'

'This bastard was on board that navy steamer we led on a wild-goose chase a couple of months ago,' snarled Coffin, glaring at Killigrew with

265

hate-filled eyes. 'What was she called?'

'The *Tisiphone*,' Killigrew offered helpfully.

'It's all right, Manoel,' said Madison. 'You can release Mr Killigrew.'

'You *knew?*' Coffin asked Madison in disbelief.

Madison smiled. 'Mr Killigrew is no longer in Her Majesty's service, Eli. It seems he's been ... how can I put this? ... guilty of an indiscretion.'

'The hell he has. You're not serious about having this whoreson on board, are you? He'll betray us to his friends at the first opportunity! He's probably here to spy for his navy!'

Madison shook his head. 'Calm down, Eli. Mr Killigrew here's seen the light. Acts, chapter nine, verse eighteen: "And immediately there fell from his eyes as it had been scales: and he received sight forthwith". It's oh-kay, I've made some enquiries and his story's on the level. I had a difficult enough job persuading him to join us. Don't mind Eli, Mr Killigrew. He hates the English, so don't take it personal. Once you two have had a chance to get to know one another you'll get along fine.'

'I'm sure,' Killigrew said drily.

'Don't count on it,' snarled Coffin.

'You'll get along with him, Eli, or I'll know the reason why. You've known me long enough to know that when I've made up my mind, it stays that way. Killigrew replaces that good-for-nothing Cutler until I say otherwise, you hear me?'

'Aye, aye, sir,' Coffin said surlily.

'Oh-kay, let's get to work. There's plenty to be done before we set sail. You've seen the ship, Mr Killigrew? Good. Take him to the chart room,

Manoel. Eli, you come with me.' Madison headed out of the hold and Coffin made as if to follow him, but turned back to address Killigrew in a low, menacing voice.

'Now you listen to me, you Limey sonuvabitch. I don't know what your game is, but if you're on the level then I'm a Dutchman's uncle.' He touched Killigrew under the jaw with the coils of his whip. The bull-hide felt cold, coarse and dry, like the scales of a snake. 'Sooner or later you're going to slip up, and when you do I'll be waiting.' He turned away and went out of the hold, chuckling to himself in anticipation.

Duarte took Killigrew to the chart room. It was well ordered, and the relevant charts for their forthcoming voyage were easy enough to find. The route was straightforward: out into the Irish Sea, through St George's Channel, around Land's End, across the mouth of the Bay of Biscay, past the coasts of Spain and Portugal and south-sou'-west to the coast of Africa. The course veered well away from the Guinea Coast, presumably to evade the Royal Navy vessels which patrolled off-shore, and terminated vaguely somewhere near Sierra Leone, as if Madison had not been bothered to think that far ahead; evidently he did not trust Killigrew enough to reveal the precise location of their destination before they had even left port.

He made his way up on deck to where Madison and Coffin stood on the quarter-deck close by the helm. 'Ah, Mr Killigrew,' said Madison. 'You approve of the course I've plotted?' he asked with a smile.

'Yes, sir,' said Killigrew. 'Although it seems to be incomplete…?'

Madison's smile did not alter. 'Our destination is a month's sailing away. We'll concern ourselves with that nearer the time. All ready, Mr Duarte?'

'Aye, aye, *senhor capitão.*'

'Then we'll waste no more time. Perhaps you'd care to take her out, Mr Killigrew?'

'Very well, sir.' Killigrew guessed that Madison was testing him: not to see if he was up to the task, if he had doubted that for a moment then he would never have taken him on as his second mate; more to assess his style of ship-handling – and crew-handling. 'Let go the bow-fast!' When the crew did not obey at once, he repeated his order in Portuguese, but still they exchanged glances of mocking bewilderment as if Killigrew's command of the language was wanting, which he knew it was not. It was not just the master of the *Madge Howlett* who was testing the new second mate.

'You are responsible for discipline on board this vessel, are you not, Bosun?' Killigrew asked Duarte.

'Yes.'

'Then see to it that my orders are obeyed promptly,' Killigrew said mildly.

Duarte glanced at Madison, who nodded almost imperceptibly. 'You heard Senhor Killigrew!' Duarte roared at the hands. 'Let slip the bow-fast!'

'Hoist the jib and foresail,' ordered Killigrew, glancing sidelong at Madison. The master was smiling faintly, indicating approval of Killigrew's handling of the reluctant seamen. The brig's bows turned away from the pier. 'Now let go the stern-fast and brace up the sails. Meet her,' he added to the helmsman, who nodded and span the helm to stop her head from coming around any further.

The mooring lines cast off, the *Madge Howlett* slowly gathered way, moving out from the dock into the Mersey. The tide was approaching the high-water mark so there was no approachable current, and the wind coming in from the brig's port quarter made her easy to handle.

'Port the helm... Ease her... Help amidships... Steady as she goes.'

'Steady it is, sir.'

The actual task of conning the brig into the channel was child's play for Killigrew, and with a fresh breeze blowing across the Wirral peninsula they had soon passed New Brighton, the North Fort and the South Fort, crossed the bar, and emerged into Liverpool Bay. They hoisted all canvas, sailing close-hauled towards the setting sun. At seven bells Madison ordered Coffin to take the con and, after reminding Killigrew dinner was at eight, went below.

Killigrew returned to his cabin for a quick shave, a change of shirt and a brush-up before dinner. The hair he had left on his sea-chest had been dislodged, but it had been unnecessary: the searcher, prevented from concealing his search by an impulsive rage, had screwed Killigrew's mocking note into a tight ball. Somehow he knew it was Coffin who had done the searching. There was a feeling of violence about the chief mate,

269

and not very deep below the surface, either. Of all the men on the *Madge Howlett* – including the chunky Duarte – Killigrew feared Coffin most of all.

Making his way to Madison's cabin he encountered a small man, dressed as smartly as his obviously cheap clothes would allow, with a sallow complexion and a bulging, watery-looking pair of eyes. 'You must be Senhor Killigrew,' said the man. He had a nervousness about him, and a voice like egg-white poured over sandpaper.

'If you insist,' Killigrew responded lightly. 'I fear you have the advantage over me, Mr...?'

'Pereira. Cirungião Antônio Pereira, at your service.' He extended his hand, and Killigrew shook it. It was like touching the petals of an orchid, the feel of clammy, dead flesh. If Pereira was the ship's surgeon, Killigrew was determined not to fall ill on this voyage.

He gestured at the door to Madison's cabin. 'Shall we go in?'

'To be sure, to be sure.' Pereira raised a hand, swallowed hard, and tapped gently.

'Come in, Pereira,' Madison called from inside. 'I'd recognise your weak-livered scratching at my door any day. And Mr Killigrew,' he added, seeing Killigrew enter behind the surgeon. 'Come in, gentlemen. Take a seat.'

Coffin was already there, seated at the table. There were only four of them to dine that night, which was just as well for the table only seated four; there was not room for a bigger one in the cramped cabin. One wall was dominated by the window which gazed out from the stern, while the remaining three were decorated with samplers: 'They that go down to the sea in ships, that do business in great waters; These see the work of the LORD, and his wonders in the deep – Psalm 107, 23-24'; 'It is good for a man that he bear the yoke in his youth – Lamentations iii, 27'; 'Judge not, that ye be not judged – Matthew vii, 1'.

Killigrew took them in as he seated himself opposite Pereira. The samplers reminded him of the sampler on the wall of Eulalia's bedroom, which reminded him of Eulalia, and he felt a fleeting pang as he thought of how much he would have preferred to be with her than in the company of these murderous rogues. He forced himself to put all thoughts of Eulalia from his mind: he would need his wits about him if he was going to stay alive for the next few months.

A black steward – Killigrew wondered if he were a slave or a freeman – stood by with a bottle in one hand, and as soon as everyone was seated he began to pour out the wine: first Madison, then Pereira, then Coffin. When it came to Killigrew's turn, he almost forgot to put his hand over his glass. He suddenly realised he had not had anything alcoholic for several hours, and regretted not being able to drink now. He wondered how long it would be before he could have another drink, and the thought made his mouth water.

'What's the matter, Killigrew?' sneered Coffin. 'Not drinking? You're missing out. It's a good year. What are you afraid of? There are no little girls for you to run down out here in the Irish Sea.'

'All right, Eli,' growled Madison, although secretly Killigrew welcomed Coffin's taunting: it would make it easier for him to abstain, if by doing so he would be disappointing a heartfelt wish in Coffin that he should fall off the wagon.

But the chief mate would not be silenced so easily. 'Or maybe he's afraid that he'll get drunk and let something slip. Like what he's *really* doing on board this ship.'

'I said *that will do*,' Madison said firmly, and Coffin lapsed into a sullen silence. 'Mr Killigrew will have a cup of coffee,' Madison told the steward, who nodded and went out. When he returned with a pot and a china cup and placed them in front of Killigrew, the latter hesitated before drinking. If they wanted to poison him, he had given them a perfect opportunity: it could be doctored without the others having to drink it; and the bitter taste would mask any poison. But then, if they wanted him dead he had given them all the opportunity they would ever need simply by coming aboard.

Madison turned to Killigrew with an apologetic smile. 'I noticed you admiring my wife's handi-work when you came in, Mr Killigrew.'

'The samplers?'

Madison nodded. 'A woman's touch. Are you a married man yourself?'

'I do not have that pleasure,' said Killigrew.

'That's a great pity,' said Madison. 'A man should be married. Proverbs, chapter five, verse eighteen: "Let thy fountain be blessed: and rejoice with the wife of thy youth."'

'Since we're playing at Bible quotes, Cap'n, I

have one for you,' said Coffin. 'From the book of Jeremiah, I think: "Can the Ethiopian change his skin, or the leopard his spots?"'

That pointed barb effectively stifled any further attempts at polite small talk at the dinner table, but service as an officer in the Royal Navy prepared a man for many things, and stilted table talk in an uncomfortable atmosphere was one of them. The steward served them a simple but hearty meal of beef, carrots and potatoes and Killigrew tucked in with vigour, apparently oblivious to Coffin's hostility and the discomfort of Madison and Pereira, enthusiastically asked the steward to pass on his compliments to the cook. Finally Coffin muttered that he had had enough and went below.

'You'll have to forgive Mr Coffin, Mr Killigrew,' said Madison. 'As I said, he hates the English.'

'Any particular reason?'

'Just family tradition. His grandfather was killed at the battle of Trafalgar.'

'On which side?'

'The British side. Against his will.' In those days it had been the habit of the Royal Navy, forgetful of the United States' new-found independence, to stop American merchant ships and press their seamen into service aboard British men-o'-war; this had been the main cause of the War of 1812. 'But he's a good man.'

'A good man? Or a good seaman? The two are not necessarily one and the same, in my experience.'

'Aye, true enough. I'd say he's both, when he

doesn't let his prejudice get the better of him. You'd be wise to try to win him over, Mr Killigrew. He's not a good man to have for an enemy.'

'You speak from personal experience?'

Madison chuckled. 'There's not a man who's experienced Eli's enmity who's lived to tell the tale,' he said. Killigrew, sensing the captain spoke the plain truth, felt a shudder run down his spine. 'Fortunately for me, Eli and I have always been friends.'

'Until now?'

'Oh, we don't always see eye to eye, but we can usually agree to differ.' Madison snipped the ends off a couple of Havana cigars and handed one to Killigrew. 'I don't know. Maybe he *is* right about you. What do you say?'

'I say you should trust your own judgement first.'

'Aye, well, the jury's still out on that one. You've still got to prove yourself to me, Mr Killigrew. But help us pick up our cargo from the Guinea Coast and get it across the Atlantic to the slave markets of Havana, and perhaps then you'll have my trust.'

'I hope I can win it. I'm not so sure about Mr Coffin's. I never was one for visiting the sins of the fathers upon the sons myself. My own father was killed in a fight with the Ottoman fleet, but that didn't stop me from fighting with the Turks in Syria.'

'I understand you distinguished yourself considerably in that campaign?'

'I only did my duty.'

'In support of a crumbling Empire which your father once fought against?'

'You should judge each nation by the cause it is fighting for at any one moment in history, Captain Madison. My father fought for Greek independence. I fought for the freedom of the Lebanon from the Egyptians. The Lebanese may have had no great love for their Ottoman overlords, but, believe me, they preferred being ruled from Constantinople to the rule of the viceroy in Alexandria.'

'Your father fought as a mercenary?'

'As a sailor of fortune. He served Admiral Cochrane against Napoleon's navies, and when Napoleon was beaten they went wherever there was a just cause to be fought for: Chilean and Brazilian independence, then for the Greeks.'

'And you wanted to follow in his footsteps? Is that why you went to sea?'

'Yes. What about you? What made you go to sea?'

'The same thing as you, the same thing as Mr Coffin. We followed in our father's footsteps. Mr Coffin and I served together aboard a whaler until we realised the advantages of blackbirding.'

'And they are?'

'Money, Mr Killigrew,' said Madison. 'I know the Good Lord taught us that love of money is the root of all evil, but a man must make a living. Besides, it's charitable work, too. As you said yourself, we're rescuing the niggers from a life of ignorance and Godlessness and taking them to a new life in the New World.'

Killigrew forced a smile on to his lips to conceal

his revulsion. 'Of course,' he said. Madison could be dangerously likeable at times, and Killigrew was glad when he expressed such opinions. It would make it easier for him when the time came for him to bring Madison down.

'I say, Sir George!'

Emerging from the portals of the Reform Club with one of his parliamentary colleagues, Sir George Grafton heard his name called out and glanced down Pall Mall to see Rear-Admiral Sir Charles Napier limping towards him. 'Oh, Christ,' he muttered. 'Look out, William, it's that lunatic Napier. I thought we'd seen the last of him.'

Unsmiling as ever, his companion merely inclined his head with a dour expression.

Sir George pasted a broad smile on to his face. 'Why, Sir Charles! Good morning to you, sir. May I be one of the first to congratulate you on your recent appointment to the command of the Channel Fleet?' *God knows, I worked hard enough to get you sent back to sea so you'd keep your interfering nose out of parliamentary business.*

'Why, thank you, Sir George, thank you. Although I must say, it did come rather un-expectedly. And just when I was starting to find my feet in the House of Commons, too.' He chuckled. 'You know, if I didn't know better, I'd say one of my political enemies was trying to get me out of the way.'

'Nonsense, Sir Charles. There are no enemies in the House of Commons. Only adversaries.'

'I fear my command of the finer intricacies of

Shakespeare's tongue is not up to the task of discerning the difference. But then as you know, I'm just a simple, bluff old sailor at heart.'

In a pig's ear, thought Sir George, and indicated his companion. 'You've met Mr Gladstone, I take it?'

'I know of his father,' said Napier. Mr Gladstone senior owned a plantation in the West Indies and profited from the trade in apprenticed labour, shipping coolies from India in conditions little better than slave ships.

'Mr Gladstone is one of the rising stars of our party,' said Grafton.

'Our paths have crossed,' said Napier. 'Although not yet our swords.'

'And nor will they ever,' sniffed Mr Gladstone junior. 'I have always felt that duelling is the kind of childish behaviour that gentlemen should avoid. And, I might furthermore add, contrary to the laws of our nation.'

'I was merely speaking metaphorically, Mr Gladstone. Of our parliamentary swords.'

'Oh,' sniffed Gladstone.

Napier turned back to Grafton. 'Sir George, I wonder if I might have a word with you *in camera.*'

'By all means, but I pray you be brief. I have important business to conduct...'

'As have I. Channel fleets don't run themselves, you know.'

'You must excuse me, Mr Gladstone. I'll speak further on this matter with you at a later date.'

'I shall look forward to it,' said Gladstone. 'Good day to you, Sir George, Sir Charles.' He doffed his top hat to them, and wandered off in the direction of the Haymarket.

'Now then, Sir Charles. How may I be of assistance to you?'

'Shall we walk a little way?' suggested Napier. 'It's a splendid morning, and the exercise will do us good.'

'As you will.'

The two of them set off down Pall Mall towards Trafalgar Square, Napier limping. 'I'm just trying to tie up my parliamentary affairs before I raise my flag on HMS *Vincent*,' he explained. 'As grateful as I am finally to be given an important command, I am a little concerned that I shall be absent from the House of Commons at a not-entirely opportune moment. Now, while I realise that we have not always seen eye to eye over the past few years, I know I can rely on your honesty and decency as a gentleman to fight my corner for me in my absence.'

'Why, Sir Charles, I should be delighted to. And may I add that I am honoured that you should choose me for such a task?'

'Well, I have so many affairs that need to be looked after in my absence, I'm trying to spread them as thinly as possible. Most of my trusted friends have been given my more important matters to deal with, but there are still one or two insignificant ones that nonetheless would benefit from having a fatherly eye kept on them.'

'Indeed?' Sir George said drily.

'I dare say you recall Lieutenant Christopher Killigrew?'

'Ah, yes. That unfortunate young naval officer

who disgraced himself so … er … disgracefully. Drinking, I believe, and being responsible for the death of a little girl.'

'That's the way it looked,' agreed Napier. 'Sir George, before we proceed any further in this matter, I must ask you to keep what I am about to tell you in the uttermost and strictest confidence. You must swear not to reveal this to another living soul until the time is right, on your word of honour as a gentleman.'

Grafton was intrigued. 'You have it, by God.'

'Mr Killigrew did not kill that child.'

'But … did he not confess to it?'

'A ruse the lieutenant and I cooked up between us,' Napier explained smugly. 'We wanted to disgrace him.'

'I'm not sure I understand. This fellow Killigrew and yourself cooked up a calumny to blacken his name, with his consent? But to what object?'

'Through my work with the Slave Trade Department at the Foreign Office I have lately become aware that there is someone in this country who is living off the profits of that most evil trade. And, I fear, a senior member of the British Establishment. Perhaps even a member of the House of Commons.'

'That is the most outrageous suggestion I have ever heard!' blustered Sir George. 'Do you have any evidence whatsoever to back up this assertion?'

'No. But I am relying on Mr Killigrew to provide me with it. That is why we had him disgraced, you see. As a private individual he was

279

able to do what he could not as an officer of the Royal Navy: take ship aboard a slave vessel.'

'No slave vessel would ever take an ex-naval officer on as a member of its crew.'

'One already has. Even as we speak, Mr Killigrew is bound for the Guinea Coast on board the *Madge Howlett,* a suspected slave vessel. I have every confidence in that brave young man's ability to expose the name of the man who is financing the voyage.'

'The *Madge Howlett?* I cannot say I am familiar with the vessel. How many other people know about this scheme of yours?'

'No one. Except yourself, now, and once again I must entreat you to keep this matter in the strictest confidence. If word should get to the slavers that Mr Killigrew is acting as a spy aboard their vessel then his life would be imperilled.'

'To be sure, to be sure.'

Napier sighed. 'And that is why I need your help, Sir George. Both Mr Killigrew's trial and court-martial were real enough, I fear, though based only on his confession. I have promised that when he returns he will be exonerated and both his rank and good name restored. But if I'm with the Channel Fleet there will be no one in Britain who can speak up for him.'

'Say no more. You may rest assured that if ... I do beg your pardon, *when* ... Mr Killigrew returns, he shall have the full influence of my position to support him.'

'Thank you so much, Sir George.' Napier pumped Grafton's hand vigorously. 'I knew I could rely on you.'

'And now if you'll excuse me I have urgent business to attend to. Good day to you, Sir Charles.'

'What are you reading?' growled Madison, turning away from the helmsman.

'The Good Book,' said Killigrew, lifting up his Bible so that Madison could see the title on the spine.

'I never figured *you* for a religious man, Mr Killigrew. Not that I disapprove, of course. Quite the opposite.'

Killigrew smiled beatifically. '"Happy is the man that findeth wisdom, and the man that getteth understanding..."'

'"...For the merchandise of it is better than the merchandise of silver, and the gain thereof than fine gold",' continued Madison. '"She is more precious than rubies: and all the things thou canst desire are not to be compared unto her" Proverbs, chapter three, verses thirteen to fifteen.'

'He's just trying to curry favour,' sneered Coffin. 'Any fool can read the Bible.'

'Maybe you should try it, Mr Coffin,' Madison said drily.

Coffin shrugged. He and Madison had sailed together for many years and if they disagreed over the issue of Killigrew's trustworthiness, then in most other respects they were of one mind, as Killigrew had not been surprised to discover over the past few weeks.

As soon as the *Madge Howlett* had been well out into the Atlantic they had radically changed the brig's whole appearance by the simple expedient of rearranging the spars and rigging; changing the figurehead and painting out the name *'Madge Howlett'* and replacing it with *'Leopardo'* was merely the icing on the cake. After that the voyage had been as dull and uneventful as only a sea voyage could be. Killigrew's duties kept him busy. He was in charge of the boatswain's locker and it was his job to issue spun-yarn, marline, marline-spikes and serving boards to the hands. Although he was next in seniority after Coffin, there was a wide gulf between the chief mate and the second mate. Killigrew was expected to go aloft with the rest of the crew to reef and furl the topsails, and yet in spite of this he was expected to maintain his dignity before them in the interests of discipline. But in this respect his years of service in the Royal Navy put him in good stead: as a midshipman he had been expected to go aloft with the hands, and the skills of reefing and handling the sails soon came back to him. It had always been a tricky balance, maintaining one's superior dignity while working alongside men, but a good officer knew how to turn it to his advantage by showing he was not ashamed to get his hands dirty without making any pretence at being just one of the lads. Once again he found he was neither one thing nor the other, but it was a position he was growing accustomed to.

Even though he shared a cabin with Coffin he was spared the chief mate's hostility, for on the whole the two of them lived a box-and-cox existence, one working while the other slept.

When they did encounter one another, at first Coffin would growl some barbed comment, trying to provoke Killigrew into a fight. But Killigrew did not rise to the bait; in truth he welcomed Coffin's hatred, for it meant that Madison did not suspect him; if he had, then he would have taken the chief mate aside and ordered him to mask his hostility. After a while Coffin grew bored of needling Killigrew, or at least ran out of barbed comments to make, and settled for a growled acknowledgement. But his hatred remained unabated, as the occasional venomous glance he shot at Killigrew bore witness. Still, at least they made no attempt to poison him or slit his throat while he slept, and after a while Killigrew knew he could allow his vigilance to drop a little.

The days slipped by one after another as the waves were broken beneath the *Leopardo*'s prow and left churned by her wake; the future turned into the past, and the days became weeks, the weeks marked off by Madison conducting a prayer meeting on deck for the crew every Sunday morning. Attendance was compulsory. Nearly three weeks after they had sailed from Liverpool they entered the Tropics, and a few days later they made landfall at São Tiago in the Cape Verde Islands to take on board fresh water and fruit and vegetables. The *Leopardo* and her crew seemed well known there, and although it must have been obvious that she was a slaver no one made any attempt to stop her. But without the transatlantic trade the Cape Verde Islands would die, and for the moment the greater part of the transatlantic trade meant the slave trade. Killigrew realised all over again that the slave trade would never be crushed as long as men could make money out of it.

Perhaps the answer was to make it too expensive a trade to carry on.

From São Tiago they steered south-east, angling in towards the Guinea Coast, and that afternoon Killigrew was making his way to the boatswain's locker when he glanced in the galley as he passed. He was surprised to see the cook reading.

Like any cook on any ship Killigrew had ever been on, the cook was known only as 'Doc'. A short, wiry but broad-shouldered slave somewhere in his mid-twenties, with skin the colour of mahogany, Doc seemed to accept his status cheerfully. He played the guitar during his off-watches, sometimes a seaman-like shanty for the benefit of his shipmates, sometimes a haunting Spanish air which added a kind of beauty to the long watches of the night. He was always free for a chat whenever Killigrew popped into the galley for a light in the middle of the night watch, although so far he had failed to impress Killigrew with anything approaching mental acuity. Killigrew had met educated free slaves on the London lecture circuit, uneducated slaves on the Guinea Coast, African slaves and black seamen, and his experience was broad enough to suggest that those ethnologists who claimed that black people were mentally inferior to whites was so much gammon. But just as there were intelligent whites and foolish whites, there were intelligent blacks and foolish blacks. In Doc's case, there seemed to be no getting away from it: he was just plain thick.

So when Killigrew saw Doc reading, he was surprised to discover that the cook knew how. As he approached the galley, Doc quickly put the volume aside and put a pan over it to hide it.

'Good afternoon, Doc,' Killigrew said cheerfully.

Doc grinned broadly and rolled his eyes like any Ethiopian minstrel. 'Why, good afternoon, mas'er.'

'What were you reading?'

'Reading, mas'er?'

Killigrew tried to reach past and lift the pan off the book, but Doc moved to one side to block his path. Killigrew tried to reach past him on the other side, but again Doc moved to block his path, still grinning inanely. The two of them continued this comic ballet in the cramped confines of the galley for a few seconds more, until Killigrew feinted to the left and then lunged past the cook on the right. He lifted the pan and seized up the book: Shelley's *Prometheus Unbound*.

Doc actually looked ashamed.

'Heady stuff,' said Killigrew.

'Why, I can't make head nor tail of it myself, mas'er. Mr Tristão, he been learning me to read and all, but I ain't a good learner, nossir.'

Killigrew flicked through the pages until a couplet leaped out at him, and he read it out loud: '"Kingly conclaves stern and cold/Where blood with guilt is bought and sold."'

285

'I don't know what it means, mas'er, but that sho'nuff pretty,' said Doc.

Killigrew gave him back the book. 'Are you happy on board this ship, Doc?'

'Happy, mas'er? Why shouldn't I be happy? Mas'er Madison, he hardly ever beats me, and the others treat me good. 'Cepting that Mas'er Coffin…'

There was a commotion outside the galley and Killigrew left Doc to his cooking, emerging to see Duarte dragging one of the hands up the companionway to the forward hatch. Killigrew followed them up on deck.

The man staggered, partly because of Duarte's rough handling but also because he seemed to have limited control of his own legs. The man giggled at Duarte's curses, and the more Duarte cursed him the more the man giggled. At last, when the boatswain had dragged him the length of the deck, he threw him down at Madison's feet.

'Drunk, *senhor capitão*,' said Duarte.

Seeing Madison standing grim-faced over him, the man stopped giggling and the light of fear shone in his eyes as he realised how perilous his situation was. His name was Nicolau Tristão and he had a wife and baby son waiting for him in Maranhão. Killigrew had not wanted to get to know the hands other than their names: the names of men he would be sending to prison if all went well, or to their graves if anything went wrong. He did not want to know about Susana and little Rico waiting at home for a husband and father who might never return. But you could not

286

spend weeks on board ship with men without getting to know something about them. About how they had gone to sea, driven by starvation or shanghaied by crimps, or even willingly in the hope of adventure and riches.

'I don't abhor alcohol on this vessel, Mr Killigrew,' said Madison. 'Unlike your navy, I believe in treating men like equals. If I am allowed to drink, there is no reason why they should not enjoy the same pleasure. But I do abhor drunkenness.'

'Isn't that asking for trouble?' asked Killigrew. 'The one generally leads to the other.'

'I treat my men like adults, Mr Killigrew, and expect them to exert their own judgement from time to time. But tell me, what would you do with this man if you were in your navy?'

'It's not my navy any more,' Killigrew reminded him, and then continued cautiously. 'But that would depend upon the captain. There are some men who would have him flogged to within an inch of his life. And a few who would flog him beyond.'

'And you?'

'On my ship I wouldn't allow men to drink any more than their daily ration of rum. If they exceeded it – and sailors always seem to be able to exceed it – then I would hang them upside down over the side and dunk them into the sea a few times to sober them up. A flogged man cannot work.'

'And a man who cannot trust himself to stay sober cannot be trusted at all. Mr Coffin, show Mr Killigrew why there are so few cases of drunkenness on board the *Leopardo.*'

Coffin grinned. 'With pleasure,' he said, taking a crowbar from where it was clipped alongside a boat hook.

Duarte hoisted Tristão to his feet and left him standing there. The sailor had sobered up with remarkable rapidity and he turned to Madison with tears in his eyes. *'Por favor, senhor capitão* ... I will never be drunk on duty again, I swear it...'

'Damn right you won't,' snarled Coffin, circling Tristão while gently tapping the crowbar against the palm of his left hand. The sailor tried to turn to face him, but Coffin put a hand on his shoulder and span him back to face away. Then he smashed the crowbar across the sailor's kidneys.

Tristão cried out and sank to his knees, but the punishment had only just begun. A blow to the head or neck from that iron bar might have killed him at once, but Coffin was careful not to deliver such a blow: he wanted to make this last.

The bar swung down again and Killigrew winced as he heard the distinct sound of a rib cracking. Under different circumstances he would not have hesitated to intervene, but it suddenly occurred to him that Madison and Coffin had been waiting for an opportunity like this ever since they had set out from Liverpool. They were testing him once again, wondering if he had the callousness in his heart to stand by and watch a man being beaten to death. Seeing the other men on board going about their duties as if this was a not-infrequent occurrence, Killigrew tried to display the same nonchalance.

Coffin continued to swing the bar expertly, breaking Tristão's arms and legs. Duarte might have been a more suitable man to inflict the punishment, but Coffin was too obviously enjoying it.

'Proverbs, chapter thirteen, verse twenty-four,' said Madison. '"He that spareth his rod hateth his son: but he that loveth him chasteneth him betimes."'

Splintered bones burst out through the skin and blood ran across the pale deck. Killigrew felt sick and wondered when Coffin would stop. For a while it seemed as if the chief mate would not cease until he had beaten Tristão to death, but then he stopped abruptly: he had other plans for this man. He ordered Duarte to have a rope looped about Tristão's ankles, and then the sailor was hoisted from one of the yards on the foremast and swung out over the ship's side. He screamed in agony and terror. They dangled the man less than a foot above the waves, his blood dripping into the blue sea.

Those crew who were not engaged in other duties crowded the rail to watch. They were laughing and joking, betting with each other as to how long it would take, but Killigrew could see that the laughter was forced. They knew that a similar fate awaited them if they made a mistake.

As it waited for Killigrew.

The sharks did not take long to arrive. They had no difficulty keeping up with the ship, their dark blue-grey fins cleaving effortlessly through the water. One burst out of the water, jaws snapping, and narrowly missed Tristão before crashing back down into the waves.

Tristão screamed. He was blubbering in terror now, pleading for Madison to forgive him. But Madison was not even paying any attention to him, instead discussing something with the helmsman. Killigrew wondered which was the more repulsive, Madison's indifference or Coffin's enjoyment.

By glancing at Madison, Killigrew was mercifully spared from witnessing the end. There was a splash and a cheer, and when he glanced back Tristão's head had been bitten clean off at the neck. Blood gushed from the torso. Killigrew choked back the bile that rose to his gorge.

The corpse was brought in to the ship's side and cut loose. The sharks closed in and tore the body to pieces. Coffin indicated the pool of blood on the deck. 'Have that mess cleaned up,' he ordered Duarte.

'You see, few of my men try to thwart my will,' Madison told Killigrew. 'And no one does it more than once.'

'You should be careful,' Killigrew told him with a beguiling smile. 'There's a first time for everything.'

Madison's own smile did not falter, although he knitted his eyebrows. 'Not on this ship, Mr Killigrew.'

Killigrew knew he could not afford to look too shocked by what had happened so he remained on deck for a while, fighting the urge to go below and wash the taste of bile from his mouth. After about half an hour had passed, he went down to his cabin, stopping off at the ship's barometer to check the atmospheric pressure. It had dropped alarmingly in a short space of time.

'Looks like we're in for a storm,' he remarked to no one in particular.

XII:

Force Twelve

If Killigrew had had a farthing for every old sea dog who had told him that the sea was like a woman and needed to be respected by those that would earn their living from her, he would have had enough money to buy himself several pounds of sea salt. He could only presume that they had known some pretty frightening women. He had known plenty of women – and men, for that matter – whose wrath could be unnerving, but he had yet to meet the human being whose ire could even begin to match that of an angry sea. If Shakespeare had been right when he had claimed that Hell had no fury like a woman scorned, then Hell was an afternoon boating on the Thames on a sunny summer's day compared to a storm at sea.

He had endured cyclones in the Indian Ocean and typhoons in the China Seas, and the one thing his experience had taught him was that the sea did not care if you respected it: when it made up its mind to destroy you, you were going to go down whether you liked it or not.

But there were certain precautions one could take to stave off the worst, and as the sky became overcast and the wind backed from south-east to north the crew of the *Leopardo* battened down the hatches, cleared the decks, made fast everything that could be made fast, and took in all canvas except the foresail and the main topsail, both of which were close-reefed.

The wind hovered around ten knots – force three on the Beaufort scale, barely a moderate breeze – with a gentle swell running under the *Leopardo,* but it was the calm before the storm and Killigrew knew it could not last. 'What do you think?' Madison asked him and Coffin.

Killigrew knew that a seasoned mariner like Madison would already have made his mind up about what to do next, but was looking for confirmation. 'It looks like she's coming up out of the south-east,' he said. 'If we're not careful we'll get caught in the dangerous quadrant.' A tropical revolving storm in the northern hemisphere revolved anti-clockwise, and a ship caught in the dangerous quadrant was in danger of being blown into its path.

Coffin nodded without reluctance, his hatred and mistrust of Killigrew and everything to do with him held in abeyance in the face of the coming danger. 'There's a slim chance we might make it back to São Tiago, but I wouldn't risk it. Best we run with the weather and try to get on her good side. If she catches us all we can do is turn into the seas and hope for the best.'

Madison nodded. 'Steer south-west,' he told the helmsman. 'Better break out the oilskins,' he added to Duarte. 'When his bitch hits she's going to hit fast and heavy.'

Even though Killigrew was on the lookout for clues to the coming storm's ferocity, he was caught out by the abruptness with which the sky turned dark. All of a sudden leaden clouds boiled up out of the south-east, and the first spots of rain fell on the sea, fat drops which pattered heavily on the oilskins they all wore. The sky was so dark it might have been twilight, although it was barely five o'clock and at that time of year in those latitudes it should still have been bright. Then the wind hit them, snapping at the sails and driving the rain hard against their backs. The creaking of the timbers increased in pitch as the masts and spars laboured under the increased pressure, and the wind screamed through the thrumming rigging.

'Reduce sail,' ordered Coffin. 'Staysails only.'

The wind increased steadily over the next two hours while the sky grew blacker. The gravid clouds were so low it seemed as if one only had to shin to the very top of the mainmast and reach up to touch them. The *Leopardo* scudded along with the wind full behind her. At first the gentle swell seemed unaffected and the brig rode the waves easily, but by seven o'clock the seas increased in size and she started to pitch. Killigrew watched the compass and the dog-vane: when the wind started to come from due north he would know they were clear of the dangerous quadrant.

The wind whipped Killigrew's oilskins against his limbs and forced him to lean back into it to maintain his balance. The noise rose to an ear-splitting shriek for a while and then all at once fell to a low, eerie moaning, although its speed continued to rise: sixty knots gusting to ninety, force twelve – a hurricane.

'Furl those staysails!' Madison had to shout through his speaking trumpet to make himself heard above the wind. Killigrew was not the most imaginative of men, but even he could not help thinking it sounded like the souls of mariners drowned at sea singing a dirge for those soon to join them. As the hands struggled to furl the staysails, one of them was ripped from its fastenings and whipped out to sea. A stay slashed across the face of one of the topmen and he fell to the deck with a scream which was sharply cut short.

'Cut it loose!' Coffin roared to the men trying to furl the other staysail. They would lose that one too, but better that than lose the whole mast. The topmen gladly complied and climbed down from the rigging.

The man who had fallen to the deck was not dead. Duarte ordered two of the men to take him down below to Pereira in the sick bay, although what that gentleman was supposed to do for the seaman – whose back was clearly broken – was beyond Killigrew.

The seas rose to forty feet and started to break over the *Leopardo*'s stern. Killigrew braced himself as the water on the deck surged between his legs. It ran out through the scuppers, but not quickly enough for his liking. 'All hands to the bilge pump!' he ordered.

As the seas increased in height they came closer together, thus steepening between crest and trough. As each wave broke over the brig's stern she laboured to rise over the crest. As the waves passed under her she slipped easily down the back of the wave, her stern pounding the trough with a shudder which ran the whole length of the ship; then the next sea would break over her and they would go through it again, each time worse than the last. There was nothing they could do now but keep pumping out the bilges, hang on for dear life, and pray.

Forked lightning shattered the sky, like bright limelight behind cracked, black-painted glass, but the rumble of thunder was masked by the wind's ululating threnody. The gale blew the rain at such an angle it was impossible to tell where the rain ended and the spume began. Water foamed and boiled across the deck. After a while it did not even break, remaining grey as it slid waist-deep the length of the ship. Killigrew could only marvel that such a delicate vessel still floated under the onslaught, although he knew it was only a matter of time.

He began to consider the possibility of his imminent death. He found he could face it with an equanimity which surprised him. He felt a pang at the thought of never seeing Eulalia again in this world, but apart from that he had little to lose. He thought of the Chinese he had met, with their philosophy of 'joss': either he would survive the storm, or he wouldn't – it was as simple as that. There was little he could do about it and no point whatsoever in worrying: now his fate was in the hands of the gods.

The *Leopardo* was lifted on another crest and exposed to the full fury of the wind. It was like a living thing, full of rage and hatred and determined to sink this ship which defied its capricious will. It slammed into Killigrew's body and would have knocked him off his feet if he had not been gripping the rail tightly. He heard a shout behind him and turned his head, tears coming at once to his eyes as the wind stung them.

Coffin had raised his face to the black, lightning-slashed sky and shook his fist at it. As the brig slipped down into the next trough, sheltering them from the worst of the wind, Killigrew could just catch his words: 'Come on, you bastard! Do your worst! I'm ready for ye!'

'Don't you think that's rather asking for trouble?' Killigrew asked with a wan smile. But Coffin could not hear him above the noise.

Incredibly, conditions worsened. More incredibly, the *Leopardo* stayed afloat. But she could not take much more of this pounding. Killigrew remembered an old rhyme he had heard as a child from the fishermen of Falmouth: 'Long foretold, long last; short notice, soon past.' Experience had taught him there was truth in those words whether one encountered a storm off Lizard Point or a typhoon in the South China Sea. This tornado had risen quickly, yet after four hours it still showed no sign of abating.

His exposed skin was numb from exposure to the wind and spume and every limb in his body ached with the effort of simply remaining upright. Another wave lifted the *Leopardo* dizzyingly high – he would have said the waves were seventy feet from trough to crest if he had not known better – and then a sudden gust of

297

wind slammed into her like a giant fist. There came an horrendous crack like the firing of a sixty-eight-pounder. At first he thought it must have been the thunder, but then he realised that thunder would not have made the deck shiver so.

He looked at the foremast and saw it topple. It was snapped clean through close to the deck. It pitched forward as the next wave lifted the brig's stern, and would have toppled had not the rigging held it upright. When they reached the crest, the full weight of the wind hit the mast once again, and the braces attaching it to the mainmast made the latter bend perceptibly.

Killigrew pointed to the masts and had to cup his hands over Coffin's ear to make himself understood. 'If we don't cut it free we'll lose the mainmast as well!'

Coffin nodded and the two of them at once went forward to the mainmast. It was at moments like this that one could understand what the brotherhood of the sea was all about: Killigrew might secretly despise Coffin as a slaver, while Coffin openly detested him as an Englishman, but the two of them were instantly ready to put their differences aside and work together to save the ship; their lives depended upon it.

They hauled themselves hand over hand along the rail as the seas crashed over the deck. Killigrew indicated the stays which ran from the top of the mast down to the dead-eyes on the starboard gunwale, and made a slicing motion with the edge of his hand. If they cut the starboard forestays and timed it with the pitching

298

of the deck then the mast would topple forward and sideways overboard. That was the theory, at any rate.

Coffin shook his head firmly and pointed up to the braces which ran between the foremast and the mainmast. The important thing was to cut those first; but it would be impossible to cut them without ascending the rigging.

Killigrew nodded, jerked a thumb at his chest, and then pointed up into the shrouds.

'You're crazy!' bellowed Coffin.

'Got any better suggestions?' Killigrew yelled back.

'You'll never make it! You'll be killed!'

'Then you'll be happy, at least.' Killigrew gazed up into the shrouds once more. Coffin was right: he *was* crazy. Still, it was a sensible exchange: one life for two dozen.

One honest man for the life of two dozen slavers, he reminded himself. *If you're going to die, wouldn't it be better to take the bastards with you?* Was it his place to judge these people? Surely that was the Lord's decision. But he had taken that decision into his own hands when he had executed da Silva. Perhaps this storm was God's way of punishing him. *One murderer and two dozen blackbirders,* Killigrew told himself. No wonder God wanted this ship sunk with all hands. *Watch it, Kit my bucko: you've been spending too much time with Madison you're starting to think like him. You've never been a Jonah before now, and this is hardly the time to start!* He found himself grinning as some of the defiance Coffin had expressed earlier infected him with its violent energy.

'Come on, then!' he roared at the heavens. 'Take me, if you want me!'

And with that he hauled himself up into the ratlines.

He ascended a step at a time. It seemed to take all of his strength just to cling to the sodden rigging, never mind to pull himself up at the same time. The rain hammered him and the wind sought to tear him away. He was glad it was so dark, for he could hardly see the mountainous seas around him and the deck pitching below; occasionally a flash of lightning would pick out the white caps of the wave crests, but Killigrew had enough to do without worrying about that.

The mainmast creaked threateningly. It was the only thing keeping the foremast up, and soon it too must snap. Killigrew forced himself to climb faster, throwing caution – literally – to the howling winds. The rain soaked clean through his oilskins and seemed to slice into the skin underneath.

Before he realised it, he had reached the doubling where the topmast reached the top-gallant mast. Up here the wind was even stronger. He lost his footing and slipped, dangling from his arms. The strength of the wind seemed to make gravity irrelevant: everything span around him and he no longer knew which way was down. The wind blew him forward at an angle, and nothing he could do would get his feet back on to the ratlines. He thought about pulling himself across the shrouds hand-over-hand, but knew that as soon as he released the grip of one hand, the other would be broken by the strength of the wind.

Then the *Leopardo* sank into another trough and the mast swung backwards, swinging Killigrew with it until he could entangle his legs in the ratlines once more. *Just a few more inches,* he told himself. He climbed up: one step, two, and then he could see the brace less than a foot away through the stinging rain.

He wrapped both legs and arms around the shrouds, clinging on with all his might, then eased a hand into his pocket and took out his clasp knife. *Whatever you do, don't drop it,* he thought to himself with a grim smile. The rain was like a thousand white-hot needles against his flesh and his hands were so numb he could barely open the knife. But at last the blade snapped into view. He reached across with one hand and started to saw at the thick rope which ran from the mainmast to the foremast. The blade was razor sharp and quickly parted the strands. It was hard work nonetheless, and it seemed to take for ever before the weight of the foremast was enough to break the strands which remained. There was a snap like a pistol-shot and the rope snaked away into the night.

Killigrew closed the knife and began to descend, grateful for every step with took him a foot nearer to the safety of the deck. Only one other brace ran between the foremast and the mainmast, where the topmast met the lower mast. He swung himself underneath the ratlines and lowered himself to the maintop. He missed his footing in the darkness and the wind, and his sea-boots slipped on the rain-washed planks. He scrabbled desperately at the boards, his numbed fingers searching for a grip. He felt his feet slip out over the leading edge, then his calves and his knees, and then he had hooked one arm around the mast itself. Half dangling over the edge, he braced himself where the mast itself afforded him some protection from the murderous wind.

He risked a glance down to the deck. He could just make out pale faces staring up at him, while the deck itself was awash with soaking waters which sloshed between the bulwarks. Each time a wave broke over the *Leopardo*'s stern the faces would be buried beneath a maelstrom of white water, but they were still there when the waters receded. Coffin was at the foot of the starboard forestays, already hacking through them with a hatchet.

Killigrew took out his clasp knife once more and reached down towards the brace with the blade. His arm was just an inch too short. He withdrew it and altered his grip on the haft of the knife so that he held it between his fingertips. That way he found he could reach the rope, but the amount of pressure he could apply was negligible. The strands parted, but slowly, far too slowly.

The rope snapped so suddenly that Killigrew lost his grip on his knife and it was whipped away into the darkness. Coffin had hacked through the forestays and as the ship was lifted on another wave the foremast toppled forwards and then swung sideways as the port-side forestays took up the strain. There were still plenty of braces running from the foremast to the bowsprit, but

Killigrew could not cut those in time and could only hope that they snapped. There was a chance the bowsprit itself would be ripped away, but better that than losing the mainmast.

The foremast crashed into the sea and was swallowed up by the blackness at once. Coffin lunged through the knee-deep water on deck to hack at the port-side forestays which still attached the mast to the ship's side. A moment later there was a great crack as the jib-boom snapped off the bowsprit, and then the last of the ropes snapped and the danger from that quarter was gone.

Killigrew descended to the deck feeling shaken and used-up. He crossed to where Coffin hacked through the last of the forestays, but the job was done by the time he got there. Coffin did not even acknowledge him.

As the brig descended stern-first into the next trough Killigrew turned aft and then froze in horror.

A rogue wave rose up behind them, towering, mountainous. An immense wall of water a hundred feet tall if it was an inch. Such a wave could not support its own weight and Killigrew saw foam at its peak as it began to topple forward on to the poop deck. Either it would snap the ship clean in two or else flip it stern over bows: either event signalled the death of the *Leopardo*.

'Hold on!' he yelled as the vast breaker tumbled down towards the brig's stern like the jaws of some vast leviathan of the deep closing on its prey. He felt the whole ship shudder and pitch crazily as hundreds of thousands of gallons of water slammed on to the poop. The deck fell away sickeningly from beneath him and he went over backwards, splashing into the knee-deep water. Still the breaker descended, a vast wall of cascading water eating its way up the length of the deck from stern to stem.

Towards Killigrew. Floundering, he rolled on to his front and half crawled, half doggy-paddled towards the stump of the foremast. He threw his arms around it, took a deep breath, and then the water crashed down on him. The weight of water drove the breath from his body and seemed intent on pushing him clean through the deck. It was strangely silent beneath the water after the howling of the wind and the crashing of the waves.

The pressure on his back slowly receded, and then the waters surged about him, transferring the weight to his arms and shoulders as the flood tried to drag him away from the mast-stump. Even if he had been at full strength he could not have hoped to resist that pressure; as it was, his trip into the rigging had left him hopelessly drained. His arms gave way and the water swirled him away: up, down, sideways, it was impossible to tell. Something heavy slammed against him, and then a fresh surge of water span him through its inky depths.

He thought about swimming towards the surface, but dismissed the idea as nonsensical: he did not even know which way the surface lay. There was nothing he could do but enjoy the strange feeling of peace which filled him as the water swept him where it would. Was he drowning? Probably. He had always supposed that one day it would come to this, but he had never thought it would happen this early in his career. There had been so much he wanted to do with his life, so many battles left unfought, it seemed a shame it should all come to an end now. Others would remain to fight those battles, of course, but he was not sure he could trust them to do the job properly. And then there was Eulalia waiting for him in London...

Something else slammed against him, and he clung to it instinctively, just as he clung on to his life by holding on to what little breath remained in his lungs. The water tried to pull him away again, but with less determination now. Then a roaring filled his ears. At first he thought it must be the blood roaring in his head as he died, but then he realised it was just the turbulence of the storm-tossed waves.

A moment later whatever he clung to broke the surface, and Killigrew surfaced with it. The wind, rain and spindrift stung his face and he gulped air into his lungs.

He was clinging to the rails of the head. By a miracle, he was still alive. By an even greater one, the *Leopardo* was still intact and afloat. Shaking his head to clear the rain and hair out of his eyes, he saw other members of the crew on deck looking about them with wonderment as if astonished to find that they still lived, and he shared in that wonderment.

'Man overboard!' boomed Duarte.

No rest for the wicked. Killigrew pushed himself to his feet and crossed to where the boatswain stood at the rail, pointing out into the inky blackness beyond. Killigrew could just make out a figure floating level with the storm-tossed ship, perhaps thirty yards from the side. At that distance his face was no more than a white blur, but Killigrew somehow sensed that it was Coffin. If he had thought about it he would have left the chief mate to drown. Not even Madison could have blamed him for doing nothing after all he had already been through, and trying to save the chief mate was suicide anyway. But there was no time to think. He quickly unwound a coil of rope which had been wrapped tightly around a belaying pin. He gave one end to Duarte and tied the other around his waist.

'Make that fast!' he snapped at Duarte, and then jumped overboard thinking: *There's trust for you.*

His narrow escape from the rogue wave had filled him with a sense of exhilaration, as if part of him had got the impression he was indestructible. He knew the idea was false, and yet somehow it filled him with renewed strength. He started to swim out with a strong, easy crawl-stroke to where Coffin struggled in the water. But his strength had deceived him and quickly gave out. *Just a few more feet*, he thought, as his exhaustion caught up with him.

He reached Coffin as the chief mate was going down for the third time. Killigrew caught him underneath the chin and dragged him back to the surface. It was all he could do to float on his back supporting Coffin. Then the rope around his chest tugged against him and he realised that the muscular boatswain was hauling them both back to the ship.

'You'll die when I decide it, and not before,' he heard someone snarl at Coffin, and it was only by process of deduction he realised it must have been himself. If the half drowned chief mate heard him, he gave no indication of it.

Then they bumped against the *Leopardo*'s side and strong arms hauled them both over the bulwark. The storm seemed to have abated a little. Killigrew hoped it was over now, rather than a temporary lull. Coffin sprawled on the deck, vomited sea water, and lay still.

'Is he dead?' asked Madison.

Duarte put an ear to Coffin's chest, and then shook his head. 'He lives.' The brawny boatswain lifted Coffin in his arms and carried him almost tenderly below deck to the sick bay. Killigrew followed.

Pereira looked distinctly seasick in the dim glow of the oil lamp which swung wildly from an overhead beam. There was only one cot in the sick bay, and it was already occupied by the man who had fallen from the rigging earlier. But from the way Pereira had pulled the sheets up to hide the man's face he was no longer in need of a comfortable bed. Killigrew hoisted him out unceremoniously and Duarte lay Coffin in his place.

Before Pereira could do anything, a spasm shook Coffin's body and he leaned over the side of the cot to fetch up more sea water. Gasping for breath, he looked up at the boatswain. 'What happened?'

'You were washed overboard,' said Duarte. 'Senhor Killigrew saved you.'

Coffin glanced across at him. If Killigrew had expected gratitude he was disappointed, but even he was stunned by the look of sheer venom in Coffin's eyes, as if the chief mate would have preferred to have been left to drown. Then Coffin turned his eyes on Pereira. 'Brandy,' he gasped.

'I have none,' said Pereira.

'There's a bottle of *aguadiente* in Madison's cabin,' said Coffin.

'I'll fetch it,' offered Killigrew.

As he made his way aft below decks he thought about Coffin's reaction on hearing who had saved him, and began to understand it. How hateful it must have been to a confirmed anglophobe like Coffin to owe his life to an Englishman! The thought afforded Killigrew a small modicum of amusement, but it was short lived. He remembered how the Chinese believed that if one saved a man's life, one was responsible for that man for the rest of his existence; a very Chinese logic, but a kind of logic nonetheless. Any atrocity Coffin committed from now on would lie on Killigrew's head. It was a thought which filled him with a distinct feeling of unease.

He went into Madison's day cabin. Despite the tarpaulin which had been stretched over the skylight in the deck head, the glass had shattered under the pressure of the waves and now lay in shards all over the floor, while water dripped steadily from above. In spite of this, the shutters which protected the windows were still in place, and the oil still burned in the lantern which swung from an overhead beam, casting eerie, swaying shadows across the scene.

By some miracle the bottle of *aguadiente* in a drawer of Madison's desk had not been broken. Killigrew took it out and pulled out the stopper, pouring a generous and – in his opinion – well-earned measure down his throat. He gasped with pleasure as the fiery liquid burned its way down to his stomach.

So much had happened during the past few hours that he had forgotten he was on board the *Leopardo* for a specific purpose, and it was only in that instant he remembered it. This was the opportunity he had been looking for from the moment he had joined the crew. He went to the door and glanced out. Seeing no one, he closed the door and went to work.

He carefully searched the other desk drawers, taking care not to drip water on to the papers within, but found nothing to indicate who the financier behind this slaver was. Then he turned his attention to the safe. It was locked, of course, and the key was doubtless on Madison's person. Killigrew did not know anything about picking locks, but there was no harm in inserting the key to his own sea-chest to see if that fitted: it would only take a couple of seconds.

But a couple of seconds can mean the difference between life and death. Just as he was trying to withdraw the key, having failed in his attempt, the cabin door opened and Duarte's massive bulk filled the frame.

XIII:

Flotsam

'So!' snarled Duarte. 'Senhor Coffin was right about you! You *are* a spy!' He quickly pulled his pistol from its holster. 'No tricks. Keep you hands where I can see them.'

'Certainly.' Killigrew raised his hands.

Duarte crossed the cabin and came around the desk, keeping his pistol on Killigrew the whole time. He gestured for Killigrew to back away from the desk. 'There's a perfectly good explanation for all this,' said Killigrew. 'But I'm sure it will sound better coming from your lips, Captain Madison,' he added, with a nod of acknowledgement towards the door.

Duarte only half-turned before he realised he had been tricked, but it was all the time Killigrew needed. He snatched the bottle of *aguadiente* from the top of the safe and smashed it over Duarte's head.

The boatswain straightened and turned away from the desk, the liquor running down his face. He levelled the pistol between Killigrew's eyes and pulled the trigger.

Killigrew did not even flinch. 'I've yet to see the pistol that still worked after the kind of drenching we've both had.'

Duarte threw the pistol at his head. Killigrew

ducked and then lunged at the boatswain's throat with the jagged remains of the bottle. Duarte knocked his arm aside with one hand and drove his other into Killigrew's stomach.

It was like being butted by a charging bull. Killigrew doubled up in agony. Then Duarte caught him by the arm and dashed his wrist against the side of the safe. Killigrew dropped the broken bottle. Duarte lifted his knee into his face, smashing his head back against the safe door.

Killigrew slumped to the deck. Duarte reached down and seized him by the lapels, lifting him to his feet once more. The boatswain was bigger and stronger than Killigrew and furthermore he had not spent the past hour climbing about the rigging in a force-twelve hurricane, or swimming in tempest-tossed seas. Killigrew knew that if he was going to survive this encounter then he was going to have to kill Duarte as quickly as possible, while his little remaining strength held out.

He drove one fist into the boatswain's stomach with all his might, and then the other. Duarte grunted, and then hoisted Killigrew's feet clean off the deck, swinging him around and slamming him against the far bulkhead. Killigrew punched him on the jaw, snapping his head around, but when it came back to face the young Cornishman it was still smiling. Duarte punched him in the stomach again, following it up with a hammer-like blow to the back of the neck as he doubled up.

Barely conscious, Killigrew fell face down on

the deck and tried to crawl away. Duarte stood over him and rolled him on his back before wrapping his massive hands around Killigrew's throat, squeezing.

Killigrew felt himself choking. He flailed wildly at the boatswain's torso, but it was like trying to dig a tunnel through a mountainside with his fists. His vision swam and he felt himself suffocating as Duarte increased the pressure on his windpipe.

A red mist filled Killigrew's eyes. He fumbled blindly about him on the deck for something he could use as a weapon, anything. His searching fingers found the pistol. He gripped it by the butt and thumbed back the hammer.

Duarte laughed. 'That won't do you any good, *inglese*. Wet powder, remember?'

Killigrew brought the pistol up between Duarte's legs with his final reserves of strength until it slammed hard against the boatswain's crotch. Then he pulled the trigger. The hammer fell and Duarte screamed in agony. He released Killigrew and the Englishman broke away and pulled himself to his feet.

He snatched up a chair and brought it down against Duarte's head. It was the boatswain's neck rather than the sturdy chair which snapped, silencing his screams.

Killigrew quickly closed the door and prayed that the noise of the storm had muffled the sounds of the struggle from the rest of the ship. If it had not, he was a dead man. But if he did not move quickly he was a dead man anyway. He opened the windows at the rear of the cabin. In the flashes of lightning he could see that the seas were still mountainous; no sooner had he opened the shutters behind the window than a wave crashed against the stern, drenching him.

He picked up Duarte and dragged him across to the window. It was almost impossible to fit him through. 'Why the devil couldn't I have got into a fight with Pereira?' he wondered out loud. He gave a final push and the corpse popped out like a cork out of a champagne bottle to be swallowed up by the sea.

Killigrew closed the shutters and the windows behind them, turning to survey the cabin. It was a mess, but no more than could be accounted for by storm damage. Ditto his own face, which he supposed was no oil painting after the beating Duarte had given it. An inch of water sloshed about his feet; Killigrew could only pray it would be put down to the water dripping through the tarpaulin over the smashed skylight.

He adjusted his neckcloth and returned to the sick bay. 'What happened to you?' asked Pereira, wide-eyed.

'I slipped and fell in the dark as the ship lurched,' Killigrew explained glibly. 'Where's Mr Coffin?'

'He went back on duty. Said the ship needed him.'

'The same goes for me.'

Killigrew went back on deck and found Madison and Coffin standing on the quarter-deck. Lightning still flashed in the heavens, but further away now, and the wind had died down to a shriek. Killigrew checked the compass and the dog-vane to make sure they were not in the eye of the storm; if they were, then the worst was yet to come. To his relief he saw they still headed south-west while the wind came steadily off the starboard beam: they were out of danger and putting distance between them and the tornado with every passing minute.

'What happened to you?' grunted Coffin.

'Slipped and fell,' said Killigrew.

'Holding the bottle of *aguadiente*, I suppose, since you haven't brought it with you.'

Killigrew nodded. 'I'm afraid the cabin's rather a mess. That rogue wave must have smashed in the skylight. There's glass and water all over the place.'

'We can clean up in the morning,' said Madison. 'Where's Mr Duarte?'

'I don't know. I left him with Mr Coffin in the sick bay.'

Madison glanced at Coffin, who shook his head. 'He went out after Killigrew.'

'He's probably somewhere down below,' said Madison.

'I'm sure you're right,' agreed Killigrew.

'*Coisa* ho!' cried the lookout at the masthead.

Coisa, coisa ... what the devil is a "*coisa*"?' Madison demanded irritably.

'It's Portuguese for "thing",' offered Killigrew.

'I'm aware of that, Mr Killigrew,' Madison said irritably. 'What I meant was, what kind of a "*coisa*" is he referring to?'

'Let's find out, shall we?' Killigrew tilted back his head to call up to the lookout. 'Where away?'

'Fine on the port bow!'

Madison, Coffin and Killigrew levelled their telescopes in that direction and searched the horizon for the unidentified floating object, but saw nothing. 'Has the fool been drinking?' wondered Madison.

It was the morning after the storm. The sky was clear and the air fresh, the waves choppy. The dawn had revealed the full damage to the *Leopardo:* both to the ship itself and to its crew. In addition to the man who had been killed in his plunge to the deck, three men were missing presumed swept overboard, Duarte included. Now the crew were hard at work trying to jury-rig the spars and rigging to compensate for the loss of the foremast and the jib-boom. With her spread of canvas thus reduced, the *Leopardo* was making poor speed as she resumed her south-westerly run to the Guinea Coast. Now she responded sluggishly to her helm and was almost impossible to steer. Madison would have given anything to have lost the mainmast rather than the foremast, but it had been the storm's decision, not his, and there was nothing for it but to make the best of a bad job. In addition, the storm had sprung several timbers, and while the carpenter and sailmaker laboured to plug the gaps other crewmen worked at the bilge pumps.

Killigrew realised he was making the mistake of looking for a ship, which in those conditions would have been visible the moment its sail rose above the horizon if the lookout were attentive. But the lookout had not cried 'sail ho!' but *'coisa ho!'* Killigrew lowered his telescope accordingly, looking for something smaller. He found it almost at once.

'It's a mast.'

'Ours?' asked Madison.

'If it is, it's acquired some extra appurtenances.' There were three figures clinging to the floating mast. Somehow Killigrew doubted they were the men missing from the *Leopardo*'s crew, unless Duarte had been blackballed from entry to Davy Jones's locker.

'Castaways,' said Madison. 'From some other ship that foundered in last night's storm, I suppose.'

'We should leave them,' said Coffin. 'The last thing we want is strangers sniffing around on board. We've already got one of those,' he added, 'and as far as I'm concerned that's one too many.'

Madison said nothing, chewing over Coffin's proposal as if giving it serious consideration. The suggestion was anathema to Killigrew. If the castaways were left to their fate their chances of survival would be non-existent that far out from the coast, and Killigrew had been brought up to believe it was the duty of every seaman to go to the help of those in peril on the sea regardless of all other considerations. But he was not sure a slave crew would operate under the same strictures.

'We can't leave them to die,' he said. 'It would be damned unchristian of us.'

Madison nodded reluctantly. 'Mr Killigrew's right, Eli. We can't be like the priest and the Levite and pass on by. Matthew, chapter seven, verse twelve: "Therefore all things whatsoever ye

316

would that men should do to you, do ye even so to them: for this is the law and the prophets.'"

'And what if they find out we're blackbirders?' demanded Coffin. 'As soon as we put them ashore we'll have every navy vessel on the coast searching for us.'

'Then we'll have to make sure they don't find out, won't we?' Madison said crisply, and turned to the crewman he had appointed boatswain in Duarte's place. 'Lower the jolly boat, Mr Covilhã. We'll have that mast, too, to replace the one we lost last night. We'll drop them off a few miles down the coast from Freetown, within easy walking distance of one of the settlements but not close enough to excite the attention of any navy vessels in the harbour there.'

As the jolly boat picked up the castaways, Killigrew was aware that for them it was a case of out of the frying pan and into the fire. He was beginning to understand Madison's warped idea of morality: while the slave captain would pick up castaways out of Christian charity, he would not hesitate to have them murdered later if that was the best way to protect his own interests. But with any luck it would not come to that.

As the *Leopardo* hove to alongside the floating mast the jolly boat bumped against the brig's side. There was a stir on deck as the hands gathered around the rail to help the three castaways over the bulwark, in particular the one that was female and pretty. They gathered around her, grinning inanely and knuckling their foreheads. But Killigrew was more concerned about the man who was barely conscious and had

317

to be lifted over the rail. He seemed to be delirious, babbling away in a daze, quite oblivious to what was going on around him.

As the man was laid on the deck, Killigrew crouched over him. The man was in his late twenties, fair-haired, his smooth, pink face sunburned and now salt-blistered. He wore a dog collar.

The woman pushed her way through the crowd of sailors around her and Killigrew was aware of the hem of her dress at the edge of his vision, but he was too busy trying to ascertain what was wrong with the man to look up at her. 'Oh, you will take care of my brother, won't you, sir?' she asked. Like her brother, she spoke with a distinct American accent. *More damned Yankees,* thought Killigrew.

'We'll do our best, ma'am,' he said. 'What happened to him?'

'He got hit on the back of the head by a … by one of those things as our ship went down.'

Killigrew was finally forced to glance up at her. That she was the delirious man's sister there could be no doubting, but the features looked better on her than they did on him, for all that her lips were blistered, her eyes gummed with sea salt, and her blonde hair straggled wetly across her shoulders.

She was pointing to a block and tackle in the ship's rigging. Killigrew nodded. 'That's a block, ma'am.'

'It's "miss", not "ma'am",' she told him.

'Pleased to meet you, miss, though I wish it could be under more fortuitous circumstances.

318

My name's Killigrew, by the way. Kit Killigrew.'

'We're just glad that your ship came along when it did,' said the woman. 'This is my brother, the Reverend Chance.'

'Which would make you...'

She nodded with a grimace. 'Miss Chance. No jokes, please. Believe me, Captain Killigrew, I've heard them all.'

He found himself warming to her at once. 'Then I'll have to see if I can surprise you. And it's just "mister", I'm afraid, not "captain". Captain Madison over there is the master of this vessel,' he explained, pointing to where Madison stood on the quarter-deck with Coffin. Both of them were avoiding the castaways, perhaps fearing that their faces might be identified later.

He turned to the nearest sailor. 'Carry the reverend down to the sick bay. Miss Chance, you and your friend here...'

The third castaway tugged his forelock. 'Donohoe, sir, Able Seaman Clem Donohoe,' he announced in an Irish brogue.

'One-time navy?' Killigrew asked him.

'As is yourself, sir, unless I'm very much mistaken.'

The presence of an able seaman who had served on one of Her Majesty's ships was a reassurance to Killigrew, a potential ally if things turned nasty. 'Very well, Able Seaman Donohoe. You go below with Miss Chance here so the quack can make sure you're both all right. I'll have some hot food brought to you.'

As the three castaways were taken below, Killigrew turned to Doc. 'Some hot broth,

Mas'er Killigrew?' suggested the cook.

'Good idea, Doc.'

As the cook made his way to the galley, Killigrew crossed to where Madison and Coffin waited. 'Well?' demanded Madison.

'Well what?'

'What did you find out?'

'The clergyman and the woman are brother and sister...'

'We saw that much for ourselves,' sneered Coffin.

'The reverend received a blow to the head when their ship went down. He looks like he might be in a bad way. Their names are the Reverend and Miss Chance.'

'Miss Chance!' guffawed Coffin. 'It was sure as hell a mischance that brought them on board *this* vessel.'

Killigrew smiled thinly. 'Yes, well, if I were you I should avoid making that joke in her presence. I got the feeling she might not see the humorous side of it.'

'What about the other one?' Madison demanded impatiently.

'His name's Donohoe. An Irishman – from County Cork, unless I'm mistaken. He's served in the navy.'

'Another goddamn Limey tar,' muttered Coffin.

Madison half-turned towards his chief mate. 'Haven't you got duties to be seeing to, Mr Coffin? Like getting that mast lashed up in place of the one we lost?'

'Aye, aye, Cap'n.' Coffin headed forward with

a crooked grin.

'You were saying about this Donohoe fellow?' Madison asked Killigrew.

Killigrew shrugged. 'I suppose he was a sailor on board their ship.'

'Which was?' asked Madison.

'I didn't enquire. They've all been through an unpleasant ordeal and I thought the first priority was to make them comfortable.'

'Quite right, of course, Mr Killigrew. All the same, I'd feel a good deal happier if I knew a little bit more about them before I put them ashore.'

'I'm sure they don't represent any kind of threat—'

'I'm sure they don't intend to,' Madison cut in firmly. 'But of all the captains in the slave trade today, no one's got a longer record of avoiding capture than me, and that's because I take precautions. Find out more, Mr Killigrew.'

'Aye, aye, sir.'

'You seem to have a talent for … shall we say social chit-chat? Putting on a polite face for the gentry?'

'My grandfather made sure I was brought up correctly, if that's what you mean.'

Madison gestured dismissively. 'Whatever you want to call it. It was your suggestion that we pick them up instead of leaving them to their fate. I'm making you responsible for them. I'll tell Mr Covilhã to have the men watch what they say when our "guests" are around. And I don't want them sniffing around the hold, understood? They go in the sick bay, the officers' accommodation or on deck, but nowhere else. If the reverend is indisposed he'd best stay in the sick bay, and I suppose Mr Donohoe had better sleep with the other lads. Miss Chance can have my cabin.'

'And where will you sleep, sir?'

'I'll have your bunk, Mr Killigrew. You can bunk up with Pereira.'

'What a delightful thought,' Killigrew said drily.

'And Killigrew?'

'Sir?'

'I guess Miss Chance might scrub-up real pretty. But I don't want you trying to take advantage of her, you understand? Treat her with respect.'

Killigrew bridled. 'You forget. I used to be an officer and a gentleman.'

'I forget nothing. "Used to be" is right.'

Killigrew made his way down below. Half a dozen sailors crowded around the entrance to the sick bay. It was the first time any of them had seen a woman since they left Liverpool, Madison having made sure that few of them left the ship at São Tiago and none of them had left the dockside. 'Haven't you men got work to do?' snapped Killigrew. 'Mr Coffin could do with a hand lashing up the new mast.'

'*Sim*, Senhor Killigrew.' The men scurried away and Killigrew slipped into the sick bay. Pereira was examining the back of Reverend Chance's head while Miss Chance sat on the chair, a rough blanket thrown around her shoulders. Donohoe sat near her on the floor. If the *Leopardo* was poorly equipped with medical facilities, it was infinitely better than other slavers Killigrew had encountered, most of which did not even carry a surgeon on their books in order to save on expense.

'How is he?' Killigrew asked Pereira in Portuguese.

'Not good. He has a bad concussion, and fever too perhaps. I have given him a little laudanum to help him rest.'

'Is he going to be all right?' Miss Chance asked in English.

'The surgeon's doing his best for him,' said Killigrew, and she nodded. 'How about you two?'

'I'm fine,' she said. 'Well, still a little shaky maybe. I was ready to commend our souls unto God just before this ship turned up.'

'Didn't I tell you we'd be fine?' said Donohoe.

'How about you, Mr Donohoe?' asked Killigrew.

'Oh, I'll be right as rain, Mr Killigrew, sir. I've been shipwrecked before. It'll take more than a few big waves to be putting an end to Clem Donohoe.'

'Were there many others on board your ship?'

'Seventeen of us in the crew, all told.' Donohoe smiled wanly, although he was obviously upset at the thought he would never see his shipmates again. 'The reverend father and Miss Chance here were our only passengers. I think maybe some of the others managed to get into one of the boats, but when she foundered she went down so fast…' He let the sentence trail off and gestured helplessly, hopelessly.

'Which ship was it?'

'The *Belinda Lovelace*, out of New York. Bound for Sherbro Island with supplies and mail.'

'My brother and I were on our way to join the American Mission there,' explained Miss Chance.

Killigrew nodded. He knew Sherbro Island, or at least he had seen it a few times: a large island immediately off the Guinea Coast. It was there that the slaves who had revolted against their captors on board the *La Amistad* had settled after their trial in the United States had cleared them of the charges of mutiny and murder a few years earlier. Many of them had become Christians during their incarceration in the States, and they had helped the newly formed American Missionary Association set up the Mende Mission at Komende on the island.

'I'll see if I can persuade Captain Madison to drop you off there. It's on our way.' As a matter of fact the course Madison had plotted – which had yet to be completed – trailed off immediately to the west of Sherbro Island, and Killigrew knew that Madison would be far happier to drop off his passengers at a Christian mission than he would at a British Crown Colony and naval base.

Doc turned up with three bowls of steaming broth on a tray and handed two to Donohoe and Miss Chance. 'What about him?' he asked, nodding at the recumbent reverend.

'He'll be asleep for a few hours,' said Pereira, taking the third bowl for himself. 'A pity to let it go to waste. You can make him another bowl when he awakes.'

'Doc, could you fetch our guests some dry clothes from the purser's slops?' suggested Killigrew, and the cook nodded and went out. 'If you two are both comfortable, I'll leave you to Senhor Pereira here.'

'About accommodation…' said Donohoe.

'That's been arranged,' said Killigrew, and filled them in on the arrangements.

'I'm sorry if we're an imposition,' said Miss Chance.

'Don't be ridiculous,' Killigrew told her with a smile.

He reported to Madison in his day cabin. The captain was already packing up his things to make room for Miss Chance. 'Well?' he grunted.

Killigrew related the gist of his conversation with Donohoe and Miss Chance, and Madison nodded. 'We'll make better time once Mr Coffin gets the new mast in place. We should be within sight of Sherbro Island in just over a week if all goes according to plan. You'd better get some rest now. I want you to take the middle watch tonight.'

'Jesus!' Killigrew gasped when he came up on deck to take over from Madison as officer of the watch.

Madison grinned, his face turned into a ghastly devil's mask by the phosphorescence of the sea which cast its hideous glow over the ship. 'You never seen this before, Mr Killigrew?'

'After three years on the West Africa Station? But it still gives me the creeps.'

Above the sky was as black as the Earl of Hell's waistcoat, without a star to be seen in the heavens. A few lanterns swung above deck. But their illumination was hardly needed: the whole sea was aglow with phosphorescence, from horizon to horizon, a bright, eye-searing pale green. It looked as if they were sailing through a sea of fire.

'Revelation, chapter fifteen, verse two: "And I saw as it were a sea of glass mingled with fire".'

Killigrew nodded. 'No wonder the ancients believed that a belt of flame circumscribed their world.'

'I'll bid you goodnight, Mr Killigrew. See you in the forenoon.' Madison went below.

Killigrew was left alone on deck with the helmsman and the look-outs. Apart from the hideous glow of the sea, all was well: a strong breeze blew from the south-west, carrying the *Leopardo* towards her destination on a starboard tack. Despite the jury-rigged foremast, the vessel rode easily on the broad swell of the ocean.

Miss Chance emerged from the aft hatch. When she saw Killigrew she smiled at him, but knitted her brow at the peculiar quality of the light. As soon as she was fully out of the hatch she saw the sea and her expression changed to one of wonderment.

She crossed to where he stood, treading carefully on the deck as if she feared that the ship might vanish from beneath her and plunge her into the glowing sea. She was dressed in clothes from the purser's slops, outsized and baggy on her slight figure, making her look even smaller and more vulnerable. She had somehow managed to wash her hair, and while she had been unable to have it properly coiffed, it spilled across her shoulders in a way which was natural and attractive.

'Am I dreaming?' she asked him.

He shook his head. 'Phosphorescence, miss. It looks eerie, I'll grant you, but it's common enough and quite harmless.'

They leaned against the rail, side by side, and stared down to where the ship seemed to strike veins of glowing gold from the green-tinged light. 'What causes it?' she asked.

'I've no idea. To tell you the truth, I don't want to.'

'Because you might fear the explanation?'

Smiling, he shook his head. 'The only thing I fear about the explanation is that it will prove to be perfectly banal and ruin the magic of it. How is your brother?'

Her face fell. 'Feverish. I'm afraid the blow to the head he received may have permanently addled his brains. Is ... what kind of surgeon is Mr Pereira? I mean, is he a good one?'

'He's no better nor worse than any surgeon you'll find on a ship like this,' said Killigrew, meaning he was neither better nor worse than having no surgeon at all.

'What kind of ship is this, exactly?'

'A merchantman. Trading manufactured goods to the Guinea Coast in return for palm oil.' He felt more uncomfortable lying to her about the purpose of their voyage than he did lying to Madison about his motives, but it was for her own safety.

'An American master and chief mate, an English second mate, and the rest of the crew Spanish or Portuguese,' she mused. 'Are all merchantmen as cosmopolitan as this, Mr Killigrew?'

327

He shrugged. 'It's not uncommon amongst merchantmen, or even navy vessels. A ship may be registered in one country and owned by a merchant in another, but the men aboard her don't much trouble themselves what flag they serve under. If they loved their countries so much, they'd've stayed in them instead of running away to sea. Unless they've been shanghaied, of course, but all the hands aboard this vessel are willing enough.'

'Why did *you* run away to sea, Mr Killigrew?'

He chuckled. 'With my family background, running away would have meant staying on shore. The Killigrews have been making a living from the sea since the fifteenth century. What about you, miss? What brings you so far from home?'

'I just want to help our black brethren, that's all. William – my brother – was the first to get involved in the Missionary Association, but I've always supported him in everything he's done.'

'Wouldn't you rather have a life of your own? Or is that an impertinent question?'

She shook her head. 'This is the only way I can have a life of my own. If I stayed in America my folks would press me to marry, and then I'd have to subsume my life into that of my husband. At least this way I get some choice of my own. And the condition of the Africans is something I care about passionately.'

'Ah, yes. Converting our heathen brethren to the path of righteousness.'

'From your tone I take it you do not approve?'

'I've not had much experience of the effects of

missionary activity in Africa. In Guinea there's so much tribal warfare it's impossible to tell how much is caused by missionaries and how much is caused by the economic demand for prisoners of war.'

'The economic demand for prisoners of war? Is there one?'

'Slaves, miss.'

'Oh, of course. You seem to think that all of Africa's problems are caused by whites.'

'I wouldn't go that far. But Africa has more problems caused by Europeans and Americans than Europe and America have problems caused by Africans.'

'But surely you can't approve of the Africans living in unenlightened ignorance?'

'What you call ignorance is subjective, miss. Take the Chinese, for example. We call them heathens, but to them we're the uncultured barbarians. Who's to say we're right and they're wrong?'

'Surely common sense dictates–'

'European common sense, miss. The Chinese were living in ignorance of the teachings of Christ for thousands of years before missionaries arrived in China to convert them. Were all those who lived before now to be condemned to an eternity in Hell simply because God himself made them Chinese?'

'They are all God's children, Mr Killigrew.'

'True. But you cannot deny that God seems to have represented Himself in different ways to the different races on His earth. Since they are God's ways, can they be wrong?'

329

'You'd have to ask my brother, Mr Killigrew. He's the theologian, not me.'

'I think of myself more as a philosopher than a theologian, miss.'

'But you can't deny that the heathens of this world live in a state of wretched poverty and constant warfare?'

'There's plenty of poverty in Europe and America. And as for war, is there really that much difference between the tribal wars in Africa and the wars between nations in Europe and the Americas? Except that more people are killed in our wars, because we are more civilised and therefore better organised and efficient at killing.'

'But at least we know that to kill is a sin.'

'And yet still we do it. Does that make us better or worse? When I was in the navy–' He broke off and smiled. 'But I'm lecturing you, miss, and that's deuced tedious of me.'

'Mr Donohoe said something about you having the carriage of a naval officer, Mr Killigrew. Why did you leave the navy for the merchant service?'

'It's a long story, and not one that I'd want to bore you with.'

'Aren't you going to tell her?'

Killigrew turned and saw Coffin standing there.

'Tell me what, Mr Coffin?' she asked.

'Why, tell you about why he was kicked out of the Royal Navy, Miss Chance. About his drinking problem. About how he got drunk one day and decided to race his carriage down Pall Mall, and in so doing knocked down an innocent child and killed her.'

She stared at Killigrew with an expression of shock and horror.

Coffin grinned. 'Not so much the gentleman he seems now, is he?'

She gave the chief mate an icy look, and then turned back to Killigrew with what might have been a hint of sympathy in her eyes. 'That's a terrible thing to have on your conscience, Mr Killigrew. I'll pray for your eternal soul.'

'Pray for us all, Miss Chance,' Coffin called after her as she headed back below. 'Did Mr Killigrew here neglect to mention this is a ship of the damned?'

Killigrew was woken by the sound of someone hammering on the door of the cabin he shared with Pereira. He rolled out of his hammock, landing lightly on the balls of his naked feet, and jerked the door open. 'What?' he snapped.

Miss Chance stood there. 'Please come quickly, Mr Killigrew!' she said in a rush. 'It's Mr Coffin! He's beating one of the sailors and if someone doesn't stop him I fear he may ... oh! Mr Killigrew! Oh!' She raised a hand before her eyes and averted her gaze, blushing crimson.

'Oh! Sorry.' Killigrew stepped behind the door to cover his nakedness, reflecting that Miss Chance was going to have to get used to the sight of the naked human form if she was going to do missionary work in Africa. 'Go on.'

'Mr Coffin was beating one of the sailors. I fear that if someone doesn't stop him he'll beat the poor man to death!'

'All right, I'll come right up.' Killigrew quickly

331

pulled on his pantaloons and shirt. The ship's bell rang urgently as he laced his half-boots, summoning the hands to their quarters.

It was a week since they had rescued the three castaways from the sea. Dawn was lightening the sky, revealing the coast of Africa off to port. And there, off the port bow, a frigate less than three miles away was running to intercept them. Covilhã was ordering men to cram on all canvas, even at the risk of breaking the jury-rigged foremast, while Madison ordered the helmsman to steer a course to the south-west to avoid the frigate. 'Stand by to tack ship!' called Covilhã.

The object of Coffin's wrath lay at the foot of the mainmast in a pool of his own blood. He lay so motionless it was impossible to say whether he lived or died, but Coffin continued to kick him in the head regardless. 'You want to sleep, you idle, good-for-nothing sonuvabitch? I'll put you to sleep! I'll send you to sleep with the fishes!' He reached down to grab the man by the collar and dragged him across to the rail.

'For the love of God, Mr Killigrew!' pleaded Miss Chance. She stood by while Donohoe struggled to go to the aid of the unconscious man, held fast in the grip of a burly sailor. 'Stop him! Don't you see this is your chance to redeem yourself in the eyes of the Lord?'

But Killigrew was powerless to intervene.

'Take our guests below, Mr Killigrew,' Madison ordered gruffly.

'Please,' said Killigrew. 'You'd better do as the captain says.'

'Aren't you going to stop him?'

'Please, miss. For your own good.'

Coffin reached the side of the ship and lifted the man above his head with all the strength his insane rage gave him. The man went over the side without a scream and hit the water with a splash. Killigrew could not see the sharks from where he stood in the middle of the deck, but he knew they would be there.

'Oh, God!' sobbed Miss Chance. 'Heaven help us! Did you see that? He murdered him! Mr Coffin murdered that poor sailor, for the love of God! Just because he fell asleep on watch!'

Donohoe stopped struggling. 'Of course. Because that allowed the frigate to get so close without anyone on board this ship knowing about it.'

'So? What does it matter?' asked Miss Chance. 'That's not a reason to kill a man.'

'It is if they're slavers,' spat Donohoe.

'Sl-slavers?' stammered Miss Chance, as if she had believed that the slave trade had ended forty years ago when Denmark, the United States and Great Britain had all declared the trade illegal.

'Quite right, Mr Donohoe,' said Madison. 'I'm afraid this is a slave vessel you find yourself on, my dear,' he explained to Miss Chance. 'Take them below, Mr Killigrew.'

'Please,' insisted Killigrew, gesturing to the hatch. 'For your own safety...'

'Blackbirders!' spat Donohoe. 'I'd expect nothing less of these foreigners, but I'm surprised at ye, Mr Killigrew. I took ye for a Christian gentleman.'

Killigrew smiled wanly. 'You wouldn't be the

first to make that mistake, believe me.'

Donohoe rammed an elbow into his captor's chest and broke free. He snatched a belaying pin from the bulwark.

'No!' shouted Killigrew.

Coffin heard footsteps on the deck and turned in time to see Donohoe running towards him, brandishing the belaying pin above his head. The chief mate pulled his pistol from its holster and shot him in the chest. The Irishman fell back to the deck, dead.

Miss Chance groaned and her eyes rolled up in her head. Killigrew had to move fast to catch her before she fell. 'Goddamn it!' he muttered.

'Take her below and put her somewhere out of harm's way, Mr Killigrew,' ordered Madison. 'I strongly advise you put her in irons. Then come straight back on deck.'

Killigrew nodded and carried her below decks. As he carried her to the orlop deck her eyes opened. Seeing Killigrew carrying her she began to pound at his face with her fists. He put her down, but with her feet on the deck it was only easier for her to beat him. He grabbed her by the wrists and tried to still her, but her face was twisted with hatred and loathing.

'You rats! You evil, murdering rats.'

'Listen to me! Stop it!' he pleaded. 'Listen to me, as you value your life!' But she continued to struggle in his grip. Nothing he could say could get through to her, so he kissed her on the forehead.

She stopped struggling and stared at him in astonishment.

'Listen to me,' he said, more calmly. 'You have to trust me. I can't explain now, there isn't time, but you must trust me. Do you understand?'

She nodded, wide-eyed. 'You ... you're going to have to kill me, aren't you?'

'Not if I can help it,' he told her. 'That's a promise.' He steered her down to the orlop deck and gestured to a set of irons. 'Sit down.'

'You're going to shackle me here?'

He nodded. 'Please believe me, I beg you. It's for your own safety.'

As he clipped the fetters over her ankles the reality of her predicament hit her with its full force. 'What if the ship sinks? I'll drown!'

'The ship won't sink. That frigate won't fire at the hull. They probably don't think we have slaves on board but they'll want to find proof that we're slavers before they condemn us. So they'll aim at the spars and rigging. Believe me, this is the safest place to be. If they catch us, Madison won't want a dead American citizen on board, so you'll be safe enough.'

'And if they don't catch us? What then?'

Killigrew had no idea. 'I'll protect you. I promise. You've got to trust me, that's all.' He headed back towards the companion ladder.

'Mr Killigrew?' she called after him. He turned back. 'I ... I don't know why ... I've no reason to ... but ... I *do* trust you.'

He grinned ruefully. 'Yes, well, don't tell any of those scum up there you said that, or we'll both be as good as dead.'

XIV:

Barracoon

Killigrew returned on deck and studied the frigate through Madison's telescope. 'Do you know her?' asked Madison.

Killigrew nodded. 'She's the USS *Narwhal.*' He did not add that less than four months ago he had been drinking on board her with Lieutenant Lanier and his friends.

'Can she catch us?'

'I don't know. Before we lost our foremast she wouldn't have stood a chance, but now with this jury-rigging...'

It was strange to find himself being on the other side in the war against the slavers, running with the hare after spending so many years riding with the hounds. It would be embarrassing for him if the frigate caught them. He was not confident he could convince Lanier that he was working as a secret agent for Rear-Admiral Napier; also if there was nothing in Madison's safe to identify the man behind the slavers then this whole enterprise would have been for nothing, and he would never be able to redeem himself and be reinstated as an officer of the Royal Navy. Worse than that, if the Americans saw fit to hand him over to the authorities in Freetown as a British citizen caught on board a slave vessel, there was a good chance he would be hanged for it. So from Killigrew's point of view there was nothing to be gained from trying to sabotage the *Leopardo*'s efforts to escape the *Narwhal*.

But now he had Miss Chance's safety to think of. Madison would not let her and her brother go now that they knew they were on board a slaver. Was there any way he could keep them alive and help them get to safety? It seemed impossible. But was his mission more important than their lives? If he succeeded he would be saving thousands of Africans from being condemned to a life of slavery; but only if he succeeded. How could he balance that against the life of one man and one woman? And was it the Africans he was concerned about, or his own skin?

He wondered if Miss Chance could swim, at least long enough to stay afloat until she could be picked up by the crew of the *Narwhal.* Perhaps he could put her and her brother into a boat while everyone else was busy? But they would see what he had done sooner or later, and know he was up to no good. Unless…

'Perhaps we can buy ourselves some time by putting the Reverend Chance and his sister in the jolly boat and leaving them for the *Narwhal* to pick up?' he suggested to Madison. 'That way we get them out of our hair and force our pursuers to slow down at the same time.'

'Aye, and hand over a woman who can easily identify every manjack of us to the authorities, Mr Killigrew. You'll have to do better than that.'

A cannon boomed distantly and Killigrew saw a plume of pale grey smoke rise from the

Narwhal's side. There was no answering splash of shot landing in the water closer to the *Leopardo* – it had been a blank.

'They're asking us to show our colours,' grunted Coffin.

Madison nodded. 'Hoist the Union Jack from the jackstaff, Mr Covilhã. If they get within hailing distance you can do the honours with the speaking trumpet, Mr Killigrew. Maybe that Limey accent of yours will throw them off the scent.'

Close-hauled, the two ships raced to windward. Each time the *Leopardo* changed tack the *Narwhal* mirrored the manoeuvre barely seconds later. There was no doubting the American sailors knew their business, but it was impossible to say which of the two vessels was the faster.

The *Narwhal* came within a mile of the *Leopardo* as the latter ship tried to slip past her and at once one of her pivot guns boomed and raised a huge plume of water from the waves barely a cable's length to port of the brig. The Americans had used round shot and for a moment Killigrew panicked, thinking the *Narwhal* meant to sink them after all. He thought of Miss Chance, whom he himself had chained on the orlop deck. Then he realised that the Americans would know the range of their guns to within a few yards, even taking the wind into account. It had just been a warning shot.

Then the two ships were level, only three-quarters a mile of ocean separating them. The frigate veered towards the brig, but for every yard towards the slaver she gained sideways, she fell a yard astern. When she was almost directly abaft the brig her bow-chaser boomed, sending up a fountain of water which showered the men on the quarter-deck.

'We'll use the sweeps,' decided Madison.

There were six sweeps on board the *Leopardo,* three for a side. There were not enough men on board to have more than three men to each sweep. Even Killigrew had to help, leaving Coffin to take the helm while Madison had the con. The sailors stripped down to their waists and hauled away to the strokes called out by Covilhã like the galley slaves of old, praying that the sweeps would give them that extra burst of speed they needed to elude the *Narwhal.*

It was hot and sultry, and the sweat soon poured from the backs of Killigrew and the others as they rowed under the blazing tropical sun. Working with his back to the bows, Killigrew could just see the sails of the *Narwhal* beyond the *Leopardo*'s stern. If the frigate were falling behind, it was doing so so slowly it was impossible to discern. His back and arms soon ached from the exertion.

'We're losing her,' opined Madison, staring aft through his telescope.

Coffin glanced over his shoulder. 'Aye, but they ain't giving up yet. They know we can't keep this up for ever.'

'Pace the men, Mr Covilhã,' ordered Madison. 'We may have a way to go yet.'

The sun climbed towards its zenith until it beat down mercilessly on the men labouring on deck. Madison disappeared below. Killigrew wondered if he had given up hope of outrunning the frigate and was going to burn the papers in the safe; if he did, then the chances were that Killigrew's mission was doomed to failure and he would have to live the rest of his life in disgrace. He was toying with the idea of leaving his place at the sweeps and going below to stop Madison when the slave captain reappeared a few moments later carrying a pail in one hand and dragging Miss Chance by the arm with the other.

'Fill the pail at the water butt and give the men some water,' ordered Madison.

'Do it yourself,' she snapped back. 'You think I want to help scum like you escape from justice?'

He thrust the pail into her hands, making her stagger. 'You'll do it, missy, or I'll have you pulling on one of those sweeps yourself!'

She glared fiercely at him for a moment as if defying him to do it, and Killigrew suppressed a smile, torn between admiration for her spirit and a throat-burning thirst. Then she glanced at the men at the sweeps and saw Killigrew amongst them. Her shoulders slumped and she crossed to the water butt. He was glad she had sense enough not to make straight for him, instead serving the men on the port-side sweeps first.

'Is there anything I can do to help?' she murmured as she lifted the ladle to Killigrew's parched lips. He swallowed the water – it probably had not even been that fresh when they had taken it on board at São Tiago eight days earlier, but it was still the sweetest liquid he had ever tasted – and then just shook his head, conserving his breath.

Madison suddenly peered forward, and raised his telescope to his eye, staring ahead. Then a grin spread across his face, and he lowered the telescope. 'Three points to starboard, Mr Coffin, if you please. Keep pulling boys! There's a smoke a couple of miles ahead. If we can make it there's a chance we'll be safe.'

The men at the sweeps pulled even harder, knowing that the end was in sight. It occurred to Killigrew that Madison might have lied to the men in order to get them to pull faster, but he could not twist his head around far enough to check. Covilhã and five others shipped their sweeps briefly to trim the sails to their new heading, and then resumed rowing.

They had put another half-mile between themselves and the *Narwhal*, but still the frigate did not give up. It was rare for a frigate to fall in with a slaver it had a chance of catching – such ships usually only ended up on the West Africa Station because their navies had no other use for them – and, having smelled blood, it was reluctant to give up the chase.

A few minutes later the brig slid into the fog bank and the men gasped with relief as the low cloud masked them from the worst of the sun's rays. Killigrew felt the moisture prickle his bare skin.

'Keep pulling!' ordered Madison. 'We're not out of it yet. Hard a-port, Mr Coffin. Port-side sweeps back water!'

The *Leopardo*'s head came about in the opaque mists, and with the oarsmen on the port-side reversing the ship almost turned on her axis.

'Now forward again! One ... two ... three ... four ... five ... way enough! Toss and ship sweeps. Way aloft! Take in all canvas! We'll drift with the smoke. Silently, now silently!'

After pulling at the sweeps for the best part of three hours, the hands climbed into the rigging like octogenarians, but the sails were soon furled. 'Pipe down! Not a sound out of any of you, d'ye hear? The next man to make a sound other than me or Mr Coffin goes the same way as Tristão did, follow me?'

Coffin took his whip from his belt and looped it around Miss Chance's neck. 'That goes for you too, missy. One peep and I'll snap that pretty little neck of yours like it was driftwood.'

The hands climbed silently down from the rigging and tip-toed across the deck. The frigate would not have chased them so far if it was going to be put off sailing into a little low cloud, but Killigrew guessed Madison was counting on their last manoeuvre inside the fog to throw the Americans off the scent.

They waited. Everything was silent but for the creaking of the timbers and the gentle slap of the waves against the brig's sides.

'Heave to!' a voice with an American accent boomed barely two cables away. Killigrew thought he recognised Boatswain Charlie's voice. 'Counterbrace them yards!'

Everyone turned to look in that direction, and they could see a pale shadow looming through the mist behind them. Then a boatswain's whistle sounded the order to pipe down. The Americans had guessed that the slaver was hidden in the fog bank, and they were listening for a clue which would give away its location. All that was needed was a sudden gust of wind to tear a rent in the fog and the *Leopardo* would be exposed to the view of the *Narwhal* within point-blank range of her port broadside.

There was silence for one minute, two, three. Harsh laughter, faint muffled, and Boatswain Charlie hissing for silence, threatening dire warnings against the next man to make a sound. Coffin pulled tight on the whip he still had coiled around Miss Chance's neck, as if sensing that she was tempted to call out to the men on the frigate. She glanced across to where Killigrew stood, looking at him from under her eyelashes. He gave his head an infinitesimal shake.

'Ah, to hell with it!' said someone on the frigate. 'They're probably miles away by now. Belay that last order, men. Brace in the sails!'

The shadow moved on through the fog, but Madison quickly raised a hand, signalling for his crew to remain silent. It might yet be a ruse by the captain of the frigate to trick them into betraying their position.

They waited. An hour passed, then another. No one went near the ship's bell. As the afternoon wore on the mist slowly evaporated, until all of a sudden it was gone. There was no sign of the *Narwhal,* but the African coast was visible directly ahead.

Madison took a sighting with his sextant and then went below to check the chronometer. He returned on deck a moment later. 'Take the con, Mr Covilhã. Lay in a course east by north. Take

343

the girl below and put her in irons, Eli, then join me directly in my cabin. You too, Mr Killigrew.'

Madison went below followed by Coffin dragging Miss Chance by the arm. Killigrew shrugged his shirt back on and gazed towards the bows. They were heading in towards the African coast. By his own dead reckoning they had passed Sherbro Island during the chase and now lay somewhere off the Guinea Coast to the south. Did that mean they were close to their destination?

He buttoned his shirt and went below, tucking it into the waistband. Madison was already waiting for him in his day cabin, poring over a chart. He said nothing apart from to respond to Killigrew's knock on the door, and from the tone of the captain's voice Killigrew deemed it wisest to stand back and say nothing until Madison looked up and addressed him.

Presently they were joined by Coffin. 'Well?' Madison asked him.

'We've no choice, sir. She was dead the moment her ship went down. You know it and I know it. Only this dumb Limey thought he could prolong her life.'

Madison sighed. 'You're right, of course, Eli. All the same, she is a woman.'

'All the more reason to kill her, sir.' Coffin grinned. 'You can't trust a woman to keep her mouth shut. I'll do it, if you like. I'll see to it she don't suffer too much.'

Killigrew was a patient man, but he had been subjected to Coffin's needling for over four weeks now, and the callous way in which he spoke of murdering an innocent woman in cold blood was more than he could bear. 'You'll enjoy that, won't you?'

Coffin turned to him. 'Perhaps you'd rather do it yourself, mister, since it was your idea to bring her aboard in the first place?'

'All right, you two, that's enough,' snapped Madison. He massaged his temples and sighed again. 'There ... there is another way,' he said hesitantly. 'I'm not sure that I care for it overmuch, but at least it doesn't mean killing her.'

'Cut her tongue out?' suggested Coffin. 'Too risky. She'd still be able to write down all she's learned.'

Madison scowled at him. 'I was thinking of giving her to Salazar.'

Coffin pursed his lips, and then nodded. 'That's not a bad idea. All them nigger whores he keeps in his harem, I reckon he must get a hankering after a bit of white meat every once in a while.'

'What do you say, Mr Killigrew?'

Killigrew shrugged. 'Who's Salazar?'

Coffin chortled. 'Why, ain't you never heard of Salazar? No wonder you navy boys are always a-running round in circles. You don't know anything about the slave trade if you don't know about Francisco Salazar.'

'And he is...?'

'You'll find out soon enough,' said Madison. 'As we should make landfall at the Owodunni Barracoon by nightfall.'

The sun was sinking into the ocean by the time the *Leopardo* anchored half a mile from the coast, casting an orange light like fire across the sky and sending a flaming path across the waves to where the brig floated. Killigrew stood on deck and gazed towards the land. Even with the telescope he could see nothing, but that did not surprise him. For most of its length the Guinea Coast presented nothing to the seaward observer but an unbroken barrier of impenetrable green foliage, but Killigrew knew that the foliage hid deltas and mangrove swamps, a hundred thousand tiny creeks and inlets which made ideal hiding places for the slavers' barracoons.

'They're all asleep,' sneered Coffin.

'Then let's wake them up, Mr Coffin,' ordered Madison.

They fired a blank shot from the *Leopardo*'s bow-chaser, and ran up some signal flags. A few moments later a flag appeared on the shore, barely visible even through a telescope in that light. It seemed to flutter over the jungle in the evening breeze, and Killigrew could just make out the design: a yellow and black leopard on a white background.

Madison closed his telescope with a gesture of satisfaction. 'That's the signal. Lower the gig, Mr Covilhã. Fetch the girl, Mr Coffin.'

'Where are we?' she demanded as she was handed down into the gig. 'Where are you taking me?'

'Somewhere where you'll be made comfortable,' said Madison.

Killigrew suspected that was far from true and

wished there was some way he could warn her, but thinking about it he decided it would be better if she was allowed to remain calm for now. There were eight of them in the gig altogether: Madison, Coffin, Killigrew, Miss Chance, and four oarsmen. Coffin was carrying a sample of the *Leopardo*'s cargo, one of the rifled muskets they hoped to exchange for slaves.

The gig shoved off from the brig's side and they rowed across the bar which prevented ships of any reasonable draught from getting any closer into shore. Once they were across the bar a creek suddenly appeared as if from nowhere amongst the trees which crowded the edge of the stretch of white sand on the beach. The jungle seemed impenetrable on either side of the creek, and the tangled roots of the mangrove trees which clawed at the mud looked eerie in the falling light. Strange tropical birds cried out in the darkness, and mosquitoes buzzed infuriatingly about the heads of the people in the boat. Submerged shapes glided silently through the water without even causing a ripple. Killigrew took them for logs, until he realised they moved against the current: crocodiles.

Then they turned a bend in the creek and a wooden jetty came into view. Three men stood on the jetty, two rough-looking mulattos wearing broad-brimmed straw hats and cradling rifles, and a European, tall, lean-built, dressed all in white and bare-headed.

'Salazar? Is that you, you old son of a gun?'

'Captain Madison.' There was a hint of a wan smile and no trace of any particular accent in the man's rich and sonorous voice. 'Welcome back to the Owodunni Barracoon.'

The gig bumped against the jetty and two of the oarsmen quickly went ashore to make the painter fast, while the guards helped Madison and the others on to the jetty. 'And Mr Coffin, of course. And who are these?' asked Salazar, indicating Killigrew and Miss Chance.

'This is Mr Killigrew, my new second mate, who's been good enough to fill in for Mr Cutler, who was careless enough to get himself shanghaied aboard the *Ophelia*. And the lady is Miss Suzannah Chance, of whom more later.'

Salazar smiled. 'A woman of mystery. How intriguing. And a beautiful one at that,' he added, kissing her hand to her evident distaste.

Salazar was a younger man than Killigrew had expected, in his late thirties or early forties. Flecks of grey showed prematurely at the temples of his leonine head, and high cheekbones and a thin jaw gave his face an angular look.

'So, have you anything in stock, Salazar, or are we going to have to look elsewhere?' asked Madison.

'My dear Captain Madison, when have you ever known me have nothing in stock? The question is, what have *you* got for *me?*'

'The usual. Guns, powder, textiles.' He handed Salazar a sheet of paper which the barracoon owner tucked inside his shirt without bothering to read.

'Shall we get in out of this unhealthy night air?' he suggested, slapping at a mosquito on the back of his neck. 'Dinner is almost ready. I do hope

348

you will join me. I have the finest chef on the Guinea Coast in my employ, Miss Chance, and an excellently stocked wine cellar.'

Madison ordered the oarsmen to stay by the boat and one of the guards stayed with them while the other led the way up a short dirt track to an arch in the hedge which bordered the creek. Killigrew stepped through it into another world.

There were dozens of buildings: long, low barracks; workshops; clusters of mud huts; bungalows built in the colonial style; a huge stockade off to the left, and at the centre of it all what looked like an Italianate *palazzo*. There were guards everywhere, and Killigrew suddenly noticed a wooden watchtower a hundred feet tall growing up out of the jungle on a neighbouring island, largely camouflaged by the creepers which had been trained to climb up it.

'I had no idea there was such a large settlement in these parts,' said Killigrew.

'That depends how you define a settlement, Mr Killigrew,' said Salazar. 'All this is my barracoon. All these islands belong to me. My own private kingdom, if you like, in which I am master of all I survey.'

Killigrew was stunned, partly by the size of the barracoon but mostly by the fact that Salazar was obviously some kind of megalomaniac. 'It must be the biggest barracoon on the Guinea Coast?'

'In the world, Mr Killigrew. I employ over three hundred people here: guards, servants, clerks, lawyers, administrators, workmen. I pay them well, and in return I get their total and unquestioning loyalty.'

'And if you don't?'

'Every kingdom must have its laws, Mr Killigrew, and those laws are useless if there is no penal code to back them up.'

'A place like this must be very expensive to maintain.'

'It's all relative. I am a businessman first and foremost. I do not run my little kingdom simply for my own aggrandisement.'

'You don't?'

'This barracoon has a turnover of three and a half millions a year, Mr Killigrew. That's pounds sterling. And most of that is clear profit.'

The barracoon was much bigger than the Slave Trade Department had estimated. 'That's a lot of money,' said Killigrew.

'Mr Salazar does very well for himself,' observed Madison.

'Yes. But not nearly as well as your owners do. I fear that is where the real money lies: transporting the slaves across the Atlantic.'

'The profit lies with the risk, Mr Salazar.'

'Indeed it does. I tell you, Mr Killigrew, when Great Britain declared the slave trade illegal it was the best thing that ever happened to our trade. Mr Madison can purchase a slave here for twenty to thirty thousand *reis* depending on its quality and sell it in the Americas for ... how much would you say?'

'We expect to make a nine hundred per cent profit,' said Madison. 'That's before you deduct the cost of the voyage, of course.'

'Of course. But even so we can still afford to

have two out of every three ships caught by the Royal Navy and the whole operation will still be worth while. Since the proportion of vessels actually caught by the navy is pitifully small, you can imagine what kind of profits we are looking at.'

They approached the colonnaded portico of the *palazzo* at the centre of the settlement. 'Welcome to my humble abode,' said Salazar. 'It was built in Umbria in 1502 as a summer residence for Duke Valentinois. I had it dismantled brick by brick and shipped out here to be reassembled as you see it now.'

'Gives a whole new meaning to the term "conveyancing",' remarked Killigrew.

They ascended the steps to the portico and a black butler emerged to hold open the door for them. Inside it was no more opulent than some of the grander governors' residences Killigrew had visited in some of Britain's better-established and more profitable colonies. Thick velvet drapes hung over the windows and the floor was marble. On the walls, magnificent oil paintings depicting scenes from classical mythology vied for space with hunting trophies in the most ghastly lapse of taste – gazelles, leopards, even a huge rhinoceros's head stuffed and mounted over the Adam fireplace.

Salazar turned to the butler. 'Inform chef there will be six of us to dinner. Shall we say half past eight? That will give my guests time to freshen up after what I'm sure was a long and tedious voyage.'

'It was long,' admitted Killigrew. 'I'm not so

sure about "tedious". I had no idea dinner was going to be so formal, otherwise I'd have brought some evening clothes...'

'You can borrow some of mine,' said Salazar. 'We look to be about the same build. And I don't think finding clothes for the lady is likely to present a problem. Henriques, show the gentlemen and the lady upstairs,' he added, snapping his fingers at a liveried black footman.

'I'd rather we kept an eye on the lady, Salazar,' said Madison. 'She's kind of by way of being a prisoner.'

'A prisoner!' exclaimed Salazar. 'Even more intriguing. I shall not press you on the matter, Captain Madison, since I know you well enough to know you will reveal all at the appropriate time. I shall make sure she is watched.'

'If you think I'm going to get changed with one of your guards watching me...' she protested.

'Oh, heaven forbid, Miss Chance! I think I can provide you with a suitable escort. Henriques, summon Assata directly to escort Miss Chance to her chamber.'

Killigrew studied the paintings while they waited.

'I see you are admiring my Titian, Mr Killigrew,' said Salazar.

'Wasn't that one stolen from the Louvre a couple of years ago?'

'It may have been,' Salazar admitted with a dismissive gesture. 'I paid full price for it, however, I assure you. When one has earned one's first million it becomes very difficult to find new ways of spending one's money.'

Killigrew smiled thinly. 'How you must long for a life of simple poverty.'

Salazar shrugged. 'I happen to like the best of things in life. Am I to be blamed if God has smiled on my enterprises over the years?'

'What about the stuffed heads? Yours?'

'Yes indeed, Mr Killigrew. Are you a hunting man?'

'I'm inclined to agree with Shenstone.'

'Shenstone?' asked Salazar.

'A British poet. What was it he said? Ah yes. "The world may be divided into people that read, people that write, people that think, and fox-hunters."'

Salazar gestured dismissively. 'Foxes are vermin, Mr Killigrew, and their extermination should be left to the lower orders. You cannot know the full thrill of hunting until you have hunted big game. Take this fellow, for example,' he said, indicating the rhinoceros head. 'Five years ago, it was. Can you have any conception of the thoughts that go through a man's mind as one of those beasts bears down on him? At one hundred yards I fired my rifle, but it misfired. He lumbered on. I pulled my pistol from my belt, aimed, and fired – got him right between the eyes. I'll swear he ran on another fifty feet before he realised he was dead.' Salazar's eyes glittered as he recollected the event. 'When his body finally crashed to the ground, he was as close to me as I am to you now. I tell you, Mr Killigrew, one cannot appreciate the true exhilaration of life until one has looked death between the eyes.'

In the *aide-memoire* of his mind, Killigrew

scrawled the words: *Mad as a March hare.*

Henriques returned with a tall, muscular black woman wearing a blue-and-white striped tunic belted at the waist and a white cap with a leopard device on the front. A carbine was slung over one of her shoulders, and a large dagger hung at her side along with a brace of pistols. 'Ah, Assata,' said Salazar. 'One of my personal bodyguards, gentlemen, a gift from King Gezo of Dahomey.'

'And all I got for Christmas was a cravat,' sighed Killigrew.

'Assata, take Miss Chance here up to the Chinese room. See that she is given a chance to wash and change for dinner. There are plenty of clean clothes hanging in the closet, Miss Chance. You should be able to find something to fit you.'

Madison and Coffin watched open-mouthed as Assata escorted Miss Chance up the grandiose staircase. 'Tell me, Salazar,' Coffin asked with a leer, 'is guarding the only thing she does with your body?'

Salazar smiled thinly, unimpressed by Coffin's rough manners. 'Believe me, Mr Coffin, it would be a foolish man who tried anything untoward with Assata. When one has seen a woman crack a man's ribcage between her thighs, one becomes very reluctant to place oneself in that perilous position.'

Henriques escorted Madison, Coffin and Killigrew upstairs and showed them each into a room. The rooms were large and every bit as richly appointed as the rest of the house, with large four-poster beds and marble washstands in a corner. Presently Henriques returned with hot water and towels. It was the first chance Killigrew had had to wash properly in weeks, and he made the most of it, washing the salt out of his hair and scrubbing himself from head to toe. There was a complete supply of toiletries on the shelf above the washstand: macassar oil, pomade, eau-de-cologne. By the time he had finished, Henriques returned with underclothes, a clean shirt and a pair of white pantaloons. Killigrew dressed and went outside where he encountered Miss Chance emerging from another room, followed by Assata.

'You look ravishing, Miss Chance, if I may be so bold,' said Killigrew. It was true enough. She wore a pale-blue evening gown of light silk which swished and rustled with each step she took.

'I only wish you were the only one in this place with the word "ravishing" on his mind, Mr Killigrew,' she responded. 'There are hundreds of dresses in that closet, some of them the very latest fashions from Paris. Why do I get the feeling I'm not the first woman to visit this place? It gives me a creepy feeling.'

'I think it's rather charming myself,' said Killigrew, admiring the interior decoration. 'I'll say one thing for Salazar, his taste is impeccable – barring the dead animal heads on the wall downstairs, of course.'

'I suppose *you'd* like to live like this.'

'Who wouldn't? Although I think I'd grow tired of it after a while. My own tastes have always run to colonial simplicity.'

'After a week on that hell-hole you call a ship, this is all too good to be true.'

'I wouldn't disagree with you there.' He wanted to say more, but suspecting that Assata knew more English than she let on he thought it wisest not to. 'Shall we go downstairs?'

Madison, Coffin and Salazar were already waiting for them with a fourth gentleman, a huge African dressed in a curious combination of clothing: a spotless red tunic with enough gold braid on it to suggest it had once been the property of a brigadier-general if it had not been so obviously first-hand, white breeches, and sandals, the whole topped off with a leopard skin, the head resting on top of the man's shaven scalp, giving an even greater impression of height to his six and three-quarter feet. He was perfectly proportioned too: broad-shouldered and muscular of build, like an ebony sculpture of a Greek athlete.

The African held the rifled musket Coffin had brought from the ship and was turning it over in his hands, gazing down the barrel and snapping the hammer expertly.

'That's the latest in European military armaments, your highness,' Madison was telling him. 'The rifling in the barrel makes the bullet spin in flight, increasing the range and improving accuracy remarkably. You see, I don't try to fob you off with out-dated, second-hand muskets. I've got five hundred more like that on board the *Leopardo*, every one of them fresh from the manufactory where they were made. I'll let you test it tomorrow before I ask you to commit yourself. I hear you're a pretty good shot with a musket? Well, I'm a lousy one. But you use a musket, I'll use that rifle, and I'll beat you ten times out of ten against any target you choose to pick. Even British line infantry don't have rifles as good as that. Those weapons will make your leopard warriors the envy of the finest armies in the world.'

Salazar glanced up and saw Killigrew and Miss Chance descending the staircase. 'Ah, Miss Chance. May I introduce you to Prince Khari? Your highness, this is Miss Chance.' The prince bowed stiffly and clicked his heels, like a Prussian drill instructor. 'And of course may I present Mr Killigrew, your highness? Mr Killigrew, this is Prince Khari.'

'Charmed, I'm sure,' said Killigrew. 'I take it the two of you have a business association?'

Salazar smiled. 'It is thanks to Prince Khari's constant warring with his neighbouring tribes that I am never short of merchandise.'

'They are not "neighbouring tribes", as you call them,' Khari reminded Salazar. He spoke good English with a rich and melodious timbre. 'They are tributary states of my father's empire.'

'Of course, of course.' Salazar seemed amused, as if he was used to pandering to the pride of native chieftains. 'Prince Khari is the son of King Nldamak,' he added to Killigrew and Miss Chance.

'Ah,' said Killigrew. 'And there I was thinking he must be one of the Buckinghamshire Kharis.'

A footman emerged from a small doorway and held up a small bronze gong, which he struck. 'Dinner is served.'

'Shall we be seated?' Salazar, as host, led the

357

way into the dining room, followed by Khari, Miss Chance, Madison, Coffin and Killigrew. A long mahogany dining table large enough to seat two dozen people stretched the length of the room, while another gilt-framed old master hung above the cold hearth at the far end. The furniture, as far as Killigrew could tell, was Louis–Quinze. The whole scene was dimly yet warmly illuminated by the many candles burning in the three candelabra on the table; the candelabra might have been silver-plate, but given Salazar's attitude to spending money Killigrew was ready to bet they were solid silver.

Salazar sat at the head of the table while the others searched for their place cards. Killigrew found himself seated at Salazar's left while Miss Chance sat opposite him. Assata entered the room and stood just inside the doorway with her arms folded, unsmiling, watching Miss Chance.

'I'm sorry I'm not wearing a coat or cravat, Mr Salazar, but these were the only clothes your footman brought me,' Killigrew said apologetically. 'However, I see from your own apparel you prefer a more casual approach to dress?'

'Indeed I do, Mr Killigrew. I find the heavy clothes worn in Europe quite unsuited for these tropical climes. I trust you have no objection?'

'None at all. A very sensible policy, if I may say so.'

'You may, and I shall take it as a compliment that you do. I trust that the clothes are a suitable fit?'

'Well enough. They're a little tight around the chest and shoulders.'

Salazar shrugged. 'That is to be expected. I fear I do not get as much exercise as I used to when I was a sailor. I try though, exercising with the foil. Do you fence, Mr Killigrew?'

'A little,' Killigrew admitted cautiously. 'I'm more used to a cutlass.'

Salazar tutted. 'Such a clumsy weapon. Hardly suited for a gentleman, I would have thought.'

'But more practical than a foil when boarding a hostile ship.'

'Mr Killigrew used to be an officer in the Royal Navy,' explained Madison.

'Indeed.' Salazar seemed completely untroubled by this revelation. That worried Killigrew at first, until he realised that in the heart of his own private kingdom a man like Salazar had nothing to fear from a lone man, ex-navy or otherwise.

'You used to be a sailor, Mr Salazar?' asked Miss Chance.

He nodded. 'Oh, yes. Once I was the captain of a slaver, just like Mr Madison here. I soon made so much money I was able to start building this place. How long until you can retire, Mr Madison?'

Madison smiled. 'With any luck I'll be able to retire after this voyage. I've got my eye on some land on the western frontier of the United States. Good cattle-farming country, I'm told.'

'Exchanging one form of cattle for another?' Killigrew suggested drily.

Madison beamed. 'Exactly so, Mr Killigrew. But cattle are a lot easier to handle than niggers. No offence intended, your highness.'

Prince Khari inclined his head regally.

'Ah, the wine,' said Salazar, as another footman entered and started to pour white wine into the crystal goblets. 'Graves. The best dry white in my cellar. A good vintage, and an excellent complement to the *consommé d'été*. You will have a glass, won't you, Mr Killigrew?'

'Mr Killigrew doesn't drink,' said Madison.

Salazar smiled broadly. 'Oh, but I think he does, Captain Madison. Don't you, Mr Killigrew? Or should that still be *Lieutenant* Killigrew? I'm afraid my informant was rather vague on the matter of whether or not you retain your rank while you're working as a spy for the Slave Trade Department in Whitehall.

XV:

Bad Medicine

'What?' Salazar said with amusement. 'No heated denials? No protestations of innocence?'

'You seem to be pretty sure of your information,' Killigrew said mildly, although his mind was reeling. 'May I enquire how you came by it?'

'So you can return to England and exact your revenge on the one who betrayed you? Put such thoughts from your mind, Mr Killigrew. You will not be seeing England again.'

'You mean to say he was a spy all along? Spying on me?'

'Spying on us, Captain Madison,' said Salazar. 'It's the name of your financial backers he's really interested in, although I'm sure his navy would be grateful for the name of your ship and the location of this barracoon.'

'Goddamn it, didn't I always say that sonuvabitch wasn't on the level?' exclaimed Coffin, banging his fist on the table.

'Is it true, then?' Madison asked Killigrew, more in sorrow than in anger. 'Have you been a viper in my bosom all this time? I am sorely disappointed in you, Mr Killigrew.'

'I think we should congratulate him for carrying out his imposture so successfully,' said

Salazar. 'It was a courageous effort, although doomed to failure. I must say, Mr Killigrew, you seem to be taking your defeat with remarkable composure.'

'I've lost this trick, but not the hand.'

'I think you'll find that you've played your last card.'

'Oh, I may have a few more left up my sleeve...' Killigrew suddenly leaped up from his chair, knocking it over backwards, and whirled, snatching the carving knife from the sideboard behind him. He hauled Salazar out of his seat and held the knife's serrated edge to his throat.

Madison, Coffin and Khari all jumped to their feet, but they were too slow. Too slow, that is, compared to Assata. In the blink of an eye she had drawn both her pistols and now levelled them, unwavering, at Killigrew's head.

'No!' Salazar called to her in panic. 'Don't shoot.'

Killigrew grinned nervously. 'Don't worry, Mr Salazar. If Miss Assata knows how to use those things – and from the look of her, she does – then she knows she's got as much chance of hitting you as she has of killing me.'

'I doubt it,' Salazar returned mildly. 'Assata is an excellent shot and she would have no difficulty putting out both your eyes at that range. No, my concern was for the Tintoretto on the wall behind you. So please, Mr Killigrew, do both art and yourself a favour and resume your seat so we can finish dinner like civilised gentlemen.' He held out a hand, palm upwards, and Killigrew, seeing the futility of further resistance, hesitated only for a moment before he surrendered the carving knife. Everyone sat down once more, the footman hurrying forwards to right Killigrew's chair for him.

'Better we kill him now and be done with it,' snarled Coffin. 'I'll do it myself if you like.'

'Please, please!' said Salazar. 'Nothing so uncouth as bloodshed at the dinner table, I pray you. Besides, I think it would be better if Mr Killigrew here informed us exactly how much Rear-Admiral Napier knows of our activities before we see to it that he takes his final leave of this world.'

'Torture, I suppose,' Miss Chance said coldly. 'Have you people no consciences?'

'I used to have one,' said Salazar. 'But I outgrew it. The vast wealth I have earned as a consequence is more than adequate compensation.'

Coffin shook his head. 'He won't tell you a thing. I know his sort. He's dangerous. Better to kill him now and be done with it.'

'Oh, I'm sure Mr Killigrew can be persuaded to tell us everything he knows. Have you ever studied the history of the Spanish Inquisition, Miss Chance? Some of the techniques they used were really quite sophisticated. But tell, Captain Madison: you have still not yet revealed the reason for Miss Chance's presence.'

'It was sheer mischance which brought Miss Chance to us, if you'll pardon the pun,' said Madison, oblivious to the look she shot him which suggested that pardoning the pun was not on her personal agenda. 'Her ship went down in a storm about a week ago. We found her, her brother and a sailor floating in the water the next morning. Mr Coffin was for leaving them to their fate; foolishly, I chose to be guided by Mr Killigrew's advice. I should have guessed then, when I realised he was still a sentimentalist at heart, that he was up to no good. Mr Coffin was kind enough to dispose of the sailor as soon as they realised we were slavers. Miss Chance's brother, the Reverend Chance, is so sick he doesn't even know his own name, so he's no threat; in fact I've a feeling he won't last the night,' he added with a sly smile which made Killigrew fear for the missionary's life.

'But as for Miss Chance herself, well … you can see we have a problem. Call me old-fashioned, Mr Salazar, yet I still baulk at the thought of killing a woman. But as you can understand, we can't very well let her go. Least of all now that she's been here and seen this place. Then I thought of you. Might there be a place in your harem for her?'

Miss Chance leaped to her feet and flushed bright crimson. 'What? How dare you!' Assata quickly stepped up behind her and forced her back down into her chair. Miss Chance struggled against her, but the Dahomey amazon was bigger and stronger than her, and twisted her arm up into the small of her back until she cried out in pain. 'Let go of me, you … evil woman!'

'Enough, Assata!' snapped Salazar, and the woman released Miss Chance with a contemptuous curl of her lip.

'Let the girl go on her word of honour that

she'll breathe nothing of what she's seen to a living soul, and I'll tell you everything you want to know,' Killigrew said tightly.

'But you are going to do that anyway, whether you like it or not,' Salazar pointed out reasonably. 'You are in no position to bargain, Mr Killigrew.' He turned back to Madison and Coffin. 'It is a generous gift, my friends.'

'The least we can do, under the circumstances,' said Madison. 'If it hadn't been for your informant in England, my carelessness in having Killigrew in my crew could have ruined us all.'

'Then I shall accept your gift. She will be a fine addition to my little menagerie.'

'For the love of mercy, Mr Killigrew!' implored Miss Chance. 'Surely you cannot mean to sit there and say nothing while these evil swine treat me like … like some kind of chattel?'

'There is not a lot Mr Killigrew can do about it,' said Salazar. 'If I were you, Miss Chance, I should not look to him for help. He is as good as dead. Whether that death comes swiftly and painlessly, or lingering and agonising, is entirely up to him. The sooner you accept that and resign yourself to your fate, the happier you will be, I assure you. I pride myself on how well I treat my concubines, and I hope I am not without my charms…'

'You have all the charm of a rattlesnake, Mr Salazar. I wouldn't willingly associate with you if you were the last man in the world.'

Killigrew chuckled.

'That amuses you, Mr Killigrew?' said Salazar, evidently hurt by her rebuff. 'Laugh while you can. You will have nothing to laugh about to-morrow, I assure you.'

'I believe it is customary to give the condemned man a last request?' asked Killigrew.

'Of course, within reason. Perhaps you would like the pick of my harem? I often treat honoured guests so, and your bravery deserves reward. But not Miss Chance, however. I prefer my meat fresh, and do not care to taste of another man's leavings.'

'What a charming way of looking at things you have, Mr Salazar. Actually, I was thinking more along the lines of something to drink, since I've been on the wagon for about a month now and there's no longer any need for me to maintain the pretence of being teetotal.'

Salazar laughed. 'Of course. Some wine for Mr Killigrew, Henriques?'

'Actually, I know it's a little early in the meal, but I wondered if I might trouble you for something a little stronger? To help calm my nerves, you understand.'

'Then I entreat you to try my cognac. It was left in the cellars of Bonaparte's home on the island of Saint-Helena. I purchased it at auction for no less than five thousand pounds per bottle. A fitting last request, would you not say?'

'Genuine Napoleon brandy,' Killigrew re-marked with a smile, as Henriques leaned over him to place a balloon glass on the table.

'It was well worth every penny I paid for it,' said Salazar. 'It has a splendidly smoky flavour.'

As Henriques leaned over the table with the bottle of cognac, Killigrew shifted his chair slightly and a moment later the footman had dropped the bottle and was hopping about, clutching his foot.

'Oh, I'm sorry, did I hurt you?' Killigrew quickly righted the bottle and mopped up the puddle of spilt cognac from the surface of the table with his napkin. 'My apologies. How clumsy of me.' He made as if to wring out the napkin, twisting it between his hands, and then thrust it into the neck of the bottle and touched the cognac-soaked cloth to one of the candles in the nearest candelabra. The cognac flamed at once and then Killigrew hurled the bottle at Assata. She ducked and the bottle smashed against the wall, spraying the far end of the room with flaming cognac.

Killigrew rammed his elbow into Salazar's face, knocking him backwards over his chair, and then tipped the table over sideways against Coffin, pinning him in his seat. He grabbed Miss Chance by the wrist and dragged her through the door leading to the kitchen before any of the others could recover in time to react. They slammed the door behind them and a moment later two bullets smashed the panels in quick succession.

A tall wooden dresser piled with crockery stood beside the door, and Killigrew at once tried to pull it over in front of the door. Seeing his intention, Miss Chance helped him and a moment later it crashed into place, scattering shards of broken crockery across the floor. The door opened an inch a moment later, and was then brought up short as the dresser blocked it. On the other side, someone started to throw their shoulder against it.

Killigrew and Miss Chance turned away from the door to see a heavily build chef with a scar down one side of his face staring at them in astonishment. Recovering quickly, the chef snatched up a large triangular-bladed knife and lunged at them.

Killigrew dodged the thrust and backed away around the kitchen table. A cauldron of consommé was gently warming over the hearth; Killigrew grabbed a butcher's hook, using it to tip up the cauldron so that a tidal wave of soup splashed across the floor towards the chef. Even further enraged at seeing his creation treated in such a cavalier manner, he charged forwards. As he thrust at Killigrew's throat, Killigrew caught him by the wrist. The two of them struggled chest-to-chest with the knife between them. The chef was the stronger of the two, and he forced Killigrew back into the flames in the hearth at the same time that he turned the blade's point towards Killigrew's left eye.

Then there was a dull thump and the chef's head jerked. His eyes rolled up and he slid down to the floor to reveal Miss Chance standing behind him wielding a heavy wooden chopping board in both hands.

The men on the other side of the door had stopped trying to open it and were now trying to smash it, the panels splintering as they attacked them with some sharp, heavy object. Killigrew grabbed Miss Chance by the hand. 'Come on.'

There was another door on the far side of the kitchen. It was locked but the key was in the hole.

Killigrew unlocked it, took out the key and hustled Miss Chance through, before following her out and locking the door behind them. He looked around to get his bearings, and then dragged her after him as he dashed across the lawn. There was a brick wall nearly eight feet high at the far end of the garden. He leaped up and got his hands over the top of it, his feet scrabbling against the bricks until he was able to pull himself up. Sitting astride the wall he glanced down to help Miss Chance up after him, but there was no sign of her.

'Miss Chance?' he hissed urgently into the darkness.

'Behind you.'

He twisted, and saw her seated on the wall beside him. 'How did you...?'

'What?'

'Never mind.' His hand found hers in the darkness and the two of them jumped from the wall, rolling over on the compacted earth below.

A bell tolled sonorously in the darkness, some kind of alarm, and in the glow of torches off to their right they could see armed men emerging from the low barracks they had seen earlier. 'Maybe they don't want us to leave after all,' mused Killigrew, leading the way between two single-storey thatched buildings.

Behind them torches and lanterns were being lit throughout the barracoon. Killigrew was tempted to find the slave pens to release all the slaves, using the confusion he would thus cause to effect his own escape. But the slaves would be locked in, fettered and shackled and under heavy guard. Releasing them would have to wait for another day, when he came back with reinforcements to destroy the barracoon once and for all. The only way he could make sure of that was to get out alive.

They plunged into the bushes beneath some trees, blundering through the thick undergrowth until he was sure they had lost their pursuers. He became aware that Miss Chance was pulling back against him, trying to slow him. 'Stop!' she hissed. 'We can't go anywhere without my brother!'

'I don't intend to.' He stopped to get his bearings. All around them the jungle was alive with the croaking of frogs and the chirruping of insects, but the sounds of pursuit were distant. 'They can't search the whole jungle for us and they won't be able to follow our tracks until it gets light, so we've got a few hours at least. They'll expect us to make for the shore and follow the coast south to Monrovia.' He glanced around. There were no less than four watchtowers, one at each corner of the barracoon, and he could just make them out against the purple night sky. Using his trained seaman's eye, he took a bearing on each of them so he could find his way back to where he stood now.

She suddenly pecked him on the cheek. He regarded her with gentle amusement. 'What was that for?'

'Thank you. You were wonderful back there.'

'You were rather splendid yourself, if I may say so. Can't say I've known many young ladies who'd've handled themselves as well as you did tonight. But we're not out of it yet. Do you think you can climb up this tree?'

She looked up at the branches overhead. 'Certainly, but why?'

'You'll be safe up there. If anyone does come by, just stay very still and keep quiet. You'd be amazed by how few people ever bother to look upwards when they're searching for someone.'

'Where are you going?'

'To fetch your brother. And to make sure they don't use the *Leopardo* to ship any slaves out of here before I can come back to destroy this place.'

'Why can't I come with you?'

'Do you think you can swim half a mile?'

'No,' she admitted. 'Can you?'

'I'll have to. Sit tight. I'll be back, I promise,' he added, conscious that time was against them.

Fronds and creepers lashed at him as he stumbled through the darkness. He knew he might blunder into the trunk of a tree at any moment, but he was racing against time now, knowing he had to get well away from the barracoon with Miss Chance and her brother by sun-up. The unmistakable sound of the surf booming on the shore guided him. He crashed through the undergrowth, tripped over a root, and suddenly found himself rolling over and over on fine, dry sand.

He stopped himself and scrambled back into the trees in case anyone was watching the beach. A full tropical moon cast its pale yellow light over the scene, and he could see the *Leopardo* anchored about half a mile out to sea. He hoped that the Reverend Chance was sufficiently recovered from his blow on the head for Killigrew to get him off the ship.

He sat down and unlaced his half-boots. He was not worried about sharks, at least not much. He was more worried that Salazar's men might be expecting him and Miss Chance to make for the beach; perhaps they were already watching the sand from the trees further up the beach, with their rifles primed and loaded. Still, the longer Killigrew left it the greater the danger became. He knew his chances of salvaging any kind of victory against the slavers were now slim, but he had reached the stage where there was nothing he could do but plough on and hope for the best. It was his duty to get out of this alive, not only for his sake and that of the Chances, but also for the slaves in the pens, both present and future.

He dashed out of the trees and sprinted across the white sand, half expecting a fusillade of shots to blast out of the night behind him. But there were no shots, no shouts, nothing. When Salazar and his men came to the beach – as they must do, sooner or later – they would see his footprints in the sand. What would they make of them? Would they guess what he was up to? Perhaps not: it was so bold, he could hardly believe he was attempting it himself.

He splashed through the surf, deeper and deeper, until he could dive into the water and pull himself through the breakers with a strong crawl stroke. There was a strong current running across the coast and he had to stop every few minutes, pacing himself and redirecting himself towards the ship again. When it was only a cable's length away he used a silent breast-stroke so as not to alert anyone on deck of his approach, but as the *Leopardo*'s hull loomed above him a better idea occurred to him.

He trod water alongside the hull and waved an arm above his head. 'Hey, Covilhã! Ahoy there! Anyone up there?'

A man's head appeared silhouetted above him. 'Who's there?'

'That you, Covilhã? Throw me a line, for God's sake. Then weigh anchor and make sail. We've got to get out of here.'

A rope was thrown down from the side and Killigrew pulled himself up it, his stockinged feet braced against the brig's side. He was surprised by how much effort it took him just to climb aboard: the swim had drained him more than he had realised. As he scrambled over the bulwark, he saw the other members of the crew gathered on deck. 'Don't just stand there, for Christ's sake! Man the capstan! We've got to get out of here.'

'I take my orders from the *capitão*, not you,' snarled Covilhã.

'Not any more. He's dead. So are Coffin and the others. Wake up and look lively there, man. It's an ambush – the British were waiting for us. They've must've taken the barracoon before we got here. There's no sign of Salazar and the others. I was lucky to get away with my life.'

Killigrew managed to project the right amount of urgency and panic into his voice to convince the boatswain, who turned to his men: 'You heard Senhor Killigrew! Man the capstan!' he ordered. 'Away aloft! Which way do we sail?'

'I don't know,' snapped Killigrew. 'Away from the coast, out to sea, to start with. There's probably a British cruiser waiting up the coast to close the trap, a steamer like as not. I'll go down to the chart room and plot us a new course.'

Covilhã nodded and Killigrew left him and the crew busily preparing to set sail while he went below deck. He made his way forward to the sick bay where the Reverend Chance lay on the cot. Dr Pereira was dozing in his chair. Killigrew went to the cot and tried to shake Chance awake, but at once saw by the light of the oil lamp that nothing would ever wake the clergyman again. He was dead, as stiff as a board, his face twisted into a ghastly rictus. He had not died easily.

Pereira stirred and looked up at him. 'What ... what's wrong?'

'What happened here?'

Pereira looked puzzled. 'He ... he's dead, *senhor.*'

'I can see that,' snapped Killigrew. 'How?'

'I used the strychnine.' He gestured to where a brown bottle stood on a shelf. 'Isn't that what Capitão Madison wanted?'

Killigrew felt sickened. He regarded the surgeon in contempt. 'You murdered him? In cold blood?'

'I ... I was only obeying orders, *senhor!*' protested Pereira.

'Well, I've got new orders for you.' Killigrew took the bottle from the shelf and removed the stopper. There was plenty of poison left. He held it out to the surgeon. 'Drink.'

Sweat broke out on Pereira's brow. 'Please, *senhor* ... no!'

'Drink it! All of it.'

'Please, *senhor*, I beg you...' Pereira tried to dodge past Killigrew in his panic but Killigrew tripped him up. Pereira sprawled on the deck and as he rolled over on his back Killigrew sat on his chest. As he tried to pour the poison between Pereira's lips, the surgeon clamped his mouth firmly shut. Killigrew punched him in the throat and when he opened his mouth to gasp Killigrew thrust the neck of the bottle between his teeth. He pinched the surgeon's nose, closing his nostrils and forcing him to swallow.

'Have a taste of your own medicine,' Killigrew suggested grimly.

Pereira thrashed about wildly, first in terror and then as the spasms gripped his body. Fortunately the sound of the anchor chains rattling through the hawse-hole smothered the hammering of the surgeon's limbs against the deck. His teeth clamped down so hard on the neck of the bottle they smashed it, but by then he was already as good as dead. Killigrew snatched the pillow from under Chance's head and smothered it over Pereira's face to stifle his horrid gurgling and retching. After a few moments he lay still.

Killigrew stood up, as sickened by what he himself had just done as he had been by the Reverend's murder. Was he any better than the slavers were, at heart...?

'*Que...?*'

He whirled to see Covilhã standing in the entrance to the sick bay, staring down at Pereira's body. Killigrew glanced around for something he could use as a weapon, but Covilhã quickly pulled his pistol from his belt and levelled it at him. 'I do not know what you are doing, *senhor*, but I think you were lying about the Royal Navy ambushing *Capitão* Madison and Senhor Coffin. I think it is you who is working for the Royal Navy...'

Killigrew raised his hands. 'You have to trust me. You don't understand. It was Pereira who was the spy, not me...'

'I have had enough of your lies, *senhor*.' Covilhã raised his arm and levelled the pistol between his eyes.

Killigrew braced himself for the shock of the ball smashing into his skull and prayed that the pain would be short-lived.

There came the sound of a soft 'clunk' and Covilhã's grip on the pistol faltered as blood trickled down his face. Killigrew stared in astonishment and saw a butcher's cleaver embedded in his skull. The boatswain's knees gave way and he crumpled, revealing the broad-shouldered shape of the ship's cook standing behind him.

'Doc,' said Killigrew. 'I can explain everything...'

'Don't bother. I know exactly who you are and what you're up to. You're working for Rear-Admiral Napier, aren't you?'

'No, that's a...' Killigrew frowned. 'How the devil do *you* know?'

Doc grinned. 'Because I'm working for him, too.' Doc's pidgin-patois was gone, replaced by what sounded suspiciously like a London accent. 'Able Seaman Wes Molineaux, at your service, sir. The rear-admiral asked me to keep an eye on you. Looks like it was a good thing he did, too.'

'He might've let me know.' Killigrew eyed Molineaux dubiously. God knows, he needed all the friends he could get right now, but he was not sure if the black could be trusted. Certainly Molineaux was not on the side of the slavers, for if he had been he had had nothing to gain and everything to lose by killing Covilhã; and it would not have been unlike Napier to have set Killigrew such an unusual guardian angel. He decided he had no choice but to trust his new-found friend.

Molineaux eyed Chance's corpse on the cot and then lowered his gaze to where Pereira lay beneath Covilhã. 'Did you hush the quack?'

'Yes.'

'Plummy for you. Never did like him. What's the plan, boss? You *have* got a plan, haven't you?'

'Yes. And it's "lieutenant" or "sir" to you, Able Seaman. Not "boss".'

Molineaux grinned. 'I know all about you, Killigrew. You may not have killed that ankle-biter, but it was a real court-martial that cashiered you. So until the day you get your rank back – if it ever comes – I'll call you what I like. In fact, seeing as how I'm an able seaman and you're just a plain civilian, I reckon it should be *me* who's giving the orders.'

'We'll worry about that later. First of all we've

377

got to destroy this ship. You go to the hold and set one of the powder kegs to explode in ten minutes' time; I'll see if I can break into Madison's safe and find anything interesting.'

'You know all about cracking peters, do you?'

'How difficult can it be?'

'Bearing in mind a safe is a box which has been specifically designed to stop people from breaking into them–'

'And you're an expert, I suppose?' Killigrew snapped impatiently.

'As it happens, yes. That's why the rear-admiral chose me for this job.'

Killigrew nodded. He had already guessed from Molineaux's use of thieves' cant that the seaman had not always worked on the right side of the law. 'I'm surprised he bothered to involve me in this at all. You seem to know all the wrinkles.'

'The rear-admiral figured a ship's officer would have a better chance of learning something from Madison than a black cook. Seems he was wrong, though.'

'Save the sass for later. We've got work to do. I'll meet you in Madison's day room in five minutes.'

Molineaux had sense enough not to argue. As he headed aft, Killigrew took down the oil lamp and fetched a candle from the purser's store and a coil of rope from the boatswain's locker. He looped the coil over one shoulder and slipped into the hold. He could hear the sailors moving about on deck above, and the timbers began to creak as the masts took up the strain of the billowing sails.

Killigrew put the oil lamp down on one of the kegs of gunpowder stowed in the hold and took his clasp knife from his pocket. He broached the top of another keg, wincing at the sound of the wood splintering, and prayed that no one on deck had heard it. Then he stirred the powder in the keg with his hands, hoping it had not separated into its constituent parts during the voyage. He scooped it up to one side, so that the surface of the powder in the keg formed as steep a slope as possible.

Now for the delicate part.

He took the candle out of his pocket, and cut it all off but for one inch. Lifting the glass cover from the oil lamp, he lit the stub of the candle. Holding his breath, he planted it in the powder. As the candle burned down, the powder would slide down to fill in the void, until at last it came into contact with the flame.

Still holding his breath, he replaced the glass cover on the oil lamp and backed away from where the candle flickered over the charcoal-covered powder. As the deck rolled the candle listed slightly and Killigrew's heart leaped into his mouth. Then it seemed to settle down. He hurried out of the hold and headed aft to Madison's day room.

Crouched in front of the safe, Molineaux was inserting a couple of picklocks into the keyhole when Killigrew entered. The seaman glanced up in alarm, but then recognised him and relaxed. 'Get it open?' Killigrew asked him.

'Not yet. These things take time.'

'Time is the one thing we don't have. There's

enough powder in the hold to blow up this ship and ten more like her.' Killigrew crossed to the window and opened it, before tying one end of the rope to an overhead beam.

'If we don't find something in here to tell us who's behind this Bay Cay Trading Company, you can kiss goodbye to your commission.'

'And if we don't get out of here now you can kiss goodbye to that part of your anatomy on which you sit. And every other part of your anatomy, for that matter.'

'Got it!' The tumblers of the lock clicked, and Molineaux swung open the door.

The safe was empty.

Salazar reined in his horse on the beach to the south of the barracoon, where Madison and Coffin headed southwards with a band of Salazar's men, holding burning torches aloft. 'Any sign of them?' asked Salazar.

'No,' snapped Coffin. 'We're wasting our time here. Killigrew won't come this way, because he knows it's the first place we'll look.'

'It is the only sensible way for him to come,' Salazar pointed out reasonably. 'The nearest settlement is Monrovia, fifty miles to the south. Either he comes this way or he makes for Freetown, which is nearer a hundred miles to the north.'

Coffin hawked and spat upon the sand. 'You seem pretty sure he'll stick to the coast.'

'Of course he will. What chance do a young European and an American lady have of getting anywhere in the interior? They would not last five minutes. It would be complete madness to try that way.'

'It was complete madness for him to try to pass himself off as a slaver,' said Coffin. 'But he tried it – and almost pulled it off.'

'Prince Khari will take his leopard warriors into the interior to search for him,' said Salazar. 'If Killigrew has headed inland, he will not get far.'

'I wouldn't trust the uppity nigger and his goddamned leopard warriors to catch a dose of the clap,' snorted Coffin. 'Face it, Salazar. You let the Limey bastard get away.'

Salazar shrugged. 'Perhaps. It does not matter.'

'Doesn't matter!' exclaimed Madison. 'And just how do you figure that, Mr Salazar, bearing in mind that once he gets back to civilisation he'll tell the authorities everything: about you and me, about my ship and your barracoon...'

'*If* he gets back, which I very much doubt. And if anyone will believe him, which I also very much doubt. You forget: in England he is disgraced as a drunk and a child-killer.'

'He won't be when Rear-Admiral Napier speaks up for him.'

'Which is why I suggest someone goes to England and makes sure that an accident befalls the rear-admiral. Something fatal. Who will pay any attention to Killigrew if he does not have Napier to back him up?'

A smile spread slowly across Coffin's face. 'Maybe you ain't such a dumb sonuvabitch after all, Salazar.'

'I hope not. It would be a poor world indeed where a "dumb sonuvabitch" could amass as vast a fortune as my own. Are you volunteering to go to England to arrange the admiral's tragic and premature demise?'

Coffin grinned. 'It'll be my pleasure.'

Salazar turned to Madison. 'You see, captain? Even if Killigrew does make it back to civilisation – which is extremely unlikely – his story will not be believed. So I think that I shall be able to continue my trade uninterrupted for a few years yet, and nothing will stop you from using the profits of this voyage to fund your retirement. I don't think Mr Killigrew will give us any more trouble...'

They heard a thump from out to sea, and turned their eyes in that direction in time to see the *Leopardo* disintegrate in a huge, blossoming ball of orange flame accompanied by a tremendous roar. A thousand planks of wood were hurled in all directions, most of them high into the sky, and as the ball of fire faded into a black cloud the planks rained down on the surface of the sea, some of them landing on the beach a short distance away. Of the *Leopardo* they could see nothing, just the expanding concentric circles in the water to show where she had recently floated.

For a few moments the men on the beach stared in stunned silence. It was Madison who spoke first. 'And just in case that Limey bastard *does* get back to England,' he told Coffin with a calmness surprising for one who had just had his livelihood blown out of the water, 'make sure he suffers an accident, too. A very painful one.'

382

Both Killigrew and Molineaux duck-tailed under the water as the ship exploded less than two hundred yards behind them. The surface of the water above them burned as bright as sunrise with orange flame, and a moment later the shock wave hit them, knocking the breath from their bodies. They surfaced, gasping, just as the debris rained down about them.

'Bang go your chances of finding out who was behind the Bay Cay Trading Company,' gasped Molineaux as they trod water beside one another.

'I'll just have to hope that being able to reveal the location of Salazar's barracoon is enough to redeem myself and win back my commission,' said Killigrew.

'And we'll just have to hope that we can live that long.' Molineaux nodded to the beach perhaps seven hundred yards away where they could see torches. 'Looks like we've got a reception committee waiting for us on shore.'

'They won't be able to see us out here. Those torches will ruin their night-vision. We'll be all right so long as we steer clear of the circle of light.'

They swam across the bar, the current carrying them away from where the men on the beach spread out to meet any survivors swimming from the *Leopardo*. At last they reached the shallows and crouched low in the surf, gasping for breath. They were perhaps two hundred yards away from the nearest man, with fifty yards of open beach between them and the cover of the trees. 'Together, or one at a time?' asked Molineaux.

Killigrew shook his head. 'One at a time.

Crawling. Less chance of being seen that way. You go first.'

Molineaux nodded and slithered up through the surf and out of the water, gliding with cat-like stealth over the sand while Killigrew watched the men with the torches, waiting for one of them to cry out at any moment. But they moved further away now, heading back towards the barracoon, as if they had given up any hope of catching Killigrew returning ashore; perhaps they thought he had been blown up with the *Leopardo*.

When he glanced back at Molineaux he saw the seaman was already near the trees, and a few moments later the black was swallowed up by the darkness beneath the trees. Killigrew did not hesitate before following him. As he crawled along in Molineaux's tracks, he realised there was another advantage to crawling over running. Salazar's men were bound to find their tracks with the coming of sunrise and if they had found two sets of footsteps they would have realised that Killigrew had an ally now, for there would have been no chance of mistaking Molineaux's prints for Miss Chance's. But crawling just left one confused track which could as easily have been the work of one man as of two.

He reached the trees and stood up beneath their boughs, dusting off the worst of the sand which clung to his sodden clothes. 'Molineaux? You there?'

'Yeah, I'm here,' Molineaux's voice came back. Killigrew found the seaman's presence strangely reassuring. 'I mean, it's not as if there's anywhere else I could go, is there? What do we do now, head down the coast towards Monrovia?'

Killigrew shook his head. 'No. First we have to fetch Miss Chance.'

'You managed to keep her alive, then? That's good.' Molineaux grinned, his teeth showing white in the darkness. 'I was beginning to think we'd run out of Chances.'

'Very droll.' Killigrew led the way through the belt of trees which lay between the beach and the barracoon, heading parallel to the shore.

'Are you going to tell me what went wrong, then?'

'Salazar knew all about me. Someone in England talked to the wrong person.'

'Impossible. The only people who knew what you were doing were you, me, and the rear-admiral himself. And you're not suggesting *he* peached, are you?'

'No. But I'm still not sure about you.'

'Well, thank you very much! I saved your life back there, you know.'

'Anyway, several people knew about my mission,' said Killigrew. 'Corporal Summerbee and Private Whitehead, to name but two.' *And Eulalia Fairbody to name a third,* Killigrew could not help thinking as he found his half-boots and sat down to pull them on. It was inconceivable to think that she might have betrayed him, and yet...

'Who are Corporal Summerbee and Private Whitehead when they're at home?'

'A couple of Jollies who helped me inveigle myself on board the *Madge Howlett;* or the *Leopardo,* whichever you prefer. You still haven't hold me how *you* got on board her, by the way.'

'I joined her in Havana,' explained Molineaux. 'Madison went to a slave market looking for a good seaman who could cook. He chose me. At least, that's what he thinks. Actually he chose one of the other slaves and I was substituted later with the British consul's help.'

'And you mean to tell me Madison never noticed the switch?'

'Of course not. Us darkies all look the same to you people.'

'I'll thank you not to put me in the same category as Madison, Coffin and Salazar,' said Killigrew. 'So the British consul in Havana knew about our plan as well?'

Molineaux shook his head. 'He knew Napier wanted me aboard a certain slave vessel, but he didn't know why. And I didn't tell him.'

'It couldn't have been him anyway,' mused Killigrew. 'Salazar said his informant was in England... Wait a minute: if Napier had you join the crew of the *Leopardo* in Havana, he must've been setting this thing up for months. But he only told me about it two months ago.' Two months! It seemed more like two years since he had played billiards in the United Service Club in London.

'Months!' said Molineaux. 'Man, I've been on that ship for two *years*. Something went wrong, badly wrong. The cove I was supposed to protect was someone called Comber, but he never even turned up. I managed to get in touch with Napier the next time we landed at Liverpool and he told me to sit tight until he could get someone else.

When you turned up I *knew* you were one of his men straight away.'

'You've been living a lie for two years on that hell ship? I take my hat off to you. Or at least, I would if I were wearing one.'

'Yes, and it hasn't been fun either, I can tell you. You saw for yourself how Madison used to treat me.'

'You must be dedicated to the cause of anti-slavery.'

'To tell the truth I didn't have much choice. But don't believe any of that gammon I told you about not caring about the Africans. They're human beings, at least, which is more than you can say for bastards like Madison and Coffin. I don't know what made you so down on slavery, sir, but while Madison never had me flogged – as long as I toadied to him and grovelled and bowed and scraped like a bug-eyed watermelon-guzzling sonuvabitch – he weren't kind to every slave that came his way, I can tell you. Some of the things I've seen...'

'I've seen similar,' Killigrew assured him.

'So are we going to get those bastards and put them out of business for ever?'

'Damned right we are.' The two of them shook on it. 'But first we have to get to safety. Now, where did I leave Miss Chance?'

Killigrew paused to look around. He could tell from where he stood in relation to the watch-towers that he was not far from where he had left her, but in the darkness all the trees looked the same. They were too close to the barracoon for him to want to risk calling out to her.

'You mean you don't know where you left her?' Molineaux hissed incredulously.

'She's around here somewhere...'

A woman's scream, loud and shrill in the darkness, sounded somewhere off to their right.

'This way,' said Killigrew, heading off in the direction of the scream.

XVI:

The Law of the Jungle

Well, Suzannah, you wanted adventure, Miss Chance told herself ruefully as she made herself as comfortable as possible in the tree's lower boughs. *You can't say that isn't what you've got.* Shipwrecked, picked up by murderous cutthroats, chased by the US Navy, threatened with being consigned to a megalomaniac's harem and rescued by a dashing young British naval officer; if she ever got a chance to write back to her family in Poughkeepsie they were not going to believe a word of it. She was not sure that she believed it herself.

The problem was, she had had more adventures in one week than she had planned to have in the five years she intended to spend working at the Sherbro Island mission. *Serves you right. Missionary work is supposed to be a way of serving God, not of looking for adventure...*

The night sky was lit up by an explosion which hammered her ears with its roar. Mr Killigrew had said something about making sure the slavers did not use the *Leopardo* to ship out the slaves in the barracoon, but had he intended to blow the ship out of the water? It was quite likely, but until he returned she had no way of knowing whether or not he had managed to get off the

389

ship with her brother before the explosion. She hoped so. For one thing, she had little confidence in her ability to get back to safety without his help; she had studied maps of the Guinea Coast, of course, and guessed the barracoon lay somewhere between Sierra Leone and Monrovia, but which was nearest she had no idea. And for another, she found Killigrew so infuriating she was starting to wonder if she had fallen in love with him. First of all he had charmed her, then he had let her think he was a drunkard and a child-killer, then he had let her think he was a slaver, and now he had been revealed as a brave man prepared to risk everything in the noble cause of the fight against the slave trade.

'Pssssssst!'

The sound snapped her out of her reverie. 'Mr Killigrew?' she called softly. 'Is that you?'

'Pssssssst!'

The noise was close. Too close. As if it were in the tree with her…

She twisted on the bough she lay on and came face to face with a snake. She froze instantly, but her movement had already startled it and its head reared back, inches from her own, so close she could clearly see its black eyes glittering in the light and its forked tongue flickering out at her.

She caught her breath. She could feel her heart pounding. The snake only wanted to get out of the tree, she knew, but she was in its way. Why did it not have the sense to turn around and go back the way it had come?

She tried to edge back down the bough towards the trunk, but even that movement seemed to anger the snake and it reared back again. It might not be deadly poisonous, she realised, but she had no wish to find out the hard way.

She was aware of someone moving about on the ground below her, silently and stealthily. She could not look down to see who it was without taking her eyes off the snake, and that she could not bring herself to do. Its gaze was hypnotic and forced her to focus all her attention on it.

She heard a snap from below. At first she thought it was a twig breaking underfoot, but a second, identical snap followed hard on the heels of the first. It was no natural sound, but the noise of a brace of pistols being cocked. Out of the corner of her eyes she could see Assata below her, aiming her pistols up at her. The amazon gestured for her to climb down out of the tree.

'I can't move!' she hissed. 'There's a snake!'

Assata gestured with the pistols again, impatiently now. Miss Chance tried to ease her way back down the bough, but again the snake reared threateningly. Get shot or get bitten by a poisonous snake; what kind of a choice was that?

Then the snake struck.

Young ladies of genteel upbringing rarely have the opportunity to test their reflexes, so it was not until that moment that Miss Chance had any idea how good her own were. The palm of her hand hit the side of the snake, just behind its head, and without thinking about it she closed her fingers around it. It opened its jaws wide, baring vicious fangs at her, but she gripped it tightly, knowing that to let it go would be one of the last things she ever did if its bite were deadly

391

poisonous. It hissed at her, and she hoped it was not the kind of snake which could spit venom into its victim's eyes.

Then she realised she had lost her balance on the bough and was slipping over sideways. She could not use her right hand and flailed about wildly with her left, but it met only thin air. She reached the point of no return, teetered for a moment, and then fell.

The fall seemed to last for ever, and yet at the same time it was over before she knew it. What little of the world she could see in the darkness tumbled around her, and then she hit the ground below, using her left arm to break the fall and taking care to hold the snake well away from her body with her right.

Assata said nothing – she never did – but she snorted what might have been a contemptuous laugh, and gestured for Miss Chance to get up. Miss Chance tried to comply, but she could not use her right arm and she sprawled awkwardly on her left side. Assata moved in close, apparently oblivious to the particular impediment under which Miss Chance laboured, and kicked her in the side. The amazon was only wearing sandals, but she did not hold back and the blow was both painful and humiliating.

'All right, all right, I'm trying!' Miss Chance snapped irritably. 'Stop kicking me! Can't you see I've got this–'

She broke off, and looked from the snake to the amazon. Then she pressed the snake's mouth to Assata's ankle.

Assata screamed and dropped the pistols as the

snake's fangs went home. Then she turned and ran off through the trees, shrieking, doubtless hoping to find someone who would suck out the venom before it was too late.

Miss Chance snatched up the pistols and sprinted off in the other direction without really thinking about where she was going or what she was going to do when she got there. Her problem was solved for her a moment later when she bumped into a dark figure. She gasped and almost discharged both the pistols at him, when another voice called out to her. 'Miss Chance? It's all right, he's with me!'

'Mr Killigrew?' She threw herself at him and wrapped her arms around him, and he hugged her back.

'It's all right, you're safe now. We're back. We made it.'

'What about my brother? Where is he?'

'I'm sorry,' whispered Killigrew, hugging her tightly and rubbing her back. 'I'm so sorry.'

She let out a sob.

'If it's any consolation, miss, we managed to take care of the swine that murdered him,' the black man said in an English accent. She recognised him as the cook from the *Leopardo* now, although his accent had changed.

She pushed herself away from Killigrew and dried the tears that prickled her eyes on one of her elbow-length gloves before turning to the black man. 'No, as it happens it is no consolation whatsoever,' she told him coldly. 'It won't bring my brother back, will it? He was the gentlest, kindest man that ever lived. The last memorial he would have cared for is cold-blooded revenge.'

'I'm sorry, miss, but it wasn't cold-blooded, believe me,' said Killigrew, looking guilty. 'And there are plenty of other gentle and kind people out there who'll suffer if we don't put a stop to Salazar and Madison and their activities.'

She handed the brace of pistols to Killigrew. 'Who is this?' she demanded, tossing her head in the black man's direction.

'Able Seaman Molineaux,' explained Killigrew. 'It's all right, he's on the side of the angels.'

The black grinned. 'My friends call me "Wes", miss.'

'Do they indeed, Mr Molineaux?'

'Who was that screaming?' asked Killigrew.

'Assata. I was in that tree and there was a snake and then she appeared below me and pointed her pistols at me and the snake was going to strike so I grabbed it behind the head but I fell out of the tree and then she was kicking me so I made the snake bite her, heaven help me, and she ran off. I think I may have murdered her!'

'Self-defence, miss,' Killigrew assured her. 'No one will blame you for it. She'd've done the same to you, and with less provocation. But we'd better get moving. Even if that snake was poisonous, I suspect Miss Assata will live long enough to point Salazar and his cut-throats in this direction.'

No one argued with that and they set off through the trees, Killigrew leading the way. He held out one of the pistols to Molineaux. 'You know how to use one of these?'

'Just give me half a chance!'

'Well, don't. Not unless you really have to. The

sound of a gunshot will bring Salazar's men running, and right now we have more than enough problems as it is.'

The foliage grew thicker and a moment later they emerged from the trees to find themselves standing on the south bank of the creek. 'Can we swim across?' Miss Chance asked dubiously.

'Yes,' said Killigrew. 'Unfortunately, so can they.' He pointed across to where dozens of crocodiles silently patrolled the water in the moonlight.

'Then we have to go back and head south to Monrovia,' said Molineaux. 'It's closer than Freetown, anyway.'

Killigrew shook his head. 'That's exactly what Salazar will expect us to do.'

'Well, what do you suggest we do? We can't stay here, and now you tell us we can't head north or south. That only leaves swimming the Atlantic!'

'We go inland.'

'Inland! Are you crazy? Into the interior? We'll never get out alive!'

'Trust me. I know what I'm doing.' Killigrew motioned for Molineaux and Miss Chance to halt, and then pointed up ahead, to where Madison's gig was tied up to a wooden jetty which projected out into the creek. 'We'll head upstream in that.'

'Don't you think those two plug uglies with muskets might have something to say about that?' asked Molineaux.

Killigrew hefted the pistol in his hand. 'You two wait here.' He disappeared into the bushes off to their right. For a couple of minutes everything

395

was silent and Miss Chance and Molineaux were alone with the sounds of the jungle at night. Things were livelier in the direction of the barracoon, where someone was shouting orders, trying to draw order out of the confusion. On the far side of the creek she heard the mournful cry of a whippoorwill.

The two guards on the jetty stood in companionable silence, their muskets slung over their shoulders, one of them smoking a clay pipe. A moment later the pipe fell to the jetty, the guards gaped, and they both raised their hands. Killigrew emerged from the shadows, covering them both with his pistols, and motioned for Molineaux and Miss Chance to come and help him. They relieved the guards of their muskets, tied them up with their own belts, and then removed the boots of one so they could gag them with his socks.

'We'd better get a move on,' said Miss Chance, and nodded to where she could see lights in the trees further down the creek, where they had just come from. 'It looks like they're closing in.'

'All right,' said Killigrew. 'Get in the gig, Miss Chance. Cast off the painter, Molineaux.' He finished gagging the two men and then jumped down into the gig, taking up one oar while the seaman took the other and pushed them out from the jetty.

'My hands are still killing me after pulling on those sweeps all afternoon,' grumbled Molineaux.

'Mine too,' Killigrew said tightly, and nodded to where the men with torches were emerging from the trees. 'But if we don't keep rowing I don't imagine those gentlemen will be in a mood to tend to our blisters.'

'Is there anything I can do to help?' asked Miss Chance, feeling like useless baggage and hating it.

'Can you shoot?' Killigrew asked hopefully.

'I'm willing to try, but I'm afraid I'd only be wasting bullets.'

'All right. You sit tight, and maybe say a prayer for us. We'll soon have you out of here.' Killigrew and Molineaux sat side by side on the bench and hauled mightily on the oars, swiftly propelling the gig up the sluggish waters of the creek.

The men on the bank reached the jetty, stopped and levelled their muskets. Powder flamed in the darkness and a flock of ibises rose honking into the night sky as the first shots echoed over the mangrove swamps. The musket balls buzzed through the darkness, occasionally plopping into the water close to the gig, but none came too close for comfort. Some of the men tried to pursue the gig on the bank, but the undergrowth was thick and they soon fell behind.

Killigrew and Molineaux were too busying rowing to return fire. The firing died down once Salazar's men had all discharged their muskets and there was a pause while they stopped to reload. Then there was more firing, sporadic now as each man fired as soon as he was ready, but they were even further behind now and the shooting was yet more erratic. A few moments later another bend in the creek had hidden the gig from their view. Killigrew and Molineaux kept rowing, desperate to put as much distance between them and the slavers as possible before sun-up, which was only a couple of hours away now.

'Can we stop now?' asked Molineaux. 'I reckon we've lost them–'

A couple of canoes shot out of a side-channel off to their right, each containing six men. All the men had muskets slung over their shoulders, but they did not aim them yet, hoping first to overhaul the gig.

Killigrew and Molineaux redoubled their efforts, but it was hopeless. The sleek canoes were built for speed, and they had more rowers. 'Take this,' said Killigrew, handing Molineaux his oar.

'What? You're going to leave me to do all the work?'

'Trust me.'

The first canoe drew level with the gig. The men in the canoe still did not bother to unsling their muskets: presumably Salazar had told them to bring Killigrew and the others back alive if they could.

Killigrew felt under the thwart in the stern sheets and found a wooden cask. Taking it in both hands, he stood up suddenly, balancing easily in the rocking boat, hefted the cask above his head and hurled it at one of the men in the canoe. The man dived out of the way, upsetting the next man, and then the cask smashed through the bottom of the canoe. It filled with water and foundered at once.

The crocodiles in the water changed direction

and closed in on the men swimming in the water.

The gig left the sinking canoe behind, but now the second canoe was moving in for the kill. This time they did not come too close, but two of the men in the bows of the canoe levelled their muskets. Even with only four men paddling, it easily outpaced the gig.

The muskets boomed and Miss Chance gasped as a musket ball splintered the gig's gunwale close to her hand. Then Killigrew had picked up one of the muskets they had taken from the men on the jetty, brought it up to his shoulder, aimed and fired, all in one smooth motion. The first musketeer did not even cry out, just fell back silently against his mate, his arms flung wide, his musket falling into the water.

Miss Chance was shocked by Killigrew's coolness as he executed these men, even though she knew he had no choice, and yet she was also glad she had someone as proficient at killing as him to protect her. What was the phrase he had used earlier of Molineaux? 'On the side of the angels'. She thanked Heaven that Killigrew was on the side of the angels, even if he were an angel of death. He might kill just as unhesitatingly as the men who sought to capture them – perhaps even more so – but what made him different from them was that he would never harm her, was even prepared to risk his own life in order to preserve hers.

He picked up the next musket, fired again, and the second musketeer fell over the side of the canoe.

One of the men from the first canoe suddenly

got his hand on the side of the gig and tried to grab Miss Chance. She shrieked in alarm and kicked him in the head. Another man appeared on the other side of them, and Killigrew smashed the butt of the musket into his face. A third tried to swim after them, but a crocodile surfaced behind him, its jaws gaping, and a moment later the man was dragged under. Horrified, Miss Chance covered her eyes.

'It's all right,' said Killigrew. 'It's just the law of the jungle. Kill or be killed.'

'Cannibalism, if you ask me,' said Molineaux. 'I've never seen reptiles eating reptiles before.'

Another shoot rang out from the second canoe, which was still overhauling them even with only three men paddling now. Killigrew braced his feet on the bottom boards and took careful aim with his pistol. Another man died, and Miss Chance quickly snatched the other pistol from Molineaux's belt and handed it up to Killigrew. He took careful aim again, but then hesitated.

'Shoot, for Christ's sake!' urged Molineaux, still heaving on the oars.

'It's our last shot,' said Killigrew. 'And there's three of them. Miss Chance, could you look in the bow locker and tell me what you find?'

She opened the locker. 'There's a bag of tools ... something made out of canvas ... some rope ... and a bag filled with water.'

'That'll be the sea-anchor, miss.' He tucked his pistol in his belt and reached into his pocket. 'And it isn't water. Pass it here.'

He took the bag from her and held it out over the side of the gig, puncturing it near the top

400

with his clasp knife. A little liquid dribbled down the side and dropped into the river. Killigrew took the pistol from his belt and held the flash pan against the hole in the bag. He pulled the trigger. The bullet went wide, but the flash ignited the liquid. It flamed quickly, and he tossed the bag at the canoe. The bag burst against the prow of the canoe and sprayed the three remaining men with burning oil. They screamed and beat at their burning clothes and hair, before jumping into the water. The crocodiles closed in, and the burning canoe drifted away with the sluggish current.

Killigrew's own hand was on fire. He doused it in the river, and then resumed his place on the bench beside Molineaux, taking up the other oar. A couple of minutes later they had left the scene of carnage behind them.

'Now all we have to do is find our way overland to Monrovia,' said Killigrew.

Molineaux rolled his eyes. 'He makes it sound so easy.'

Killigrew grinned. 'Trust me.'

They did not stay in the boat much longer. About half a mile further on the channel widened where the river led out of the mangrove swamps and shortly afterwards they came to some rapids. In other circumstances Killigrew would have suggested they carry the gig between them to the head of the rapids; the fact was that his hands were in no condition to help carry a boat several hundred yards through thick jungle with the prospect of more rowing at the end of it, and he

401

doubted Molineaux's hands were any better. The blisters they had developed pulling on the sweeps earlier had burst now, and their palms were raw and bloody. He wanted to get away from the water as quickly as possible anyway. In another hour it would be first light, and dawn was when the miasma overlying tropical rivers and swamps which caused malarial fevers were at their worst.

They rowed into the river bank, where thick foliage overhung the water. Killigrew tested the depth of the water with an oar and then jumped over the side, landing chest-deep in the water. 'Come on,' he told Molineaux.

The seaman was about to follow him when he hesitated. 'What about the crocs?'

'I think we left more than enough to keep them occupied down river.'

Molineaux cast his eyes over the water as if to make sure there were no crocodiles now rushing through the river towards Killigrew, and then realising he had no choice he swallowed hard and followed Killigrew over the side. Between them they pushed the foliage aside and pulled the gig hard against the bank, handing Miss Chance out and on to dry land. Molineaux followed her up, and Killigrew tried to angle the gig's bows up on to the bank. 'Molineaux, take the prow and pull, I'll get behind and push.'

'Wouldn't it be easier just to sink it?'

'Yes, but if this turns out to be an island we'll only have to refloat it. Once we get it on the other side of these bushes it'll be invisible from the river, even in daylight.'

Molineaux pulled, Killigrew pushed, and between them they managed to drag the gig up the bank and through the bushes. A short distance from the bank the undergrowth thinned out and disappeared altogether, but so few moonbeams could penetrate the canopy it was pitch black beneath.

Killigrew wanted to get as far away as quickly as possible, but their chances of navigating through the trees in the darkness were non-existent. 'It'll start getting light in an hour,' he said, gazing upwards towards the canopy. 'We'll be able to get going then. Until then, two of us can sleep. Who's going to keep watch?'

'I'll do it,' said Molineaux. 'You swam from the beach to the *Leopardo* and back again, I only swam back. Stands to reason you'll be more in need of a doss than me.'

'All right,' Killigrew said gratefully. 'We'll sleep in the gig,' he told Miss Chance. 'We'll be more comfortable there.' Which was not entirely true, but he did not want to worry her by telling her that in the boat they would be marginally safer from snakes and spiders and scorpions and whatever other nasty stinging things inhabited the jungle.

Killigrew had no recollection of actually getting into the boat; the next thing he knew, he was awoken by a piercing shriek. Lying next to him, Miss Chance awoke too and clung to him in alarm. 'What was that?'

Killigrew shook his head woozily. He had had so little sleep he felt as if he would have been better off not sleeping at all. 'I don't know...'

There was another ear-splitting shriek, and

then the whole jungle seemed to come alive with howls and screams. Although it was still dark, there was enough light to see by now, and they could make out the trees stretching high overhead, like the pillars of some great Gothic cathedral, reaching up to the vaulted forest canopy perhaps a hundred and fifty feet above them.

Miss Chance seemed to realise that she was clinging to Killigrew more tightly than propriety would have approved of, and let go of him quickly with a sheepish grin. 'Where's Molineaux?' Killigrew asked her. She shrugged.

There was no sign of the seaman. Had he headed back to the barracoon to lead Salazar and the others to where they were hidden?

A moment later Molineaux appeared, running through the trees with a look of sheer panic on his face. 'What the hell's that sound?' he demanded of Killigrew.

'I don't know. Whatever it is, it isn't human.'

'Is that good or bad?'

'It's probably just monkeys or something. Where did you go?'

'I had to pump ship.'

'"Pump ship"?' asked Miss Chance.

'Answer the call of nature,' Killigrew explained delicately, feeling guilty for having suspected Molineaux of betraying them.

Molineaux was peering at him with a curious expression on his face. 'Sir?'

'What?'

Molineaux gestured towards Killigrew's neck. 'You've got some kind of slug sticking to you.'

A leech, Killigrew realised with revulsion, and reached up to pull it off before remembering that it you did that they were supposed to leave their heads inside you. He quickly rummaged about in the gig's emergency supplies and came up with a box of brimstone matches, and handed it to Molineaux. 'It's a leech. Burn it off.'

'You sure about this?'

'Just get on with it.'

'Hold still.' Molineaux struck one of the matches and held it under Killigrew's jaw until the leech curled up and fell off.

'You'd better avert your gaze, miss,' said Killigrew, stripping off his clothes. 'There may be more of these things. They must have stuck to me when I went in the water last night. You too, Able Seaman. Strip. You check my back, I'll check yours.'

'You're clear,' Molineaux told him at last. 'How about me?' He glanced down at himself. He was covered in them. 'Oh, yeuch! Gerremoff me!'

Killigrew painstakingly worked his way around Molineaux's body. He noticed that there were scars on Molineaux's back. 'I thought you said Madison never flogged you?'

'He didn't. I got those courtesy of the Andrew Miller.'

'The Andrew Miller?' asked Miss Chance, sitting in the gig with her back to the two naked men.

'He means the navy, miss. What did you do to deserve those?' he added to Molineaux.

'Sassed the bosun on my first ship.'

'Why am I not surprised? Why did you join the

navy in the first place?'

'Just between the three of us?'

'Just between the three of us.'

'I signed on one step ahead of the peelers. I used to be a cracksman. The rear-admiral found out, I don't know how, but that's how he picked me for this job. Careful with them lucifers,' he growled, as Killigrew removed the leeches from his inner thighs.

'All right, I'm done. You're clear.'

'Those things aren't poisonous, are they?' asked Molineaux, as they got dressed once more.

'They're not venomous, if that's what you mean. They're even used in medicine sometimes.'

'Plummy,' sneered Molineaux. 'Maybe we should have left them on, if they're good for us.'

'All right, miss, you can open your eyes again,' said Killigrew when they had finished dressing. He raided the gig's emergency supplies to see if he could find anything else of use. The only things which might conceivably be worth taking were some hard tack and salt junk, a lead-line, and some rope. 'Right, let's get going.'

'Which way?' said Molineaux.

'We'll follow the river until the sun comes up. Then we'll head east for a day, towards the sunrise, and then turn south until we hit the coast again.'

They set off walking beneath the trees. Killigrew was in a hurry to make good time but he did not force a punishing pace, knowing that their European constitutions were not up to the task of overexerting themselves in the tropical heat. The sun came up and the screeching of the monkeys died away to be replaced by a brooding and oppressive silence. The weather grew hotter and hotter, until the sweat dripped off them. A couple of hours after noon, they heard rushing water and followed the sound until they came to a pleasant glade where a cataract cascaded from a rocky precipice into a crystal-clear pool. Molineaux at once started to take off his coat as if to plunge into the refreshing water, but Killigrew laid a hand on his arm.

'What's the problem?' demanded Molineaux. 'No crocs, no leeches, no sharks, just lovely cool clear water...'

Killigrew pointed to where a leopard sat watching them from a rock overlooking the pool, its haunches tensed as if ready to spring. 'I suggest we keep very, *very* still.'

'I second the motion,' muttered Molineaux.

'Oh, don't be ridiculous!' said Miss Chance, pushing between the two of them. 'It's just a big pussy cat.'

'A big pussy cat that can rip a man's throat out in the blink of an eye,' Killigrew warned her.

She ignored him, gesticulating at the leopard. 'Shoo! Scram! Go away!'

The leopard snarled at her, a cross between a roar and a miaow, showing sharp fangs. She bent down, picked up a stone, and lobbed it at the leopard.

'No!' yelled Killigrew.

The stone bounced off the rock near the leopard and it sprang to its feet, backing away a little before it held its ground and snarled again. Miss Chance picked up another stone and this time hit the leopard on the nose. It turned and sprinted off into the undergrowth with an amazing turn of speed.

'Plummy,' said Molineaux. 'What if it comes back with its mates?'

'Leopards hunt alone, Mr Molineaux,' said Miss Chance, easing herself into the water, her gown billowing out around her. 'And they almost never attack humans.'

'You're an expert on leopards, I suppose?' asked Molineaux.

'I've read about them,' she returned, striking off across the pool with a sedate breast-stroke. 'I may only be a woman, but I'm not addle-headed enough to decide to spend five years in Africa without reading a little about the country.'

'It'll be getting dark soon, and I don't expect it find a better place to camp for the night than this,' said Killigrew. 'I'll see if I can get us something to eat.' He put down the bag he was carrying and took out the lead-line and some ship's biscuits.

'You want me to keep an eye on the lady?' asked Molineaux.

'I think it would be better to ask her to keep an eye on you,' Killigrew returned with a smile.

'Hey, you were just as scared of that leopard as I was!' Molineaux called after him as he headed off into the trees.

Killigrew had learned how to snare birds from the natives in the jungles of Borneo. Although most of the forest's inhabitants had avoided the three intruders, he had glimpsed several birds during the day, either fluttering through the tree canopy or running along the ground. Finding a likely-looking spot, he broke up a ship's biscuit and scattered the crumbs on the forest floor. Then he made a noose from the lead-line and laid it on the ground, running the line up to the hiding place he had chosen behind a tree. Then he settled down to wait.

He did not have to wait for long. A plump-breasted bird with brightly coloured plumage and a glowering expression which reminded him of Standish strutted along the ground, bobbing its head like a pigeon. It saw the crumbs, studied them with its head cocked on one side, and then edged cautiously closer to investigate. It stepped on the noose, and Killigrew was tempted to pull on the snare there and then, but forced himself to be patient and waited until it took another step, putting a claw fully within the circle of twine.

He pulled. The bird squawked and fluttered into the air, but the noose was fast around its leg and Killigrew had a firm grip on the line. He pulled it in and wrung its neck.

'What've you got there?' Molineaux asked when he returned to the side of the pool.

'Supper,' said Killigrew. 'I'll pluck it. You see if you can find some firewood and get a fire going. Don't go too far, though: I reckon you could only be a hundred yards off through the trees and still get lost in this jungle.'

'I ain't going to get lost,' Molineaux muttered under his breath, heading off into the trees.

Killigrew sat down on the pebbly beach at the side of the pool and began to pluck the bird, uncertainly at first but with growing confidence as he discovered there was a technique to it. Miss Chance climbed out of the water and shook herself off. The wet cloth of her gown clung to her body, outlining her figure alarmingly. Killigrew looked away, but she lay down beside him. 'Do you want a hand with that?'

'Have you ever plucked a bird before?'

'Have you?'

'No, but I seem to be managing.'

'Good heavens, look at your hands! Did you do that rowing?' she asked. He nodded. 'Here. Let me bandage them for you.'

'Have you got any bandages?'

'I'll use my petticoats. Avert your eyes.' He glanced away and heard the sound of material tearing. 'All right, now give me your hands. Here, wash them in the water first.'

He was overwhelmingly aware of her proximity as she bathed his hands in the cool water. 'You should have said something earlier,' she said. 'How typical of a man to suffer in silence, to no good purpose other than the protection of his pride. I don't suppose poor Mr Molineaux's palms will be in any better case than this. Really, the two of you are as bad as each other! There,' she concluded, tying off the makeshift bandage. 'You'd better let me pluck that bird after all. I don't know where you men would be without a woman to look after you.'

'In the navy we usually make do with a jolly.'

'I beg your pardon?'

'A Royal Marine. Every vessel has a squad of marines on board, usually with nothing better to do than to stand around getting in the way. We keep the private soldiers employed by using them as servants for the ship's officers. Most of 'em retire and become gentlemen's gentlemen.'

'And that makes up for the lack of feminine company, does it?'

'Oh, there are plenty of opportunities for that, if you know where to look for it.'

'A wife in every port, is that it?'

He grinned. 'Well, I wouldn't say that. I've never been to New York.'

She slapped him playfully on the shoulder. 'Not when you're at sea, though.'

'You'd be surprised. I've known ships where the captain took his wife to sea. It's not allowed, of course, but they do it anyway and everyone turns a blind eye. Sometimes they take their whole families.'

'But you're not a captain.'

He smiled. 'Not yet. Give me a few years. I've only just made lieutenant.'

'So what do you do for feminine company?'

'Sometimes the captain's daughter can be a comely lass,' he told her, with wistful remembrance.

'And when the captain doesn't have a daughter?'

'A cold shower-bath every morning. Um ... that bird's not getting plucked, you know.'

'Oh!' Miss Chance at once set to work, which was just as well because a couple of minutes later Molineaux returned, backing slowly out of the trees.

'Did you get some firewood?' Killigrew asked him.

411

'Uh-hunh.'

'"Uh-hunh"? What does "uh-hunh" mean? Did you or didn't you, man?'

'I got some firewood, but I had to drop it when I put my hands up.'

Killigrew glanced up and saw that Molineaux had his hands raised over his head. The reason for this was the tall African, naked but for a breech-clout and with a necktie of cowrie shells, who followed him into the clearing with a spear levelled unwaveringly at the seaman's chest.

Killigrew and Miss Chance leaped to their feet. Another spear buried its head in the ground at Killigrew's feet, and he twisted to see a dozen more native warriors standing on the rocks overlooking the pool.

XVII:

The Leopard People

Killigrew thought about plucking the spear from the ground but decided against it in case the natives interpreted that as a hostile act. Instead he raised his hands above his head.

'Speakee Krio?' he hazarded, without much hope, a lack of hope which proved to be justified when one of the warriors jumped down from the rocks and moved across to face him, brandishing his spear and shouting angrily in a language which Killigrew could not understand. All of the warriors looked extremely hostile.

'Say something to them, Molineaux,' he hissed. 'These are your people.'

'*My* people?' spluttered the seaman. 'My people were prigging culls in St Giles. I don't understand these people's mumbo-jumbo anymore'n they'd voker the flash patter.'

The warrior shouted at Killigrew again and waved his spear in his face. Killigrew found his eyes transfixed by the spear's point. 'I don't suppose you caught any of that?'

'I think it was an invitation to dinner,' said Molineaux. 'With us as the main course.'

One of the warriors tried to grab hold of Miss Chance. She pushed him away. Killigrew moved to defend her, but before he had taken a couple

413

of steps she had started shouting back at the men – in the same language. Their expressions showed as much astonishment as Killigrew felt. One of them responded, glowering, but she kept up the tirade. At length the natives began to look sheepish and lowered their weapons.

'You can speak their language?' asked Killigrew.

Miss Chance nodded. 'Fortunately they're Mende. I learned some of their language from an ex-slave I met in New York who was born in these parts.'

'You seem to be rather fluent.'

'Well, I only learned the basics, but I seem to be making myself understood. They thought we were slavers; that's why they were so hostile at first.'

'You put them straight, I take it?' asked Killigrew, and she nodded.

The man who appeared to be in command of the natives spoke to her again, more politely now. 'I think he's saying we're free to go, but they'd be honoured if we'd be guests at their village for dinner tonight.'

'I knew it!' groaned Molineaux. 'No prizes for guessing who'll be on the menu.'

'Oh, don't be ridiculous,' said Killigrew. 'There aren't any cannibals on the Guinea Coast.'

More words were exchanged between Miss Chance and the leader, and suddenly all the warriors burst out laughing at something she said. 'What's so amusing?' asked Killigrew.

'I told them Mr Molineaux was afraid they wanted to eat him.'

Grinning, the leader said something. 'He says

his village would soon starve if they had to live off something as scrawny as Mr Molineaux,' explained Miss Chance.

'Scrawny?' spluttered Molineaux. 'Who's he calling scrawny?'

Killigrew smiled. 'Tell them we accept their invitation.'

Miss Chance made the introductions, but the only name Killigrew caught was that of the leader, Ndawa. In turn, the two Englishmen were asked for their names. The Africans laughed heartily on hearing them.

'What do they find so amusing?' asked Killigrew, not a little put out, as they set off through the jungle once more.

'They say we have strange names.'

'Tell them theirs sound peculiar to our ears.'

'They want to know what our names mean. Especially Mr Molineaux's. They say an African should not have a white man's name.'

'You can tell them I'm proud of my name,' Molineaux protested indignantly. 'It was given to my father by my grandmother, who was a close personal friend of Tom Molineaux.'

'Not Tom Molineaux the celebrated pugilist?' exclaimed Killigrew.

Molineaux grinned. 'Well, I hear Mr Molineaux was what you might call something of a ladies' man, and my grandma wasn't exactly what you'd call a lady...'

'A pity you didn't inherit his physique as well as his name,' Killigrew remarked drily.

Miss Chance explained to the natives that Molineaux had been named after his grandfather, a great warrior, and Ndawa nodded approvingly. 'He says he shall call you "Sekou", which means "fighter".'

'"Sekou",' mused Molineaux, and nodded. 'I like that.'

Ndawa asked Miss Chance a question, and Killigrew recognised his own name. 'He wants to know what it means,' she said.

'It's the name of a place in Cornwall. I suppose one of my ancestors must've come from there.'

This provoked further howls of laughter from the natives. Another exchange passed between Ndawa and Miss Chance. 'He says that life must have been very confusing in your ancestor's village, if everyone was named after the place they lived in,' she explained.

The undergrowth became thicker, and a few moments later they emerged from the trees to find themselves at the edge of a broad savannah through which a wide stream meandered sluggishly. A village of clay huts with conical thatched roofs stood on the bank of the stream about half a mile away. There were fields around the village where men and women worked, and they all stood up as the party of hunters returned with two whites and a black man in white man's clothing.

By the time they entered the village itself there was quite a crowd of people gathered to stare at them. Like Ndawa, men and women alike were naked from the waist up but for bracelets, necklaces and head-dresses of cowrie shells. Chickens roamed freely within the confines of the village, marked out by a seven-foot-high fence, and there were goats everywhere. The place was dusty, but a lot cleaner than most parts of London. And the air was a damned sight fresher, too, reflected Killigrew.

He felt something touch the back of his hand and glanced down to see a small boy, completely naked, rubbing his hand to see if the white would come off. Ndawa chased the boy away with a cuff around the back of the head, shouting at him angrily.

'Tell him I don't mind,' said Killigrew.

'Actually, from what Ndawa said, I think he was afraid that the boy might get the idea that white men weren't dangerous after all,' said Miss Chance.

Killigrew nodded. Ndawa did not want the boy to go near white men because in this part of the world, most white men were slavers.

Killigrew, Molineaux and Miss Chance were ushered into the largest hut, towards the centre of the village. This, they learned through Miss Chance, was the home of Ndawa's father, Momolu, the head man of the village. Momolu himself was there, a tall, plump, grey-haired man with a cherubic face. He rose to his feet to greet the guests, speaking the language with a deep, rich and melodious bass.

'He says we are welcome under his roof, and we are to stay as long as we wish,' translated Miss Chance.

'Will he be offended if we say we only want to stay for one night, but must be on our way to-morrow? Every day we delay increases the chances of another ship reaching Salazar's barracoons to carry off the slaves there.'

'That depends how I put it, I suppose.'

'Tell him we're extremely grateful for his hospitality, but I'm worried that if we stay too long we'll be in danger of outstaying our welcome.' Killigrew shot a hard glance at Molineaux, who was exchanging smiles with one of Momolu's daughters, a pretty young girl somewhere in her late teens. She smiled back at him shyly.

'He says we can stay for as short or long a time as we desire, and if we let him know when we want to leave, he will send guides with us to help us get to where we want to go.'

'Ask him how far it is to Monrovia.'

Momolu did not understand the question at first, so Killigrew drew a sketch map of the Guinea Coast in the dust with a stars and stripes where Monrovia was. Momolu chuckled and nodded, marking the location of his own village on it, and said something to Miss Chance.

'He says it is three days' journey from here, and if we wish to leave tomorrow he will arrange for a guide to take us there. And he likes your drawing of a canoe-house. I think he means a ship.'

'That's not a ship, that's a whale,' protested Killigrew, who had gone to some trouble to make it quite clear where the land ended and the sea began on his map.

'Looks like a ship to me,' said Molineaux.

'It's a whale!'

'It does look like a ship,' admitted Miss Chance.

So there was something else Killigrew was no good at: drawing. Eulalia would be delighted when he told her.

Food was brought in wooden bowls, rice with a sauce of fish, cassava and sweet potatoes. It was pleasantly spicy and none of the Europeans would have had trouble finishing it, had not Miss Chance warned them to leave just a tiny morsel in their bowls. 'In many African cultures it's considered bad manners to eat all the food that's put before one. It suggests that one's host has not provided one with enough.'

The meal was washed down with some kind of palm wine served in wooden cups, and all that was lacking in Killigrew's opinion was a cheroot to round off the meal.

A thought occurred to him. 'Ask him what he knows about the leopard people.'

Miss Chance nodded, and at once passed on the question to Momolu. The chief's reaction was astonishing, both angry and fearful, and he raised his voice for the first time since Killigrew had met him. 'What's wrong?'

Miss Chance had knitted her brows as if struggling to follow what Momolu was saying. 'I'm not sure, but I think you've said something improper. Something that isn't supposed to be discussed in front of the women and children.'

Killigrew was not satisfied, but did not want to be a bad guest by pressing the issue. 'You'd better give him my apologies. Tell him I'm an ignorant white man, that I didn't know any better.'

Miss Chance managed to mollify Momolu somewhat, but the chief did not recover his

419

earlier good grace and sat there glowering. After that the atmosphere in the hut was unbearable and Killigrew made his excuses – through Miss Chance, of course – and went outside. He sat on the low clay wall which surrounded the village well, sipping his palm wine and trying to ignore the women who peered at him out of the doors of their huts, giggling. It was a beautiful evening and he gazed across the savannah, enjoying the sunset. Knowing that for now there was nothing he could do to help the slaves in Salazar's barracoon, he tried to put them from his mind.

Certainly his surroundings were pleasant enough, and he would have enjoyed a slightly longer visit, although he knew he would soon grow bored in such a place. He had always preferred the hustle and bustle of cities to idyllic rural villages, and the noisier and more crowded, the more he preferred them.

After a while Miss Chance emerged and joined him at the well. 'Our sleeping accommodation has been arranged,' she explained. 'We'll each be sleeping in separate huts to avoid overcrowding; several people have offered us places, I've left it to Momolu to worry about who has the dubious honour of being our respective hosts. The chief seemed to think that I was your wife and suggested that if we wanted he could arrange for us to have a hut to ourselves, but I soon put him straight on that score.'

'Good,' said Killigrew, thinking: *pity*.

She fanned herself with her hand. 'I can't say I blame you for coming outside. It really was getting rather stuffy in there. I was beginning to feel quite faint.'

He smiled and said nothing. He was lost in his own thoughts, and while he was happy to listen to her prattling on, he did not feel inclined to say much himself. 'It's a beautiful night, isn't it?' she ventured.

'A beautiful night, a beautiful country,' he told her.

'And the people are so kind! I wonder how many Africans would get the same kind of welcome in our countries as we have in theirs?'

'You know how your country treats Africans,' said Killigrew.

She lowered her eyes. 'That's not fair. You know I don't approve of slavery any more than you do.'

'I'm sorry. I just can't help thinking that the only way we're going to stop the slave trade for good is to abolish slavery in the Americas.'

'You're right, of course. Perhaps instead of dedicating my life to converting these people to Christianity I should instead try to convert my own countrymen. These people seem less in need of moral guidance than we Americans do.'

Killigrew shrugged. 'You can't blame yourself for being American. People are people. Some are good, some are bad. It's got nothing to do with where they were born or what colour their skin is. The one thing I've noticed, from Falmouth to Nanking, is that nearly every culture seems to arrive independently at some system of morals which allows them to live in peace with one another. The real problems only start when those cultures clash head to head.'

'You're certainly right there. You know, I asked

Chief Momolu what the names of the gods were in his religion. The books I've read about Africa always say that the natives are simply heathens, so I'd always assumed they were pantheists. It turns out the Mende have only one God, the same as Christians and Moslems.'

'There you are, then. God is God in any language.'

She pressed an arm to her forehead. 'Oh! This heat!'

Killigrew frowned. It did not seem that hot to him, and he wondered if he had a chill. He glanced across to where Molineaux was talking to Momolu's daughter. 'He's not going to get us in trouble, is he?' he asked Miss Chance.

'The chief seemed to be quite pleased at Mr Molineaux's evident interest in Abena.'

'In what?'

'Abena. That's her name. Seems he wants to marry her off.'

'To a British sailor? You must be joking!'

'The chief seems to think Mr Molineaux has come a long way in the world. He thinks that Molineaux has come to Africa to settle in the land of his ancestors.'

'I doubt it. I've known Englishmen – white Englishmen, I mean – who were less proud of their British heritage than Molineaux seems to be. I don't know him that well, but he doesn't seem to be the kind who'd want to give up all the luxuries of European life to live in Africa.'

'You might be wrong about him.'

'I might be, but I don't think so. I've known plenty of seamen his age, miss, and apart from

422

the colour of his skin he's no different from the rest of them. At least, no different than they are from each other.'

'Supposing he did want to settle down in Africa? Would you stop him?'

'He's a rating of the Royal Navy. Settling down here would be desertion,' Killigrew said firmly, but then smiled. 'Of course, since I'm not currently a commissioned officer of the navy, I'm not under any obligation to try to stop him from deserting. Just so long as he doesn't stop me from getting to Monrovia.'

'And what then?'

'I'll get passage to Freetown, make a report to the senior naval officer present, and press for an expedition to the Owodunni Barracoon to see that vile place wiped off the face of the earth.'

'You make it sound so easy.' A look of panic suddenly appeared on her face and she bit her lip. 'You … you'll have to excuse me for a moment.' She hurried back towards the huts and accosted one of the women. The woman nodded and led her away, smiling. *Gone to pump ship*, thought Killigrew with a smile.

Killigrew spent the night on a rush mat in Momolu's hut. The hut was more than big enough for the chief, his wife and daughter, and their guest. Miss Chance was the guest of Ndawa and his wife, while Molineaux was put up in the hut of one of the other village headmen. The African night was cooler than the day – to the extent that the villagers put on long, lightweight gowns of fine country cloth – but it did not trouble Killigrew. In spite of all his worries, he

423

had no difficulty getting to sleep.

He was awoken in the small hours of the morning and found Ndawa shaking him by the shoulders. The African said something in Mande, the language of the Mende, his face concerned but his words intelligible to Killigrew.

'What is it? What's wrong? It's no good, I don't understand. You'll have to get Miss Chance. Me no hear, you fetchee Missy Chance for to jam heads talkee Mande,' he said at last, lapsing into the pidgin English of the coast in frustration.

But Ndawa no more understood that than Killigrew understood Mande. He spoke again, and this time Killigrew caught Miss Chance's name amongst all the unfamiliar words. A trickle of cold sweat ran down his spine. Perhaps the reason Ndawa had not brought Miss Chance was because he could not bring her. Perhaps the problem had something to do with her.

A small oil lamp, such as the Arabs used, provided light in Ndawa's hut, and by its warm glow Killigrew could see that Miss Chance looked ghastly. Her face was ashen and beaded with sweat, and while Ndawa's wife had covered her with blankets and the night was still warm, she was shivering uncontrollably and her teeth chattered. Ndawa's wife now knelt beside her, mopping her brow with a damp cloth.

Ndawa spoke some more. Killigrew did not understand the words, but the meaning was plain to see. Miss Chance was seriously ill.

He knelt down beside her. 'Miss Chance?'

'Mr Killigrew?' she reached feebly for his hand and he took it at once, squeezing it affectionately.

424

'I think it might have been something I ate.'

'It's just a fever,' he told her. 'It'll pass.'

She smiled, but he could see in her eyes that she knew he was lying.

'Ask them if they've got any cinchona bark,' he said.

'I don't know how to say that in Mande. Will it help?'

'I've heard it can often help in cases like this,' he said. 'Try Jesuit's powder.'

She spoke to Ndawa's wife, and Killigrew recognised the words 'cinchona' and 'Jesuits', but neither seemed to elicit any understanding from the woman. 'She says they've already sent for the witch doctor, but he lives in a village a day's journey from here so it will be two days before he gets here.'

Killigrew did not argue. It was an African sickness, so perhaps it needed an African cure. If she had been in Europe a doctor would probably have prescribed leeches, and nothing an African witch doctor could prescribe would be much worse than that, in Killigrew's opinion. 'Just hang on. You'll be all right.'

Ndawa's wife said something to her husband, and he gently took Killigrew by the arm, lifted him to his feet and dragged him away. Probably telling him that she needed rest, which Killigrew agreed with.

As he emerged from the hut Molineaux arrived with a small boy. 'What's wrong?'

Killigrew led him some distance away from the hut, so there was no danger of Miss Chance hearing them speak. 'It's Miss Chance. She's contracted yellow fever.'

'Oh, Jesus!' groaned Molineaux. 'She'll be all right, won't she? I mean, people get yellow fever and survive, don't they?'

'Sometimes. If they're strong.'

There was no question of Killigrew leaving the village while Miss Chance was too ill to be moved. He spent the rest of the day moping around, worrying. Without her to translate there was no one he could speak to but Molineaux, and he felt strangely excluded. The people of the village were clearly sympathetic, but the language barrier was all but insurmountable.

He felt so impotent. He wanted to do something for Miss Chance, but the only thing he could think of was going to Monrovia to see if any apothecaries there could sell him some cinchona bark. That was three days' journey away, and there was no guarantee that there would be any cinchona when he got there, or that she would still be alive when he got back six days later. But at least he would be doing something.

Her condition deteriorated during the course of the day, and that night Killigrew slept fitfully.

The witch doctor arrived late the next morning by dint of travelling all through the night. If Killigrew had expected some outlandishly dressed man with a demonic horned mask, he was disappointed: the doctor dressed little different from any of the other Mende, except for the bag of charms and talismans he carried.

Rather more remarkable was the witch doctor's travelling companion, an individual Killigrew immediately recognised as a member of the Kru race, a people renowned throughout the world as expert sailors and equally skilled linguists, these talents making their services as pilots, casual labourers, interpreters and boatmen much in demand from European vessels which operated along the Guinea Coast. If most of the Krumen Killigrew had met spoke pidgin rather than English proper, it was because they had been given the impression that pidgin was the only language British sailors spoke and understood.

The witch doctor's companion was recognisable as a Kruman from the tribal markings on his face, a line of blue cuts from his forehead to the tip of his nose and arrows on his temples, and the sharpened teeth he revealed whenever he grinned, which, like most Krumen, he seemed to do a great deal. He wore a white top hat, a size too large for him so that it rested on his ears rather than the top of his head, a white cravat, and a white-and-pink chequered loin cloth; he was otherwise naked but for an ivory bracelet and arm- and ankle-bands of leopards' teeth and cowrie shells threaded on string. He carried a notched fighting-stick over one shoulder as a young Englishman might carry a cricket bat as he sauntered to the crease.

'Speakee English?' this apparition enquired of Killigrew, who nodded. 'Me Tip-Top, me speakee man.' Killigrew guessed that like most Africans, Tip-Top had two names, a real name and the name given to him by white sailors who were too lazy to try to remember African names. The Kru in particular seemed to revel in the ridiculous names with which white sailors christened them, in a way which suggested to Killigrew that somehow they were having the last laugh on the white men who sought to mock them, as if it was hilarious that these ignorant foreigners could not cope with Kru names, but the least the Kru could do was to tolerate their stupidity. 'You speakee what bad for white puss, Tip-Top speakee medicine feller.'

Killigrew related Miss Chance's symptoms to Tip-Top, who relayed them to the witch doctor. 'Me thinkee yellow jack,' concluded Killigrew. 'Savvy yellow jack?'

Tip-Top nodded, his top hat jiggling on his head. 'Medicine feller hear, him savvy yellow jack good. White feller's sickness. White puss live, done live, who savvy, can?' He went into Ndawa's hut with the witch doctor, who did not look optimistic. Killigrew realised it was too much to hope that the doctor would know a cure. He stood outside the hut and waited, pouring himself his third cup of palm wine of the morning.

Molineaux approached. He had 'gone native' – sensibly considering the heat of the day – and was wearing only his undershorts. Killigrew wiped sweat from his own brow and held out the gourd to him. 'Drink?'

'It's a little early in the day for me,' said Molineaux, eyeing the gourd dubiously. 'Sun not over the forearm, and all that. Are you sure you haven't had enough?'

'Yes.' Killigrew drained his cup in one draught, and refilled it. 'This is my fault. I should have listened to you. This would never have happened if we'd stayed on the coast.'

'If we'd stayed on the coast we'd've been nabbed by Salazar's patrols. You can't blame yourself.'

'Then who else am I going to blame?' Killigrew demanded savagely.

They heard shouting from the far end of the village, and looked up in time to see a boy running between the huts, his feet muddy from the rice fields where he had been working. He was shouting something.

'What's the palaver, d'you think?' asked Molineaux.

'I don't know, but I've got a bad feeling,' said Killigrew, throwing away his cup and gourd.

The two of them ran towards the entrance of the village in time to see a large group of strangers approaching, some of them mounted on small but sturdy horses, the rest following on foot. Killigrew still had his pocket telescope on him and he took it out to study these new arrivals more closely.

They were warriors, bearing muskets and spears and wearing an odd mixture of African clothing and European uniforms, but all of them wore leopard skins in one form or another. Focusing on the lead horseman, Killigrew at once recognised Prince Khari.

'Slavers!' he roared to the villagers. 'Slavers!'

They did not need to be told. Some of them ran to fetch their spears and bows, other readied the farming implements they held to use them as weapons. Killigrew wished he had a pistol or a cutlass, anything he could use as a weapon. The villagers gathered at the entrance to the village and formed a defensive line. They at once began to loose their bows, sending their long arrows whipping through the air towards the leopard men.

The horsemen reined in and the men on foot spread out on either side of them, bringing their muskets up to their shoulders. Prince Khari bellowed an order and the muskets crackled, a cloud of pale grey smoke rolling across in front of each fusillade as the villagers fell dead and wounded on all sides. As unreliable a weapon as the musket was, it had nonetheless achieved and maintained its place in the soldier's armoury for hundreds of years thanks to its ability to wreck havoc amongst closely packed bodies of men.

Those villagers who survived the initial onslaught continued shooting their bows, but the effect was negligible. The horsemen goaded their horses on, hoofs pounding the earth, and levelled their spears while the musketeers dropped their weapons and charged forwards with swords and war-clubs. A moment later the two sides slammed into one another.

Killigrew had found himself caught in mêlées before, and he did not much care for them. There was too much going on: no opportunity for skill or intelligence to keep a man alive. All one could do was lash out at the bodies that pressed close around one, and hope that one only hit the enemy. A man could be killed as easily by a blow aimed at another as by a blow aimed at himself, a blow from a friend as from an enemy. A man who walked away after such skirmish might simply be lucky, rather than a good fighter.

And that was just a fight between Europeans, where the colour of a man's coat might at least give you some indication as to where you should direct your blows. Here the best Killigrew could do was to lash out at any leopard skins he saw. Mêlées were confused enough at the best of times, but at least in the battles he had known in Syria and China he had caught the occasional command shouted in English or French to guide him. Here, where all commands were given in unknown tongues, he was completely lost. The only thing he could judge was that whichever way he turned, the leopard men seemed to be gaining the upper hand.

A leopard man swung a club at him. Killigrew ducked beneath the blow and rammed a fist into the man's stomach. The two of them grappled, and the leopard man pushed Killigrew back against the wall of a hut and pressed his club against his throat. Then a horseman galloped past, inadvertently bumping into the leopard man and giving Killigrew a chance to snatch the club from his hands. He swung the club and struck the man to the ground.

He heard more hoof-beats and started to turn, but something heavy slammed into him from behind. He sprawled in the dust alongside the man he had just clubbed unconscious. He was aware of hoof-beats pounding the earth all around his head, and managed to crawl out of the way.

The leopard men had fought their way through the entrance to the village and now they rode amongst the huts, setting the thatched roofs ablaze with torches. Killigrew pushed himself to his feet and saw Ndawa fighting off two leopard men at once. He brought down the club on the head of one, allowing Ndawa to finish off the other with a spear-thrust. He thanked Killigrew with an upraised hand, and then ran off to help some of his fellow villagers.

Killigrew looked around for another enemy and saw no shortage of them. As the women and children of the village ran from the blazing huts, the leopard men herded them down the main thoroughfare, guiding them towards the entrance. One of the women – Ndawa's wife – fought back, trying to snatch a spear from a leopard man. Another leopard man rode up behind her and clubbed her down.

Something inside Killigrew snapped.

The man whose spear Ndawa's wife had tried to take grabbed her by the ankles and began to drag her through the dust towards the village entrance. Killigrew stepped into his path. The man did not see him until he bumped into him. He dropped her ankles and began to turn, only to receive the full force of the club in his face.

The horseman saw this and charged forwards. Killigrew waited for him, readying his club. The horse reared in front of Killigrew, hoofs flailing wildly. Killigrew side-stepped and dashed the club against the side of the horse's head. The horse went down on its forelegs and pitched its rider over its head. He tried to get up, but Killigrew did not give him a chance.

He glanced up and saw Miss Chance, asleep on

her feet, being dragged out of Ndawa's hut between two leopard men, supervised by Prince Khari. Killigrew tried to run to her, but another leopard man blocked his path. Killigrew smashed his skull in.

As Killigrew charged forwards once more, Prince Khari glanced around and saw him. Recognising Killigrew, he grinned broadly and pulled a pistol from his belt. The pistol brought Killigrew up short, frozen in panic. Khari levelled the pistol and was about to fire when suddenly Tip-Top stepped out from behind a hut and gave the prince's horse a sharp thrust in the hindquarters with his fighting stick. The horse reared as Khari squeezed his trigger and the shot went wide. Khari landed on his back in the dirt and Tip-Top was about to strike him on the head when another leopard man brought him down with a blow from a war-club, crushing his top hat. Khari jumped athletically to his feet, and another horse was brought for him.

Killigrew gazed about through the drifting smoke and dashing bodies, but Miss Chance and her captors had disappeared. He jumped on to the wall around the well to get a better view. Wherever he looked the young men, women and children of the village were being ridden down and caught in nets strung between two horsemen. He glimpsed Miss Chance being slung across the rump of a horse. He was about to jump down and go to her when another leopard man ran at him. Killigrew kicked him in the face. He saw a horseman about to ride past, and grabbed the rope by which the well's pail was suspended from the primitive wooden derrick. He swung himself out from the well, caught the rider in the chest with both feet and knocked him clean out of the saddle. The rope swung back, and Killigrew dropped to the ground, kicking the dismounted rider in the side as he tried to get up.

By the time he got to the horse another leopard man was trying to climb into the saddle from the other side. Killigrew ducked underneath the horse and grabbed the man by the ankles, pulling his feet out from beneath him so that he cracked his head on the ground.

Killigrew got a foot in the stirrup and swung himself into the saddle. The whole village was ablaze now. The acrid smoke stung his eyes and clawed at his throat. Whichever way he turned the horse, he found his path blocked by the flames. The only way out – using the phrase 'way out' in its wildest possible sense – was a fence, five feet high and burning fiercely. He tried to ride the horse at it, but it balked and almost threw him from the saddle. He backed it up as much as possible, until it's rump was scorched by the hut burning behind it. It broke into a gallop without any goading. Within seconds it was upon the fence, but by now it was moving too fast to have any chance of stopping or swerving in time.

It leaped.

For a moment smoke and flames filled Killigrew's vision, and then he was treated to a grandstand view of the savannah stretching beyond the fence. A moment later the cassava field immediately below the fence hurtled up to meet them, and he was jerked viciously in the

434

saddle as the horse's hoofs hit the soft earth. The horse stumbled, and Killigrew almost fell to the ground, righting himself in the saddle at the same time that the horse regained its footing.

He looked around. The leopard men had got what they had come for and were herding their captives back towards the trees while a few of their number fought a rearguard action against Ndawa and the other men who had managed to avoid being taken. Killigrew dug his heels into the horse's flanks and galloped towards them.

'Ndawa!' yelled Killigrew. The young man turned and saw him. 'Spear!' Killigrew made a throwing motion. Ndawa understood, and tossed a spear up to him as he rode past. Killigrew caught it by the shaft and urged the horse onwards, towards the rearguard. Seeing him bear down on them, they scattered. Beyond them he could see Prince Khari seated astride his horse, riding alongside the horse over which Miss Chance was slung.

'Khari!'

The prince twisted in his saddle, saw Killigrew, and turned his horse to meet his charge. Killigrew readied his spear to launch it at Khari's chest, and saw the prince pull a second pistol from his belt. The pistol came up unwaveringly. Killigrew knew he was too far away, but hurled the spear anyway, trying to give it some spin in flight the way he had seen the Africans do, so it would fly further and straighter, like a bullet from a rifle.

He missed Khari by about three inches, the spear sailing past his head to bury itself in the ground behind him. Khari did not even flinch. A moment later he pulled the trigger and disappeared in the puff of blue-tinged smoke which burst from the muzzle of his pistol. The next moment everything went crimson and Killigrew was blinded. He felt his horse stumble beneath him and then he was thrown forwards. The ground slammed into him and he rolled over and over. Wiping the horse's blood from his eyes with his sleeve, he tried to get up but his ankle gave way beneath him. He tried again, and stood up just in time to be slammed to the earth as Khari rode him down. He crawled a short distance, and felt rather than heard the hoofbeats pounding towards him as Khari rode him down again. Through the muzziness which clouded his vision, he just managed to glimpse the horse's fetlocks, and then something smashed into his skull.

XVIII:

Coffle

Half a mile into the jungle they came to where the leopard men had left their mules, and the captives were reorganised into a proper coffle. Men, women and children alike had their wrists tied behind their backs, and the men were yoked in pairs, one behind the other. A rope ran from the wrists of the rearmost man in each pair to the wrists of the next captive, a woman, who had her hands tied behind her; another rope, tied around her neck, ran back to the wrists of the next man behind her, the first in the next pair with his neck in turn in one end of a double-ended yoke. The children were mixed in with them.

The leopard men reloaded their muskets to keep the slaves covered, and exchanged war-clubs for cat-o'-nine-tails which they used unstintingly on any slave who even looked as if he or she might try to cause trouble, lashing them until the blood poured from their flayed skin.

Molineaux saw Miss Chance pulled from the rump of a horse and then placed in a litter made by stretching a pole between two mules and slinging a hammock from beneath it. She looked unharmed, but it was obvious she was in no condition to travel. He wanted to go to her to give her a few words of reassurance, but he was in the coffle at the front end of a yoke, his wrists tied before him and linked by a rope to a noose around the neck of Momolu's daughter Abena. As the coffle got under way he had no choice but to follow her or else risk choking her. He gagged as the man behind him was slow to keep up, pulling back on the yoke which cruelly chafed both their necks.

So far none of the leopard men seemed to have noticed that whereas all the other male captives wore breech-clouts, Molineaux was wearing a pair of white cotton undershorts purchased from Mrs Cropper's penny bazaar in Liverpool. He thought about pointing out that he was not an African and that the leopard men had no right to enslave him, a British citizen, but decided against it. They had no right to enslave any of these people, but that had not stopped them from doing so. Any demand to see the British consul in Monrovia would be received at best with jeers and at worst a swift death to stop him from causing trouble.

Not that he was in a position to cause much trouble. The unspoken language of ... well, not love, perhaps, but a certain mutual attraction ... which had served him so well with Abena the night before last, was useless in any attempt to plot an escape with the other slaves. They called out to each other in Mande, words of hope and encouragement to give one another strength, he supposed. Not understanding, he felt horribly isolated.

He wondered if Killigrew was all right. Probably. White men always managed to survive somehow, and compared to the rest of his pasty-faced brethren, Killigrew had struck him as being particularly adept at looking after himself. Would Killigrew try to rescue him? Certainly he would not allow Miss Chance to be carried off by the slavers; and, to be fair, he would probably try to free Molineaux and the other captives if he could. But could he? Molineaux doubted it. No, if he was going to get out of this, he would have to do it himself. Secured to Abena in front of him, and another man behind him, under the vigilant eyes and guns of the leopard men, there was nothing he could do but watch and wait and bide his time until a better opportunity presented itself.

Some of the leopard men shouted at the captives and lashed them angrily. For some reason Molineaux was spared; when the other captives fell silent, he realised that the leopard men were ordering them not to talk.

Two of the leopard men fell into step alongside Abena, joking in whatever language it was they spoke, and laughing. It was obvious they were referring to her, and one of them reached across to grab one of her breasts. She shrank away, and the man grabbed a fistful of her hair at the back, pulling her head back to tilt her pain-ridden face to the sky, snarling something at her.

Molineaux was perfectly positioned to kick him in the crotch from behind, and saw no reason to refrain.

The man clutched at himself and sank to his knees, sobbing in agony. His friend turned and smashed Molineaux in the face with the butt of his musket. The side of his face exploded in pain and he went over sideways, jerking the man behind him forwards and twisting his own neck in the yoke. He lay there, half-throttled, unable even to move, let alone defend himself. The man stood over him and lashed at him with a cat-o'-nine-tails, and Molineaux cried out as the knotted thongs lacerated his skin. 'Ow! Jesus Christ! All right, I'm sorry, I'm sorry!'

The man stopped and stared at him, before whirling to where Prince Khari rode at the head of the column. He shouted something, and Prince Khari wheeled his horse and rode back to where Molineaux lay. 'You speak English?' Khari asked, reining in.

Molineaux said nothing, and shrugged as if he did not understand.

'You shrug like a white man,' spat Khari. He made it sound like an insult.

'And you've got a face like a warthog's arse,' Molineaux could not resist replying, 'but you don't hear *me* complaining.'

Khari said something to the leopard man, who lashed at Molineaux again, once, twice, three times. Molineaux bit his lip in spite of the pain, determined not to give them the satisfaction of crying out a second time. 'What's the matter?' he taunted Khari, when the leopard man backed away to admire his bloody handiwork. 'Haven't you got the grit to get down off that prad and fight me yourself? And me yoked and bound and all.'

'Where did you learn to speak English?' demanded Khari.

440

Molineaux decided this would not be a good time to speak of his British parentage. 'From a missionary. Where did you learn yours? 'Cause I'd ask for my money back if I were you, you big ignorant hunk of shit.'

Khari repeated his order to the leopard man, who lashed at Molineaux again. 'Brave feller, eh? I'd like to see you try that if I wasn't bound,' Molineaux spat through the pain.

Khari leaned on the pommel of his saddle to address him. 'You were not born in Africa. Perhaps you are a runaway, who was shipped back to Sierra Leone or Monrovia? I cannot place your accent, but it does not matter. I ought to kill you for your impertinence towards a prince of royal blood, but a slave who already speaks English will fetch a good price at market in the United States.'

'Yeah? Well, when I've finished with you, the only market you'll fetch any kind of price in will be a meat market.'

Prince Khari chuckled, and ordered the leopard man to give Molineaux another half a dozen lashes before riding back to the head of the coffle and ordering them to move on.

Killigrew heard voices. They did not make any kind of sense. He wondered if it was because they were speaking in a foreign language, or because the blow to his head had deprived him of his senses.

His senses certainly felt addled, at least those of them he was using. Apart from his hearing, he could taste the dust in his mouth, could smell the smoke and blood, and could feel the hard earth pressing against his body and the agonising throbbing in his skull. He could not see because his eyes were shut. He kept them shut because he was afraid that if he opened them he might find that he was blind.

He felt hands on his shoulders, turning him on his back. He rolled over and opened his eyes. If he was blind, then keeping his eyes shut for the rest of his life was not going to make a – he winced – blind bit of difference.

He could still see. All he could see was blinding white light, but it was better than nothing. Then Ndawa's head eclipsed the sun.

'*O-ke?*' asked Ndawa, his face full of concern.

'No,' said Killigrew. He raised a hand to his head and discovered with astonishment that his skull had not been caved in, although a huge lump had risen on one side of it. The horse's hoof must have stuck him a glancing blow. 'Not "*o-ke*".'

Ndawa helped him up. Killigrew tried to stand on his own two feet, but his left ankle gave way the moment he put his weight on it. He would have fallen if Ndawa had not caught him. Ndawa put one of Killigrew's arms across his shoulders and helped the white man limp back towards the village.

A scene of carnage greeted them. There were corpses everywhere: several of them leopard men, but not nearly enough to put out the rage that smouldered within Killigrew. Like a moorland fire it had gone underground and seemed to be extinguished, but in time it would burst out afresh, more fierce and destructive than ever before. And when the reckoning came someone, Killigrew was determined, was going to get very, *very* badly burned indeed.

Most of the people left in the ruins of the burned-out village were the elderly ones, too weak and feeble to be worth taking away as slaves. The women moved amongst the bodies of their sons and grandsons, weeping, while the men went to work, trying to clear up the mess.

Killigrew had hoped that the witch doctor would be able to give him some kind of ointment to put on his twisted ankle to take away the pain – he had tried heathen remedies in the past and found them at least as effective as the latest European techniques – but the doctor was dead, run clean through the body with a spear which had grotesquely pinned him to the side of Ndawa's hut. At least Ndawa's wife was there, and not too badly hurt. Then Killigrew remembered Miss Chance and his heart filled with despair. They had taken her. She was not well enough to travel; she would be lucky if she survived the journey back to Salazar's barracoon; he had no doubt that was where Prince Khari would take her. And even if she did live that long, what kind of a fate awaited her when she arrived?

'Where's Molineaux?' he asked Ndawa. The young man shrugged, not understanding. 'Sekou,' said Killigrew. Again Ndawa shrugged. He did not know. He turned away and went to help tend the wounded. These people had enough concerns of their own, without worrying about a British seaman and an American missionary. Killigrew tried to go in search of a horse, but before he had taken two steps his ankle gave way beneath him and he collapsed against the wall of the hut, sliding to the ground with a sob of frustration.

'*Ce n'est pas bon,*' said a voice beside him, and he turned to see Tip-Top standing over him, knocking his battered top hat back into shape.

Killigrew looked up at him in surprise. 'You speak French?'

'A little,' admitted Tip-Top. 'As you do, evidently.'

'I wish you'd said something earlier. It's better than messing about with pidgin English.'

Then Killigrew saw Momolu. There was a bloody graze on his temple and his face was ashen, but his voice remained strong as he said something bitterly to Killigrew. 'What did he say?' Killigrew asked Tip-Top.

'He says: "Now you know what the leopard people are."'

That evening Momolu held a palaver which all the remaining villagers attended. Killigrew went along and watched from the sidelines. He could not understand a word that was being said, but it was clear that passions ran high. 'Can you tell me what they're saying?' he asked Tip-Top.

'They are discussing what is to be done. Italo – the young man who speaks now – is saying they must gather together their kinsmen from the neighbouring villages and pursue the leopard people to their lair and rescue the prisoners before they are spirited off to Hell.'

Killigrew smiled without much humour. 'I

think it more likely they'll end up in the Americas – not that there's much difference between Hell and the Americas for those condemned to a lifetime of slavery.'

Italo sat down, and Momolu rose to his feet. 'He is saying that he would do anything for the return of the captives, but attempts have been made to track the leopard people to their lair before; those that set out to find it never returned,' translated Tip-Top.

'Tell them I know where the captives have been taken,' said Killigrew. 'Tell them I have been there myself and barely escaped with my life, but I am willing to return to help them free their kinsfolk, if they will help me.'

Tip-Top stepped forward and removed his hat, holding it in front of him like a petitioner. They heard him out as he translated what Killigrew had said, but as soon as he had finished Italo leaped to his feet and spoke so angrily that spittle flew from his lips, gesturing at Killigrew the whole time.

'I don't like the sound of that,' said Killigrew.

'He says it is your fault that the leopard people came to the village today,' Tip-Top murmured out of the corner of his mouth. 'That they came here searching for you and your friends.'

'He's probably right,' said Killigrew. 'Tell him–' He broke off when he saw the Italo's tirade had finished and Momolu was gesturing for his son to speak.

'Now Ndawa is defending you. He says that although your skin is white your heart is pure, and the way you fought today proved that. You saved him from being killed and his wife from being taken by the leopard people, and for that he is always in your debt. You fought as a lion, and the lion always defeats the leopard. If they listen to you, there is perhaps a chance you can show them a way to defeat the leopard people.'

Killigrew flushed. He pushed himself to his feet and leaned against the side of the well for support. 'Now tell them this: the leopard people are working together with white men. White men who make me ashamed to be a white man. There are other white men, like me, who would like to destroy the white men who bring shame upon my race by helping the leopard people carry your kinsfolk into slavery; but we cannot do it without the help of the Mende, just as the Mende cannot defeat the leopard people and free their kinsfolk without the help of the white men. By working together, we can destroy the leopard people and the white men who would help them.'

When Tip-Top had finished translating all this into Mande, Killigrew was surprised by the lack of reaction on the part of the villagers. He had thought it a fairly capital speech, and was disappointed. He could only assume it had lost something in the translation.

Momolu rose to his feet and spoke very briefly indeed, although his dry tone was unmistakable. 'He wants to know if you've got a plan,' explained Tip-Top.

Killigrew grinned with relief. 'Now he's talking my language.'

As it happened he did have a plan, and he explained it at length through Tip-Top. There was approval on the whole, but Italo was not entirely satisfied. 'He wants to know how they can be sure you will meet them when and where you say you will, and whether you can guarantee to bring the help of the white men with the great canoe-houses.'

'Tell him I cannot guarantee the help of other white men, although I will do everything I can to bring it about. But whether I come with help or alone to the place we have arranged, I *shall* come, on my word of honour as an English gentleman.'

Italo had one more question. Instead of translating it to Killigrew, Tip-Top looked about until he saw a solid-looking rock on the ground nearby. He picked it up and showed it to Italo, answering his question. That seemed to satisfy Italo, who nodded and sat down once more.

'What was all that about?' asked Killigrew.

'He wanted to know what the word of a British gentleman was,' explained Tip-Top, and grinned. 'I showed him.'

They had given him five days. Killigrew knew it would take him three days to get to Monrovia, even with native bearers carrying him in a litter; with his ankle twisted, he would not make it otherwise. He knew that the remaining two days would not give him much time to fulfil his side of the bargain, but it would have to suffice; every day's delay before putting their plan into action increased the chances that more ships would come to the Owodunni Barracoon and carry off the slaves imprisoned there.

He set out with Tip-Top and Ndawa's cousin, Dguma, acting as bearers, as soon as they could rig up a litter; even before they left, runners were sent out to the neighbouring villages to call for the help of their warriors. Tip-Top and Dguma, used to the stifling tropical heat, carried Killigrew at a pace that would probably have killed all but the fittest Europeans. As they rested at villages along the way each night, Killigrew exercised his twisted ankle as much as he dared. He was determined to be in shape for the attack on the Owodunni Barracoon, but did not dare over-exert the joint for fear of making it worse rather than better.

Monrovia, the capital of Liberia, had been founded a quarter of a century earlier. Like Sierra Leone, Liberia had been set up as a homeland for Africans and their descendants who had been slaves but now, being free, wished to return to live in Africa. But while Sierra Leone was a British Crown Colony, Liberia had been founded by Americans. The United States constitution forbade – for obvious reasons – the ownership of colonies, so quite what the Liberian state was in legal terms was not fully defined; the US Government, however, embarrassed by this colony that was not a colony, had decided that it was time Liberia stood on her own two feet and declared her independence, whether she liked it or not. Killigrew had heard that a convention had been called in Monrovia for the following month so that the settlers of the non-colony could discuss their future. But when he arrived, borne between Tip-Top and Dguma, the place seemed as sleepy as ever.

Even though they had been founded for the

same purpose, Freetown and Monrovia were the complete antithesis of one another: where Freetown was a riotous, ramshackle town where alcohol-consumption and prostitution were the order of the day, Monrovia was God-fearing, decent, orderly, alcohol-free and all in all the kind of place that only Yankee evangelists could create.

Killigrew hated it.

But he forgot all his loathing the moment he spied the frigate moored in the harbour. 'We're in luck, Tip-Top,' he exclaimed.

'A British ship?'

Killigrew nodded. 'HMS *Thor*. I know her captain.' Whether the captain would be prepared to listen to the disgraced Killigrew was another matter entirely.

Tip-Top and Dguma finally stopped on the waterfront and Killigrew climbed down from the litter, hobbling on his ankle but able to move around unsupported now. He pointed to the Kru bumboats tied up below the wooden jetty. 'See if you can persuade one of them to take us out to the frigate,' he told Tip-Top.

The Krumen manning the bumboats took little persuading. They had doubtless already visited HMS *Thor* many times since she had anchored in the harbour, but they were clearly glad of another excuse to visit the ship and ply the crew with their wares. Killigrew picked the likeliest, to the disappointment of the other boatmen, who nevertheless rowed out to the *Thor* with their rival, so that Killigrew arrived with a commercial flotilla of honour.

As they drew near, a lieutenant about the same age as Killigrew crossed to the rail to wave them away, and Killigrew guessed they had suffered the bumboat boys smuggling alcohol on board to the crew. Prohibition might be about to become inscribed in the constitution that was being drawn up for Liberia, but Killigrew expected that that was one law which might well prove to be unenforceable, even in the face of evangelical zeal.

'Clear off, you wretches! We've already got all the cassava, sweet potatoes, spices, rum, peppers, rice and mangoes we need. Go on, get away!'

'That's no way to greet an old friend, Matt,' chided Killigrew.

Lieutenant Matthew Masterson performed a double-take. 'Killigrew? What the deuce are you doing here?'

'It's a long story and I haven't much time. May I come aboard?'

Masterson frowned, torn between loyalty to an old shipmate and the knowledge that Killigrew was *persona non grata*. 'Look, Killigrew, I heard about what happened in London and I'm dreadfully sorry, but–'

'It's urgent, Matt. Many lives are at stake. You have to believe me, I didn't kill that girl. I've been spying for the Slave Trade Department. Rear-Admiral Napier will confirm my story.'

'Napier's here?'

'No, he's in London.'

'It will take weeks to get confirmation–'

Killigrew pounded a fist against the side of the hull. 'Damn it, there isn't time! You'll just have to

450

trust me, Matt, I know where the Owodunni Barracoon is.'

Masterson stared. 'You've been there? I was starting to think it was a mythical place, like an El Dorado for slavers.' He hesitated only a moment longer. 'Throw down a ladder for him, Bosun.'

Killigrew heaved a sigh of relief. 'Is it all right if I bring my friends aboard?' he asked, indicating Tip-Top and Dguma.

'Of course! Come on up.'

'Is Nose-Biter still captain of this tub?'

Masterson nodded.

'You think he'll be willing to sail there and help me destroy the place?'

Masterson looked uncertain. 'This isn't the old days, Killigrew. We can't just go charging into barracoons, freeing slaves and bombarding them the way we used to. After the legal wrangle Denman got himself into at the Gallinas river...'

'At least let me speak to him.'

Masterson took a deep breath. 'All right, Killigrew. But this issue isn't as straightforward as it seems...' He motioned aside the marine who stood on duty at the entrance to the roundhouse and ushered Killigrew inside. They made their way to the captain's day room and Masterson saluted the marine who was likewise on duty there. A low murmur of voices could be heard coming from the other side of the door.

'Sorry, sir, but Captain Crichton says he's not to be disturbed,' said the marine.

Masterson cleared his throat. 'My apologies to Captain Crichton, but I think he will want to hear what Mr Killigrew here has to tell him.'

The marine knocked on the door. 'Captain Crichton, sir? Lieutenant Masterson apologies for the interruption but says he thinks you'll want to hear what Mr Killigrew has to tell you.'

The door was jerked open and Captain Crichton stood there, glowering at the marine. He was in his late fifties but despite his age he was of tall, imposing build with wild white hair and watery eyes which bulged from his fish-like face. 'Killigrew? Lieutenant Kit Killigrew? Or perhaps I should say ex-lieutenant?'

'It's a long story, sir.'

'Well, you'd better come in.' Crichton stood aside and allowed Masterson and Killigrew to enter the day room. As Masterson closed the door firmly behind them, Killigrew saw that Crichton's guest was a tall African with widely flared nostrils, low brows and a pair of eyes which glinted like polished Minié balls. He was dressed smartly in European clothes: black pantaloons and frock coat, white shirt, waistcoat and cravat. What brought Killigrew up short was the leopard skin draped over his shoulder. He rose to his feet and bowed without taking his eyes off Killigrew for a moment.

'Your Majesty, may I introduce Mr Christopher Killigrew?' said Masterson. 'Late of Her Majesty's Royal Navy and currently working for the Slave Trade Department of the British Foreign Office. Killigrew, this is His Majesty King Nldamak.'

Killigrew knew the name, although it took him a moment to recall where he had heard it before, and even then he only did so because of the leopard skin.

Nldamak was Prince Khari's father.

The slave coffle had reached the delta at the mouth of the Owodunni river two days earlier. They had only marched for a day, but it had been a gruelling march nonetheless and no less than seven of the captives had died: three dropped from exhaustion and were left for the vultures with their throats slit, the other four were murdered with shocking casualness for showing the least resistance. After seeing that Molineaux had shown his captors considerably more respect than before, but had been even more determined than ever to see the slavers put out of business for ever.

They could not see the barracoon at first – unlike Killigrew, Molineaux had not got a clear look at the place when they had been there a few days earlier – for the place was screened by the thick bands of jungle which grew all around the channels and swamps of the delta. But Molineaux saw the four watchtowers silhouetted against the sky – in the direction of the sea, he supposed – and knew they had arrived.

They came to where one of the channels barred their way. A wooden landing stage reached out into the brackish waters. Crocodiles sunning themselves on a nearby mud-flat seemed to pay the slavers and their prisoners no attention. There was no boat tied up at the stage, just a tall wooden post set in the earth with an ivory horn hung from it. One of the leopard men took the horn and blew into it, a series of resounding notes which startled a flock of ibises to flight. Molineaux tried to imprint the sequence in his memory; it might come in useful later.

They waited. Some of the leopard men lit pipes. At length Molineaux heard a gentle plashing and gazed down the channel in time to see a large canoe appear around a bend, manned by four mulattos. They quickly reached the landing stage and tied up. One of them eyed the slaves. 'Not a bad looking lot, your highness. Not the best I've ever seen, but they'll do, I'm sure. Every slave has his price. Senhor Salazar is keen to know if you got Killigrew and the Chance girl.'

Khari gestured to where Miss Chance lay in the litter. 'I have the woman. Killigrew is dead, as Salazar requested. I rode him down myself and crushed him beneath the hoofs of my horse, as I crush all my enemies.'

The man nodded and turned away, but Khari seized him by the arm, making him wince. 'I expect to be paid well for this, Tobias. If not in guns, then in gold.'

'You'll have to discuss that with Senhor Salazar,' said Tobias. 'But I'll tell you one thing: word is there's another ship due in in a few days' time.'

'With rifles?'

'Rifles, gunpowder, rum, the lot. Don't you fret, your highness. You'll get paid.'

Khari folded his arms. 'I hope so. Senhor Salazar seems to think he can order me around as if I were another one of his lackeys. There are plenty of other barracoons where I can sell my captives.'

Tobias chuckled. 'Maybe so, your highness, but not this side of Cape Palmas, there ain't. Come on, let's get the first batch in the canoe.'

The first batch comprised Miss Chance, Molineaux, Abena, and five other captives. Tobias got in the boat with Prince Khari and three of his leopard warriors. They cast off from the landing stage, paddled off down the channel and left the others to wait.

For the first time since their capture, Molineaux was close enough to Miss Chance to talk to her. 'Miss Chance? You all right, Miss Chance?'

She muttered something without looking at him. He caught Killigrew's name, but the rest of it made no sense. She was clearly delirious, and the pallor of her skin was ghastly.

Something smashed into Molineaux's back, and he sprawled at the bottom of the canoe. He rolled on to his back and found himself staring up at Prince Khari. 'You may have the gift of speaking English, but I did not say you could use it.'

With his hands now tied behind his back, and consequently twisted under him at an awkward angle, Molineaux winced. 'You didn't say I couldn't.' He was perfectly positioned to tip Khari over the side with a kick to his knees, in the hope of feeding him to the crocodiles, but with the leopard men covering him with their muskets he would gain little from that other than his own death in return for the possibility of Prince Khari's. He decided to wait for a better

455

opportunity to kill him.

Khari gave him a half-hearted kick to ram home the point and turned away. Molineaux managed to sit up and tried to memorise the route they took through the channels, but the delta was like a watery maze, and one jungle-covered river bank looked much the same as another to him. Finding the way out of the delta the other night had been easy: it had simply been a case of heading upstream until they reached the main body of the river; but finding the way to the barracoon at the heart of the delta would be impossible for a stranger. Salazar had chosen the location of his lair well.

At last another landing stage came into sight, and Molineaux began to appreciate just how big the barracoon really was. Most of the island where they landed was covered by a huge stockade surrounded by a wooden palisade at least twelve feet high. From inside the stockade he could hear pitiful groans and the rattle of chains, like Scrooge's nightmare of Marley's ghost multiplied a thousand times. The mangrove swamps did not smell sweet at the best of times; here the stench was appalling.

The captives were dragged out of the boat. 'Not her,' Tobias ordered when one of the leopard men made to lift out Miss Chance. 'She goes to the big house.'

The leopard man glanced at Khari, who silently nodded his acceptance, before straightening and leaving Miss Chance where she lay. Molineaux could imagine what kind of fate awaited her at Salazar's hands in the big house; he wondered if the slaver was the kind of man who would take advantage of a desperately ill woman – a man who could sell human beings by the hundred like so many heads of cattle was capable of any atrocity. Molineaux was reluctant to let her out of his sight and he pushed back against the leopard men who herded him towards the entrance of the stockade, but he was powerless.

Molineaux, Abena and the other captives were pushed into the stockade. The walls loomed over them menacingly, and Molineaux saw more guards armed with muskets patrolling the catwalk that ran around the top of the palisade. In the centre of the stockade there were a dozen sheds formed from wooden pillars lashed together with bamboo. The walls were about six feet high, and between the top of the walls and the roof thatched with palm leaves there was a gap of another four feet. The groans and rattling chains seemed to come from all around; Molineaux wanted to put his hands over his ears and scream until he had blocked out the sound of human suffering.

The captives were marched between these sheds to one towards the back of the stockade and ushered inside. As yet it was empty. A central row of wooden pillars supported the roof, and a chain ran the length of the row, with a large neck-link every two feet. The captives were each padlocked into a collar. 'Shackle him between those two,' ordered Khari, indicating Molineaux.

'You think he's dangerous?' asked Tobias. 'He don't look much.'

'No. But he is clever. Those can be the most

dangerous ones of them all.'

You better believe it, thought Molineaux, as one of his wrists was shackled to the man on his right and the other to Abena on his left.

'If he gives you any trouble, give him a good beating,' said Khari. 'But don't kill him. He speak English – he should fetch a good price.'

Khari, Tobias and the guards went out to fetch the next batch, bolting the bamboo gate to the shed and padlocking that too.

Now that Killigrew was dead it was all up to Molineaux. All he had to do was get out of his shackles, kill the guards, free the others and then use the resulting confusion to rescue Miss Chance from Salazar's salacious clutches before they all made their escape through the maze of crocodile-infested waterways and into the jungle. *Easy as caz,* he thought wryly to himself. He glanced at the padlocks on his fetters and cursed himself for leaving his picklocks at the village, not that he had had much choice in the matter. He turned to Abena. 'I don't suppose you'd happen to have such a thing as a bent nail on you?'

She looked at him blankly.

He sighed. 'Didn't think so.' He lay back on the planking which formed the floor of the shed, trying to feign calmness in the face of adversity, but his own frustration got the better of him and he pounded the planks with his fist.

XIX:

A Lamb to the Slaughter

'I had a dream,' said King Nldamak, and then grimaced. 'Well, actually it was more of a nightmare.' He glanced at the three white men in the cabin bashfully, as if worried they might be laughing at him for being superstitious, but all three met his gaze gravely. He continued. 'I dreamed that one day the white man would rule all of Africa, from the Barbary Coast to the Cape of Good Hope.'

'Great Britain has no territorial ambitions in Africa,' Killigrew assured him, truthfully enough. 'Colonies are expensive to run and more trouble than they're worth.'

'Expensive to run, Mr Killigrew?' mocked Nldamak. 'Has not your country plundered India for its riches? Is it not Indian wealth which has made Britain great, while enslaving the Indians?'

Killigrew flushed. 'Britain only wants to trade. Fair trade is mutually beneficial to both parties. Sometimes it is necessary to displace corrupt local rulers and set up an administration until such time as government can be handed back to the local people...'

'And how long until you hand back local government to the Indians, Mr Killigrew? Ten years? Fifty years? A hundred years?'

459

Killigrew held up a hand. 'I'm not saying that the East India Company hasn't made mistakes by allowing itself to be drawn into a greater and greater role in the government of India, your majesty. But we British have learned from that experience. We won't make the same mistake again.'

'Won't you? Perhaps you are wise enough to see that, but what about your government? Is that wise?'

Killigrew thought of men like Sir George Grafton, and decided it was probably best to say nothing.

'Africa is a rich land, Mr Killigrew. One day your people, and the people of the other nations of Europe, will realise that. Some already do. The only thing which prevents the white man from penetrating further into this continent is the white man's fever. But I hear now that Jesuit's bark is being proved to be a cure for the fever. The bad airs which now prove so fatal to the white mans constitution will not protect us for ever, and when the time comes the white man will come in force to plunder Africa's riches. Africa must defend itself, Mr Killigrew. Not just the Vai, the Mende and the Temne, but *all* the peoples of Africa. We must stop allowing the white man to carry off the best and strongest of our people to slavery in the Americas.'

'I couldn't agree with you more, your majesty. That is why I must fight against your son.'

Nldamak looked away. 'Khari and I went our separate ways many years ago, Mr Killigrew. He believes the only way the African can defeat the white man is to accept the white man's ways and learn to beat him at his own game. But the white man's ways are not the ways of Africa.'

'There was slavery in Africa long before the white man came, your majesty,' said Masterson.

Nldamak looked up at him sharply. 'If a wrong has been done for hundreds of years, Lieutenant, does that make it more or less of a wrong? Let Africa make her own mistakes. If she must suffer, let it be through her own fault rather than the fault of the white man. But my son – who is no longer my son – does not see these things the way I do. He has spent too much time in the company of white men, and it has corrupted him. Now his cause is the white man's cause, and he would betray his own people if it were to his own advantage. I do not mean to insult you gentlemen. I know that your hearts are good. I thank you for working to stop the slave trade; you have seen for yourselves the suffering it causes. But there are others in your country who do not understand and do not care. *They* are the ones I fear. They are the ones who will one day decide that Africa must be plundered for her wealth, as she has already been plundered for her people.

'And as for my son, who is no longer my son … he chose his path a long time ago. Let it lead him where it will. He must do what he must do, just as you must do what you must do. If you kill him, I shall grieve, as any father must. But I will not stand in your way. And now, gentlemen, you must excuse me.'

They ushered him out of the great cabin and stood and watched from the deck as Nldamak climbed down to the captain's gig and was rowed back to the waterfront, his shoulders slumped dejectedly. Killigrew saw a man who predicted only pain and suffering as the future for his people, and his heart went out to him.

'He speaks well enough, I'll grant you,' said Masterson. 'But can we be sure he won't send word to Khari and Salazar to warn them of our imminent attack?'

Captain Crichton nodded slowly. 'Oh, I think we can trust him, Lieutenant.'

Killigrew nodded. Nose-Biter Crichton might have a reputation for being as mad as a hatter, but Killigrew knew the captain was a good deal wiser than he let on. 'Besides, if we set sail at once we can attack the barracoon long before he can get word there,' he said. He was concerned that every moment they delayed increased the chances of more slavers coming to take away the captives in the barracoon's stockade.

'Weigh anchor and set sail, Masterson,' ordered Crichton. 'Set a course for the Owodunni Barracoon. Mr Killigrew here will give you directions.'

Within an hour they gathered together in the day cabin for a council of war: Killigrew, Crichton, Masterson, Tip-Top, Dguma and the captain of the *Thor*'s marines, Captain Reynolds. Killigrew showed them the sketch map he had just finished.

'This is the barracoon, or at least as much of it as I saw. Salazar gave me a pretty good guided tour. The sandbar here prevents any ships from approaching within half a mile of the coast. There are watchtowers here, here, here and here. The men in them have telescopes, so it's a fair bet they'll see you coming the moment you round the headland two miles to the south. Salazar's house is here, at the centre. Over here we have administration blocks, these are the barracks, and this is the harem.'

'Sounds to me like this fellow Salazar knows how to live,' remarked Masterson.

Killigrew nodded. 'Let's just hope he knows how to die. If he doesn't, I know how to teach him.' He was aware of Crichton and Masterson exchanging worried glances at his bloodthirsty talk, but pretended not to have seen and concentrated on the plan. 'Over here is the stockade where the slaves are kept, at the eastern end of the delta, away from the shore. The barracoon's well laid out and easily defensible – Salazar's no fool – but he's made one fatal flaw. Provided you don't elevate those eight-inch shell guns of yours above five degrees, if you anchor just outside the bar you can bombard the whole barracoon and hit everything but the stockade itself.'

'What about the harem?' asked Crichton. 'Wouldn't want to bombard innocent women.'

'And Miss Chance,' added Masterson. 'Odds are she'll either be in the harem or in Salazar's house.'

Killigrew nodded. 'That's where your marines come in, Captain Reynolds. I'll go with you to guide you. Ndawa – Chief Momolu's son –promised to meet me there with some of his men and enough canoes to get us through the creeks. We'll hit the barracoon at midnight. We use stealth. With any luck we'll be able to get the women out of there before Salazar even knows we've been and gone. The other slaves will be safe in the stockade. At two bells in the middle watch you can start the bombardment.'

'Then you'd better make sure you're out of there by then,' said Crichton. 'Because I'm going to throw every shell I've got on board at that barracoon, and when I'm done there won't be so much as a termite left alive in that delta.'

Captain Reynolds nodded. 'If there are any survivors amongst Salazar's men, we'll pick them up. I've done this kind of thing enough times before.'

Killigrew shook his head. 'Make no mistake, gentlemen. This is far and away the biggest barracoon I've ever seen. Salazar himself told me he employs over three hundred men.'

'That's a lot of people,' said Crichton. 'What arrangements are we going to make for prisoners?'

Killigrew looked up at him, his dark eyes glittering coldly in the light of the oil lamp. 'Who said anything about taking prisoners?'

HMS *Thor* hove to a few miles to the south of the Owodunni delta at sunset the following evening and the anchor was dropped into the sea with a splash. The crew prepared to lower the launch.

'Remember, you've got to be out of there by two bells in the middle watch,' Masterson told Killigrew. 'Do you have a watch?'

'Yes, but it's broken. I think some water must have spoiled the workings. Damn it, you'd think someone would come up with a way to make these things impervious to water.'

'You'd better take mine. Shall we synchronise watches, sir?'

Crichton checked his own watch. 'I make it six thirty-seven, on the dot.' Six hours and twenty-three minutes to one o'clock, or two bells in the middle watch.

'Same here,' said Masterson, and handed his watch to Killigrew, who tucked it into the fob pocket of the borrowed waistcoat he was wearing along with a borrowed dirk and a borrowed cutlass. 'You'd better take this as well,' he added, handing Killigrew some kind of pistol.

Killigrew studied the weapon curiously. It was like a pepperbox, but whereas the pepperbox had six distinct barrels for each shot, this weapon had only one barrel, with a cylinder in the middle containing several chambers, each of which was brought into line with the barrel as the cylinder turned. He had seen such weapons before, but this one had six chambers rather than five.

'Colonel Colt's invention,' explained Masterson.

Killigrew cocked the hammer experimentally, saw that it worked, and then lowered the hammer back into place. 'Ingenious.'

'Each chamber's already primed and loaded. All you have to do is cock, aim and fire. Effective range is about fifty yards.'

'Thanks, but if I have to use it I'll have failed. Stealth is the order of the evening, gentlemen.'

465

'Take it anyway,' said Masterson. 'Just in case.' Killigrew nodded and buckled on the gun belt Masterson handed him before climbing into the launch. 'Good luck,' Masterson called down to them as the boat was lowered to the water.

'I'll see you in seven hours,' Killigrew told him.

Masterson grinned. 'I'll have a bottle of whisky standing by.'

'I'll probably need it by then.' In fact Killigrew would have liked to have a drink or two there and then, to stiffen resolve, but he knew he needed to keep a clear head.

It was a tight squeeze in the launch with Tip-Top, Dguma and Reynolds and his squad of twenty marines. The Jollies looked smart in their red coats and white crossbelts. They rowed proficiently across the bar and through the breakers, jumping out to drag the boat a few feet up on to dry sand so that the officers would not have to get their feet wet. The squad moved quickly across the beach with Tip-Top and Dguma while Killigrew gave one last glance to where the *Thor* rode at anchor, silhouetted by the last rays of the sunset.

'No turning back now,' said Reynolds. 'We're going to have to move fast now to get to the barracoon in time. My men are in first-rate condition, Killigrew. You'd better not slow us down.'

'I'll certainly try to keep up,' Killigrew promised him gravely. 'Let's just hope this breeze keeps up, otherwise we'll be left without naval support at the eleventh hour.' Without the bombardment from the *Thor*, even if the marines

466

did succeed in rescuing the slaves from the barracoon, there was nothing to stop Prince Khari's leopard men from pursuing them as they escaped.

'I just hope that these natives are there with the canoes,' grunted Reynolds.

Dguma and Tip-Top exchanged a few words. 'What did he say?' asked Killigrew.

Tip-Top grinned, his pointed teeth showing white in the bosky gloom. 'He says the word of a Mende is as good as the word of an Englishman. They'll be there.'

As the light faded they headed inland through the jungle. Dguma led the way, used to moving stealthily through the forest at night. It was a clear night and a half-moon rose shortly after sunset, but beneath the trees it was pitch black. The marines were well disciplined and they marched silently, without talking. However irritating the Jollies might be on board ship, there were no soldiers in the world Killigrew would have preferred to have around him in a scrap.

Nevertheless it took them nearly five hours to cover the few miles to the edge of the delta. They paused by a thick band of undergrowth beyond which Killigrew could hear the gentle trickle of water.

'Well, we're here. Where are they?' His ankle was throbbing again after the trek and he unlaced his half-boot to massage it.

Reynolds looked at him. 'Are you sure you're up to this, Killigrew?'

'Never felt better.' Killigrew laced his boot up tightly.

Tip-Top translated his question into Mande for Dguma.

Before Dguma could reply, a voice hissed at them in some African tongue, suspicious and full of menace. The marines quickly unslung their muskets, but Dguma answered the voice, and a moment later a shadowy figure emerged from the darkness. 'One of their watchers,' explained Tip-Top after a brief exchange with Dguma and the stranger. 'Ndawa and the others are about five hundred yards off that way.'

They followed the man through the trees. Killigrew kept one hand on the butt of the revolving pistol holstered at his side in case the stranger should turn out to be one of Salazar's men, but before long they were surrounded by about a dozen Mende armed with spears, bows and war-clubs. Ndawa clapped Killigrew on the shoulders, and even Italo seemed pleased to see him. One of the Mende cupped his hands to his mouth and made some kind of bird-call, doubtless the signal to summon back the other men who had been watching for Killigrew and his companions.

Tip-Top asked Ndawa a question, to which the Mende replied evenly.

'What did you ask him?'

'I wanted to know if this was all the men he had with him,' said Tip-Top. 'He says more wanted to come, but twenty was enough.'

'He's right,' said Killigrew. 'Salazar's men might have noticed a larger force of Mende approaching and hiding here in the woods. Tell him that the naval bombardment has been arranged.' He hoped it was true. His worst fear – that the breeze might die and leave the *Thor* becalmed – had come true. But he sensed that Crichton and Masterson would not let him down and would get the frigate into position, even if that meant putting all their boats into the water to tow it.

Led by Ndawa, the Mende picked up the five bark canoes they had brought with them and moved off through the trees until they came to a spot Ndawa had reconnoitred earlier, where the bushes at the side of the channel thinned out enough for them to reach the water's edge. With Tip-Top's help, Reynolds and Ndawa organised their men, dividing them between the canoes. One canoe would head downstream and the men inside would silence the guards in the two watchtowers to the west, which would be the first to spy the approach of the HMS *Thor* as it rounded the headland to the south; another would take care of the guards in the easternmost watchtowers, which dominated the harem and the stockade. The remaining three would attack the barracoon and rescue the women in the harem.

'Fix bayonets, men,' ordered Reynolds. 'No shooting unless you have to. We don't want to raise the alarm.'

The Mende got into the canoes first and held them steady for the marines, but the marines were used to working with small boats and climbed in without fuss, four marines and four Mende to each canoe. Killigrew climbed into the largest canoe with Tip-Top, Ndawa, Dguma,

Italo and Reynolds with three marines.

The canoes slipped silently through the water, the paddles making barely a sound. The jungle on either side of them was alive with the croaking of frogs and the chirruping of insects, while the sound of distant laughter floated through the night from the direction of the barracks. One of the canoes headed off down one of the main channels towards the coast, bearing the men who would kill the guards in the westernmost watchtowers; the rest headed inland, towards the harem.

Ndawa held up a hand, and the lead canoe slowed to a halt, the others doing likewise. Then he signalled one of the canoes forward to where a watchtower loomed over them about a hundred yards away. It tied up directly beneath the tower, and two of the marines got out. Killigrew took out his pocket telescope and was able to follow their progress as they ascended the ladder stealthily, silhouetted against the purple night sky. They were at their most vulnerable now, and Killigrew expected someone to see them and raise the alarm at any moment. His heart pounded in his chest, but his earlier fear had melted away and now only excitement filled him. He had been waiting for this night for a long, long time.

This was the night of the reckoning.

The first marine reached the top of the ladder, bayonet in hand. If either of the two guards made any sound as they died, Killigrew did not hear them. Their silhouettes disappeared and were quickly replaced by the marines, who put on the guards' broad-brimmed straw hats and assumed their positions.

Ndawa signalled again and the remaining canoes glided forwards. One moved on to deal with the second watchtower, the other three passed the stockade. Killigrew could smell the stench of excrement and hear the groans of the slaves and the occasional clank of their chains. *Just a few more minutes,* he thought, *and then you'll be free. Just hang on until then.*

The three canoes tied up at the next island, at the far end from the long, low building which formed the harem. Two guards stood on duty with muskets over their shoulders at either end of the building, but they looked relaxed. Ndawa was about to ease himself out of the canoe when Killigrew put a hand on his arm to stop him.

'Tell him to kill the guards, but not to enter the building,' he asked Tip-Top in a low voice. 'The women may all be there against their will, but we don't know that for sure, and it will only take one of them to raise the alarm.'

Tip-Top passed this on, and Ndawa nodded before climbing out of the canoe with Dguma, Italo and another man. They split into two pairs, tackling each end of the building silently. The guards never knew what hit them, and Killigrew could barely hear the soft thud of the bodies as they hit the ground with arrows through their throats.

Killigrew, Tip-Top and the marines climbed out of the canoe and hurried through the moonlight to join the others outside the building. Killigrew tried the front door. It was unlocked.

471

He eased it open a crack and peered through. A long corridor ran the length of the building, illuminated by an oil lamp hanging from the ceiling, and a guard dozed in a chair towards the middle with his straw hat tipped forward over his eyes, snoring loudly. A door led off the corridor every six feet on either side, and Killigrew could hear sobbing coming from more than one of them. He eased the door shut once more.

'Two minutes,' he whispered to Reynolds. Tip-Top passed the word on to Ndawa.

Killigrew made his way around the outside of the building. Each room had a small barred window set in it. Most of the rooms were dark, but even without light he could see that none of them contained Miss Chance: all the captives of the harem were black. A light showed in one window, and as Killigrew peered through he could see a fat white man he did not recognise – his bronzed face and hands in obscene contrast to the white rolls of flab of the rest of his body – holding down a slender young black woman, bending her over the grim cot which served as a bed as he thrust himself into her from behind.

Filled with revulsion, Killigrew felt himself trembling with rage, but held himself in check. Being raped was probably traumatic enough without having someone kick down the door to witness your humiliation before brutally and bloodily murdering the man who was raping you.

He finally returned to where Ndawa waited with the others. 'No sign of Miss Chance,' he whispered to Reynolds. 'Salazar must have her at the house.'

'And you're going after her, I suppose?'

Killigrew nodded. 'Besides, I've got a score to settle with Salazar.'

'Want me to send some men with you?'

'No, thank you. I'll manage. Give me ten minutes, and then start getting the women out of here.' No matter how stealthily they were, Killigrew could not imagine that releasing the women from the harem and getting them through the delta was a task which could be performed without the alarm being raised.

Ndawa nodded as Tip-Top explained, and then asked a question. 'He wants to know what he should do if you're not back by the time we're ready to get back in the canoes,' said the Kruman.

'You go without me,' Killigrew said simply. He checked his watch. It was a quarter past midnight. 'You've got three-quarters of an hour before the bombardment starts.' *If it starts*, he added to himself: there was no sign of the breeze picking up again, and the night was deadly still. 'Don't be here when it does.' He hurried off into the darkness before Reynolds, Ndawa or Tip-Top could protest.

A water channel separated the island with the harem from the main island at the centre of the barracoon where Salazar's house and the administrative blocks stood. A narrow wooden bridge arched over the water, and another guard stood on duty there with a musket over his shoulder, smoking a clay pipe. Killigrew decided to adopt the bold approach and strode up the bridge as if he had every right to be going where he was. The man looked up as his footsteps sounded on the planks of the bridge.

'*Boa noite,*' said Killigrew.

'*Boa noite, senhor.*'

Killigrew produced a cheroot Crichton had given him earlier. '*Tem lume, por favor?*'

'*Sim, senhor.*' The guard produced a box of lucifers, struck one on the wooden handrail of the bridge and lit Killigrew's cheroot for him.

'*Obrigado.*' Killigrew surreptitiously took out his dirk and held it behind his back.

'*De nada.*'

'*Onde está a casa de Senhor Salazar?*'

As the guard turned away to point out Salazar's house, Killigrew clamped a hand over his mouth and slit his throat. '*Obrigado,*' he murmured, propping the man's body against the handrail so it looked as though he was staring into the water below the bridge. He kicked the man's pipe, which had fallen to the planks of the bridge, into the water, and wiped the blade of his dirk clean before replacing it in the sheath at his side.

He crossed to where the *palazzo* stood, keeping to the shadows. There were no guards here. All the downstairs rooms were dark, although lights showed in some of the upstairs windows. He crept around the back and tried the kitchen door. Locked. Kicking it open would raise the alarm. He looked around for another way in, and saw a drainpipe leading up to the roof. He looked around again to make sure no one was watching, but a hush lay over the barracoon. Everything was preternaturally quiet. Killigrew prayed he was not about to walk into a trap.

Or rather, climb into a trap, to be precise. Ignoring his throbbing ankle, he shinned up the drainpipe to the ornate stone balustrade that ran around the top of the *palazzo* and scrambled over it. There were perhaps a dozen skylights set at various places across the roof, but they were all locked and barred. Making his way around the edge of the roof, he came to where a balcony jutted out in front of some French windows that were dark. He lowered himself over the balustrade and dropped. He landed lightly on the balls of his feet but pain shot through his ankle nonetheless. He crouched there for a moment and peered through the glass. The room beyond was unoccupied. He tried the handle. The door was unlocked but the catch was on. He slid his dirk into the gap and jiggled it until he was able to raise the catch, slipping inside and closing the door behind him.

He crossed to the far door and pressed his ear to it. No sound came from the other side. He opened it a crack and peered out. A single oil lamp illuminated the landing. There was no one in sight. He slipped out of the room and crept cat-footed across the carpet to the door opposite. Light shone underneath the door. He crouched down to peer through the keyhole and saw Captain Madison sitting up in bed, reading the Bible. *I'll deal with you later,* Killigrew thought to himself.

Voices came from a door further down. He peered through that keyhole. The occupants of the room were out of sight this time, but he could hear them talking. He recognised Salazar's voice:

'You should be grateful to me, Miss Chance. If it had not been for the Jesuit's powder I gave you, you would be dead by now.'

'If you think I'm going to surrender to your disgusting embraces just because you saved my life – after first endangering it, of course – you've got another think coming, Mr Salazar.'

So at least one of the captives had not been violated; that was some small relief at any rate.

'You should be good to me, Miss Chance... May I call you Suzannah?'

'You may not. Don't touch me! Get your filthy hands off me!'

Killigrew straightened and was about to burst through the door when he felt a hand on his shoulder. He straightened, turned and found himself staring at Prince Khari's chest.

'I never took you for a peeping Tom, Mr Killigrew.'

'I'm a man of many parts,' Killigrew told him with a shrug, and tried to stab him in the stomach with his dirk.

But Khari's hand swept down as fast as a striking mamba and gripped him by the wrist, halting the dirk's point an inch from his skin. He span Killigrew around, slammed him against the wall and twisted his arm up into the small of his back until Killigrew gasped and dropped the dirk.

Two of the bedroom doors opened and Salazar and Madison emerged, the former in white pantaloons and shirt, the latter in a blue-and-white striped nightshirt and tasselled nightcap. 'What's going on?' demanded Salazar.

476

'I found an intruder,' said Khari.

'Good evening,' said Killigrew, speaking with difficulty because of the way Khari was pressing his cheek against the wall.

Recognising him, Salazar relaxed and smiled, leaning negligently against the wall. 'Mr Killigrew. I've been expecting you...'

Killigrew groaned. 'Somehow I had a feeling you were going to say that.'

'...in spite of what his highness here told me about having killed you.'

'You don't have to call him "your highness", you know,' said Killigrew. 'His father's dis-inherited him. He won't even inherit a cracked chamber-pot when King Nldamak dies, never mind a throne.'

Khari punched him in the back and Killigrew gasped as pain exploded through his kidneys. 'Do not worry, Salazar. I'll finish the job.'

'No. I'll deal with Killigrew. You go down to the pays and make sure the slaves are all safely locked up for the night. Even Killigrew here isn't foolish enough to come back alone.' Salazar relieved Killigrew of his cutlass and revolver, keeping him covered so that Khari could release him and disappear downstairs.

'I'll get dressed,' muttered Madison, going back inside his room.

Salazar motioned for Killigrew to enter Miss Chance's room. She was sitting up in bed, her face drawn and pale with heavy bags under her eyes, but it was clear she was on the mend following her illness. 'Kit!' she exclaimed, spreading her arms wide.

Killigrew saw no reason not to go to her and hug her reassuringly. 'It's all right. Everything's going to be just fine.'

Salazar tutted, seating himself in a chair by the door while keeping Killigrew covered with the revolving pistol. 'You should not lie to the lady, Mr Killigrew. Or could it be you know something which yet escapes me?'

Killigrew glanced at the carriage clock on the mantelpiece. It said twenty-two minutes to one.

Salazar examined the revolving pistol, and started to knock the bullets out of their chambers, one after another, as if daring Killigrew to come around the bed at him; but the cutlass was propped against the wall close by Salazar's hand. 'I admire your spirit, Mr Killigrew. I would like to say you have been a worthy adversary, but I fear your puny efforts to put me out of business have hardly taxed me. I noticed you glanced at the clock just now. Am I keeping you from an urgent appointment?'

'You know how it is. Things to do, people to see.' Killigrew tried to sound nonchalant, but his bravado sounded hollow even to his own ears.

'I wonder. Could it be that you managed to arrange for a naval vessel to come and bombard my little business concern? The suggestion that any man, disgraced and stripped of his naval rank, could pull off such a feat would normally make me laugh. But then, you are not just any man, are you?'

Salazar gestured with the revolver. Killigrew had counted the number of bullets he had knocked out and knew there was still one in

478

there. 'An ingenious little toy,' said Salazar, and span the cylinder, before aiming the pistol between Miss Chance's eyes. He pulled the trigger, and she flinched with a gasp as the pistol banged, flames shooting from the muzzle, but the hammer had fallen on a chamber without a bullet in it. 'So tell me, Mr Killigrew, did you arrange for a naval bombardment, or not?'

Miss Chance clung to him. 'Don't tell him anything, Kit.'

'Perhaps Miss Chance thinks I am in jest,' said Salazar, aiming and squeezing the trigger again. The pistol banged again, but again there was no bullet in the chamber. 'Let me assure you, I'm not.' He aimed again, and smiled. 'Miss Chance has four chances left. Should I make arrangements for the reception of unwelcome guests, or not?'

Killigrew knew when he was beaten. He only hoped that Reynolds's marines had been able to get the women out of the harem in time. 'Give it up, Salazar. A Royal Navy frigate should be anchoring off the shore in the next fifteen minutes: the bombardment commences at one o'clock. You can kill me if you like, but either way you're finished.'

Salazar glanced down the barrel of the pistol. 'A wise decision, Mr Killigrew. The next shot would have blown her pretty little brains out.' He picked up the cutlass in his left hand and gestured with the revolver. 'Now let us leave Miss Chance to get her rest, which she is much in need of following her recent illness.'

As they emerged from the bedchamber they

found Madison waiting for them outside. 'Well?'

'There's a British frigate coming to bombard us in a quarter of an hour.'

Madison laughed. 'One frigate? Was that the best he could do?'

Killigrew frowned. For two men who were about to be subjected to a bombardment from a broadside of a dozen eight-inch-shell guns, they were both in remarkably high spirits. 'It should be enough to turn this barracoon into so much ploughed earth,' he told them confidently.

Salazar smiled. 'I think not.'

They went downstairs and Salazar pulled on a bell rope. Henriques appeared a moment later. 'Mr Sampson and his crew are to report to their action stations at once, Henriques.'

The footman nodded and hurried outside. Salazar and Madison followed him, taking Killigrew with them. The three of them went out of the *palazzo* and approached another bridge which led on to the next island, the one which bordered the shore. 'Before I kill you, Mr Killigrew, I want you to see why your pathetic attempts to destroy me have failed, so that you may die knowing that at the end you have lost, and I have won,' said Salazar. 'When you first came here I gave you a little guided tour, and I dare say you made good use of the knowledge you thus gained instructing the gentlemen of the Royal Navy in how to bombard this barracoon. But there is one small but important detail I was careful not to show you.'

Several dozen men emerged from the barracks at the trot, and Salazar motioned Killigrew to stand back and let them pass over the bridge first. When the last of the men had passed over, Salazar, Killigrew and Madison followed.

They passed through an archway in a hedge and came to where an escarpment sloped up slightly. A creeper-covered wall ran along the top of the escarpment, and at each of the twelve embrasures in the wall a ninety-eight-pounder pointed out to sea. Killigrew's heart sank. If the gunnery of Salazar's men was up to anything, then the shore battery would blast the unsuspecting HMS *Thor* out of the water.

Salazar saw the despondency on his face, and laughed. 'Surely you did not think I would invest so much of my hard-earned money in an operation of this scale without spending something on the means to protect it?'

Some of the men took down the creeper-covered boards which shielded the embrasures from the sea while others crossed to a bunker about fifty feet behind the battery. One of them unlocked the door and carried an oil lamp inside. The others followed him, and had soon formed a human chain, passing out round shot and cartridge bags. As one group of men piled the shot and cartridges outside the bunker, others from the gun crews came down and fetched the first load for their cannons. They worked with startling efficiency and were clearly well drilled.

'I told you before,' said Salazar. 'I like the best of everything in life. That extends to my gunners. Mr Sampson was trained in gunnery by the best teachers in the world, Mr Killigrew: your own Royal Navy. I don't think my men will have any

481

difficulty reducing one frigate to so much matchwood,' he added with evident relish at the forthcoming slaughter.

Salazar stepped up to the wall and motioned for Killigrew and Madison to join him. Below the wall Killigrew could see the steep slope of the escarpment stretching down to the beach, thick with foliage. Out to sea, HMS *Thor* was getting into position, towed by the ship's boats in the absence of any wind.

'Perfect,' said Salazar. 'With so many men in their boats, it will take several minutes to get them back on board and ready to fire a broadside. She's a sitting duck. Fire your first broadside as soon as you're ready, Mr Sampson!'

'Aye, aye, Mr Salazar!'

Killigrew had only one last card to play. 'If you sink a British frigate, the Royal Navy is going to come looking for you. And we've already left word with the authorities in Monrovia as to exactly where they can find you.'

Salazar smiled. 'I dare say you have. But I'll be long gone by then. Sinking this ship will buy me all the time I need to clear out of here and set up my operations at a new location. It will cost me a great deal of money, but that will be a drop in the ocean compared to the profits I make from the trade. You see, Mr Killigrew, your schoolboy heroics will result in nothing more than the loss of one year's profit for me, and the deaths of the crew of a British frigate. Oh, and your own death, of course. Which, I might add, is long overdue. Perhaps you'd like to do the honours, Captain Madison?'

'With pleasure.' Madison levelled the pistol at Killigrew's forehead. 'No pithy last words, Mr Killigrew? You disappoint me. Then let the Good Book supply your epitaph. Isaiah, chapter fifty-three, verse seven: "He was oppressed, and he was afflicted, yet he opened not his mouth: he is brought as a lamb to the slaughter".'

'Amen,' said Salazar. 'Goodbye, Mr Killigrew.'

XX:

The Reckoning

'Pull,' hissed Molineaux. 'Pull, damn your eyes!' He knew the other slaves could not understand his words, but he hoped they would get the general idea.

The captives pulled on their fetters, seeking to break them away from the wooden pillars which supported the roof. If they succeeded the whole roof would probably come down on their heads, but it was only made of palm leaves and a few bamboo poles, and a few cuts and bruises were preferable to a life of perpetual slavery. But the wooden beams were fixed deep in the ground, and they could not be budged.

Molineaux heard voices outside. He quickly motioned for everyone to stop pulling and resume their earlier positions. A light showed through the gate of the shed, and he saw Prince Khari standing on the other side with Tobias, who held an oil lamp aloft. 'See, your highness? There's no one here but these slaves, and they ain't going anywhere.'

'I want to be sure. Open the gate.'

The two men entered the shed, and Tobias moved the light of the lamp over the slaves, moving along the row. Khari eyed them warily looking for anything which suggested that all was not well.

Molineaux rose up on his knees as they approached him, his hands clasped together. 'Please doan' make me no slave, mas'er! I beg you! I ain't no African, I is a freeborn Englishman! Oh lawdy, please doan' send me to th' Americas, please!' He grabbed Tobias by the belt in supplication. The slaver slapped him across the face with his left hand, and Molineaux fell back to the floor.

'Shut your noise, you crazy nigger sonuvabitch!'

'Poor dumb white trash,' Molineaux muttered under his breath, as Tobias led Khari to the end of the row. Khari heard him and glanced over his shoulder with one eyebrow raised, but he did not see that Molineaux had expertly filched the ring of keys from Tobias's belt.

'All right,' said Khari. 'Salazar was wrong. He *did* come on his own.'

The two of them turned and strode back towards the gate. Molineaux did not bother to wonder who had come on his own. He had about fifteen seconds. He inserted the key into the padlock on his left manacle. The other slaves shifted where they lay, clinking their fetters so that Khari and Tobias would not hear the keys jingle in Molineaux's hands.

The first padlock snapped open and Molineaux's left hand was free. Two more to go, but Khari and Tobias were only a few feet from the gate now. The right manacle was trickier, because he had to use his left hand to unfasten it. His hands were trembling so much he could barely get the key in the hole. He dropped the keys, cursed himself silently, and tried again. The key turned at once.

Khari and Tobias had reached the gate.

Now the neck-collar. But the first key did not fit. Molineaux tried the next one, and again found it did not fit.

Khari and Tobias went outside and closed the gate behind them. Tobias snapped the padlock on the gate back into place and then reached for his keys to lock it.

Molineaux inserted a third key into the padlock on his collar.

'What's wrong?' Khari asked Tobias.

'My keys ... damn it, I must have had them a moment ago, otherwise how did I let us into the shed...?'

Khari looked up and Molineaux saw his eyes peering through the gate. Their eyes locked in the same instant that the padlock on Molineaux's collar came free. Khari patted Tobias on the shoulder and pointed through the gate at Molineaux.

'Kill him. I'll raise the alarm.'

'What the... Goddamn it!' Tobias jerked the padlock off the gate just as Molineaux tore the collar from his neck and handed the keys to the next slave in the row.

As Khari disappeared, Tobias charged towards Molineaux, reaching for the pistol holstered at his side. Molineaux ran to meet him. The two of them clashed just as the pistol came out of its holster, and they struggled for a moment with the gun between them. Molineaux managed to force the muzzle down towards the ground and it went off with a flash that was blinding in the darkness of the shed. He broke free of Tobias's grip and threw him towards the row of chained slaves. One of them stood up to receive him, looped his fetters over the slaver's head and drew the chain hard against his throat. Tobias gurgled horribly as the slave throttled him.

'I'm going after Khari…' Molineaux told the slaves, and then gestured dismissively and turned and ran for the gate. 'Ah, what the hell. You can't understand a word I say anyhow.'

He emerged from the shed in time to see Khari sprinting towards the entrance of the stockade. The guards silhouetted on the catwalk peered down into the darkness below, trying to work out what was going on. One of them called down in Portuguese.

'Sound the alarm!' shouted Khari. 'Slave rebellion!' He reached the gate of the stockade and hammered on it. The gate was opened, and Molineaux saw two guards standing there in the moonlight with muskets in their hands. Khari shouted something at them in Portuguese and dodged past.

The guards raised the stocks of their muskets to their shoulders and levelled them at Molineaux. His eyes widened, and he threw himself behind the shed just as the muskets flashed and two bullets thrummed in his direction.

He rolled over on the compacted earth, picked himself up and ran around the far side of the shed nearest the main gate. The guards there were still trying to reload their muskets.

Molineaux charged towards them, his naked feet pounding the earth. One of them raised his musket and fired. Molineaux swerved and felt the bullet sing past the side of his head. The other was still ramming his next shot home with the ramrod when Molineaux reached him.

The seaman snatched the musket from his hands and smashed the butt against the side of the guard's head. The guard went down, and Molineaux turned the musket on his companion, shooting him through the chest with both ramrod and ball at point-blank range.

The guards on the catwalk were shooting down into the stockade now, but not at Molineaux. The slaves were pouring out of the first shed, one of them unlocking the gate to the next and disappearing inside with Tobias's keys. Molineaux snatched a Bowie knife from the belt of one of the guards and went after Khari. Emerging from the stockade he glanced around, wondering which way the so-called Prince of the Leopard Men had gone. The tolling of the alarm bell soon told him.

The bell hung from a wooden pin between two tall upright posts on the next island. Molineaux sprinted across the bridge. Already the guards were pouring out of the barracks to suppress the rebellion. He cursed himself for his stupidity. Armed with muskets, they would easily slaughter the slaves. Molineaux's one consolation was that he would at least be able to kill Khari.

But as he drew near to Khari the leopard prince turned and saw him. Molineaux slashed at him with the knife, but Khari caught him by the wrist and twisted his arm up into the small of his back. Molineaux cried out and dropped the knife, and Khari threw him towards the reeds which lined the bank of the nearest waterway.

Molineaux rolled over, stood up quickly and turned to meet Khari's next attack. Khari had picked up the knife and now he advanced on Molineaux, taking his time. 'I knew you were trouble the moment I laid eyes on you,' he snarled as the two of them circled. He lunged, slashed at Molineaux's throat. The Englishman leaped back and landed amongst the reeds on a mud back. Khari came at him unhesitantly and thrust at his stomach. Molineaux tried to catch him by the wrist, but the thrust was only a feint and Khari at once followed it up by slashing Molineaux across the chest. He hardly felt a thing other than a slight burning sensation, but when he glanced down at himself he could see a thin cut across his chest weeping blood.

Khari moved in for the kill.

Madison would have been less than human not to have turned his head when the first shot sounded from the direction of the stockade. An opportunity like that came along once in what would be a very short lifetime if one was careless enough to let it slip past. Killigrew seized it in both hands, along with the pistol Madison held to his head. He pushed the muzzle aside and the two of them struggled chest-to-chest for a moment. Killigrew twisted Madison around until the gun pointed at the stack of powder cartridges outside the bunker. He pressed down on

Madison's trigger finger and the revolver discharged its single remaining shot harmlessly into one of the cartridges.

Snarling with rage, Madison threw the gun away and seized Killigrew by the throat. As his hands crushed his windpipe, Killigrew saw the slaver's eyes flicker past his head, and glancing at the ground he saw Salazar's shadow in the moonlight, poised to swing the cutlass at his back.

Killigrew whirled Madison around as a human shield. The slave captain gasped as the heavy blade bit deep into his spine. Then his legs crumpled and he fell to his knees. Killigrew watched him without compassion. 'Ecclesiastes, chapter three, verses one to two,' he said coldly.

Madison puckered his brow. 'Ecclesiastes...?'

'"To everything there is a season, and a time to every purpose under the heaven: A time to be born, and a time to die".'

Madison nodded, and died.

Salazar stared down at Madison's body, and then levelled the point of the cutlass at Killigrew's throat. 'You are going to spend a long, long time dying for that, Mr Killigrew.'

Killigrew tried not to stare as behind Salazar, one of Sampson's men picked up the powder cartridge that had been pierced by the bullet from the pistol. As the man carried the cartridge on his shoulder, he was oblivious to the gunpowder which spilled out of the bullet-hole and left a trail in his wake. 'Do I get a last request?' Killigrew asked Salazar.

'Such as?'

'A last cigar.'

Salazar shook his head. 'My cigars are back at the house, and I don't intend to give you a chance to think up some new trickery while I send someone to fetch one.'

The man carried the powder cartridge to the cannon closest to where Killigrew and Salazar stood, only ten feet away.

Two more shots sounded in quick succession from the direction of the stockade, followed by a whole fusillade, but Salazar did not take his eyes off Killigrew for a moment. 'Mr Sampson, be so good as to send someone to find out what all the shooting is about,' he called impatiently.

'Aye, aye, sir. You heard him, Caspar. Go down to the stockade and find out what the problem is.' One of Sampson's men nodded and ran off as the alarm bell sounded. The rest of them ran out the guns and aimed them at the frigate anchored beyond the bar.

'We're ready to fire, sir,' reported Sampson.

Killigrew glanced to where Madison had thrown the revolver. It lay between him and the trail of powder leading back to the stack of cartridges outside the bunker. But Salazar stood between Killigrew and the revolver with a cutlass in his hand.

'Then what are you waiting for?' Salazar snapped over his shoulder at Sampson.

Killigrew ducked underneath the blade of the cutlass and dived for the revolver. He snatched it up, rolled over and came to a halt by the trail of gunpowder.

Salazar whirled around. He swung the cutlass but the blade met only air.

491

Pointing the muzzle at the charcoal-grey dust, Killigrew cocked the hammer and pulled the trigger. The cartridge in the chamber fired and spat flames down the barrel. The trail of gunpowder sparked and ignited at once.

'Look out!' shouted Sampson, as a white flame burned rapidly down the trail and the air filled with acrid smoke.

'Will someone *please* put that fire out?' Salazar snapped in exasperation, swinging the cutlass back over his shoulder to aim a blow at Killigrew's neck. Killigrew threw the revolver at his head. It struck Salazar in the middle of the forehead and he blinked once and went down.

Sampson tried to stamp out the burning trail of gunpowder as it raced towards the stack of cartridges outside the bunker; then he thought better of it and turned and ran for his life. So did his men.

Killigrew picked himself up and ran to the wall, vaulting over it. He dropped about fifteen feet and landed heavily amongst some bushes. He clasped his hands over his head and waited for the explosion.

Seconds came and went. Nothing happened. Perhaps the gunpowder trail had not reached as far as the cartridges. Killigrew unclasped his arms and glanced up in disappointment.

On the quarter-deck of the *Thor*, Lieutenant Masterson watched as the last of the frigate's boats was swung back aboard in the davits and the men went below to man the guns. He reached for his watch for the sixteenth time in the past

492

hour, only to remember yet again that he had loaned it to Killigrew.

'Three minutes to two bells, lieutenant,' said Captain Crichton, seeing the motion. 'We'll be on time. We'd better pray that Killigrew, Reynolds and the others got out of there.'

'They know what they're doing,' Masterson said tightly, hoping it was true.

'And the consequences of failure,' agreed Crichton.

The ports on the gun deck were opened and the shell guns loaded and run out. 'Ready when you give the word, sir,' reported the gunner.

'Very well, Mr Andrews,' said Crichton, and checked his watch again. 'One minute...'

There was a bright flash from the coast, and everyone turned with a gasp. A moment later there came a terrific boom as a cloud of fire mushroomed up from behind the low ridge above the beach. The roar of the explosion echoed with a rumble like thunder off the hills behind the barracoon. A vast cloud rose slowly into the night sky.

'What in God's name was that?' spluttered Masterson.

Crichton smiled. 'That, lieutenant, I believe to have been Mr Killigrew's handiwork.'

At the foot of the wall, the flash of the explosion was blinding, as bright as the sun, and the blast was deafening. Killigrew hurriedly clamped his arms over his head once more and rolled in against the foot of the wall as the flames shot out over his head with a roar. The very earth seemed to shake around him, and then the wall crumbled and cracked. Chunks of masonry rained down on the slope of the escarpment, bouncing and spinning amongst the undergrowth, and one of the cannons crashed down inches from where Killigrew huddled.

The roar faded slowly as dust sheeted down from above and thick smoke filled the still air. As it slowly disseminated, Killigrew glanced up and saw only flaming wreckage where the battery had previously glowered over the beach. It took him all of his self-control not to whoop with exultation in an undignified manner.

But it was not over yet. Out at sea, he could see the *Thor* waiting to do its share of the destruction. He glanced at his watch. One minute to one: and Miss Chance was still locked in her room in the *palazzo*, right at the heart of the barracoon. He scrambled up the rubble of the shattered wall to where the battery had stood. A huge, charred crater marked where the cartridges had been stacked, and the bunker had been completely flattened. There was no sign of anyone except for one or two grisly remains of those who had not managed to get clear of the explosion.

An echoing boom sounded from the *Thor*, and he turned to see a great bank of cloud rising from her side. A split second later the scream of a dozen shells hurtling through the air filled his ears. He threw himself flat on the ground as the shells screeched overhead, and a moment later a vast wall of flames burst out of the ground, completely obscuring the rest of the barracoon from his sight. The multiple explosions seemed even louder than the stack of cartridges going off, and chunks of soil and mud rained down all around him.

He did not wait for the dust to settle but at once got up and ran into the cloud of smoke. If the *Thor*'s gunners were up to snuff – and he had a feeling they would be – then he had about one minute before they reloaded and fired again.

The first broadside had left no trace of the bridge which led to the central island, and precious little trace of the watercourse it had crossed. Killigrew stumbled through the mud and sprinted across the grass to the *palazzo*. The door was wide open. He dashed up the steps and inside. A moment later a blade swung at his head. He ducked down, rolled over on the marble floor, and twisted in time to see Salazar standing there with the cutlass still in his hand. The slaver's clothes were torn and scorched and his face was blackened, but he did not appear to have suffered any kind of serious injury; he had the devil's own luck, Killigrew mused grimly.

'I hope you weren't thinking of depriving me of my guest,' said Salazar, swinging the cutlass as he advanced.

In the distance, Killigrew heard the sporadic boom of the *Thor*'s guns as her men fired independently, as soon as they were ready. Once again the air was filled with the screech of shells. One landed on the lawn in front of the *palazzo*. There was a blinding flash followed by a roar, and the windows all exploded inwards. Killigrew flinched as shards of glass flew across the room.

Salazar, who had instinctively ducked, straightened and resumed his advance. He charged forwards suddenly, hacking at Killigrew's head, and Killigrew barely ducked aside in time. Salazar slashed at Killigrew, the point of the cutlass slicing through his shirt and scoring a line of blood from his shoulder.

Molineaux and Khari broke off their desperate struggle for a moment to gape in astonishment at the great plume of flame which rose up from where the battery had been.

Molineaux was the first to recover from the initial shock. He lunged forwards and seized Khari by the wrist. Khari stumbled under the onslaught, his feet slipping on the mud-bank, but he quickly rallied and twisted Molineaux this way and that. The leopard prince was easily the stronger, and he grinned as he forced Molineaux over backwards. Molineaux sprawled in the mud and Khari fell on him, plunging the Bowie knife down towards his chest. Molineaux rolled to one side and managed to kick Khari in the ribs, but without any appreciable result.

As Molineaux tried to crawl away, Khari picked himself up and stood over him. Molineaux rolled on to his back and seized a fistful of mud, staring up at where Khari towered over him and feeling like David facing Goliath. He flung the mud at the giant's face.

Blinded, Khari grunted and raised an arm to wipe his eyes. Molineaux jumped to his feet and leaped into the air, delivering a flying kick to Khari's chest. As Molineaux fell to the mud once more, Khari staggered backwards. His feet scrabbled for purchase in the slippery mud and he fell into the water with a terrific splash. The low profiles of crocodiles cruising through the channel at once changed direction.

Molineaux would have liked to stay around to see Khari's grisly demise – if only to make sure the crocodiles did not turn their noses up at him – but at that moment the *Thor*'s first salvo landed. The sky lit up orange, and he felt the ground tremble beneath his feet.

A crackle of muskets sounded behind him: not the sporadic firing of the guards, but a well-disciplined volley. He turned and saw a squad of ten marines there, giving the slaves covering fire as they ran for the canoes. The slavers turned and ran, only to find themselves face to face with another squad of marines. They threw down their muskets and raised their hands.

Feeling a wave of relief wash over him, Molineaux stumbled down towards the stockade. It was the first time he had been glad to see marines. So it was Killigrew who had come back, and he had brought some friends with him.

He had barely got as far as the alarm bell, however, when he felt burning pain explode through his right thigh. His leg crumpled beneath him and he fell against the wooden posts supporting the bell. Sobbing with agony, he glanced down and saw the haft of the Bowie knife embedded in his leg. He twisted and saw Khari advancing once more. The leopard prince leaned over him, grabbed the haft of the knife and twisted it in the wound. Molineaux screamed in

497

agony. Khari pulled the knife out with one hand, grabbed Molineaux with the other, hoisted him to his feet and slammed him back against one of the posts. He raised the knife above his head to plunge it into Molineaux's chest.

With one final effort, Molineaux lifted his knee into Khari's crotch and broke free. Khari grunted and brought the knife arcing down. The tip slashed across Molineaux's shoulder blade, and then his leg gave way beneath him and he fell. He reached out to grab something and caught hold of the bell-rope. But the pin supporting the bell had not been designed to take the weight of a man. The bell gave a half-hearted clang which broke off, along with the bell itself. Khari frowned at the sound and looked up. Molineaux stared in horrified fascination as the heavy brass bell crushed Khari's head like an eggshell. He winced.

Then the shells of the next salvo began to fall across the barracoon, shooting great plumes of fire into the night sky and hurling clumps of earth through the air. One shell landed in a nearby mud-bank and Molineaux was splattered with mud.

He started to crawl towards the landing stage where the marines were rounding up the slavers beyond the extreme range of the frigate's guns.

But his progress was agonisingly slow. He was not even halfway when the shells of the third salvo rained fire on the barracoon. He wondered if Madison was able to see this; if he had been, the slave captain would doubtless have had some pithy Biblical quote about a hail of brimstone and fire on Sodom and Gomorrah.

He felt footsteps pounding the earth behind him and twisted in panic, wondering if Khari had somehow managed to survive having his skull smashed in, but it was only a Kruman wearing a top hat. Molineaux recognised him from somewhere, and after a moment's thought placed him as the interpreter who had arrived at the village with the witch doctor the day Prince Khari had attacked.

In the darkness the Kruman almost ran straight past Molineaux on his way to the stockade. 'Hey!' Molineaux called out after him. 'Don't leave me!'

The Kruman twisted and skidded to a halt. 'You Killigrew friend?'

Molineaux nodded, and ducked his head as another shell burst nearby. 'Was it Killigrew who arranged the fireworks?'

The Kruman grinned and nodded, and helped him to his feet. 'Come, we go, plenty quick.'

'Wait a minute, what about Miss Chance?'

'White puss in big house. Mas'er Killigrew, he go fetchee. Come, we go!'

'What about Killigrew? Will he be all right?'

'Mas'er Killigrew worry 'bout Mas'er Killigrew. You, me, worry 'bout me, you. He be fine.'

Molineaux allowed Tip-Top to help him down towards the landing stage. 'Yeah,' he sighed. 'He certainly seems to have a talent for survival.'

The whole house shuddered as one of the shells scored a direct hit on the roof. The chandelier over the receiving room shivered and tinkled, and the ornate rococo moulding fell in pieces from the ceiling. A big chunk of plaster hit the marble floor between Killigrew and Salazar.

Killigrew still backed away before the relentless sweeps of the cutlass in Salazar's hand. He looked around in desperation for something he could use as a weapon, but there was nothing. He bounded on to the mahogany table and kicked the candelabra at Salazar's head.

Salazar ducked to one side and the candelabra crashed against the wall before falling to the floor. 'I should have finished you off when I had the chance,' he snarled, and swung at Killigrew's knees. 'This is all your doing.'

Killigrew jumped over the slashing blade. Salazar leaped on to the table. Killigrew backed away until he came to the far end of the long table and almost stepped out into space. He teetered and barely managed to regain his balance.

Salazar laughed. 'No place left to run to, Mr Killigrew.'

'Then come and get me.'

Salazar lifted the cutlass and flexed his fingers around the hilt, clearly wondering if Killigrew had any more tricks up his sleeve. Then he charged the length of the table, swinging the blade of the cutlass behind his head. Unarmed, Killigrew waited to receive the attack.

Salazar swung, Killigrew ducked at the last moment and the blade swished above his head.

Salazar's momentum kept him going until he careered into his opponent. Killigrew caught him around the waist and straightened, flinging him over his shoulder. Salazar screamed, and abruptly fell silent.

Killigrew turned. It had been his plan to throw Salazar into the fireplace, but his aim had been too high. Instead Salazar's rhinoceros head had killed its killer five years too late, its horn piercing his throat underneath the jaw. Now Salazar hung grotesquely over the fireplace, the final trophy in his own collection. His arms hung limply by his sides. After a few seconds' pause the cutlass finally slipped from his lifeless fingers and clattered to the floor.

Another shell burst outside. Killigrew jumped down from the table and sprinted up the stairs. 'Suzannah!'

'In here!' She hammered against the door. 'The door's locked, I'm trapped inside!'

'Stand back!' He lashed out at the edge of the door with his foot, just below the lock. Agony exploded in his ankle, but the door snapped open. Miss Chance ran out into his arms.

Another shell smashed into the house and a huge chunk of masonry crashed to the landing. The shuddering impact hurled them both to the floor and showered them with dust. 'Are you all right?' Killigrew asked her.

She nodded. They got up and made for the stairs. 'What happened to Salazar?' she asked.

'Don't ask,' he told her. But she glanced to her left as they went down the stairs. The lawn in front of the *palazzo* seemed to be on fire, and the flames cast a hellish glow over the grisly scene of Salazar's death.

He tucked her head against his shoulder. 'Don't look.'

501

'I already did.'

'Come on. We'll go out the back.' He pushed her through the door to the dining room. They left the house as the last echoes of the bombardment died away and made their way down to the beach where Masterson and a squad of seamen were landing in one of the launches to help the marines round up any surviving slavers.

Epilogue:

The Final Hurdle

JUNE 6 – HMS *Thor* (26 guns, Captain C. Crichton) was instrumental in the destruction of a slave trader's barracoon on the Guinea Coast. A large number of slaves is known to have been freed. There were a number of arrests, although many of the slave traders are believed to have been slain in the attack. None of the marines taking part in the action were killed. The site has been razed. Lieutenant C.I. Killigrew of Her Majesty Royal Navy was mentioned in despatches.

This small snippet at the bottom of the 'Naval Intelligence' column was the only mention of the affair in any of the London newspapers. Rear-Admiral Napier folded his newspaper and glanced across to where Killigrew sat opposite him in the carriage, staring moodily out of the window as they rattled down Pall Mall. 'Well, the newspapers have decided that you should have your commission restored, at any rate.'

'Will that cut any ice at the Admiralty?'

'Public opinion is a powerful weapon, Mr Killigrew. More powerful even than the shell guns of HMS *Thor*, perhaps. I've spoken to the First Lord. He scowled a good deal, of course, but he muttered something about seeing what he could do. Cheer up. You mark my words, you'll be back in uniform before you know what's hit you.'

'I just wish I could have found out who was behind Salazar and the Bay Cay Trading Company.'

'Ah. Yes, well, we'll come to that presently. Here we are,' he added, as the carriage pulled up outside the Reform Club. He took a pinch of snuff, sneezed explosively, and then preceded Killigrew out of the carriage, limping up the steps. 'Rear-Admiral Sir Charles Napier and Mr Christopher Killigrew to see Sir George Grafton,' he told the porter.

'You're expected, gentlemen. Sir George is waiting for you in the smoking room.'

Sir George rose to his feet as Napier and Killigrew approached, and glanced pointedly at his watch. 'I don't know what this is about, Rear-Admiral, but you'd better be brief. I have an appointment with the Earl of Auckland at three.' He plumped himself back down in his chair and motioned for Napier and Killigrew to likewise be seated.

'We shan't keep you any longer than is absolutely necessary, I assure you, Sir George,' said Napier, lowering his bulk into a chair. 'By the way, you've met Mr Killigrew, haven't you?'

'Ah, yes. The young man who helped to destroy the Owodunni Barracoon. If you want me to press the Lords of the Admiralty to overturn the verdict of your court-martial, young man, you can put aside any such hopes. As far as I'm concerned that trial was properly convened and carried out. The navy can hardly be held responsible if you saw fit to give a false admission of guilt.'

'That's all in hand,' said Napier. 'I think Mr Killigrew has proved his value to the navy, and I'm currently trying to come to an agreement with the First Lord regarding his reinstatement.'

'More than the blighter deserves,' muttered Grafton.

'I think you do Mr Killigrew an injustice, Sir George. But then, you may not know exactly how much he achieved by his adventure. You see, the aim was not just to find one single barracoon and destroy it, although that was what you might call by way of an added bonus. No indeed. What our colleagues at the Slave Trade Department wanted to know was: who was the man who financed the ships that carried the slaves to the Americas? And thanks to Mr Killigrew here, I think I can point the finger at that man right now.'

'Oh?' Grafton said cautiously. Killigrew was equally surprised, but he held his peace, suspecting that Napier knew what he was doing.

'Yes. You see, someone tipped off Salazar that Mr Killigrew was working for me. And that was a secret very few people were in possession of. I'd made sure of that; that was the very reason I arranged the whole thing without getting the Admiralty's approval first.'

'How many people knew?' asked Grafton.

'Well, just myself and Mr Killigrew. And two soldiers of the Royal Marines who helped us

505

could have guessed, of course, but they're above suspicion. Oh, and yourself, Sir George. Or had you forgotten our little conversation of the twenty-fifth of June?'

Grafton rose to his feet angrily. 'Sir Charles, I sincerely hope you are not insinuating what I think you are.'

'Oh come now, Sir George. Do you take me for a child? I've suspected you were behind the slavers for years. Now Mr Killigrew – not to mention yourself – has kindly provided me with the proof I need to secure a conviction–'

'Call that proof?' roared Grafton. 'By God, that's the grossest slander...!' he spluttered apoplectically. 'Sir, I demand you retract that last statement at once, or else I shall have no choice but to ... but to...'

'Call me out?' Napier suggested hopefully.

'No. To litigate, damn your eyes! I'll sue you for every blasted penny you've got!'

'I must compliment you, Sir George. I had no idea you were such a fine actor. But you're wasting your breath. Dead men cannot litigate, and you know as well as I that the penalty for slaving in this country is death... For Heaven's sake, Mr Killigrew, what on earth are you counting on your fingers? That's very distracting, you know.'

'Excuse me, sir, but could I have a word?'

'Not now, Killigrew! When I've finished with Sir George here–'

'No, sir. *Now.*'

Napier smiled thinly at Grafton. 'You must excuse me for a moment, Sir George.' He rose to his feet and allowed Killigrew to take him to one side, leaving Grafton fuming in his seat. 'Now what is it, Killigrew?' he demanded irritably.

'You did say you told Sir George on the twenty-fifth, didn't you?'

'The twenty-fifth of June, yes. What's that got to do with it?'

'It's just that Salazar knew when I arrived at the Black River Barracoon on the first of July. Which means that if Salazar learned it from Sir George, then his messenger travelled from London to the Guinea Coast in less than a week.'

Napier stared at Killigrew. 'Why on earth didn't you say something before?'

'Because I didn't even know you'd said anything to Sir George.'

Napier turned back to Grafton. 'My apologies, Sir George. I seem to have made a terrible mistake.'

'A mistake? A *mistake!* I'll say you've made a mistake, you slanderous poltroon! You're finished, d'ye hear me? The pair of you! I'll have you thrown out of the navy, I'll have you blackballed from every club in town, why, I'll have you hung, drawn and quartered...!'

'Shouldn't that be "hanged", sir?' said Killigrew.

'Get out!'

Napier fled as fast as his gammy leg would carry him, followed by Killigrew.

The two of them drew breath on the pavement outside. 'I'm awfully sorry about that, Mr Killigrew. I'm afraid I made rather a fool of myself there. Still, it's not the first time and I dare

507

say it won't be the last.'

Killigrew smiled ruefully. 'It was a good plan, sir. It would have just worked better if we'd compared notes before our meeting with Sir George.'

Napier shook his head. 'I don't understand it. I was certain it must be him... Oh, well, never mind. Some you win, some you lose, eh, Mr Killigrew? Can I offer you a ride somewhere?' he added, climbing back into his carriage.

'Thank you, sir, but no thanks.' Killigrew was seething that Napier had risked his life by using him as human bait and did not trust himself to hold his tongue during the ride. It had probably never occurred to the old fool that he might get killed. The Rear-Admiral had probably thought he had been doing Killigrew a favour by adding that extra touch of peril. It was flattering that Napier seemed to think him so indestructible, but that did not alter the fact he might well have been killed. Besides, he had another matter to attend to. 'There's a personal call I'd like to make,' he told Napier.

'A young lady, eh, I'll warrant! Wedding bells in the air soon, perhaps? Well, good luck to you.'

'Thank you, sir.'

'Driver! Drive on!'

Killigrew watched the carriage until it disappeared down a side street, and then hailed a passing hansom. 'Knightsbridge,' he told the driver.

The hansom dropped him off outside Sir Joshua Pengelly's house. He walked slowly down the drive to the front door and pulled the door-bell. A footman answered.

'Yes?'

Killigrew handed him his card. 'Mr Christopher Killigrew calling for Mrs Fairbody.'

'I'll see if the young lady is at home, sir,' said the footman, and closed the door in Killigrew's face.

A moment later it was flung open and Eulalia ran out. 'Kit!' she exclaimed, and embraced him shamelessly on the doorstep. 'When did you get back? I was so worried for you … and then I saw the piece in this morning's paper! Come in, come in! Fleming, would you ask cook to make some tea for myself and Mr Killigrew? We'll take it in the parlour.'

Killigrew followed her into the parlour. 'Actually, Eulalia, it was your father I wanted to see.'

'My father? You go swanning off risking your neck on the high seas for absolutely *weeks*, and when you finally get back and show up on my doorstep, it's my father you want to see instead of me? Shame on you! And after the things that passed between us the last time we saw one another,' she added coyly, toying with the lapels of his frock coat.

When he did not reply, she looked up at his face. 'Kit, what's wrong? You're acting very strangely. Did … did you have a bad time in Africa?'

'It wasn't a picnic, if that's what you mean. The slavers found out about my being a spy for the Slave Trade Department.'

509

She gasped, and her hand flew to her mouth. 'My word! They didn't try to harm you, did they?' she asked, and then her features softened into a smile. 'But so what if they did try? Nothing could hurt my Kit.'

He shook his head. 'You're wrong there, Eulalia. I can be very, very deeply hurt indeed. By something like betrayal.'

She knitted her brows. 'Betrayal? What on earth are you talking about?'

'Only five people knew of my mission, or even knew enough to guess what it was, in time to get word to the slavers. Three of them were above suspicion. The fourth was myself.'

'And the fifth?'

'Was you, Eulalia.'

She shook her head. 'No, Kit. You're mistaken. I wouldn't do anything to harm you, you know that. I love you.'

'But you love your father more. Is he in?'

Her eyes flickered up towards the ceiling, and she bit her lip.

'I'd better go and have a word with him.' He went out into the hallway once more.

She caught up with him halfway up the stairs and grabbed him by the arm. 'Please, Kit. You're wrong about this, I promise you. If you love me, you'll forget about my father and leave him out of it. What's done is done. You're here and in one piece and that's all that matters. No one else was hurt.'

He turned to face her. 'No one else was hurt?' he echoed incredulously. 'What about all the Africans that have been enslaved and carried off to the Americas?'

'What about them? For Heaven's sake, Kit! They're only niggers.'

He raised a hand to strike her in a sudden access of rage. She stared at him in horror, but he caught himself. He had never struck a woman in his life and he did not intend to start now. Instead he looked down at her, not with pity but with loathing and contempt. Then he turned and continued up the stairs.

She ran after him and caught him at the half-way landing. 'No, Kit. Please. Not my father. Whatever it is you think him guilty of... Please, Kit, no. Don't do this...'

Killigrew continued implacably up the stairs. He glanced up and saw Sir Joshua standing there, gazing bleakly down at him. Then Pengelly turned abruptly and disappeared into his study, slamming the door behind him.

Killigrew broke free of Eulalia and ran up to the door, but Pengelly had locked it. Killigrew threw his shoulder against it, once, twice, and then stood back to kick it open.

A shot rang out on the other side. Killigrew flinched, half expecting a bullet to come flying through the planks, but this was Kensington, not the Guinea Coast.

He kicked the door open and at that moment Eulalia reached his side. She took one look through the door and turned away with a sob.

'Christ!' whispered Killigrew. He was used to bloodshed, but that was on active service, not in a genteel suburb of London.

Eulalia suddenly flung herself at him, clawing

511

at his eyes. 'You … you bastard! You killed him, you bastard! You did this! *You did this!*'

He caught her by the wrists and held her at bay, alarmed by her fury. The servants came rushing up the stairs. The footman and the butler took Eulalia between them while the housekeeper glanced into the study. 'Holy mother of God! Is it the master?'

The butler glanced at the body. 'It looks like it.'

Eulalia was still struggling in the footman's arms, screaming and lashing out at Killigrew with her legs. 'You'd better leave, sir,' the footman said disdainfully. 'I've got your card for when the police get here. I dare say they'll want to speak to you about this.'

'I dare say,' agreed Killigrew.

He wandered out of the house in a daze, crossed the road, and entered the park opposite. He sat down on a bench overlooking the Serpentine, buried his face in his hands, and wept.

Before he had set out on his mission, he had told Napier he would give anything to see the slave trade stopped. Now he realised just what that had meant.

'I still can't believe you used me as human bait to draw out Sir George Grafton,' Killigrew said bitterly. He had to raise his voice above the clamour of the engine and the plashing of the paddle-wheels as the ferry steamed east past the Naval Dockyard at Woolwich, bound for Gravesend and Chatham. 'I could have been killed!'

'Oh, don't be like that! I knew you'd pull

through somehow. Besides, I made sure Able Seaman Molineaux was in place to watch your back, didn't I? How is Molineaux, by the way?'

'Doing well. Mr Strachan says he'll have full use of his leg again in no time. And he did save my life. In fact I couldn't have done it without him.'

'There you go then. I knew I could rely on that fellow. Just goes to prove that a blackamoor can be just as clever and stout a chap as any, eh? Must make sure I get Molineaux a berth on a decent ship, come to think of it.'

'Come to think of it, you should make sure *I* get a berth on a decent ship.'

'One thing at a time, Lieutenant. I got you back your commission, didn't I? So where would you like to go next? Another crack at the slavers? We may have rooted out one nest of the vile scum, but I suspect there are plenty more where they came from.'

Killigrew shook his head. 'I think I can rest contented that I've done my share against the slavers, sir.'

'So, which cause do you wish to turn your attentions to now, eh?'

'Now that you mention it, sir, I did hear that they're having problems with pirates in the China Seas.'

'China,' said Napier, and sighed. 'I'll see what I can arrange.'

'You might also care to pay me that one hundred guineas you owe me.'

'Good Heavens! I'd forgotten all about that. Will you take a cheque?'

513

Killigrew nodded. 'Better make it out to Sir Andrew Strachan, QC. By an unfortunate coincidence, one hundred guineas just happens to be the retainer he's demanding before he'll act as my counsel in the Videira action.'

'You haven't heard, then?'

'Heard what?'

'It seems Videira's new ship got stopped off the coast of Liberia with a hold full of slaves by the USS *Narwhal*. Apparently the testimony of one Lieutenant Lanier went a long way to convincing the court of his guilt.'

'Good old Lanier,' said Killigrew. Since slavery was equated with piracy, the captain could only have received one punishment for his crime. 'But what about his family? Don't they want to take up the case?'

'Videira didn't have any family, so his lawyers will have to drop the action.'

'Thank God for that,' sighed Killigrew. 'Lord knows how I'd've paid Sir Andrew's fees. My agent tells me that my share of the prize money for all those slaves we rescued at the Owodunni barracoon comes to precisely sixteen pounds, three shillings and six pence.'

'You never were in it for the money.'

'It's just as well,' Killigrew said bitterly. It was reassuring to know there was some justice in the world, but that was small compensation when he remembered Eulalia and thought of what he had lost. But that was just the price he had to pay for being a slave to his principles.

'Oh, buck up, man!' said Napier. 'I know we never did find out who was behind the slavers.

But we'll get him one day.'

'I wasn't thinking about that, sir.'

'What, then? No, wait: let me guess. It wouldn't have something to do with that young lady you went off to see after we spoke with Sir George, by any chance?'

Killigrew smiled sadly. 'I think you can safely say that.'

Napier glanced to where Miss Chance stood in the bow of the ferry, gazing with the rapture of an excited schoolboy at the ships in the docks. 'It wasn't ... ah...?'

'Miss Chance? No, it wasn't her.'

'Well, when I was your age and I was jilted, I used to say that being in love was like steeplechasing. Ever done any steeplechasing, Killigrew? Capital sport. If you take a tumble, the important thing to do is not let the experience put you off. Got to get straight back in the saddle, eh?' Napier winked, and nudged him in the ribs.

Killigrew smiled. 'Miss Chance will make someone an admirable wife one day, if she chooses to,' he admitted. 'But I fear our paths go separate ways. We had a good heart-to-heart over dinner at Rules last night. She's determined to go back to Africa to do missionary work in Liberia.'

'After all that she's been through?'

Killigrew nodded. 'Now more than ever. And it wouldn't be fair for me to expect her to marry a naval officer.'

Napier sighed, doubtless thinking of the family he was leaving behind as he returned to the flagship of the Channel Fleet. 'You're right. It's a

515

hard life for the womenfolk, being married to us naval officers. A crotchety old fool like me in particular. Oh, by the way, did you hear about Sir Joshua Pengelly? Terrible business. Something to do with irregularities in his financial affairs. Still, I dare say they'll be plenty left in the coffers for his daughter to get by on. What's her name? Euphemia?'

'Eulalia.'

'That's it. Eulalia. You used to be a friend of the family, didn't you?'

'Used to be. Excuse me a moment, sir.' Killigrew moved aft to where one of the hands was lowering the accident boat in its davits. 'Good morning,' he said, talking to the boatman more as an excuse not to talk to Napier than because he was particularly concerned in what the man was doing.

The man was bent over the taffrail with his back to Killigrew. When he turned, Killigrew found himself staring into Eli Coffin's venomous eyes and the muzzle of a pistol.

'*Don't* put your hands up,' snarled Coffin. 'Just put 'em in the pockets of your pants nice and easy, as if we're shooting the breeze. That's it. Now let's go down below and I'll show you the engine room.'

The engine room was noisy, even by engine room standards. The piston arms were a blur, and the whole engine seemed to be working much too quickly for its own good, shuddering and vibrating. Killigrew glanced at the pressure gauge and saw that it was way too high.

'Keep moving,' ordered Coffin, and prodded

him in the back with the pistol. He had to shout to make himself heard above the din of the engine.

As Killigrew moved around the back of the engine space he found the ferry-boat's engineer. His throat had been slit from ear to ear. 'Your handiwork, I suppose?' he shouted.

With his left hand Coffin reached into the pocket of his coat and pulled out a pair of manacles, tossing them to Killigrew. 'Attach one cuff to your wrist and the other to that pipe there,' he bellowed into Killigrew's ear.

Playing for time, Killigrew clipped the first bracelet over the pipe, removing the key from the cuff to lock it in place. 'You do realise that the pressure is far too high, don't you?' he roared. 'If you don't open the release valve soon, the boilers will explode.'

Coffin grinned. 'That's the general idea. Mr Salazar asked me to kill the rear-admiral, and to make it look like an accident. That's exactly what I'm going to do. And as an added bonus I get to kill you and that bitch Miss Chance.'

'Salazar's dead,' shouted Killigrew. 'And Madison.'

'Oh, I heard all about that, you Limey sonuvabitch. This here's what you might be calling my revenge.'

Light fell on them both as the door leading up on deck opened and Napier stood there. 'Hullo, Killigrew. Come to look at the engines? Mind if I join you?'

Coffin started to turn the pistol on him. Killigrew reached up and pulled down the handle on one of the release valves. A jet of steam shot out and Coffin screamed as his face was scalded. Killigrew grabbed him by the wrist and forced the gun to one side. They struggled chest to chest for a moment in the cramped space alongside the machinery, Killigrew slowly forcing the muzzle of the pistol towards the blur that was the piston arm. There was a clang and the pistol was snatched from Coffin's grip.

Killigrew at once broke free and grabbed hold of an overhead beam, pulling himself up to kick Coffin in the chest. The American was thrown back against the bulkhead and cracked his head. Killigrew grabbed him while he was still dazed and clipped the second bracelet of the manacles over his wrist.

Napier hobbled down the steps. 'What in the world...?'

As Coffin pulled frantically on the manacle, glaring and spitting at them both, Killigrew backed away, wiping his mouth on his sleeve. 'One of the slavers, sir,' he shouted to Napier. 'He came here to kill us both in revenge.'

He turned his attention to the engine, pulling on the handle of the main release valve, but it was jammed. 'The swine's sabotaged it!'

'Can you fix it?' shouted Napier.

'Not enough time. Tell everyone to abandon ship!'

Napier hurried up the steps to the door, and Killigrew was about to follow him when Coffin shouted after him.

'Killigrew! Shipmate! You ain't gonna leave me here, are you?'

Killigrew glared at him, and then noticed a toolbox at his feet. He gave it a kick so that it slid along the floor and came to rest by Coffin's ankles. 'You broke it. You fix it.'

By the time he emerged on deck everyone was leaping over the sides without bothering to lower the accident boats; they were only a hundred yards from the river bank. Only Miss Chance dithered by the rail.

Killigrew charged towards her along the length of the deck. 'Jump! She's going to blow!'

'I can't swim!' she wailed.

'I won't let you drown!' he shouted, and launched himself at her. He caught her around the waist. The two of them went over the side and hit the water with a splash. At once Killigrew supported her, keeping her head above water as he towed her clear of the paddle-wheel which bore down on them. The ferry had just passed them when there was a loud clang and a moment later there came a sound like a huge bell cracking followed by an ear-splitting roar. The midships section of the paddle-boat disintegrated in a sudden bloom of steam, while jagged fragments of iron hurtled in every direction, raining down on the water like a thousand musket balls. The twin smoke stacks shot straight up into the air, and then dropped down once more, spinning lazily until they splashed into the river to windward.

'Are you oh-kay?' Killigrew asked Miss Chance.

'Yes,' she gasped.

The ferry had been ripped in two as if it were

519

no more than a flimsy child's toy which had been smashed in a childish fit of temper. The two halves rapidly began to sink, bows and stern tilting up towards the sky. The accident boat still floated, attached to the taffrail by its painter. Killigrew swam across to it and got Miss Chance to hold on to the boat's gunwale while he took out his clasp knife and sawed through the painter moments before the stern sank.

Soon there was no trace that the ferry had ever existed except for people swimming in the water and Killigrew and Miss Chance clinging to the accident boat. Fortunately they were in the middle of the busiest waterway in the western world, and within seconds a coal lighter was adjusting course and heaving to in order to rescue the survivors.

Killigrew held the accident boat steady so that Miss Chance could climb in. He scrambled over the gunwale after her and glanced to where Napier and several others were being helped aboard the lighter. 'Did everyone get off in time?'

'I think so,' she told him. 'What happened?'

'It was Coffin. Are you all right?'

'Well, this dress is ruined and my hair's a mess, but I think I'll survive. And I expect I'll miss the packet to Monrovia now.'

'Don't worry. They'll be another one in a month.'

'A month,' she echoed, and lay back on the bottom boards. She smiled up at him archly. 'Whatever shall I do for a whole month?'

He grinned. 'Have you ever tried steeple-chasing?'

Afterword:

Larger Than Life?

This story may seem far-fetched, but ninety per cent of it is based on historical fact. The Royal Navy never – as far as I am aware – used undercover spies to provide information about the slavers (although they did benefit from many ex-slavers who turned informer), but otherwise the methods used by the Royal Navy in the suppression of the slave trade, and those of the slavers they pursued, are authentic.

The climax of the story is inspired by a true incident which took place in 1847, when a slaver's barracoon was destroyed by an alliance of the Royal Navy and local people with the connivance of the captain of the USS *Dolphin;* as Hugh Thomas points out on page 692 of his authoritative work *The Slave Trade,* (Simon and Schuster Inc., New York, 1997) this was 'an unusual example of British-North American collaboration'.

Francisco Salazar is fictional but he is based on Pedro Blanco, a slaver whose barracoon at the mouth of the Gallinas river was destroyed by Captain Joseph Denman of HMS *Wanderer* in 1841, although by then Blanco had already retired a millionaire. Very few of the men who profited from the slave trade were ever brought to justice. Although slave trading warranted the death penalty under British law, there is no record of it ever having been carried out.

The Owodunni Barracoon is based on Blanco's barracoon, harem and all. When Denman heard that two British subjects – a black woman named Fry Norman and her child – were being held prisoner by the King of Gallinas, who was probably supplying slaves to Blanco's successor, Denman used this as an excuse to attack and destroy the barracoon. One of the slave traders found at the barracoon, a Señor Buron, although not a British subject and not therefore subject to British law, begged Denman to take him away with him for fear of what the natives would do to him if he was left behind. Denman agreed, and in return for his kindness Buron sued him for the destruction of his goods which had been at the barracoon. The case dragged on for years, Denman having to defend himself as the navy did not support its officers when they were subjected to such legal attacks; fortunately Denman's father was a chief justice and he won the case in the end. It was while he was in England fighting the case that he wrote and had published his *Instructions for the Guidance of Her Majesty's Naval Officers Employed in the Suppression of the Slave Trade,* presumably to help his fellow officers avoid falling into the same legal snare as himself.

In the meantime, sad to say, the Gallinas barracoon was rebuilt and resumed its slave-trading operations; it was destroyed again in another attack by the Royal Navy in 1849. Other barracoons, at the mouths of the Sherber and

Pongas rivers, likewise received the attention of the Royal Navy.

Three of the characters featured in this book were real characters. Neither Isambard Kingdom Brunel nor William Ewart Gladstone need any introduction from me, although it is only fair to say that while Gladstone did speak out against the maintenance of the West Africa Squadron, he was a lifelong opponent of the slave trade. The third, Rear-Admiral Sir Charles Napier, is less well known, which is a pity. Napier was a popular hero, something of a legend in his own lifetime. He had been promoted to post-rank after taking on three French ships of the line in nothing more than a brig during the Napoleonic Wars. In 1828 Dom Miguel usurped the throne of Portugal from the rightful heir, his niece Maria da Gloria. Captain Napier was employed as a sailor of fortune to command Queen Maria's fleet. To the despair of the British Foreign Office and the concomitant delight of the British public, Napier not only thrashed Dom Miguel's fleet but, fancying himself a general as well as an admiral, helped to trounce the Miguelites by land as well.

Napier's greatest moment came in 1840, after Ibrahim Pasha, the Viceroy of Egypt – a vassal of the Ottoman Empire – rebelled against the sultan in Constantinople and invaded Syria. The people of Syria, Christian and Muslim alike, preferring the less exacting regime of the Ottomans, in turn rebelled against the Egyptian invaders. Fearing the break-up of the Ottoman Empire – if only because its fall would give the Russians free access to the Mediterranean – the British government sent a fleet to the Levant to support the Ottoman sultan and his oppressed subjects in Syria. Napier was promoted to commodore and was appointed second-in-command of the fleet. But if the Admiralty hoped that the years might have mellowed him to the point where he would be prepared to take orders from someone as cautious as the commander-in-chief of the fleet, Admiral Stopford, they were disappointed. Before long Napier was playing at being a general again – and just as successfully as before – leading a naval brigade in action in the Lebanon fighting alongside the Turks.

The British Government was not entirely happy with the high-handed way in which Napier imposed a peace settlement on the viceroy which was far more exacting than the one they had intended. When the viceroy asked him what his authority was, he is said to have replied: 'My credentials are the double-shotted guns of the *Powerful* and the honour of an Englishman.' But the British public welcomed Napier back as a hero once more, and if there was one thing the government was not prepared to do that was fly in the face of public opinion. Becoming the independent member of parliament for Marylebone in the general election of 1841, Napier was effectively kicked upstairs by his appointment as naval aide-de-camp to Queen Victoria until his promotion to the rank of rear-admiral in 1846 and his appointment as commander-in-chief of the Channel Fleet in 1847.

If Napier is less well known today than even Admiral Rodney, Hood or Cochrane, despite having been a national hero in his day, it is because his career effectively came to a dead end in the Baltic during the so-called Crimean War, where Napier was in command of the British Fleet. The British public expected great things of a man with Napier's reputation for succeeding in what most other people would not even have bothered to attempt, and he disappointed them. But it was not his fault if the Russian Fleet refused to come out of the harbour to fight. He certainly did the best he could ... but that's another story.

Men like Napier, larger-than-life characters who were prepared to risk everything out of motives that were one hundred per cent pure and noble, simply don't seem to exist any more; they are relics of a bygone age, which is a great pity. I for one have always had an admiration for the early Victorians – the more liberal sort of them, at least – and can only lament that their reputation has been dragged into the mire by scurrilous politicians who sought to identify themselves with Victorian values.

Nowadays when we think of the Victorian era we tend to think of the child labour, the appalling working conditions, the poverty and squalor; we tend to forget that it was an era of social reform, and that the Britain they left behind them in 1901 was a far better place than the one they found in 1837. In enforcing the *Pax Britannica,* the Royal Navy made the seas safer for trade. Their main aim, of course, was to make the seas safer for *British* trade; but making it safer for all was a side effect of which they could be justly proud. And if that most hated of bugbears, the British Empire, reached it zenith under the Victorians, then it must be remembered that the great age of colonialism and the scramble for Africa belonged to the later Victorians. Men like Napier and Killigrew, students of Adam Smith, believed in fair and equal trade, and in respecting all nations and races; they would not have approved of what was to come. It is true that sailors in the Royal Navy received prize money for each slave they helped to free, but the more active members of the West Africa Squadron were undoubtedly motivated by idealism rather than greed.

And what of Killigrew himself? He is a fictional character, of course, but inspired by extraordinary characters who nonetheless lived and served in the Royal Navy during this era: men like Denman, Henry Keppel and Astley Cooper Key – gentlemanly swashbucklers who fought with revolvers in one hand and cutlasses in the other and carried the day against pirates and slavers because they never worried about the consequences of failure. Such men and their deeds are largely forgotten today, perhaps because in the public's consciousness they – along with everything else to do with the Victorian Age – are inextricably and unjustifiably bound up with the atrocities of imperialism. They were the last of a dying breed and could not exist in a world where old-fashioned virtues like courage, idealism, fair play and good manners have been replaced by arrogance, selfish ambition and unthinking political correctness. We shall not see their like again, which is a great pity.

This Large Print Book for the partially sighted, who cannot read normal print, is published under the auspices of

THE ULVERSCROFT FOUNDATION